W. Stephen Gilbert

W. Stephen Gilbert has worked widely in television,
having produced several dramas including the acclaimed
King of the Ghetto and *Only Connect* for BBC2. He is also
a novelist, critic and journalist, contributing to the
Independent, the *Observer* and *Time Out* among others.

SCEPTRE

Fight and Kick and Bite

The Life and Work of Dennis Potter

W. STEPHEN GILBERT

SCEPTRE

Copyright © 1995 by W. Stephen Gilbert

First published in 1995 by Hodder and Stoughton
First published in paperback in 1996 by Hodder and Stoughton
A division of Hodder Headline PLC
A Sceptre Paperback

The right of W. Stephen Gilbert to be identified as the Author
of the Work has been asserted by him in accordance with the
Copyright, Designs and Patents Act 1988.

10 9 8 7 6 5 4 3 2

British Library Cataloguing in Publication Data

Gilbert, W. Stephen
    Fight and Kick and Bite: Life and Work
        of Dennis Potter
I. Title
822.914

ISBN 0 340 64048 0

Typeset by Palimpsest Book Production Limited,
Polmont, Stirlingshire

Printed and bound in Great Britain by
Mackays of Chatham PLC, Chatham, Kent

Hodder and Stoughton
A division of Hodder Headline PLC
338 Euston Road
London NW1 3BH

For my father Stanley and in memory of my mother Enid
. . . and for my mother in the business, Betty Willingale

Contents

'To pin a man down in a few hundred pages
takes a certain callousness as well as
a modicum of love – a little in the same way
that a boy will cheerfully hold up a dragonfly,
crucified on a postcard with drawing pins,
for the admiration and enlightenment,
or even sometimes the pity,
of his companions.'

Dennis Potter[1]

List of Illustrations

xi

Kika Markham in *Double Dare (BBC)*
Michael Gambon in *The Singing Detective (BBC)*
Cheryl Campbell and Bob Hoskins in *Pennies From Heaven (BBC)*
Janet Henfrey, Johnny Wade and Keith Barron in *Stand Up, Nigel Barton (BBC)*
Janine Duvitski, Helen Mirren and Dinah's pram in *Blue Remembered Hills (BBC)*
Hywel Bennett and Megs Jenkins in *Where the Buffalo Roam (BBC)*
Patrick Malahide and Janet Suzman in *The Singing Detective (BBC)*
Gina Bellman and Michael Gough in *Blackeyes (BBC)*
Robert McNaughton and Glynis Barber in *Visitors (BBC)*
Four consultants in *The Singing Detective (BBC)*
Five officers in the Ministry of Defence in *Lipstick On Your Collar (Photograph by Stephen Morley for Channel 4)*
Arthur consults his bank manager (Peter Cellier, Bob Hoskins) in *Pennies From Heaven (BBC)*
Louise Germaine in *Midnight Movie (BBC)*

Acknowledgements

Books of this kind depend on generous helpings of other people's time and trouble, experience and advice, access and organisation. I have interviewed many who knew and worked with Dennis Potter. Rather than gather their names in a list both indigestible and fraught with the dangers of unintended implications of precedence, I would rather suggest that these individuals' quoted contributions within the text be taken as indicative of my gratitude. Some of those who kindly talked to me have not in the end been quoted directly, omissions dictated by the needs of my narrative or the inadequacies of my conduct of it rather than by any judgement of the value of their contributions. I content myself with the belief that, as they are all 'in the business' in one capacity or another, they will perceive the importance of subtext and understand that their input was in no sense wasted.

If I single out four individuals here, those not so favoured will not be dismayed. Dennis Potter's mother, Mrs Margaret Potter, and his sister, Mrs June Thomas, made me welcome in their home with great good humour, open-hearted trust (which I hope I have not let down) and encouraging enthusiasm for my project. Miss Iris Hughes, Potter's school teacher, was no less kind and informative. And Kenith Trodd, Potter's most frequent and enduring collaborator, fielded my every trivial query with patience and gusto, despite being successively in production with *Karaoke* and in pre-production with *Cold Lazarus* (his assistant Alexandra Harris was a brilliantly intuitive go-between).

With characteristic self-effacement, John Wyver allowed me to make off with the manuscript of his unpublished book about Potter and with his accumulated research. This is a flying start in anyone's language. My own researches made me dependent upon the sympathetic efficiency of several great institutions. Not the least of these was the BBC where Nicholas Moss, Head of Policy and Management, smoothed the path of access; Paul Almond and his assistant Shelley

Simmons patiently arranged for me to see recordings, many of which fell well outside their natural purview; and the top-of-the-range staff at the BBC Written Archive Centre at Caversham, led by Jacqueline Kavanagh and (in my case) featuring Jeff Walden, gave me unflaggingly sunny and expert service.

At Channel 4 Chris Griffin-Beale, with unrivalled ebullience, went into immediate action; his assistant Nick Dear kindly did the chores. The ITV companies have become much more difficult (more business-like?) for a freelance to bend to his will, but I am at least grateful to Richard Cox at LWT for his good-natured account of the ways of the world. (Clare Telford of *The South Bank Show* sprang to my assistance, however.) It was the British Film Institute which more readily (and economically) screened Potter's ITV work for me and I am indebted to Briony Dixon and the BFI staff. Gratitude also to Christopher Robinson of the University of Bristol Theatre Collection.

Much of the assistance I received was of the anonymous kind that researchers are apt to take for granted. But the patience and professionalism routinely offered in the following institutions lightens one's task immeasurably. I would like to thank the staff and officers of the Independent Television Commission Library; the Bodleian Library, Oxford (with a mention for Simon Bailey of the Oxford University Archives); the Oxford Union, the Oxford University Labour Group and the Oxford University Dramatic Society; the British Newspaper Library at Colindale; the British Library at the British Museum; the Westminster Reference Library; the Westminster Music Library; the Senate House Library, University of London; and the *New Statesman*. I am grateful to the following for their permission to reproduce copyright material (see Notes and Sources for details): BBC Written Archives Centre at Caversham Park, Reading, Financial Times Limited, Guardian Newspapers Limited, Isis Publishing Limited, Mirror Group Newspapers PLC, Newspaper Publishing PLC, Times Newspapers Limited.

For selfless advice, I thank Mark Le Fanu of the Society of Authors. For unknowing inspiration, I salute Garry O'Connor, the late Richard Ellmann and my old acquaintance Simon Callow. For personal encour-agement, I embrace Tony Coult, Roy Battersby, Richard Krupp, Diane Millward, Eric Davidson, Susan Jeffreys, Lynne Truss, Beth Porter, John Lyttle, Anne Karpf and David Yallop. Without the utter inflexibility or the precisely-apportioned praise of my editor, Roland Philipps, the inspired guidance of my agent, Tony Peake, always supplying what I need, whether caution or stimulus, and the gentle understanding of my partner, David James, through this strange preoccupation with somebody else, this book would certainly not have been written.

Preface

'Quotations can be used like bludgeons in insensitive hands.'

Dodgson, Alice[1]

The newcomer to biography enters two territories, both of which look relatively familiar and yet are full of traps for the unwary. One of them is the world of the book's subject, much anticipated and yet (thankfully) full of discovery. The other is the strange biosphere of biography itself.

This book is a *critical* biography of Dennis Potter. That is not to say that it is an attacking portrait; rather that it attempts to analyse and evaluate Potter's work in the context of the circumstances of his life. I hope many other books and studies of all kinds will come to be written about an artist who takes his place among the most significant of the second half of this century.

One of the more alarming outcrops in the biographical biosphere is the literary estate. The would-be biographer approaches it with trepidation for it guards the paper leavings, both grandiloquent and trivial, of the departed. In my case, I have not asked for access to any material that has not already been exposed to public view. My analysis is of what is on the record. To the 'official' biographer goes the honour (or the exhilaration or the responsibility or the chore) of examining the private papers, insofar as the estate permits. I wish him only joy of them.

But there are more ways of killing a cat, Charles Kingsley argued, than choking her with cream. My own draws heavily on what my subject himself wrote and said, on the assumption that the actual top-of-the-milk is always going to be preferable to any manufactured cream-substitute of my own. In my defence I call up no less an authority than Dennis Potter himself: 'Sometimes, at the nice times, it is tempting to abdicate the occasional solemnities of criticism and just orchestrate a series of quotations from the book being reviewed.'[2]

I believe I have offered rather more than 'just ... a series of quotations' within these covers. But many of the words are Potter's own and those of his collaborators. The literary estate holds copyright on the works themselves. As this book is not 'official' (that is to say, commissioned by the estate), formal leave to draw on those works has not been granted. So be it. Between them and me is a no man's land called 'fair dealing'. By this convention – to which I have enthusiastically subscribed – I am entitled to draw a single extract of up to 400 words or a series of extracts to a total of 800 words from each of Potter's works without seeking the estate's permission.

The matter is worthy of note for the simple reason that the Potter estate has acted in an unusually protective manner towards its literary demesne. More than one person who worked with Potter has said to me, 'I have been asked not to speak to you.' For whatever reason, my requests for interviews have been widely declined or ignored.

It may seem to the reader, as it seems to me, that a critical biography of this kind is in no sense calculated to, or likely to, devalue the literary estate or the reputation of Dennis Potter. Rather the reverse. Perhaps when the executors examine its contents, they will recognise that there is nothing to fear. Potter argued his own case robustly and he fiercely opposed the censorship of views and the repression of freedom of debate. And he leaves behind a robust *oeuvre*. From my efforts to elucidate it, he needs no protection.

W. Stephen Gilbert
Crouch End, London
June 1995

Introduction

Live and Kicking

British television at the end of the 1950s was different in every
particular from the medium we know today. There were just two
channels. One was delivered to 98 per cent of the United Kingdom
by the British Broadcasting Corporation, whose old wireless heart was
slowly reconciling itself to the ascension of the irresistible force. The
other went to 93 per cent from the private-sector confederation known
as ITV, then administered by the Independent Television Authority
and parcelled out by franchise to eight regional companies, only half
of which made regular programming for the whole network.

In the mid-1990s, on the other hand, the choice is dizzying. As
Rowland Morgan put it in his Digitations column in the *Guardian*,
'Satellite TV viewers will be able to zap a different channel every five
minutes for more than seven hours', a calculation expounded thus:
'Non-domestic satellite broadcasting channels licensed by the ITC:*,
87.'[1] And 147 cable services fall under the ITC's ægis too.[2]

Thirty-five years ago, most of ITV's output and virtually all of the
BBC's was made in-house, that is to say in the production offices
and studios owned and staffed by the broadcasting companies. The
programmes were received only in monochrome in return for a
mandatory licence fee of £4 per annum made over to the BBC,
after extracting £1 in excise duty, to finance both its television and
its radio programming.[3] ITV's income derived wholly from advertising
and sales; it still does.

In the 1990s the studio system is breaking down much as it did
in Hollywood in the fifties. Independent companies account for an
increasing proportion of production across the industry and for
practically everything on satellite and Channel 4. Still mandatory
despite the BBC's decreasing share of the audience, the licence fee

---

* The Independent Television Commission replaced the ITA's successor, the Independent
Broadcasting Authority, in 1991, simultaneously subsuming the Cable Authority.

at the beginning of 1995 was £84.50;[4] as a somewhat illogical gesture to the past (illogical because related to the domestic equipment rather than to the material broadcast), there is a licence rate of £28 for diehards and indigents viewing in monochrome.[5]

Many programmes of the 1950s were broadcast live in the true sense of being enacted at the moment of transmission rather than in the contemporary sense of being pre-recorded before a 'live' audience. So, for instance, if a play went out live, as most did, appearances by a character in successive scenes would need to be accommodated in the shooting plan. Dashes across the studio on tiptoe, being sure to avoid the camera cables, were the order of the day for actors, often shedding one garment in favour of another as they went.

Contemporary television 'as it happens' really only occurs in the presentation of news bulletins and on-the-spot reports, sports relays and those low-budget magazine shows that characterise out-of-peak programming for adults and children alike. Except for soap operas and children's serials which are pre-recorded on tape, the lion's share of drama is now made on film. An intriguing vogue for live relay from viewers' homes has led a couple of entertainment shows (*Noel's House Party, Don't Forget Your Toothbrush*) to embrace the rough edges of the old era and go truly live.

The sheer amount of broadcast television shrinks radically as the perspective lengthens. On 6 July 1959, for instance, the BBC scheduled just 460 minutes of programming, or seven hours and forty minutes, beginning at 13.00 with a meagre half-hour of Test Match coverage followed by a regional opt-out, then closing down for a puzzling quarter-hour before *Watch with Mother*, going off-air again until 16.30 when another thirty minutes of cricket was vouchsafed, then transmitting uninterrupted until closedown at about 23.10.

ITV, ever ready to steal a march, opened at 12.45 with homely fare until 13.25, draped round two minutes of news at 13.00, returning at 17.05 with *Small Time* and a continuous line-up until 23.30, a total of seven hours and five minutes. The whole day's television adds up to 885 minutes, an unimaginably modest total of fourteen and three-quarter hours. Even had it been possible to lay it end to end, there were still more than nine television-free hours in the day. How different were demands in those days.

As to the statistics of present schedules, Rowland Morgan again bends them his own way: 'TV offers 53 hours of illusion for each hour of life. Hours of programmes weekly in multi-channel UK homes: 9,000. Real-time hours in a week: 168.'[6]

The fare transmitted on 6 July 1959, a Monday, typifies the period. The BBC imported two western series, *Wells Fargo* (suitable for young viewers so shown at 17.10) and *Bronco* at peak (19.55–20.45, much the longest programme on the channel). Home-produced programmes included an hour of drama from 20.45: *The Case Before You*, a recreation of the workings of a magistrates' court (made by Elwyn Jones who three years later was to launch one of television's most significant creations, *Z Cars*) and *The Widow of Bath*, a conventional thriller serial.

Light entertainment comprised *Juke Box Jury* at 19.30, with 36-year-old comic Eric Sykes on the panel, and *A Song for Everyone* at 22.00, with Kenneth McKellar and the BBC Scottish Variety Orchestra, two examples of the Reithian BBC's safely middle-aged and middle-of-the-road notion of popular music.

There was improving culture from 22.30 until 23.00, a visit to the Royal Scottish Academy, in the company of John Betjeman and an Outside Broadcast (OB) unit, to admire its summer exhibition. The schedule's interstices were occupied by such gems as *Three Little Kittens* ('a film about a cat family on a farm, previously shown last year'), *Australian Walkabout* (a travelogue and another repeat), *Kay on the Keys* ('Kay Cavendish presents entertainment with the light touch'?) and, of course, news bulletins with sports reports and weather forecasts at 14.00, 18.00, 19.25, 21.45 and 23.00. But doubtless the event of the night was the return of the popular magazine *Tonight* (18.45–19.25), its presenter Cliff Michelmore being the *Radio Times* cover star.

Elsewhere that July week of 1959, the BBC's drama consisted of *The Golden Spur* by Constance Cox, the Sunday teatime serial; a Canadian teleplay called *The Concert* as the Sunday Night Theatre;* a direct relay of a 45-minute scene from a current West End comedy; a version of Odets' *Clash by Night* with a largely American cast; *The Common Room*, eighth in a series of half-hour plays by Leo Lehman; a 45-minute play called *From Out of the West* set, like Sartre's *In Camera*, in Purgatory; a continuing serialisation of Trollope's *The Eustace Diamonds*; a teatime serial by old reliable, Shaun Sutton; schoolboy favourite *Billy Bunter*; and detective series *Charlesworth*. On the face of it, there is more variety than ambition.

The ITV schedule was comparably timid and lacking in spice. *Thought for the Day* and *Lunch Box* with Noele Gordon filled the midday session; Outside Broadcast reportage, *Sky High*, played at 17.15, then US imports took over: a half-hour of *Popeye*, the sitcom

---

* The language of the so-called legitimate stage continues to inform the marketing of drama on television up to the present day, as though the younger and more raffish medium needed to take some dignified colouring from the old, socially desirable tradition.

Private Secretary with Ann Sothern in the 18.35 opt-out slot and, the most substantial item, an hour of *Wagon Train* at 21.00.

ITA quotas on informative programming would account for the running of *Right to Reply* against *Tonight*, before schedulers turned gratefully to a panel game, *Tell the Truth*, and an hour of comedy, *Don't Tell Father*, and *Jack Hylton Presents*. The news at 22.00 (the first since the 18.15 bulletin) was followed by *Johnny Ray Sings* and an independently made spin-off of an American cop-show with its US star now based in London, *Martin Kane, Private Investigator*, and a Robert Benchley short before *The Epilogue* completed the evening. Neither channel showed a feature film.

ITV drama also touched each day and all bases and the vintage looks to have more body than its rival. The American teleplaywright Tad Mosel was produced in ABC's Armchair Theatre – the slot had offered four of his scripts by the end of the year. A decent native television dramatist, Paul Jones, was represented in Television Playhouse, while Maugham's *For Services Rendered* was mounted as Play of the Week.

Series and serials comprised Granada's *Skyport*, set indeed in an airport; ATV's ineffable twice-weekly hospital soap *Emergency– Ward 10*; a courtroom series, *The Verdict is Yours*, also twice a week; the teatime serial *Sunday's Child*; a swashbuckler for kids called *The Sword and the Lute*; and *Crime Sheet*, a series developed from *Murder Bag* which subsequently found its most successful expression as *No Hiding Place*.

Fast forward: 6 July 1994 was a Wednesday and atypical only in the relatively small number of feature films screened on terrestrial channels (four) though there were at least fifty on satellite – the Movie Channel, TNT, Sky Movies and Sky Movies Gold transmit nothing else. The familiarity of televised movies has helped to ease constraint on the length of material made for the medium. The 50- and 60-minute programmes so scarce in 1959 are standard now; on this day, ITV was running a drama series at two hours, *A Touch of Frost*, as was Sky One with *Concealed Enemies*, while UK Gold created a 120-minute *Dallas* by screening two episodes back-to-back. Schedulers of the 1950s never imagined that viewers would routinely tolerate such marathons.

Sport was shown at even greater length: on this day, BBC2 had cricket coverage from 10.25 to 12.45, then (uninterrupted save by news) from 13.20 to 19.45; and this was only a second-round trophy match. Channel 4 had two and a half hours of horse-racing from 14.00. The four-yearly Soccer World Cup was being staged (ours was a rest day) and on the Tuesday fans could have switched between BBC1 and ITV and caught around five hours of coverage. The two dedicated satellite channels, Sky Sports and Eurosport, screened thirty-seven and a half hours of continuous sports between them. This is small beer, however, when set against the round-the-clock news on CNN and Sky News, rock'n'pop of MTV or endless shopping-by-telephone available on the QVC channel; on cable there is even a non-stop country music channel, CMTE.

Transmission hours are now approaching their limit. ITV indeed transmits twenty-four hours a day. On 6 July 1994, BBC1 was broadcasting from 06.00 until 01.10, BBC2 from 06.20 until 01.40 and Channel 4 from 06.35 to 02.40, all continuously. The satellite stations vary but many start at 06.00 and go on till past midnight.

Within these much extended terrestrial schedules, there is yet a dependence on US imports similar to that which obtained in 1959: in 1994 they were *Quincy*, *The Rockford Files*, *Sesame Street*, *The Equalizer*, *Mork and Mindy* and *LA Law* as well as first runs of *The Oprah Winfrey Show* and *Frasier*. What was most noticeably absent was drama. *A Touch of Frost* was all of the drama unless the soaps, both home-grown (*Brookside*, *A Country Practice*, *Coronation Street*) and Antipodean (*Neighbours*, *Home and Away*, *The Young Doctors*), and the children's serial *Byker Grove* are counted.

Elsewhere in this July week, besides the other regular soaps (*EastEnders*, *The Bill*, *Emmerdale*) and six children's serials (four of them repeats), there were only two pieces of drama on BBC1, both made by independents: a dramatised serial of the novel *Love on a Branch Line* and an action series called *Roughnecks*. ITV had one more drama series late-night, *Moving Story*. Channel 4 transmitted two new half-hour plays from Northern Ireland and repeats of two short fantasy pieces. BBC2's whole week was a drama-free zone: satellite and cable show no new native drama.

It was not possible, I suggested above, to lay the 1959 schedules end to end. Indeed so: there were no videos. Until 1958, the only medium that could store prepared material for later broadcasting was film. There were programmes – current affairs, dramas – that incorporated filmed inserts, the former so as to take prepared reports from outside the studio, the latter to allow a modicum of location work. But repeat screenings were only possible for programmes that were shot off-air with a film camera, though this always entailed, in a nice euphemism of the period, 'added loss of picture'.

Video-recording was introduced in a gingerly fashion and it was still almost a decade before electronic editing became possible. Save in exceptional circumstances, a show was taped 'as live', re-recording being deemed inexcusably improvident.

The home video boom was twenty years away. In the early 1960s, NASA, the American space exploration centre, was the first customer for a dedicated system but it was not until 1967 that CBS, the supplier, perceived a domestic market potential. By 1971, the Japanese had bought decisively into the field. VHS emerged from fighting rival systems for market domination and began its relentless penetration of viewers' homes, the British market being an especially receptive one.

While at any one time the large contemporary audience is, like that of earlier generations, watching off-air, a growing proportion of viewers 'time-shifts' (video-records from transmission and – in theory at least – views later) or simply disregards transmission in favour of bought, rented or home-made videotapes.

A further development in the way people view entails the hand-held remote which permits the viewer to change channel or switch from transmission to videotape without getting up. Kids who live to 'zap' (switch constantly between channels) cannot imagine the long years during which the benighted viewer was obliged to stagger across the room to change channel or indeed to make any kind of adjustment to the set.

And such adjustments were needed as the picture was apt to disappear under interference like the notorious 'snow' effect. Technical breakdown at the transmission end was common in the 'live' era, quite apart from the inevitable human error or mishap on air. The musical interlude playing over a caption bearing the solemn entreaty 'Please do not adjust your set' is as distant a phenomenon as the horse-drawn milk float. Young viewers today are to be pitied for being denied the gleeful sight of a harassed presenter taking almost perceptibly hysterical instructions over a telephone and then trying to vamp till ready through the gritted-teeth rictus that cannot hide the sense of betrayal in front of millions.

On-screen presenters were always an important ingredient in television's approach to its audience, especially at the BBC where a degree of corporate identity was both sought and unavoidable. Once the arrival of ITV in 1955 had confronted the Corporation with a direct competitor, the urge to catch and keep an audience grew strongly on both channels, yielding the scheduling concept of 'channel loyalty'. Within the ITV system, the first major companies, Associated-Rediffusion, ABC Television, Associated TeleVision (ATV) and Granada TV Network aimed at branding their own programmes, both with a discernible company style and with top-and-tail logos.

6

This philosophy of distinctive broadcasting could not last. In the 1970s, media analyst Anthony Smith characterised BBC1* and ITV as 'moving towards a point of convergence'[8] as they made counter-bids for exclusive contracts with the same actors, presenters and 'personalities' and deliberately aped each other's ratings-rewarded shows. Channel 4 was launched in 1982 on a policy of acting as a 'publisher' of programmes made out-of-house, the effect of which has always been that the channel seems more like somebody's random collection of favourite videos than the provider of an organic bill of fare.

The arrival of satellite, cable and a plethora of channels with budgets tailored to the purchase of existing and hence proven programmes rather than the generation of new material (through the much more expensive and risky process of commission, development and production) has merely underlined the pith of the old saw that 'more means less'.

The independent production companies, competing in a buyer's market, necessarily tend to a market standard that lends itself to being offered to any and every broadcaster and to as many potential co-producers as possible. The phrase hovering in the wings of this situation is, of course, 'lowest common denominator'.

Moreover, changes in the economy and business practices have brought executives from unrelated industries, along with the accountants and marketing consultants, into the offices once occupied by showmen. Again, there is a parallel with the change in Hollywood, run in its heyday by inspirational despots like Louis B. Mayer and Adolph Zukor, now managed by interchangeable suits with business-school certificates.

British television, in the same way, has seen the likes of Lew Grade and Sidney Bernstein succeeded by a generation of venture capitalists to whom the medium is of interest only as long as it pulls its profitable weight in a diversified portfolio. Television and movies have become businesses for profit's sake rather than laboratories in which latter-day alchemists pursue their vocations and make discoveries. For their part, ITV and the BBC are metamorphosing, like so much else in the British economy, from manufacturing into servicing industries.

Back in 1959, plays were not only welcome but sought by television companies. Transmission hours look absurdly circumscribed from the perspective of today, but to the mandarins of the time the schedule's appetite could induce misgiving bordering on panic. 'The insatiable maw' was a phrase that stuck to television.

---

* The BBC's second channel, BBC2, opened in 1964 when the existing channel was renamed.

As John Bowen told me for a 1975 article trawling writers' thoughts on the medium:

> The great days of television drama began when commercial television began, because suddenly there was a demand for plays and the companies actively looked for playwrights. Cecil Clarke at H. M. Tennent Globe Productions (nicknamed Binkievision; it provided plays for ATV) had a system by which he contracted people to write two plays a year for £1,500 which was then quite enough to live on. David Mercer and David Rudkin wrote for him, and Peter Nichols and Ronnie Harwood and I. Sydney Newman had his own stable over at ABC and the BBC were forced to compete. At that time it was very hard to get a play produced in a theatre because the West End was as difficult then (nearly) as it is now and the Reps performed only revivals and West End successes. Only the Royal Court provided hope for the future.[9]

Interviewed for the same article, Alan Plater remembered 'a genuine and urgent *search* for new writers, at a crude level to fill up the schedules, at the proper level stimulated by a real desire to unearth new talent. Television was a real adventure playground – the early *Z Cars*, The Wednesday Play, *That Was the Week* etc – and the young writer with things to say was naturally drawn to it.'[10]

The early sixties were dubbed the 'golden age' of the teleplay. But even in the mid-1970s Howard Brenton was enthused by the possibilities of the medium: 'There is great pressure on television because it matters. As a "medium" it is still in that pristine, primitive state where it is not thought of as *art* but as *stuff*, naturally assumed by the majority of citizens as part of each day (perhaps the Globe was thought of like that). It is therefore very exciting to write for – you can get straight into the public's vein. Notice how the Whitehouse gagging lobby talks of "poisoning" and "corrupting", making a body "sick". It indicates what television is – a rich jugular straight to the heart and mind.'[11] This enthusiasm and imagery is intriguingly reminiscent of the way Dennis Potter spoke and wrote of television.

What I mean by a teleplay (or single play or one-off play) is a piece of drama written for transmission on, and production by, television, with a cast and crew assembled ad hoc and then dispersed. The piece might be a dramatisation of a short story or even a novel served up in a single encompassment; or (preferable in my view) it will be an idea conceived purely for the medium.

The methods by which plays got on to air have greatly changed over the years. In the fifties and sixties, a producer could garner considerable power, generating a substantial output with a degree of dispatch that would make the modern producer's head spin. In 1959 Sydney Newman produced forty-eight plays for the Armchair Theatre strand which ABC networked live every Sunday night. In 1994, a producer who had gone out and hustled and pitched sufficiently for her credit to appear on a total of two projects could consider it a bumper year, though she might well be looked upon as a dangerous empire-builder.

Newman, who 'couldn't make a living painting',[12] found his way into movie-making via photography. The old prophet of documentary, John Grierson, was then based in Newman's native Canada and through him the ex-painter gained a foothold in the Canadian Broadcasting Corporation where he graduated to Head of Outside Broadcasting. 'Knowing nothing about drama', he applied for and secured the post of Head of Drama. 'Contemporary relevance' was his holy grail but Thurber provided a more elegant slogan which was also the source of a famous play-title: 'Let us not look back in anger, nor forward in fear, but around in awareness.'

Teledrama, which inclined towards the stodgy and safe in Britain, was then in its heyday in the States. Work by such writers as Paddy Chayevsky, Rod Serling and Reginald Rose as well as Tad Mosel was drawing significant audiences to Play of the Week and Playhouse 90. Newman set out to emulate this at CBC.

One of his successful productions, *Flight into Danger* by his discovery Arthur Hailey, was screened on British television and as a result Newman was invited in 1958 to join ABC (the television arm of Associated British Picture Corporation) to produce the Saturday night series Armchair Mystery Theatre.

Barely had Newman got his feet under his desk when Dennis Vance, ABC's Drama Supervisor, was 'kicked upstairs'. Newman agreed to succeed him on condition that he could produce the new Sunday-night slot, retitled Armchair Theatre. As Head of Drama-cum-working producer, his chain of command was short: he simply reported to his managing director, Howard Thomas.

'Nobody in my estimation had a clue as to how to make a series of plays,' he reckoned thirty years later. 'I decided that I would do original plays about the United Kingdom today.' But first he had slots to fill. Newman had brought with him a number of scripts and he was soon joined by Canadian directors like Alvin Rakoff, William 'Ted' Kotcheff, Silvio Narizzano and the Canada-based Englishman Charles Jarrott.

He next invented the story editor, initially a research job for an enthusiast with an eye for the television potential in both established and would-be writers. Thereafter, the story editor's formal role was to work closely with the writer and represent his interests. As they proliferated, editors would routinely graduate to producing, a natural enough route that at least ensured the literacy of producers. Book critic Peter Luke was the first to be called to this crucial task.

The 1959 season of Armchair Theatre vividly reveals the developing policy: thirteen of the plays shown before a brief summer handover were North American in origin and/or subject matter; after the summer break all but two emanated from this side of the Atlantic, including a lively Irish input. Within that second batch was a significant new piece, grafting on to the American model an accurately heard native argot and reflecting a popular audience's vital daily concerns: *No Trams to Lime Street*, the first play of a Liverpudlian actor, Alun Owen.* The play enjoyed rave reviews and Newman's quest was legitimated.†

Peter Luke had discovered Alun Owen in the theatre and Newman, when he saw Owen's work for himself, endorsed Luke's judgement. Newman couldn't fathom the next play Luke recommended to him but he immediately recognised its quality. The author, a struggling actor, was summoned – 'he was poor, he was ragged, this beautiful, handsome guy' – and Newman commissioned a play but told him 'for Chri'sake I want the audience to understand it'. Understandable or not, Harold Pinter's *A Night Out* took Armchair Theatre right to the top of the ratings.

Sydney Newman had set himself to found a native teledrama. The existing American scripts allowed him the time to find it and to set a standard to be followed. By the time he left ABC in 1963, the original television play was well established in Britain. Newman's next post ('though I took a drop of £3000 a year') was Head of Drama Group at the BBC in succession to Michael Barry – 'his concern was art rather than audiences and in our business that's not good'.

In his second year, the BBC's answer to Armchair Theatre was launched: The Wednesday Play. To produce it, Newman appointed the chunky, red-haired Scot, James MacTaggart: 'Pick a good man and boy, you're away.' The arrival of BBC2 allowed for the development of the classic serial, more new one-offs and a live platform for new writers in Thirty Minute Theatre.

---

* Both Alun Owen and Peter Luke died in the twelve months following Dennis Potter's death.
† Newman tells the tale that the morning after *No Trams* he was summoned to see Howard Thomas who had with him the Head of ABPC, an American. 'What was that crap on TV?' barked the latter. 'I didn't understand a goddam word of it. My chauffeur's English. He didn't understand a word of it either.' But the play's success permitted regional accents to proliferate in teledrama.

At the BBC, Newman refined and developed his philosophy, always ensuring that the central place in the Corporation's huge programme of drama was occupied by original one-off plays written for the medium: 'the peak of drama is the single play'. In 1968 he told an interviewer: 'In television, it just isn't enough to write a beautiful play and have it performed and directed beautifully. There's an immediacy about the medium that demands that drama should grapple with problems that are urgent and of the moment. Drama must walk right into the middle of society and examine it to find out what makes people tick.'[13]

Teledrama of the mid-1990s has no such agenda. 'Immediacy', 'grappling' and 'examining' are not terms today's viewers would recognise. The malaise which Newman too optimistically discounted in 1968 is more familiar: 'When American plays lost their original vitality, the series took over as the first choice of sponsors wanting to get big audiences for their money. Instead of fighting to put the vitality back, producers went out and bought big Hollywood stars. It made no difference. Audiences just didn't care. So they got bigger and bigger stars, and more and more of them, and that's when the cost began to explode. In this country there is a divine gift of good sense which should enable us to avoid this mistake.'[14]

The system developed under Newman was admirably direct. Staff story editors went out to find scripts or simply, before the process became institutionalised, to find people who might be able to write. Staff directors then attempted to realise the writers' intentions in production. The staff producer had a certain assignment of slots and filled them either by selecting from a pile of scripts that had been submitted for consideration or by commissioning writers to attempt to dramatise particular broadly agreed ideas or (most often) a mixture of the two. Essentially the same system prevailed when I did a stint of my own producing plays for the BBC in the late 1970s, save that the staff director had gone and freelancers were hired to direct the productions.[15]

Invited in by a producer or story editor, the playwright would be encouraged to air, frequently in the vaguest terms, whatever notions might be on his or her mind. Anything that caught the producer's interest would be discussed further and then a formal commission with cash up-front would be negotiated with the writer's agent.

Based on the producer's schedule and the writer's existing commitments, a delivery date would be fixed. Assuming it was met, the script could go into pre-production as soon as any rewrites had been agreed. The whole sequence from first meeting to casting might be encompassed in a matter of weeks, so that a half-formed idea shyly put forward in January was being transmitted to an audience of millions in July.

Dear dead days. The producer of the nineties has a complex game of industry politics to play, beginning with the fact that staff producers have gone the way of staff directors. Everyone is on project-only contracts now; there are no guarantees of either jobs or slots. A producer is earning only when her project secures a backer.

Meanwhile, the story editor has lost ground. From the later sixties, the term script editor was more widely used but this changed again as some claimed, or were given, new and far-reaching functions and became 'script executives'. The non-executive, short-contract script editor found himself sliding up the end-credits, displaced by more urgently consulted specialists like the casting director. The eclipse of the script editor shadowed the decline of the writer.

The producer was, in Sydney Newman's phrase, 'the conscience of the project'.[16] The patronage wielded by the producer thirty-five years ago – even fifteen years ago – now resides with the head of department in the broadcasting company, the chief executive in the independent production company, and the representative of the financing co-producer who may have no working knowledge of television. These brokers habitually take the credit '(co-)executive producer', a title unheard of in British-made television until it began to appear in the late seventies attached to Ken Riddington's name on, of all unlikely projects, the established serial melodrama *The Brothers*.

The growth of executive power is astonishing, especially in the States which, as with so many trends, prefigures what will obtain in Britain five years later. Consider a product like *Roseanne*. It's a highly popular and well-matured US sitcom, very nearly a decade old, with a star who knows what she wants and insists on getting it. Then look at the credits on the show. An episode from the 1995 series typically lists five executive producers, two supervising producers, five plain producers and two co-producers, two creative consultants and an executive-in-charge-of-production, not to mention three executive story editors and four story editors. What do all these high-powered people do, you are entitled to wonder, on a show which ought pretty much to fuel itself, aside from get in the way of 'the talent' and pointlessly argue everything?

None of the executives proliferating through the television business needs to know much about drama or programme-making generally or, especially, scripts. This will not stop them having firm opinions on every dot and comma. In a highly expensive business like television, every dot and comma reads as money. And what those executives do know about – or rather what they control – is money.

The economic imperative is the most continuously felt of the pressures on present-day programme-makers but it is not only financial constraints, or indeed cultural or structural changes, that define the way in which television has changed in Britain. There is also an issue of political will. Television's controllers fear that they do not possess true control unless they can demonstrate that they have endeavoured to protect their resources from the interference of politicians by winning and holding easily tabulated public support. That support is measured in ratings and income from international sales.

Accordingly, almost no 'new' programmes are attempted on BBC1 or ITV unless they enjoy the safety net of co-finance and pre-sales or trail glory in another form. Popular television therefore means adaptations, revivals, copies, sequels, spin-offs, star vehicles, co-productions and imports. Anything remotely original is market-tested into insipidity.[17] This categorical expunging of originality is comparatively recent. A quite different orthodoxy held sway when there were one-off television plays in evidence, for the play was 'new' by nature, or at least it was once Sydney Newman had decreed that it should be so.

As live transmission gave way to pre-recording, plays grew in ambition. But the machinery sometimes lagged. For many years, the standard process entailed rehearsal for a couple of weeks, usually in a dowdy and draughty hall not noticeably near the studios. The floor would be blocked in a simplified version of the designer's plan for the studio so that the director could envisage where to place his cameras and the actors got a sense of how little room they had for manoeuvre.

Two or sometimes three long days in the studio were usually allotted. The studio staff – the engineers, lighting experts, camera operators, sound recordists and so on – were never drama specialists; they were *studio* specialists. They might have been recording *Blue Peter* yesterday and be working on *The Dick Emery Show* tomorrow. Some of these interchangeable workers would be stimulated and feel challenged by the one-off nature of the play, by its particular, perhaps unique requirements and become drawn into the director's often somewhat private quest to make the production memorable. Others would grumble about the temporary departure from comforting routines and affect to find (perhaps actually find) the piece impenetrable.

The director would most often have five cameras to place. Before off- and on-line electronic editing allowed post-production on a studio drama to be as extensive and detailed as in film, the editing largely had to be done live, that is to say by switching via the vision mixer from one camera's shot to that of another while the scene was being enacted. Self-evidently, pace and accuracy were sacrificed. Advocates of working on film had a decisive argument when they spoke of 'finesse'. A cut created at leisure on the bench will always be sharper and more flattering than a switch between cameras directed at screech pitch in a sweltering studio gallery.

Sixteen-millimetre telecine film (as opposed to the 35mm and later 70mm standard used for theatrically-released features) was increasingly favoured by directors who preferred location work to the 'theatricality' of studio sets, especially those like Ken Loach and others associated with producer Tony Garnett who sought to create a social-realist teledrama shot in the homes, buildings and streets where the people whose lives they would portray actually lived. There were many more directors who insisted on film for less honourable reasons, seeing television drama as a mere stepping-stone to theatrically-released movies, Hollywood and serious money, and therefore needing to demonstrate that they could shoot film.

Such people may have made more money in movies. But I could fill the whole of this page with a list of directors – and producers and designers and actors and (maybe most of all) writers – whose routine television work was infinitely more individual, thoughtful, expressive, imaginative and achieved than even the best and most successful of their feature films.

The electronic studio could be a mule to drive. The studio manager always seemed to be the dourest man in the world, never betraying the minutest reaction to anything you managed to get recorded, however heroic, then abruptly announcing in a tone of menace that ensured you knew he would brook no argument that there would be no question of an overrun. This unforgiving figure set the tone for the entire working environment.

Because it was such an unyielding process, the studio recording always entailed a degree of patch-up. The worst compromise was the naturalistic studio drama with telecine inserts: actor A in studio set of domestic hallway goes to front door in response to the doorbell; cut to actor B standing on the garden path, apparently supposed to be seen through the open door but actually shot on film three weeks earlier in completely mismatching light.

Even so, the studio was capable of sustaining great concentration and the interaction of relationships and ideas could be explored with a subtlety and resonance that the mozaic construction of film could not hope to develop. The tension and danger endemic in theatre, upon which unrepeatable heights of emotional daring or powerful outpourings are founded, could also occur under the sweaty pressure of the studio. Film is a cool medium; the stage and the studio are hot – sometimes unbearably, thrillingly.

Studio drama always *looked* as though it were happening *now*. There was a powerful sense that anything was possible, that because it might not have been shot and cut and processed weeks ago it might still escape from the institution's control. Part of the illusion was the sound quality, the studio always full of suppressed but resonating noise. A film's track, minutely reconstructed in post-production, often has a finished, deadened atmosphere.

Several writers wrote again and again for the studio, refining their techniques as its characteristics became more familiar: David Mercer, John Hopkins, Trevor Griffiths, Howard Schuman and, most doggedly of all, Dennis Potter. Fortunately for the writers there were enough directors who saw the characteristics of the studio not as shortcomings but as disciplines: men like Michael Lindsay-Hogg, Herbert Wise, Bill Hays, Philip Saville, Peter Hammond, Don Taylor, John Glenister and Jimmy MacTaggart (who directed as well as produced) along with Potter's regular directors.

In time, the studio did grow more responsive to serious work. When single-camera shooting with a full editing process began to be permitted, the studio director could observe as many niceties as his film-making rival. Richard Eyre's superb 1981 production of Chekhov's *The Cherry Orchard* used just this technique.[18]*

The development stumbled, however. Several forces came together to imperil the one-off play made in the studio. Some were technical (lightweight OB cameras allowing a different kind of location work); some institutional (the BBC, having capitalised its investment in studios, could consider increasing its work away from base); some economic (defrayal of spiralling costs through both out-of-house commissions and co-production). But most had an inevitable political nuance: the drive to maximise audiences for everything that moved making the unpredictable a liability; policy decisions, initially by Channel 4, subsequently by the BBC and the ITV companies, to seek to participate in the feature-film market; a determination to rein in drama producers who allowed writers unique privilege as suppliers of programmes from outside the institutions of television.[19]

The individuality of the writers carried the strongest political charge and therefore was always most vulnerable. It was The Wednesday Play and its successor Play for Today that saw the zenith of bolshie one-off writing. No reviewer found a more pithy image for the slot

* Eyre's cameraman, Geoff Feld, was the first to be able to specialise in videotaped drama.

than the man writing for *The Sun* (the pre-Murdoch version) in 1968: 'A Wednesday night without a Wednesday Play on BBC1 is a bit like a pork sausage without an irritating but reassuringly authentic lump of white gristle buried somewhere beneath the skin.'[20] Nobody wrote like that except this sometime critic: Dennis Potter.

It was that position of the writer outside the machine which I have always maintained is the most significant factor. The writer could be anybody. He or she did not have to be someone who had been through the institutionalising process of the television career structure as (usually) did the producer. And so there was nothing to prevent a writer's very first attempt at a piece of drama being broadcast to a seven- or eight-figure audience. Insofar as a consensus about television's function and methods holds sway within the broadcasting institutions, the playwright represented a uniquely licensed force outside that consensus.[21]

This, then, is the nub of it. The dramatist, living and working out in the world, is the sole Trojan horse of consequence and substance for interventions into television that are not born of the industry. The medium's controllers, at the BBC especially, are now apt to hail such programmes as *Video Nation* as powerfully democratising gestures, giving 'the people' unmediated 'access' to the viewing millions. I think we should be brisk with this proposal. The *Video Nation* project, charming though it might be, is a small crumb from a high table. There is all the difference in the world between a unique 50- or 75-minute play, validated by production at the highest level and run at peak, and a two-minute slot in which highly contained extracts of home-made to-camera address are played as curiosities on BBC2.

It was the once-and-for-all nature of the teleplay that gave it its unique impact and therefore its author an inimitable platform. It may be objected that series and serials writers are equally licensed but in practice this is not the case. Because of its commitment to a series or serial over several transmission weeks, the producing company needs to be much more certain of ratings success than in the case of a play which, if it fails to hold an audience, is at least mercifully over. But a series is a continuum. Hence the initiative for a series will more likely come from the company, through the executive producer, than from the writer outside.[22]

The single play explored positions and visions which no memo-scribbling executive – whose natural instinct would be to envisage any story-line fleshed out according to an industry-standard notion of professional writing – would dream of. The kind of writers who preferred personal vision to such hack-work could not be second-guessed by executives whose security depended on feeling they knew what to expect. In an industry where, to borrow William

Goldman's deathless dictum, 'NOBODY KNOWS ANYTHING' (his capitals),[23] the illusion that he is on top of it is critical to an executive's self-image and well-being.

In view of the unpredictability of the one-off play and its writer, what is remarkable is not so much that the form was abandoned but that it was ever allowed to take root in the first place. That it did indeed flourish is a tribute to the confident liberalism as well as the theatre sensibility of the early television producers and their bosses who enabled them to pursue such risky and idiosyncratic fare.

The clarion call of the BBC's Drama Department in the sixties and early seventies was 'the right to fail'. Single plays were granted a degree of exemption from the ratings war. Given the sheer width of the BBC's battlefront, it was a meagre enough concession. In the schedules, plays were 'hammocked' between more obvious crowd pleasers. There was some discreet winking between BBC and ITV over scheduling of supposed loss-leaders. And the mandarins could be consoled with awards and kudos and even reconciled to controversy if it was contained as headline-grabbing and escaped the notice of the Home Office.*[24]

Plays *did* fail commonly enough. They could occasion large-scale channel-switching, attract hostile notices and draw unlooked-for political flak upon executives. Equally, they sometimes won startlingly high ratings and rave reviews and landed industry prizes around the world, and not just because other nations' television lacked the resources or the traditions upon which to build a wide-ranging teledrama. Most significantly of all, they carried seeds which germinate right across the field. Techniques tried out in plays flower later in other forms. For instance, the gambit of direct address to camera in Dennis Potter's *Nigel Barton* plays brought much credit three decades later to avowed Potter admirer Andrew Davies in his serial dramatisations of Michael Dobbs's Palace of Westminster sagas. And, even after his death, Potter's much-favoured use of mime to vintage recordings turns up in insurance advertisements.

Many long-running and/or much-lauded drama series (*Rumpole of the Bailey, Callan, The Sweeney, Don't Forget to Write!, Boys from the Black Stuff, Gangsters, The Regiment, Z Cars*) originated in single plays; other one-offs were later remade as feature films or mounted in the theatre or both (*Up the Junction, A Suitable Case for Treatment, Whose Life Is It Anyway?, Bar Mitzvah Boy, The Apprenticeship of*

---

* Until the Department of National Heritage was set up in April 1992, the Home Office held responsibility for broadcasting.

Duddy Kravitz, Shadowlands, 84 Charing Cross Road, A Voyage Round My Father).

Because plays offered a forum for individuality, the breadth of subject and style and intent was inordinate. Some writers (David Mercer, Jim Allen, Trevor Griffiths, David Edgar, Howard Brenton) had an overtly political agenda to explore. Some had particular social concerns to express (Tony Parker, Nell Dunn, Jeremy Sandford, Barry Hines, James O'Connor). Others (Charles Wood, Clive Exton, Alan Bennett, Douglas Livingstone, Jack Rosenthal) possessed a comic spirit much too rarefied for the shallows of sitcom. Yet others were prepared to experiment with form (Rhys Adrian, Howard Schuman, Stephen Davis, Barry Bermange, David Halliwell).

But more than anything, plays were written by bewitching storytellers (John Hopkins, Alan Plater, Hugh Whitemore, John Bowen, William Trevor, Roy Minton, Peter Terson, Don Shaw, Peter McDougall, Arthur Hopcraft, Fay Weldon, Alan Bleasdale, Colin Welland, Neville Smith, Philip Mackie, Tom Clarke, Julia Jones, David Cook, Hugh Leonard, Michael Frayn, Simon Gray, Keith Dewhurst, David Rudkin: I own to, and regret, the absence of many women and any non-whites in these lists). All are possessed of relationships, aspirations, dilemmas, the stuff of humanity rather than the stereotypes common to series, soaps and sitcom.

The studio lent itself to such concerns. The most – perhaps the only – important teleplaywright to emerge in the last ten years, Malcolm McKay, put it well when I talked to him for background to an article in 1994: 'In the studio [dramas] have to be about people, about the interaction between people, rather than about the locations.'[25]

This sense of being 'about the locations' puts, in a nutshell, the objection to the film-making for television that has displaced the single play. John Hopkins memorably defined the essence of teledrama as 'two faces in conflict'.[26] Some of us cleave to the claim of the studio and tape as a still-underrated medium for one-off plays because, as Dennis Potter so often demonstrated, a contained and domestic image makes for very powerful viewing, feeling so close to the circumstances of that viewing.[27]

Nevertheless, British television systematically phased out plays in favour of film-making. It was not just a question of making teledrama on film; it was an intention to make films which could be screened on the box but which, it is implied, could have an additional life in cinemas, in film festivals, on video release. If a moment could be pinpointed as the sounding of the death-knell for studio drama and so for the one-off play, it was Gus McDonald's intended rallying cry at the Edinburgh International Television Festival which he chaired in

1977: 'The British film industry is not dead – it's alive and well and it's called television.'[28] Far from denouncing it as dangerous and false, the industry seized the cry as a mantra.

I took the view then, and hold it now, that the British film industry is, to all intents and purposes, dead. In support of my contention, I could hardly cite a higher authority than the BBC's Head of Films, Mark Shivas: 'There is no British film industry. The definition of an industry is something that makes things regularly.'[29]

But the corpse of British movies could only be made to dance on television at the expense of some creature already living there. And the survival of the one-off play had been in doubt throughout its history. In August 1964, veteran *Daily Worker* correspondent Stewart Lane quoted Kenneth Adam, Director of Programmes at the BBC, to the effect that there would be 'fewer single plays in the last quarter of this year because we are stockpiling episodes for certain series'.

Lane went on to report: 'Alarmed at a situation which could well discourage young playwrights writing for television, the Screenwriters Guild is asking Mr Adam to meet a deputation to discuss the matter.'[30] This, be it noted, was just two months before the launch of The Wednesday Play series, the first six of which went out in that last quarter.

Sensitive critics like Cuthbert Worsley saw the need to speak up for the play and its writers: 'This is a new medium and those who are writing for it are necessarily still experimenting. Those who aren't are simply using the clichés of the cinema or the stage and are not helping. But while the formal principles behind play-writing for television are still in a state of flux, so too the plays are likely to be.'[31]

In 1968 Sydney Newman left the BBC and was succeeded by Gerald Savory who, as author of *George and Margaret*, had been the white hope of the West End stage just before the war. In 1970 drama budgets were reduced and the Wednesday Play title was dropped in favour of the more portable Play for Today. Commentators were quick to make the unavoidable connection.

George Melly argued in *The Observer*:

> By allocating less money to spend on drama, you are forced to fall back on a longer and longer season of repeats . . . By creating a fluid situation, you help to conceal this, while at the same time giving yourself the right not to show a play at all . . . You confuse those viewers who regularly watched The Wednesday Play. They lose the habit, miss more plays and as a result the

drama ratings fall. This gives you further justification for more cutbacks and so on. If it's not watched, the TV one-shot play could disappear altogether in a few years, as it already has in the States. This would be a real tragedy . . . Those whom the gods wish to destroy they first muck about with.[32]

The old certainties were failing. By the autumn of 1968, when five live plays were produced by Thames, Rediffusion's successor in the London weekday franchise, filming and pre-recording were the dominant modes. The following year, the BBC ceased to put out Thirty Minute Theatre live.

Film was the coming form. Producer Tony Garnett opted for film as soon as his bosses would let him. With a little ironic licence, he recalled in 1990: 'Many writers wanted to write cinematically with fewer words and more images. Only Dennis Potter was quite happy at the time with studio dramas. He's a very conservative man but he came round in the end.'[33]

Dennis Potter had always taken a catholic view of the play's potential. 'My own attitude is that the television play is as flexible as the whole thing around it,' he wrote in 1967. 'The TV play can plunder at will, for it takes its zest and colouring and technical proficiency from the news, documentaries, sports, entertainments and sermons which surround it. The people who watch it regard it simply as a television programme, like the rest.'[34]

Nine years later, his stance was different and gloomier: 'More and more one talks of television as a *thing*, rather than of its constituent parts. I think the days of the television play are numbered; it will soon all be done on film and it'll be a director's medium like the cinema.'[35]

Alasdair Milne, then Director of Programmes at BBC Television, scanned the horizon at the beginning of 1977: 'I suspect that if in the next ten years the BBC's finances improve at all, we shall be looking very seriously at the possibility of developing our film stages at Ealing for making long programmes on film – "movies for television" as the Americans call them . . . Some of our American friends have indicated that they would be more than interested in joining in such a venture.'[36]

But it was not until the arrival of Channel 4 in 1982 that movie-making as an activity for the television industry began in earnest. It will be plain from the stance I have taken thus far that I see Channel 4's commitment to movies as another of its destructive tendencies. I ask merely: What is in it for the television industry and for the television viewer? It is not as if the movies are made primarily for transmission.

As a *Sunday Times* article woundingly put it: 'Such films as *Maurice, The Kitchen Toto* and *Sammy and Rosie Get Laid* . . . might owe their existence to Film on Four, but it is hardly the average viewer's fault if they look like old movies by the time they make the small screen.'[37]

At least Film on Four has a coherent (if base) policy: produce low-budget cinema films, give them time to make their theatrical mark, then transmit them for what they are, which is no more than low-budget cinema films, some of them now quite celebrated.

A perfect example opened theatrically in Britain at the beginning of 1995. *Shallow Grave* is directed, shot and acted by people with almost exclusively televisual credentials. It is in essence a domestic piece, located in one apartment but for a few brief 'opening-out' sequences and shot in a studio. Had not the set been constructed distortedly larger than life, it might have been an intensely claustrophobic experience. All the foregoing would suggest a standard television scenario. However, *Shallow Grave* is a genre piece which teleplays never are. Its shooting style, the vast television experience of cinematographer Brian Tufano notwithstanding, is purely of cinema; there are many shots that will not 'read' well on the small screen. And, clinchingly, it is a hermetically sealed product, an exercise with no resonance outwards. So although made primarily with television money, *Shallow Grave* is in fact a feature film, reminiscent in some of its tones of Roman Polanski's thirty-year-old cult picture, *Repulsion*. Like that movie, it has nothing to do with, and nothing to offer, television but that it will have its first domestic screening as a known quantity and with, as it happens, an enviable reputation. For although every piece of drama that director Danny Boyle made for television over some ten years has been in every way superior to *Shallow Grave*, it is the feature film that has cemented his reputation and won him awards.

These events tell much about the relative status of movie-making over teledrama. And the latter is everyone's inferior. Twenty years ago, Frank Marcus gave me a graphic example of the rewards of the theatre compared with those of television: 'My experience with my first televised play, *The Window*, was illuminating. This was originally written for the theatre. The television production was excellent – and almost totally ignored by the critics. A couple of years later, Ed Berman directed the same play, with Richard Pasco, in a restaurant basement in Queensway [the Ambiance]. Maximum seating capacity was 35; it ran for two weeks. Yet columns of reviews appeared in the press; it was even discussed on the BBC Overseas Service. As a result, it was published here and in America and has been performed extensively ever since.'[38]

It is hardly surprising that many writers found the tangible pleasures of working in the theatre, the sense of occasion and the vivid, immediate responses preferable to what could seem the soulless and robotic process of making plays for an unknowable television audience. Clive Exton declared:

I was driven from television by the fact that the play goes out and is forgotten. You're left with a manuscript and audience figures. That's not romantic, God damn it! I want to leave something behind. If I were a bricklayer, I'd be proud to have made that nice wall. I'd go and look at it occasionally. It *isn't* a job of work in that sense. That's a consciously anti-art argument. I hear that from people who write series and serials. It's a protective device – 'I'm not an artist. Contradict me, someone, please!' One wants one's work to stick around. One wants gold, glory or remembrance and in television you don't get any of them.[39]

It is clear that, while television was glad to have its writers when they were useful, the medium has rarely gone out of its way to bestow upon writers the consideration or status or rewards gladly poured over the most fly-by-night presenter. In embracing cinema values, television is without a second thought downgrading writers as an interest and writing as an art, even indeed as a craft.

If Channel 4 formulated a movie-making initiative, neither ITV nor the BBC did much more than bend in the wind of market change. In the 1980s, successive BBC drama chiefs Peter Goodchild and Mark Shivas committed the Corporation to a policy of movie-making that replaced its play tradition wholesale. There is an unresolved debate about plays-as-films, about what exactly distinguishes a drama on film for television screening from a feature film for theatrical release, about whether a piece of work can truly simultaneously encompass both functions. The BBC has never even begun to stage that debate.

Not all drama executives enthused about film. The long-serving Head of Drama at Yorkshire Television, David Cunliffe, frequently put his antagonism on record: 'It was the worst thing that ever happened to television. Every director fancied himself as a film-maker';[40] and 'We in television lurched towards the film camera . . . we let the challenge of video drama go. Now we find ourselves struggling against the Paramounts and CBS's';[41] and 'TV drama is seen as low-budget film production instead of drama skilfully custom-tailored for the home screen'.[42]

Other executives revel in their role in movieland. 'Two posters hold pride of place on Michael Grade's office wall at Channel 4' wrote Sue Summers of the Chief Executive in 1988. 'They advertise the recent British feature films *Wish You Were Here* and *A Month in the Country* – both rapturously received by the critics, both enjoying success at the box office and both backed by Channel 4'.[43] If you led a television channel, wouldn't you celebrate *programmes* on your office wall?

There is now a widespread condescension towards tape in television. Daily you can hear television professionals, people who know the difference, speak on air about 'film' when what is being broadcast is palpably videotape. 'We filmed this earlier,' they say but you look for film footage in vain. Can the explanation be that *everyone* in television, even on the News, dreams of making that Oscar-accepting speech?

Meanwhile, the film community does not unanimously sing the praises of the medium that believes it has saved the movie industry. 'There are those among the national film critics,' reports the *Daily Telegraph* film critic, 'who vent a muffled groan whenever they see the name Channel 4 on the credits of a film due for a cinema release. Asked why, they will usually reply that, whatever virtue there may be in the Channel's intentions, the results are too often "uncinematic". Cramped by the needs of the small screen, say its detractors.'[44]

And no less a figure than movie producer Sir David Puttnam sees dangers in the marriage with television: 'One scales down one's ambitions. I am worried that we've got a whole generation of film-makers whose sights have been lowered, whose cinematic thinking has been narrowed'.[45]

For its part, the BBC finally made up its mind to seek its cinematic fortune in 1988, announcing that it would back six pictures a year. I eventually saw the first, Michael Lindsay-Hogg's *The Object of Beauty*, on a transatlantic flight, in every way the appropriate fate for it. By 1990 Mark Shivas was talking of twenty movies per year: 'Getting our films into the cinema opens up a whole new area of finance for us. It also gives our films a high profile, which means that we can attract talent who otherwise might not work for the BBC.'[46] There is something amiss when a mogul can allow that his studio might not be everyone's magnet. I want to be a fly on the wall when Sydney Newman reads that. Two years later, the annual aim was revised down to five features. The BBC can confidently list only three successes *in toto*: *Truly Madly Deeply*, *Enchanted April* and *The Snapper*.

Having stopped making plays which were at a perceptible level *of* television, the BBC has set out to make movies by television rules. The result has been made-for-television films which, having no connection either overt or subterranean with the rest of the output, say little to the viewers, yet which are meant to double as made-for-theatrical release films aimed at the rumour of an international market, of which the success both box-office and critical has been only elusive.

It is not much of an overstatement to declare that there has been no true single drama from the BBC since Charles Wood's *Tumbledown* in 1988. While stray works might show individual distinction or bravery, there is no sense of the BBC having a presence in the field or a commitment to the form, no resonance for the audience or the industry about the output.

The ITV companies, pursuing a piecemeal policy of in- and out-of-house programme-making, have all but dropped one-off drama in both the home and the world markets. A brief flurry of feature-making, crested by Granada's worldwide success with *My Left Foot*, only burnt the companies' fingers.

ITV's central scheduling system, introduced in 1991, made mandatory the attachment of star names to proposals. One drama executive seems able to make the system work on her own terms, Granada's Sally Head. Much against the odds, she has built a strong run of series drama by developing writers like Kay Mellor (*Band of Gold*), Lynda La Plante (*Prime Suspect*) and Jimmy McGovern (*Cracker*). These works are shot on film and properly so. But their scale and rhythms and intensity, their resonance with Granada's committed reporting in *World in Action*, shouts televisuality.

Head left the BBC in 1989, telling the *Guardian*: 'The complexion of TV drama has changed so rapidly in the last year that people are losing sight of the writer. I believe that, even if production costs must be cut, more attention – even more attention – must be paid to the script. I would hope that Granada have recruited me to reinforce the importance of the writer.'[47] So far, so it seems.

Where else can the playwrights go? At an event hosted by the Everyman Theatre in Cheltenham, *Dennis Potter: A Fitting Memorial*, on 6 November 1994, La Plante announced that she was setting up her own company to protect her interests in her work and urged all writers to do the same. This struck me as a counsel of despair. Apart from the obvious objection that such a stance is only practicable for a small number of hugely successful writers, the assumption of corporate trappings must bring more problems than it solves unless the writer possesses self-discipline of a very high order. Other writers have turned themselves into masters of their own fate: Alan Bleasdale, for instance, and indeed Dennis Potter.

The nature of making television, however, is that it is collaborative. It works well when like-minded individuals join together with a single aim in view: to get the show done to the best of their ability. If the writer arrives with a phalanx of lawyers and accountants to spend months negotiating pre-sales and buyouts and residuals and billing and marketing and distribution, the notion of collaboration is overwhelmed by that deadly version of grandmother's footsteps, 'the deal'. Is it possible to achieve drama of daring and originality when the major creative effort is expended upon the deal? I would merely submit that the most striking and disciplined work of both Bleasdale and Potter was produced under the old, recklessly abandoned dispensation, the collaborative process.

There will be some (many?) who dismiss these thoughts as irredeemably Luddite, as whistling in the dark. How can the clock be put back? What hope of raising an audience would there be if old forms were reinstated? Who wants a political play banging on about care in the community or a stylised ecological drama set in a computer-generated rain forest in the studio when we can have Michael Caine in *Jack the Ripper*?

In a piece for *The Independent*, the BBC's Head of Single Drama George Faber wrote that 'there isn't an audience these days hungering for the studio play'.[48] This is a self-fulfilling prophesy as well as a claim built on a false premise. Of course, if you put out a short season of studio plays on BBC2 in high summer and pathetically name the series Stages (see footnote on page 3), it can easily appear that one-off plays are a disdained anachronism. But the schedulers' precious ratings record a huge and loyal audience hungering for the sitcom made in the studio, the soap on tape. Why not for drama too? Answer: Because there isn't any that is scheduled and marketed competitively. People generally want what they know rather than know what they want.

If Faber is right to say that 'it has become fashionable to knock the single play', it may be that there is an impatience in the business and among viewers with the between-two-stools vacillation of film-making for television. But it is perfectly possible for some of the lost ground to be won back and, given the power of his office, George Faber is the man who can make it happen. He could persuade the Channel Controllers that some one-off drama be exempt from ratings pressure, not such a grand gesture for the broadcaster that still supports *Panorama*. He could restore to producers the right to buy and commission work without months of meetings with battalions of executives and (worse but on the march) *consultants* who all demand their two penn'orth of unwelcome input.

He could re-create Thirty Minute Theatre's 'nursery slope' and ensure that it had sufficient slots to be effective (a minimum of twenty-six per year). He could book studios and give bold producers runs of slots on tight budgets and schedules. He could make it mandatory not only for producers but for himself too to read and decide on all but unsolicited scripts inside a four-week limit. He could create a climate wherein writers can *dare* again, be bold in style and content, yes, even be politically *engagé*. He could restore the prime ingredient that made it possible for Dennis Potter to have four plays broadcast in his first year as a playwright, twenty-one in his first decade, and so a glittering career: continuity of production.[49]

Ah yes, Dennis Potter. I have attempted in this chapter to give a partial history of the television dramatist and to indicate why I believe he is an important figure.

In the land of the teleplay, Potter was king. For a variety of reasons, some of them clearly to do with his circumstances and the accidents of his career, Potter found himself a television playwright, a role he embraced wholeheartedly.

It was on 6 July 1959 that Dennis Potter joined the industry, becoming a general trainee at the BBC. He was twenty-four years old. Earlier I compared that day's television output with the plethora of programming on 6 July 1994. On the latter date, Potter had been dead exactly one calendar month.

Between those moments – and, as we shall see, well beyond them – Potter made a more far-reaching contribution to the medium in Britain than any other individual since the BBC's founder John Reith. That, at any rate, is what I shall seek to demonstrate in the following chapters.

None of the other writers I have cited stayed as fiercely loyal to the medium as Potter did. He spelled out that commitment in 1970: 'Television is the only medium that really counts for me. It's the only one that all people watch in all sorts of situations. Television is the biggest platform and you should fight and kick and bite your way on to it.'[50]

How he fought and kicked and bit his way on to that platform and what sort of a show he put on when he got there is the burden of this book.

1

Take Your Finger Out of My Mouth

'Words themselves, . . . the very material of our discourse,
increasingly take on masks or disguises.'

Dennis Potter[1]

What writer has laid himself quite so bare, quite so unsparingly, quite
so often as Dennis Potter? His work bursts with the circumstances of
his own life. He has confronted the most intimate of human concerns
to a degree that simply could not be contemplated unless they were
deeply felt, entirely personal. In his work he stands before us naked
. . . more than naked: bleeding, his flesh flayed, his guts spilled.

At the same time, maddeningly, he juggles with fig-leaves. He
applies balm to the stigmata. 'Just kidding,' he croaks. 'I'm a *writer*.
This is art. It isn't life. Don't you *dare* jump to any conclusions
about *me*.'

Writing in 1983 for publication the following year, Potter was
forthright.

> Autobiography is by far the most boot-lickingly brutish of all the
> literary arts, especially when it purports to wrestle with personal
> motive . . . One of the reasons I chose to write 'drama' rather
> than prose fiction is precisely to avoid the question which has
> so damaged, or intellectually denuded, the contemporary novel:
> *'Who is saying this?'* . . .
>
> I do not believe what writers say about themselves, except
> when they think they are not saying it about themselves . . .
> the masking of the Self is an essential part of the trade. Even,
> or especially, when 'using' the circumstances, pleasures and
> dilemmas of one's own life. (Potter's italics)[2]

27

Five years earlier, Potter could, in speaking of his play about wartime childhood, *Blue Remembered Hills*, tell an interviewer: 'I wanted it to look as though it was autobiographical, because that's the most familiar form of storytelling – "listen, this happened to me". It could have done, it's just that sort of feel . . . I wanted it to come across in the shape of something remembered.'[3]

So much complexity, so soon. A remark of Joseph Heller's may help us here. He described his own work as 'writing autobiographically without writing autobiography'.[4] This finely-turned distinction will, I think, serve for Potter.

The attitude towards the probing curiosity of others, towards biography, is naturally self-protective. The private man defies you to prise the mask from his grasp. To analyse, he dreads (no doubt rightly), will segue into *psycho*analysing. The image this conjures up is of the defector Adrian Harris, the eponym of Potter's 1971 teleplay *Traitor*, fending off the anticipated questions of an international group of journalists come to see him in his Moscow flat: 'Bay away, my friends. I do not propose to show all of myself to you or your sort unless I can possibly help it.'[5]

It makes for a prickly and awkward subject, shielded by contradictions. I would of course be presumptuous (and verging on psychoanalysis) to start to ascribe mood-swings to the writer. That he could be afflicted by depression is well attested. How could he not be, given his intense physical afflictions?

But there are moments of sheer exhilaration, especially when he wants to tell the world how he has got off his bed and walked. His joy is infectious. Most often, though, the tone is wry or darker, the position more complex, more tentative. The masks are slipped on so expertly – or is it unconsciously? – that you lose track of where the latest transformation occurred. So the assumption of masks, the playing of games with the reader, viewer or interviewer becomes a prevailing method. It is a process of concealment by seeming revelation. He eludes as he illudes as he alludes.

The nearest Potter came to writing formal autobiography was a striking series of articles for *The Sun* in the summer of 1968, a time when the newspaper was still trading as a relaunched version of the old *Daily Herald* and before it was bought by Rupert Murdoch and transformed into the brand-leader among scurrilous modern tabloids. Potter called his column 'a mixture of self-revelation and opinionated comment'[6] and he employed it most potently as a public confessional and a platform to exorcise ghosts and get off his chest the pain both of being a writer and of being ill.

In a most playful piece from the *Sun* collection, Potter uses one of his necessary forays from the West Country to London to skate tantalisingly over details of his life. Does he calculatedly confide? Is he being unguarded?

From now on, I thought to myself, this column can be about what I *do* and not what I think. About activity, not moods. An illusion, of course. Do? Well, I got tight and walked into a fat milk machine in Gloucester Road . . . Oh, I had a good, good time all right. And spent every penny, stretched every muscle, broke a few personal taboos and forgot to ring home. Just as well. One of the kids had earache apparently. Miserable little blighter.[7]

Potter is not by nature or commonly by application a very precise writer. He does not excel at the buttonholing image, the delineation of a character that immediately strikes a chord of recognition in the viewer or reader, the shaft that illuminates in a phrase. His images are characteristically inordinate. He writes out of great passion, visceral emotion. He flails and shouts. He swamps and bludgeons.

Seeking *le mot juste*, an exercise which clearly tries his patience, he will bury it under an excrescence of related (sometimes tangential) *stuff*. Not that the stuff is not itself compelling and moving. Armed with vast quantities of alcohol and cigarettes he would work far into the night, pursuing 'that weird impulse which I can sometimes grab at when trying to write exactly the right dialogue for exactly the right character in exactly the right play; an impulse which always dribbles away uncaught, needless to say, but which still leaves the faintest aftertaste of the lost fruit in the abandoned garden.'[8]

The impulse to rewrite, to mitigate observation or stance, to hedge about and dodge behind subordinate clauses or images of eye-catching vibrancy is characteristic of Potter's writing all his life. His most famous sword-crosser at Oxford, Brian Walden, penned a gamy and rather trenchant attack on 'Potter and Potterisms' in *The Isis*: 'On those rare days when he crawls out of his cocoon . . . Potter is often forced to admit that much of what he writes and says is contradictory . . . Reasoning has never been Ishmael's forte. It is the emotional fervour which commands respect and this is not lacking.'[9]

Replying at (inevitably) more than twice his assailant's length, Potter stakes out a convoluted position, shedding Marx on one flank, Waldenite revisionism on the other, from which a candid aside leaps: 'No one can take debating speeches as definite positions, of course.'[10]

Definite positions are hard to come by and none more so than those concerning the act and art of writing. The week after that ruefully tender self-depiction as a seeker after nicety and lost fruit, Potter constructs an altogether more stonking version of himself, as if to slough off embarrassment at the humanity of what may have got away: 'Megalomania the purple monarch and its cringing, ashen-faced attendant Paranoia are perfectly acceptable bosom companions for any middle-aged writer stooped over a littered desk and an empty expanse of writing paper. Forty years old next month, I have long since given up the vain and heartless struggle to banish either of them from their poor habitation in the glittering hall of mirrors which leads from my gilded throne to the obstinate and sullen populace of words out there in the cold public prints.'[11] Remembering the constant awareness of bodily function in Potter's writing, the suspicion must hover around this ludicrous image that the gilded throne is where the middle-aged writer shits.

Consciously playing The Writer provides Potter with constant diversion and material. He apparently reveals tricks of the trade like a magician using the game of 'letting you in on the illusion' in order to cover a yet more baffling sleight of hand.

The beginning of an article for *New Society* is worth quoting at length:

Some writers are so hung up on the relationship between fiction and lying – *telling stories* is a popular description of both arts – that they insist on tightening the noose of theory about their necks. Many recent novels are stretched to allow their authors to lean in and out of the sentences, heavily breathing, obtrusive, irritating. They insist on challenging us with the fact that they really *are* there, shaping the words, manipulating the characters, conning and cajoling us, insinuating along each upward loop or downward stroke. These desperate, deliberately self-conscious interventions from the author are not usually appreciated by critics who, being conventional men with mortgages, rather dislike treacherous questions about the tensions between art and life. Novelists who set out to expose the mechanism of the story even while they are writing it are bound to seem awkward and pretentious to those who have solved the equations between the writer, the writing and the world (or between fact and fiction, truth and lies, 'truth' and 'lies') simply by taking them for granted. *Look here* – the orthodox can snarl – *I know this is a book I am reading, I know it is a story, I know it is written by someone, I know it is not, well, 'true'*. But why, then, do they get so upset when a writer goes out of his way to confirm such 'knowledge'? It is because the very act of so doing breaks open the form, construction or shape that had seemed neutral and safe and ...

I soon realised that if I went on in this vein I should lose my audience altogether. (Potter's italics)[12]

This vast paragraph is, we now learn, from a talk Potter was to give in his native Forest of Dean, a talk which, as he reports, he abandoned in favour of a spontaneous interaction with the people in the hall, some of whom he had known since childhood. The wrong-footing gambit does surely wrong-foot us. But does it nullify the foregoing argument? Are we attending the lecture seated in one of those halls of mirrors? Should we attend to what Potter says or to what his reflection says?

Some of those in the forest audience (if we are to credit his account) will have listened to him after absorbing his first novel, *Hide and Seek*, then just out in paperback. His *New Society* readers will have had the same opportunity. I open the novel at random and this paragraph falls right on cue under my gaze:

I have therefore intervened so early in my own narrative in order to stifle the dangerous kind of nonsense and critical confusion identified in the above paragraphs: the direct link, that is, between the real life of the writer and the invented life of his characters. The horrifying fact is that my erstwhile friends will seize only too eagerly upon certain possible segments of this book in order to demonstrate to the widest possible audience that the vicious things they have (to my certain knowledge) been saying about me are true. I can imagine the glee with which they will pounce upon this or that sentence, eyes bright with malice, mouths wet with cruelty. Let me emphasise again, therefore, with all the force it is possible to command, that only a fool or a charlatan will maintain that an author and his leading character are genetically or spiritually conjoined by things darker and stronger than the sweet grace of pure creative imagination.[13]

The incautious reader might suspect authorial 'leaning in' and breathing heavily. Perish the thought. Put up such a notion and the author recoils, 'Not me, guv' on his lips.

It is all good sport, bluff and counter-bluff. If you were to wish to portray Potter himself in a novel of your own and you wanted to hint at the source of your portrait but reserve the fall-back position of injured innocence, you might tinker with Potter's own name for your character. What could it be? Potter . . . some other decent craftsman, then . . . Cooper, Weaver, Thatcher (maybe not), Mason, Carpenter, Carver . . . What about Miller? And then for a first name . . . not Dennis, clearly, but something to suggest a shrewd judge: why, Daniel, of course, 'a Daniel come to judgement'.[14] And Daniel Miller is indeed the name of the hero of Potter's first novel. But he is not, oh *know* that he is not, Potter.

So we are dealing with a writer who defies us to read anything extraneous into his work, to try to part his words for a glimpse beneath, to make anything more of his own allusions to his life than what sits on the surface.

We have been warned. It is a warning that booms through Potter's writing, whether commenting on his own work or that of others. 'There was the statutory coffee-bar reference to Freud and the hero was a writer,' he notes, reviewing a television dramatisation of a John Wain story. 'The subject was writing – a combination which experience has taught us to look at with caution.'[15]

Another teleplaywright is castigated thus: 'Characters in plays may be allowed to spend time searching for their own significance. But writers should not make it so obvious that they, too, are looking desperately for it.'[16]

The ambivalence does creep in, perhaps when Potter is paying less than full attention. Reviewing *The Dick Van Dyke Show*, he makes a dangerous concession: 'A story about the life of a *fictional* comic scriptwriter written by a *real* comic scriptwriter is bound to be a curiously inbred but profitable exercise.' (Potter's italics)[17]

But what Brian Walden identified as 'contradictory' is as marked in Potter's attitude to the writing self as in any of the concerns that beset him. To reveal is at once to share generously and to expose recklessly. A note of appalled fascination sounds in his reviews of programmes in which members of the public speak frankly: 'People seem prepared to admit almost any personal weakness or sickness when the camera is on them.'[18]

He addresses the point more sardonically in one of his rangy *Sun* columns: 'Prim and proper folk, it seems, like nothing better than settling back with warm slippers and a cup of tea to watch some wretched sinner expose his weaknesses on the box. The old village stocks have shrunk to a 19-inch tube. And their one-time victims now get a cheque for 10 guineas instead of a faceful of rotten egg.'[19]

An incandescent rage at the 'intrusion' of the documentary *Marriage Guidance* (1977), made by Nick Broomfield and Joan Churchill, finally goads him into drawing a significant distinction between, in effect, biography and autobiography: 'Reticence is not necessarily a virtue for one's self but it is nearly always wiser and safer to practise it on behalf of others.'[20]

And indeed, in a rare outpouring of joyful energy engendered by remission from pain during his *Sun* season, Potter explicitly dedicated himself to the role of vessel brimming with juice which he would pour into his work: 'This column is willy-nilly turning into a weekly exercise in self-exposure. I find that in my writing I can only use myself, use up myself. So when I die I want to be completely emptied and completely exhausted. Which means, of course, that I am still rejoicing. Only a happy human being can write a sentence like that!'[21]

Must all this inhibit the aspiring analyst of the Potter canon? I leave to others the task even worse than the 'cheapest, nastiest ... most boot-lickingly brutish of all the literary arts'. This is a *critical* biography, an attempt at the life *and work* of Dennis Potter. I am concerned with his biography only insofar as the circumstances of his life inform the work. This may prove uncomfortably far.

Nevertheless, the passages I have already quoted from his writings seem to me to render the task easier. Potter presents a moving target. Deliberately or inadvertently, he shifts his ground. We are entitled to judge what he says as interim, not as definitive.

This is good. It means we need not be brow-beaten by Potter's sometimes excessive language and alarming aggression. He himself could be boot-lickingly brutish too. We can indulge him, we can make a judgement without fear of his disdain and pass on. The guard is down, the gloves are off. The monster is slain and we can enter the no longer guarded garden and seek the lost fruit. We can explore. We can have some fun too.

But compared with the licence Potter himself took with the lives of real people in his own work – Lewis Carroll and Alice Hargreaves, Edmund and Philip Gosse, Christabel and Peter Bielenberg, Giacomo Casanova and Jesus Christ – we shall be entirely scrupulous.

2

You're Sure of a Big Surprise

'Only those who were born and nourished in a small, relatively isolated community can know how strongly the day-to-day shapes of the past merge into and appear to dominate the seemingly more uncertain contours of the present.'

Dennis Potter, *The Changing Forest*[1]

Not since Hardy has an English writer's work been so suffused with a sense of place as Dennis Potter's is with the Forest of Dean. Potter passed through an extended rite of coming to terms with the land of his birth during the years after circumstances took him away. Again and again he wrote about it, either directly or obliquely. Finally, after years of being unable to settle anywhere else, he and his wife anchored themselves in Ross-on-Wye, eight or so miles from his birthplace in Berry Hill, Gloucestershire.

The best-known account of growing up in the area is *A Child in the Forest* by Winifred Foley. 'A *Royal* Forest, it had been,' she writes. 'Ten by twenty miles of secluded, hilly country; ancient woods of oak and fern; and among them small coal mines, small market towns, villages and farms. We were content to be a race apart, made up mostly of families who had lived in the Forest for generations, sharing the same handful of surnames, and speaking a dialect quite distinct from any other.'[2]

Dean's ancient royal status derives from its popularity as a hunting ground for the Norman kings. It lies between the Severn Estuary to the east and the Wye to the west. Wales is just across Offa's Dyke. In contemporary terms, the M4 bypasses to the south, the M50 to the north. But even with modern encroachment, it clings to an otherness.

34

Apart from its free-grazing sheep, the aspect of the forest that most defines it historically is its mining. The toponyms speak the legacy: Coleford, Coalpit Hill, Cinderford, Coalway. Iron was dug from the Roman occupation, coal since the Industrial Revolution, when the forest habitually yielded a million tons a year.

Until after the Second World War there were five sizeable collieries: the Waterloo, the Northern United, the Eastern United, the Cannop and the Princess Royal. But peculiar to the area are the so-called 'free miners'. Registered men, they qualify to call themselves free through being foresters by birth – precisely, born within the Hundred of St Briavels – and by working a year and a day in a forest pit. Their freedom to mine anywhere in the forest, save in gardens, orchards or churchyards, is protected by royal charter.

The free miner's is a quiet, solitary life. Typically, a lone man or a pair of workmates would open a seam. But in the boom times, the forest was dotted with such pits and hundreds of free miners operated. Now they number single figures. Locals will tell you with real bitterness that this is due to the closure of the maternity wing at the Dilke Hospital, the last place one can be born a forester if one is not to be born at home. But in truth it is the changing patterns of economic and cultural life that have starved this proud old tradition.

In his first signed piece of journalism, published by the Oxford University magazine *The Isis* in 1957, Dennis Potter wrote a romantic, impressionistic evocation of the mining village: 'The ponderous and out-of-step clamp, clamp, clamp of steel-toed pit boots could be heard minutes before the men came by, and I was able to rush to the wall, eager to see the coal-black faces, the corduroy trousers hitched and string-tied just below the padded knees, and the helmets shaped rather like those worn by the Nazi soldiers in my weekly copy of *The Champion*.'[3]

Potter's father, Walter Edward, and his father's father, George Thomas, were both colliery miners. In his teens, Walter started at the Arthur and Edward near Berry Hill, named for a previous owner's sons but known to all as the Waterloo. Then he went on to the Cannop where he stayed thirty years.

In his second book, *The Changing Forest: Life in the Forest of Dean*, published in 1962, Potter describes a visit to an old man just three months away from death by the miners' disease, silicosis, the fibrous lung growths caused by years of inhalation of silicon dioxide particles. There was 'a rattle in his chest as if the mechanism which wound him up was beginning to break down, dust in its wheel'. A further observation is the purest Potter, both with its unflinching gaze upon bodily function and in its florid, somewhat uncomfortable

35

transposition into imagery: 'A grey streak of phlegm stained the bars of the grate, slightly luminous like the path a slug has made on its morning slither across a concrete path: silicosis spit.'[4] It is this old fellow who, by the young writer's admission, gives him the quotation 'Blessed is the land between the two rivers' and who relates Bible scenes to the local landscape, magically.

The rattling chests and the cramped living conditions were taken for granted. Looking back from 1968, Potter recalled:

Even when I was fourteen (in 1949) I was still sleeping with my thirteen-year-old sister, two short steps from the bed in the same narrow room where my mother and father slept. My . grandparents were in the only other bedroom. Here, most of the time, my silicosis-ridden, illiterate grancher was painfully coughing up years of coal-dust into a huge pink po under the bed . . . Now life is better. Of course it's better. (My father is on the dole, for a start!).[5]

Walter's work at Cannop had run out in 1959 and he managed to find employment cleaning vehicles at the Red and White Bus garage in Coleford. But it was longer hours and much less pay than he had enjoyed as a miner.

His son expressed the anger at the running down of pits in his *Sun* period. 'My father's pit has been closed . . . And now a few brave shrubs cling to the poisoned soil of the undisturbed slag. Green in place of black, light in place of the darkness. It is a sort of progress. Apart from the redundancy, the fractured community, the injured pride and the cold, accountant's indignity of it all. We do not treat unwanted coal miners with the same generosity as redundant Army officers.'[6]

Walter kept the garage job into his sixties; after that, his widow remembers, 'he walked miles for jobs but people don't want you at that age. He had enough to do with his garden.'[7]

Walter married Margaret Wale in 1934. Her mother was a forester, born Jane Hawkins in Berry Hill. Like Margaret's contemporary Winifred Foley and so many girls of her own generation, Jane went to work in service in London where she met a master builder, Christopher Wale. Born in the smoke, Margaret worked as a teenager at Fuller's the cake-maker's, first on the bakehouse floor, then as a chocolate-dipper. It was on a family trip to the Forest of Dean that she met Walter.

Dennis Christopher George Potter was born on 17 May 1935, named for his grandfathers and 'Dennis for himself' says Margaret Potter. She still lives in Berry Hill. Dennis's sister June Thomas and her family share the house with her. On a glorious October day in 1994, having done a little modest research, I impertinently telephoned Margaret Potter from the call-box just across the road and was promptly invited in.

Mrs Potter is in her eighties and all but blind. Her spirit and her acuity seem intact, however, and are not unfamiliar familial qualities. She told me how she was seen as a 'foreigner'. 'That is the forest way. When I first got married, I did feel as if I didn't belong. And being a Londoner, you don't talk to everybody, do you.'

The 'forest way' was to stick with your own, who extended widely, but always to speak. 'Everybody knew everybody. You'd never go by anybody. You'd say "Morning", "Afternoon", whatever.' I found they still do, at least those over 30.

'You were all related in some way or another,' June put in.

'Oh yes,' her mother laughed. 'Millions of them.'

At first, Margaret and Walter lived in her in-laws' home. Then they moved to her uncle's house next door where Dennis and June were born. 'Brick House that was. They call it – what now, June?'

In the next room June says something I can't decipher, then looks round the door. 'Americans have got it now,' she says. 'When war broke out, the in-laws had to go up to Dean Moor. So that's when we moved in to where my dad was born on the other side of the lane. It's still there and the cousins live next door that always did live next door. Then Mum and Dad bought a house, Spion Kop, down the lane in 1952.'

'The garden there was a wilderness,' says Margaret, 'and Dennis got a spade. He always said "I was the first one to dig the garden."'

The old forest intimacy has been replaced by something different, proximity. 'Oh, strangers now,' says Margaret of modern Berry Hill. 'Some of these houses are being built in every little corner that they can find. People with big gardens sell a bit off for a bit of money and there's a house built on it. Doesn't matter where you go. Just on this little corner, there's an extra shop put up. That one's been enlarged. All those houses put up over there. The Globe's been altered. Dennis used to like that pub but since they modernised it he couldn't be bothered to go into it. He liked it with the locals sitting there talking. Now they have discos and what have you, it's not the place he knew.'

I asked Mrs Potter about hardship but she brushed it off. 'They were working short time, two days a week, when I got married. Of course the war altered all that. There was full-time work then, wasn't there.'

A woman like Margaret Potter might well make light of want but I have a nagging sense that her son perhaps selected the facts a little, building myths around himself. The grinding poverty of twenty years earlier that Winifred Foley described is certainly of a different order.

A frequent observation about Potter was that 'until he left home, he had never seen a flush lavatory or a washbasin with running water'.[8] Taken with the two-in-a-bed, four-in-a-bedroom description quoted earlier and the illiteracy of his 'grancher' that he was apt to cite,* the image suggests a deprivation at odds with appearances in the family photographs reproduced in this volume. Even if the clothes there are 'Sunday best', they are a world away from the make-do-and-mend that was all Winifred Foley ever knew.

Anthony de Lotbinière stayed at Spion Kop when he made the documentary *Between Two Rivers* with Potter in 1960 and he remembers having a room to himself.[9] So the living-on-top-of-each-other was a temporary, not a permanent condition. Margaret Potter says, 'Houses were very short then. We were living with my in-laws and it was a very small cottage.'

To solve the problem, Margaret and the children went to stay with her widowed father Christopher and her single brother and sister in Hammersmith, London. Dennis, who had passed his eleven-plus and taken his place at Bell's Grammar School in Coleford, won a scholarship to St Clement Dane's in London. Neither survives: the Coleford school became Bell's Hotel and Royal Forest of Dean Golf Club in 1973 while the Hammersmith grammar, along with Mr Wale's old home, was demolished to make way for a road.

Potter's enrolment at Bell's, about a mile and a half down the hill from home, took him into a separate circle. 'I know it's not far away,' says June, 'but Coleford was Coleford.' Thirteen months younger than Dennis, she also passed the eleven-plus, 'but they said I couldn't go to the grammar school because it was changing counties. So I had to go to the secondary modern.'

In childhood they had been close, playing together and with cousin Dawn from next door. Their playground was the forest. 'Have you seen his play *Blue Remembered Hills*?' asked his mother. 'Well, that was sort of how it was, wasn't it, June. There was that girl with the doll, what was its name?'

'Dinah. I've still got Dinah.' (She is in a different league from

---

* Interestingly, Foley writes: 'The men were all well read. With a sweep of a pit-grimed fist they dismissed bogus religious cant – and, equally, the cult of material wealth acquired for its own sake. They filled the world's belly with its properly distributed abundance, and the world's soul with the beauty of man's and nature's genius.'[10] Perhaps George Potter's illiteracy was an individual condition rather than, as I think Dennis implies, an earnest of a whole class's oppression.

Winifred Foley's doll, pathetically home-made from rags.) I wondered if it was June portrayed in the play.

'He said there was a spiteful one and that was me.' She roars. I suggest he was kidding. 'I don't know.'

'Of course,' says Margaret, 'when they were very young, she was the boss of the two. Because he was on the timid side, compared to her.'

'I was never very pushy anyway. Helen Mirren had my doll but the other one [Janine Duvitski] was the bossy one. So Helen Mirren must have been Doreen Dart. But it was based on his children's experiences as well. He mixed it all up.'

'The only bit that wasn't real was that boy being burned in the barn. That wasn't real. But you'd get little bits where you'd recognise what he was getting at. We did have Italian prisoners of war just over at Broadwell.'

'Oh yes,' says June, 'I remember them sweeping the roads with "POW" on their backs.'

Margaret never felt her son was writing about her or Walter and did not rise to my probing about the *Nigel Barton* plays which look like highly personal work about family. 'I do make comparisons, like in *Lipstick on Your Collar*. He did go to live with his aunt in London. There are little bits that help his own stories. He builds round what he knows.'

Potter often wrote about severe fathers who belittle and drive their sons but Margaret maintained that Dennis and Walter got on well. 'His dad was a shy man. Dennis was very shy at one time but mixing with all those television people he changed. And he had a very strong will. He always seemed to get things done and he could get people to do things.'

Walter died in November 1975, of a heart attack on a Sunday morning. 'I just couldn't stay in that house [Spion Kop]. I couldn't do that great big garden and there was no one else to do it so I moved here the following June.'

Writing was 'something he always did. I took it for granted. I'm still astonished at the respect that he got at the BBC and what have you.' June says, 'He used to write stories. I can remember you bought him a book called *Forward Commandoes* and he wanted to make a play out of it. He'd got it all worked out. Dawn Wilson was going to be his mum, because she'd got red hair. He was, what, perhaps eight or nine. We never did the play but he worked it all out.

'I used to see some of his stories. "Mac of the Islands" was one he wrote but I can't remember what it was about now. I used to write stories too but my talent didn't come.' She laughs. 'The teacher would read them out at school. Jane, Dennis's daughter, thought one of my stories was brilliant. I wrote it when I was sixteen. But that was it, it faded away.'

June and Dennis both attended Christchurch Junior School, as did Joyce Latham whose book *Where I Belong* is another reminiscence of growing up in the Forest of Dean, representing the generation born in the 1930s. Latham writes of 'Miss Iris Hughes, a good teacher, strict but with a great sense of humour. Even the rowdier element respected her after they had learned, to their cost, that she would stand no nonsense.'[11]

Miss Hughes still lives in the forest. 'The word "primary" hadn't come into it then,' she told me. 'I taught first-year juniors. Potter would have been seven in May 1942 and he would have come into the juniors in the September. He would have spent, or shall I say suffered, a year with me.'[12]

She remembered June as 'a gem' (agreed), Dennis as 'a quiet lad. He didn't show any of his talents then. But the scheme that was used in Gloucestershire in those days didn't really allow for self-expression. There was dictation. Or the teacher would read a story and then you were expected to reproduce it in twenty lines. If you had a good memory you produced a good composition. So you see Potter was brought up right through junior school to reproduce parrot-fashion.

'I think he must have had that creative mind at that tender age and I expect that's what made him appear quiet and withdrawn. He didn't rough-and-tumble a lot with the forest lads. As foresters we were a rough breed. They always respected one but it was a tradition. The true foresters are dying out now. We have what I call a lot of English foreigners.'

Later, in a letter, she told me of a former pupil she'd run into who, with no prompting, had offered his memory of Potter: 'He was a strange lad. Never mixed in with us. We used to try climbing some of the trees. He never joined in. Stood a little way off. Just watching.'[13]

I had wondered if Miss Hughes, who as form mistress taught the class all subjects, could be the model for Miss Tillings in *Stand Up, Nigel Barton*, who recurs simply as Schoolteacher in *The Singing Detective* and who is played in both productions by Janet Henfrey. Miss Hughes says she didn't see these works. 'I think I *was* a bit of a dragon. I was firm. I taught for forty-five years so you can tell I saw a lot of changes. Children like a certain amount of freedom but they also like to feel there's someone at the helm, someone in control. I used to say "OK, we've had our fun. Now enough is enough."'

I felt that Potter would have to be a broad caricaturist if he meant Tillings as a likeness of the warm and poised Miss Hughes. And there is a stronger candidate. Joyce Latham recalls being 'scared stiff' of the headmaster's wife, Mrs Olive Gwilliam, to whose class she graduated from Miss Hughes's Standard One: 'She had a well-earned reputation for being a strict disciplinarian, and she never shrank from using the thin brown stick she kept on top of her desk. Old Olive – except you wouldn't have dreamed of calling her that to her face – was very thin and bony, with grey hair and greeny-coloured, slightly protruding eyes which glared coldly from behind her glasses. It took only one fierce stare from her and the rowdiest class would subside into petrified silence.'[14] This surely is the dragon rendered by Potter.

Iris Hughes, herself taught by Mrs Gwilliam as a seven-year-old, says in her letter: 'I fully endorse Joyce Latham's description – she was a very hard person in all her ways. I don't think she was capable of showing any affection to child or adult, not even her mother or her husband who was a very dear man . . . She was not the type in whom a seven-year-old could "confide" if they had a "little" problem. Remember a little problem to us is enormous to a child.'[15]

Mrs Gwilliam retired at the end of 1944 when Potter was in her Standard Two class. Miss Hughes's notebook, kept since 1938, records that both Dennis and June donated 3d towards the £1 10s 0d raised for the retirement present.

The following, from 1968, would seem to be the only occasion Potter himself wrote directly about Mrs Gwilliam:

At my junior school more than twenty years ago now, an old lady used to brandish a huge pointer before a big poster map of the world. A map splotched with generous amounts of bright British red. 'That's ours!' she would say with spinsterish belligerence, using the pointer as though it was the actual instrument of conquest itself. India. Most of Africa. Australia. Canada. New Zealand. Hundreds of coral-embroidered islands. Ours, ours, ours . . . Great, great. Fancy us having all that lot then, we thought. But our school had a bucket to catch the wet from the rotting roof. And five more buckets at the bottom of the sloping yard as 'toilets'. We were only coal-miners' kids, you see.[16]

That 'spinsterish' may be a feint. It's the pointer, invoking Latham's 'thin brown stick', that persuades me.

The two governing philosophies in the Forest of Dean were politics and religion. 'It was definitely a Labour-controlled area, very much so,' said Iris Hughes.

In his highly accomplished essay on the National Coal Board and the changes in the coalfields, Potter tells his student readers: 'I was brought up to regard "tory" as the dirtiest of all oaths, and the Royal Family as useless, miserable wasters. Sir Winston Churchill is remembered today more as the man who once ordered the troops to South Wales than the great war leader intoning about the beaches.'[17]

In *The Changing Forest*, Potter describes the winter of 1947 when he was at Bell's Grammar, the NCB was newly created, Walter was full of hope and 'snow brought the lanes up to the level of their hedges', a period which 'provided my first genuine emotional and mental involvement with adult talk and hopes of politics'.[18] The running down of pits thereafter shook people's faith. 'There has been a considerable decline in the political consciousness of the area, as shown in the flavour of the talk and in the faint but discernible mental shrug with which the older concepts of "working-class" ambition and purpose are met.' And he summons a piercing and convincing depiction of the demeanour of the doomed miners as they 'appear to wait like monuments, carved out of the thick substance of the idea of a miner, the idea of the twenties and thirties, so that they will seem, almost, to be statements that have been completed, experiences that are no longer relevant or certain'.[19]

But religion caught the boy Potter even earlier than the mining culture and class politics. 'They were always Salem, the Potters,' observed Miss Hughes with perhaps a suggestion of that slight curl of the lip with which rival orders speak of each other.

Indeed the Potters were. It was Dennis's great-uncle, Harry Hawkins, who founded the Salem Chapel, in sight of where Mrs Potter and the Thomases now live. I sat in the parlour of Dennis and June's cousin Dawn Wilson (now Williams) with four generations of women descendants of Harry Hawkins, hearing what a lovely man Walter was and what a 'homely' home Margaret kept – though 'mind', as the octogenarian Hilda Wilson (*née* Hawkins) remarked, 'she's a Londoner, you know.'

When Dennis and June were small, the Salem children attended chapel three times every Sunday. Cousin Dawn, now a charming and bubbly sixty-one, still plays the organ there as she has since she was thirteen, especially from her favourite hymnal, Ira Sankey's *Sacred Songs and Solos.*[20]

Everyone who watched Potter's final interview with Melvyn Bragg broadcast two months before his death will recall his delight in a particular hymn from Sankey: 'I can think of the number before I can think of the chorus. I can see it as clear as though it were written in front of me on the slat: 787, hymn number 787.

'"Will there be any stars, any stars in my crown,
When at evening the sun goeth down?
When I wake with the blest in the mansions of rest,
Will there by any stars in my crown?"[21]

'And of course it makes me laugh and yet it tugs at me. And I see it. I see those little kids' faces singing . . . And for me of course the language of the New Testament in particular, but the Bible in general, was actually as it is to a child . . . I knew Cannop Ponds by the pit where Dad worked, I knew that was where Jesus walked on the water. I knew where the Valley of the Shadow of Death was, that lane where the overhanging trees were. As I said, I was a coward. At dusk, I'd whistle, you know, going down that particular lane.'[22]

By the Bible's language, Potter meant the language of the King James version. He once dismissed the New English Bible unanswerably as 'set not in the Forest of Dean but in Croydon'.[23]

Self-evidently Salem was woven deep in the warp and woof of his Forest of Dean nurturing. Few of his frequent impressionist displays of that childhood leave it out of the tapestry. For instance: 'For me the holiday still evokes a clean, white hanky, bowls of flowers and Sankey's floppy-covered Book of Hymns. For every Whit Sunday we Salem kids would give our Recitations. Once in the morning. Once in the afternoon. Once in the evening . . . Brass bands. Chapel. Male-voice choirs. They all hang together like the brave black-and-amber hoops on the rugby football jerseys.'[24]

Salem, a Free Church chapel, had a deadly rival in Zion, which was Methodist. Potter described them as 'twin guardians of the village . . . each a ruling centre, with a ruling cabinet and a discipline as immutable as an established natural law'.[25] But Zion is gone now and Salem, which doesn't have a resident vicar any more, is, says Margaret Potter, 'very near on its last legs. Only three or four children go for Sunday School. That's the last chapel round here.' One of the children is Nicola, June's granddaughter, rising five.

There is a passage in *The Changing Forest* which puts me in mind of Potter's own status in what Joan Bakewell and Nicholas Garnham dubbed 'the new priesthood'[26] of television:

Chapel preachers of old are talked about in the Forest of Dean with an intensity and frequency which shows that they would not be tolerated today, rather as any social unit builds up a type of nostalgic orthodoxy with which to place and feel itself as something with a specific and valuable sense of identity, never quite able to see that such an orthodoxy bears little or no relation to the conflicts and growths of the present. In Berry Hill, at least, a few of the old local preachers have long since been elevated to the legendary, or promoted to glory as more determined evangelists would have it.[27]

Researching his book, he made a Sunday visit to Salem in 1961 and was crestfallen at the small turnout. In an eerie, unknowing adumbration of what would come to him within the year, he notes an elderly worshipper's hands, 'club-like with the painful swellings of arthritis'. And he concludes, 'It does not take a religious man (which I certainly am not) to write in praise of the chapels'.[28] The religion would come too.

In a much earlier television interview with Bragg, Potter gave 'the people that I grew up with, the people whom I would want to see what I write' as his reason for using the medium he did; for those people, 'it's television or nowhere'.[29]

But even among his family, the view is that this target audience was indifferent. 'His plays, the people round here didn't understand,' his mother said sadly. 'They'd say "Oh I watched it but I didn't understand what he meant." He could *tell* you what they meant.' I asked if the foresters resented his work. 'No. It was just that they were too deep for them. I was very proud of him. I don't care what he wrote, it was my son doing it, you know. Some people say "He's always got sex in it, don't like that, too much sex". But that's life, isn't it.'

June, who hadn't heard this conversation, volunteered later that 'the foresters didn't like his plays very much. They didn't understand them. We didn't either, let's be honest. They thought he was slighting the forest all the time but he wasn't really. They're proud of him but they thought he was slagging the forest.'

As people do, the foresters certainly want to claim him. Wherever I went in the area, everyone had known Dennis or claimed they had. Ask anyone in Ross-on-Wye and they'll point out Morecambe Lodge, the house where the Potters lived. But they are not so sure what to make of him. A Coleford man, who reckoned his wife knew Dennis at school, told me that 'he must have had horrible, nasty things in his head'.

Iris Hughes confessed: 'To be quite honest, you see, I'm not awfully keen on his plays. I suppose it's as he felt. I think he was a young man full of ideas. I think perhaps a frustration at being housebound and not being able to do all the things he had hoped to do probably made him . . .' She didn't settle on a word. 'Because some of his plays are, well, a bit gruesome.

'When they used the school for *Pennies from Heaven* and some of the children were in that, the people took an interest. But when they read the reviews in the Sunday papers, some of the parents said "If I'd known it was going to be like that, I'd never have allowed my child to be in it." Well of course since that time views have broadened considerably, I suppose. But they're not everybody's cup of tea, you know. And he did tend to run the forest down. I think he realised his mistake.'

She did admire his last interview. 'To be so near to death and to take it so calmly. But I didn't like the bits where he was referring to God. Now I'm not a goody-goody but I try to think I'm a Christian. He said "God the old bugger" and I didn't like that.'

These are Potter's own people, perplexed, sometimes repelled by and resentful of his work. This book has a degree of rehabilitation to do.

3

The Varsity Drag

'I'm only just realising that it's not brains which sets the middle classes apart from yobs like me, just privet hedges'.

Nigel Barton, *Stand Up, Nigel Barton*[1]

It was the day after VE Day that Dennis Potter first went to live in Fulham with his grandfather (as opposed to his grancher). His father Walter stayed where the work was at the Cannop Colliery but Margaret and June, his mother and sister, moved too. And Dennis hated it. Hot tears were shed.

'He was homesick for the forest,' said Mrs Potter. When weeks went by and tears persisted, the boy was packed off back to Gloucestershire and for the better part of eighteen months he must have lived a very solitary life. He was ten then, 'determined to become a miner'.[2] He wrote of this time hintingly/hauntingly in 1983:

The pale, timid and precocious child, not too badly bullied, remained clever, and added aggression to a secret and misplaced arrogance . . . I don't know whether it was too obvious 'cleverness', examination salted, which ensured my early isolation, or whether, as I now dare to think but not inspect, something foul and terrible that happened to me when I was ten years old, caught by an adult's appetite and abused out of innocence. But certainly, and with a kind of cunning shame, I grew for long into someone too wary, too cut off, too introspective, too reclusive, until, finally, as though out of the blue, or the black, too ill to function properly.[3]

He fed that image of abuse into his work, perhaps nowhere more starkly than in the stream-of-consciousness voiced by the disturbed David Peters at his first session with the psychoanalyst in the 1969 play *Moonlight on the Highway*, Al Bowlly crooning over the pain in his head:

'When I was ten, there was this long alleyway, down the side of the chocolate factory, and there were very tall walls and narrow . . . and there was this man with spiky hair and eyes the colour of phlegm and he – I – there were narrow walls . . . he – smell of chocolates, that's what I remember, drifting over from the factory, sickly chocolates, there were roses on the box – "though I am wicked, I know" – just listen to his song – "come here" – "chocolate roses" he said – "we'll walk hand in hand through the ' roses" . . . "come here" – "no" I said, I shouted "Mum, Mum" – the walls were too high, nobody – Mum – nobody came – eyes – "your eyes, your fantastic nose . . . mighty like a rose"' . . .[4]

Those 'eyes the colour of phlegm' signal the unique Potter purchase on the depiction, the ingredient that turns self-revelation into imagination, the intensely felt into the graphically poetic. The act of dredging memory for experience must inform the passage quite as much as the art of *creating* memory for character. So logic would propose.

As June walked me over to see Brick House during my visit to Berry Hill, she spoke of the dangers faced by today's children even in an historically community-minded village such as theirs. I took my cue to ask about Dennis's experience. June said that he had first broached the matter in the family when he knew he would write about it in his preface to *Waiting for the Boat*. But that was all. He never volunteered and they never asked for any kind of identification. I gladly leave the tale to others.

The Potter women duly returned to the forest and the family moved in 'with Gran and Granch Potter and it was all crowded', as June recalls. In 1949 there was a further retreat to London. 'Romanies!' June's daughter Elaine declares in her scrapbook *My Family* which furnished me with a splendid historical resource.

A sufficient dwelling, Spion Kop, was finally found in 1952 and the Potters moved back to Berry Hill, but without Dennis who by then was coming to the end of his schooling. In 1953 he began two years of National Service* at the Intelligence Corps depot in Maresfield, Sussex. A fellow conscript was a refugee from a Plymouth Brethren upbringing

---

* With some exemptions, conscription for British men at eighteen was in force from 1949 to 1962.

in Southampton, the son of 'a crane driver who'd bettered himself by becoming an electrical charge-hand',[5] Kenneth Trodd.* He remembers the regimen at Maresfield as 'fairly nasty. It was routine army training, being turned into a squaddie really.'[6] After three months, both men were transferred to Bodmin, Cornwall, to take the Russian course, though still in 'a military atmosphere'.

The Russian course, if not exactly a skive, was certainly the escape route every bright recruit applied for. Alan Bennett, serving a year ahead of them, recalls that 'you knew to say "Can I be on the Russian course?" because it was a fairly cushy number and otherwise you might be on the front line. That was urgent when I went in because the Korean War† was going on and a lot of people in my intake were sent East. You didn't even have to do a test to go on the course, you just had to have School Certificate.‡ They tested you after six or eight weeks and if you passed high enough you were issued with a Woking suit, which was poor quality, and you went on to university. There were some people who were so agin the army in every respect that they wouldn't wear their own nicer clothes in the army's time. That was the hard-line approach.'[7] Bennett was sent to study at Cambridge for thirteen months before serving out his time at Bodmin, but sat his degree, like Potter, at Oxford. While Bennett translated Chekhov and Dostoyevsky at Cambridge, Potter and Trodd were sent to the War Office in Whitehall.

'Dennis was in MI3(D) and I was adjacent in MI3(C),' says Trodd. 'Then it became uniforms once a week for pay-day so it was a civil service kind of status. We were decyphering records, scraping mud off Russian soldiers' love-letters, keeping a card index of troop movements, plotting whether their units were moving towards Austria.'

At Oxford, Potter referred only to 'the sickening world of the Army'.[8] But ten years later, he coined an oxymoron for his feelings which would serve (with variations) for the rest of his life: 'Nobody who has worn a uniform can look back at his days in such an over-disciplined community without feeling affectionate contempt.'[9]

The memory was not always even half-mellow. The following is a word-picture from 1968:

'The British Empire', my old RSM§ used to bellow until a tiny

---

* Trodd changed the spelling to 'Kenith' in 1966; 'I received a letter which spelt it in that form and a girlfriend picked it up and said, "Oh, as in zenith" and I said, "All right, we'll keep that."'

† Korean War, 25 June 1950–27 July 1953.

‡ Equivalent to GSE.

§ RSM – Regimental Sergeant-Major, much heard on the parade ground.

purple vein swelled and throbbed above his left eye, 'was built on blood and guts!' Standing like a morose matchstick on the vast and unfertile acres he called a parade ground, I used to comfort myself with the alternative proposition that the Empire – of fond memory – was in reality carved out by hard-faced gents who praised God and filled their pockets.[10]

Potter portrayed the War Office period in *Lay Down Your Arms* and *Lipstick on Your Collar.* 'That boy *looked* so right,' says Alan Bennett of the latter. 'That's just how you felt in uniform, all hot and sweaty and with a terrible haircut.'

In 1956 Potter gained a scholarship to read Philosophy, Politics and Economics at New College, Oxford. Angus Wilson wrote later that 'Winchester, New College and the Treasury are the three places where they know everything'.[11]

Ken Trodd, though up at the oldest college, University, reckoned: 'New College was probably the most traditional and there'd be more isolation for a Forest of Dean boy there. It was grander than University and it had quite a number of, well, nerds.'[12] Roger Smith, taking over Potter's rooms at New College a year later, put a significantly different gloss on the college scene: 'One thing he could never admit was that most of his friends were Etonians and Wykehamists. There weren't very many other kinds there. That's what brought him and me and Ken together, a certain similarity of background. There were some grammar school boys there who were sort of grateful and there were the terrible, impossible hoorays. And then there were people like Stephen Hugh-Jones and David Cox* who made up the New College radical intellectual core and very much dominated the whole university in those years. I don't think there's been anything like that since.'[13]

Whatever you made of it – and Potter made rather a lot of it in his subsequent writings – Oxford unquestionably laid on the full panoply of stimulation and opportunity for a young man with a hunger for exploration both outward and inward. In his fresher year in the Faculty of Social Studies (which subsumed the PPE course), he could have attended J. L. Austin's legendary lectures 'Sense and Sensibilia' or heard such authoritative views of pertinent subjects as Gilbert Ryle on 'Thinking', Max Beloff on 'American Institutions' and his tutor Anthony Quinton on 'God', and sampled other such renowned minds as those of P. F. Strawson, M. R. D. Foot and Thomas Balogh.

The following year, the faculty showcased Isaiah Berlin and A. J. P. Taylor and a lecture by a Mr Thomas – 'The Relations Between

* Stephen Hugh-Jones is now a writer on *The Economist;* David Cox is a leading QC.

the Sexes in England from the Reformation to the First World War' – might have sown some seeds for Potter's work to come. Sir Keith, as Mr Thomas became, is now president of Corpus Christi College. He recalls teaching Potter 'a term or two' for PPE Prelims. 'He was a very lively member of the group, but I rather doubt whether doing British Constitutional History was a great formative experience for him!'[14] But everything is grist to a writer.

The Archives of New College, Oxford, Francis W. Steer's definitive catalogue, lists three Potters in its index:

> Potter: Jn.
>   Robt.
>   Sarah[15]

By chance, Dennis Potter's children are named Jane, Robert and Sarah. The 'Jn. Potter' cited here is in fact John Potter, Bishop of Oxford in the early eighteenth century. Robert is a farmer who sold land to the college in 1879 and Sarah a 'spinster' to whom a mortgage was surrendered in 1849. But for those to whom serendipity is less persuasive than sortilege, the knowledge that the present Sarah Potter remains unmarried will add savour to this odd conjunction.

Potter first caught attention at the fourth Oxford Union debate of the 1956–7 year. The motion was 'That the modern man does not require religious belief in order to be moral' and Trodd and Potter both spoke for the motion from the floor. According to Stephen Hugh-Jones's account in *The Isis*, 'Mr Denis [*sic*] Potter . . . made an excellent maiden speech.'[16] Another New College student telled for the Ayes: Andrew Quicke, later a director on *Panorama* and of party political broadcasts for the Labour Party, an independent producer and, interestingly enough, a Christian proselytizer. The motion was lost by 239 votes to 330.

The Union debates were fortnightly set pieces wherein wit, style, rhetoric, guile and inspiration were honed in an excitable arena by young men (women were barred) who expected to graduate to places in public life. Reputations were made and sometimes destroyed in the chamber, alliances forged and politicking learned, all in the presence of distinguished guest speakers, often front-bench MPs who might well mark one's card. The presidency of the Union, a post filled by ballot each term, conferred a fame that was at least university-wide and often of a national kind. But you had to know you wanted it and lay siege to it.

'In my opinion, for what it's worth, if his mind had gone in that direction he could have been president,' says Brian Walden, himself a holder of the office. 'He was a dazzling character, a fine and very passionate speaker. But he didn't go through the *causa sonorum*,* getting elected to all the committees. He left it too late, but he had better fish to fry and he was right.'[17]

Potter neglected to speak at – perhaps did not attend – the next debate, 'That this House finds ample evidence that Englishmen have little interest in, or enthusiasm for, the Arts'. Philip French, later a BBC radio producer and *Observer* film critic, seconded the motion and Trodd opposed. It is hard to believe that, had he been present, Potter would not have risen to a thrust from the floor by a Lincoln College student: 'Scratch an English [*sic*] mining village and you will find a Dylan Thomas.'[18] The motion was carried.

Trodd seconded the opposer while Potter and Walden (then Union Treasurer) both spoke from the floor against the next motion, 'That the Trade Union movement now includes powerful influences that effectively harm the political and economic life of this country', but it was easily carried.

The miner's son began to step blinking into the light in the Hilary term of 1957. The dramatic societies at New and Worcester Colleges collaborated on a production of Ibsen's *Rosmersholm* and Potter gave his Peder Mortensgaard, a journalist character specified as red-haired. *The Isis* described the role as 'the radical' and the performance as 'always in the right key'.[19] The production's first-time director was New College student Charles Lewsen who doubled as Brendel. One of *two* production secretaries on the Ibsen (how they lived at Oxford!) later married the aforementioned Sir Keith Thomas. Lewsen, who went on to a career as an actor and writer, played the president of the Oxford Union in Potter's play *Stand Up, Nigel Barton* eight years later.

Potter next played the Clown in one of Nevill Coghill's famous Oxford University Drama Society renderings of Marlowe's *Dr Faustus*. Coghill, introducing the work in an *Isis* spread, dubbed it 'a play of thrills'. Both his Faustus, Vernon Dobtcheff, and his Mephistophilis, Jeffry Wickham, went on to be professional thespians. His designer, Bryan Izzard, had a colourful career as a producer and executive in ITV. Shortly after this show, Potter and Trodd stood for the Union Library Committee. Trodd missed election by three votes while his ally fell well short.

For the Trinity term, Potter joined the strength of *The Isis* under the editorship of Stephen Hugh-Jones and shortly thereafter a piece about radio appeared under Trodd's byline. Meanwhile, the great issue of the

---

* I take this phrase to mean something along the lines of 'the opportunity to take soundings'.

hour was debated in the Union: 'That this House deplores the decision of Her Majesty's Government to continue tests of the hydrogen bomb.' The Magdalen student David Marquand, later an MP in the Labour and then the SDP interest, now a professor of politics, moved the motion. 'Concluding for,' reported *The Isis*, 'Dennis Potter . . . suggested that the other side give less attention to cultivating an anachronistic nationalism and more time to studying medical evidence.'[20]

Later that month, the magazine's news section carried a mug shot of the University Conservative Association's imminent guest, someone who will reappear in Potter's story; the then Minister of State at the Board of Trade, Derek Walker-Smith. Potter's first article, that piece on mining entitled 'Changes at the Top', also appeared. It contains a jocular passing thrust that actually says a lot about Potter's stance towards the youth culture of his own generation: 'Admass, of course, has seen to it that some of the changes have actually been for the worse, and I prefer the old whippet to Elvis Presley's "Hound Dog".'[21]

The next debate saw Potter and Marquand advocate the legalisation of voluntary euthanasia. The next New College Dram. Soc. production was Pirandello's *Man, Beast and Virtue*, mounted by Bryan Izzard, in which Potter played Paolino the tutor. *The Isis* pronounced, 'His interpretation, basically sound, is still ragged at the edges: he boils over once or twice too often, sometimes without motive. By the end of the week he may be raging less intensely.'[22]

Roger Smith, now a theatre director, gives a shrewd account of Potter the actor: 'He was a bit undisciplined but he was a powerful presence on-stage. I think he went through terrible anxieties before appearing, but once he was on, it was very much a Personal Appearance. I don't think he saw himself seriously as an actor though in almost everything he did there was a kind of acting.'[23]

Then came the election season. Brian Walden was elected president of the Union. Trodd came bottom of the poll for the Union standing committee but won the Treasurer's post in the University Labour Club, a significant forum. In *The Isis*, Potter essayed a risky subject in a huge article (two pages of unleavened print) on 'The Bloc Vote' and the ways in which the university's archaic rules about the conduct of elections – canvassing, for instance, was 'strictly prohibited' – were subverted. It is a candid, even gossipy *tour d'horizon* that suggests he would have made a superb political correspondent as long as the terms of the lobby system didn't keep getting him suspended. And it inevitably generated correspondence, albeit of an even-tempered sort.

Potter's second year at Oxford, 1957–8, was to raise his profile in astounding ways. He began as joint features editor on *The Isis* with a Magdalen student, Lewis Rudd (later a long-serving Controller of Children's Programmes at two ITV franchise-holders, TVS and Central), under the editorship of Robert Symmons of Christ Church who was to die distressingly young.

Unexpectedly, Potter wrote a substantial piece in reaction to the recent publication of the Wolfenden Report. He begins by making his personal position crystal clear: 'Inevitably the natural reaction of all of us who find the thought of homosexual behaviour repulsive or difficult to comprehend will be a troubled one.'[24] He will perhaps have met openly gay men for the first time in university drama circles and have pondered their distinctness from the man with eyes the colour of phlegm. In *The Changing Forest*, he will trouble to note that 'It would, of course, still be unthinkable to be a homosexual or an adulterer in the village [of Berry Hill]'.[25]

Later in the *Isis* article, he strikes a sort of liberal stance: 'The dynamic behind much . . . proselytism may disappear when the ludicrous injunctions of present laws are rectified and a hunted and despised minority have the knowledge of their personal freedom. Liberalism breeds both sense and responsibility, repression stifles both.'

The following week, Potter filed his first Union Report, roundly abusing the visiting president of the Cambridge Union ('reedy voice . . . the usual drivel . . . this silly man') and Lord Altrincham ('a very sincere but incredibly naïve performer'), crediting Roy Jenkins MP with a 'darkly elegant manner and expressive, explosive hands' and calling fellow student (but future Leader of the House) Tony Newton 'this neat, mild politician'.[26] In the next issue, a pair of Keble correspondents accused him of 'obvious political bias'.

Nothing daunted, Potter responded by accusing debaters of 'a suitably odious presentation . . . a flutteringly nervous delivery . . . the most idiotic, juvenile and sickening speech that I can remember hearing for some time'.[27] The vituperation is only slightly mitigated by the bathos.

Betweentimes, he gave stunning notice of his potential as a writer in a rumination of the 'why are we here?' kind, about student life:

Three years, you think, three years of freedom, being at last allowed to explore one's own potentialities and crystallise one's own ambitions; three years sandwiched between the past, most recently occupied by the sickening world of the Army; and the future, an approaching grey hulk of horrible respectability, set hours, even perhaps a wife, and what that bell-ringing Billy

Bunter of the Government* would have us call duty, honour and responsibility . . . a new type of undergraduate from working or lower-middle-class homes finds himself plunked down with a bank balance in what appears to be at first sight a still medieval establishment.[28]

Potter had found his first major theme and it was class. In that year, 1957, a book had been published that affected him deeply: *The Uses of Literacy* by Richard Hoggart. It was indeed an epochal book: all through the 1960s, its blue Pelican livery and Lowry cover were a familiar sight. 'Amongst the young Oxford left,' Potter wrote later, 'the name Hoggart is used as something of an incantation.'[29]

Surely Potter saw himself as one of those 'of an unusual and self-selected kind' in Hoggart's iteration of the middle-class intellectual view of them: 'exceptional individuals whom the chance of birth has deprived of their proper intellectual inheritance, and who have made remarkable efforts to gain it.'[30]

It was not merely Hoggart's insights which chimed so harmoniously with the preoccupations of the whole of Potter's *oeuvre* but the language too. Consider Hoggart's passage about 'the juke-box boys' who hang out in 'harshly lighted milk bars' which 'indicate at once, in the nastiness of their modernistic knick-knacks, their glowing showiness, an aesthetic breakdown so complete that, in comparison with them, the largest of the living-rooms in some of the poor homes from which the customers come seems to speak of a tradition as balanced and civilised as an eighteenth-century town house.'[31] That house is too neatly appropriate for a Potter comparison. But throw off the academic restraint and add some phlegmy imagery and the scholarship boy at New College might have written it.

Hoggart devotes a pertinent section to the angst of the scholarship boy (girls, it seems, do not figure). Potter will, as we shall see, live out in a highly public way this description of such a boy: 'He is in a way cut off by his parents as much as by his talent which urges him to break away from his group.'[32]

Class played its part, without naming itself as such, in the furious controversy which now engulfed the Union. It was election season again. Trodd and Potter were looking to take over the Labour Club, the former standing unopposed as chairman, the latter running for secretary.

During formal business before the Union debate on 21 November Stephen Hugh-Jones asked whether the president, Brian Walden,

---

* Believed to be a reference to the noble Lord Hailsham.

had 'suggested to Mr Dennis Potter, *Isis* Union correspondent, that he should write an article attacking a possible candidate for the presidential election'.[33] Hugh-Jones asked further whether Walden had 'supplied material' off the record for such an article.

According to a report in *The Isis*, 'Brian Walden responded that the allegations were "disgusting", that Dennis Potter's article on the matter had been rejected as "libellous" by solicitors for both *Isis* and *Cherwell* [a rival magazine] and that, as many had seen the article, he intended to sue Dennis Potter.'[34]

In the course of the hubbub that followed, Ken Trodd demanded that the 'untruth of the allegation be substantiated (cries of "shame")', Walden conceded the chair and the Union secretary gave up trying to minute the proceedings: 'at this point, matters became rather obscure,' he pleads.

In fact, Potter was summoned to shout his account above a stream of interruptions. His challenge to the Union was 'Who is lying – the president or me?' Walden then went to the despatch box to deny the allegations and to level some charges of his own. It was finally agreed that a 'tribunal of investigation', consisting of three past presidents, would be set up forthwith.

The newspapers had a field day. 'Never have such scenes been witnessed,' cried the *Oxford Mail*. 'Nearest approach perhaps was the sequel to the famous "King and Country" debate before the war.'[35] 'In the 75-minute uproar which followed,' claimed the *News Chronicle*, 'one undergraduate and two women in the visitors' gallery fainted.'[36] The *Daily Express* weighed in with a quote from Trodd: 'I have not publicly identified myself with the allegations, but the rumours are sufficiently pressing to call for the tribunal. All the people involved in this affair are officials or members of the Labour Club. But there is no political split in the Club. It has nothing to do with politics. It is a matter of personalities.'[37]

In what was flagged as an 'exclusive interview', *Cherwell* quoted Walden: 'Potter's accusation is a filthy smear and gross libel and I will not rest until I have a complete retraction and apology.' He never received either. The magazine's reporter, somewhat colourfully, added: 'Walden's words had the affect [*sic*] of splattering over the rock of Potter's obstinacy – in maintaining that he is a "backstairs intriguer".'[38]

Such excitement had the effect of drawing huge numbers to the day's debate, fortunately no sort of anticlimax. The motion was 'That homosexual practices, even in private between consenting adults over twenty-one, should remain a criminal offence' and it was proposed by an undergraduate called Kenneth Baker. Reporting for *Isis*, Trodd showed percipience in describing Baker as 'looking and talking like a fossilised Edwardian Home Secretary' for, around thirty years later, he did indeed assume that office. Baker was defeated by 'an unprecedented majority of 500'[39] but it was to be fully another decade before the Wolfenden recommendations were implemented.

The tribunal of inquiry, made up of Jeremy Lever, Edmund Ions and Uwe Kitzinger, sat the day after the rumpus. Potter, Walden and Hugh-Jones gave their evidence. It was a tortuous business and the tribunal's findings were suitably Delphic: 'We cannot wholly divorce the fault on Mr Potter's side from that on Mr Walden's . . . the sooner the affair is forgotten the better.'[40]

During the Christmas vacation, the findings fell into the hands of journalists. *The Sunday Times* reported: 'Mr Walden cannot be said to have suggested to an undergraduate journalist on the staff of *Isis*, Mr Dennis Potter, that he should write an article discreditable, or supposedly discreditable . . .'[41] But *The Observer* had it that 'Mr Walden made known a number of alleged facts concerning one of his officers, knowing that these might be published and that they might prejudice that officer's chances in a forthcoming election'.[42]

Brian Walden went on to be a Labour MP, resigning his seat to become a celebrated interviewer of politicians. Understandably, with Potter dead, he declines to comment on this stand-off forty years later. But that he holds Potter in affection cannot be doubted: 'He had a rampant feeling about class – which sounds very Marxist but I don't think he meant it in a Marxist way – that somehow there was a group of whom he was one – and I dare say he would have said I was another – who weren't allowed to express what they really were because their ethic was essentially working class. And all the time they were being asked to modify it, they were asked to behave in ways that were unfamiliar.

'My reaction to that was "So what?" His reaction was "This is appalling and something should be done about it." That was undoubtedly the engine of his left-wing politics, a feeling that there was class distinction which, if not apparent on the surface, was not far below the surface. It was incredibly inhibiting for someone like him.'[43]

Jonathan Cecil remembers the set-to as the big event of his fresher term. 'Brian Walden had all the professionalism and pragmatism of a kind of Wilsonite Labour man, as opposed to Dennis Potter who was all romantic, *écrasez l'infâme* and *à la lanterne*.* It was no contest really because Walden was a thorough pro who hadn't

---

* Two slogans from the French Revolution: 'Crush the beast' and 'to the lamp' (i.e., hang them from street lamps).

much time for romantic idealism. It was the Roundhead and the Cavalier.'[44]

Ken Trodd's gloss on the incident perhaps confirms Walden from the other side of the mirror: 'The syndrome was we-against-the-left-Establishment. The insight we had was of corruption in the place, so here are we uppity scholarship boys who in our little way have managed to conquer some of the citadels of this place. We've got to the top of this world, we've looked over the other side and found it's cardboard.

'There was a sense of "We can work this, we can play Oxford". I think that process carried on in Dennis in the utterly astute way that whenever he needed to he was able to play the press. That's where his machiavellian expertise flourished, that's where those skills came home, rather than in the House of Commons or the Labour Party.'[45]

The row still glimmered next term. The new *Isis* editor, Lewis Rudd, 'wrote a very pompous editorial – "it *is* a moral issue!" – but as far I remember the whole row didn't amount to a hill of beans. Oxford politics and Oxford journalism are very like that.'[46] Rudd quietly made changes for which the more visible Potter would be blamed later. He began a campaign to ditch the cover advertisement, set up a policy of themed issues and dropped the definite article from the magazine's title.

And he appointed Potter assistant editor. 'He was a much better writer than me, obviously. My stuff was absolute crap. It was hard, tense work, like a full-time job though we only did one issue a week. For that term, you'd go in every day and two days a week you thought of nothing else. Before the war, people like Jo Grimond edited it for the full academic year. Everybody on the staff got paid and the editor got £30 which you could probably multiply by twenty now. So it was quite a handy amount to earn.'[47]

Rudd's news section summed up the tribunal findings. Walden contented himself with noting: 'By far the worst of Potter's allegations . . . he withdrew.' Potter observed loftily, 'I am happy to emerge as a fool rather than a charletan [*sic*], the only clear alternative that had ever been open to me . . . I did what I did out of an unfortunate and misplaced sense of duty.' The report concluded with a quote from 'an optimist' on Walden: 'This is the sort of experience that can enable a man to make the Cabinet before he's forty.'[48]

In a separate item, Potter was reported to have carried a motion through the Labour Club to organise a petition urging the Government to stop manufacturing the H-bomb.

The issue also published a famous article by Potter, 'The New Establishment'. Therein he developed an argument about the trades unions: 'the old and comfortable jargon about "capitalist oppression", "working-class struggle" and "imperialist duplicity" . . . is as comforting and as relevant as passages from the Old Testament, and is not translated into the lean and abstract hate of the intellectual. The only young communists I have met do not belong and never could belong to the working classes, a body of men they insult when they saucer their tea or wear a dirty shirt.'[49]

The report of the tribunal was read at the next Union session and prompted some waspish Walden-bashing in the *Isis* editorial. The same issue carried a formal apology to Walden for a jibe published the week before. In a debate the following month, Potter found himself ranged against future Tory MPs Kenneth Baker, Paul Channon and George Gardiner on the motion 'That the present system of education is unsuited to a democratic state'. It was carried by a small margin.

Isis of 26 February was Rudd's most far-reaching but slow-burning issue, doubling the circulation and eventually bringing Special Branch men to the office to interview all concerned. Its theme was the H-bomb, it carried a Vicky cartoon drawn specially and it comprised ten unsigned and two signed articles written or commissioned by a group of named contributors. Potter was not among them, but as both assistant editor and committed disarmer, he must have been closely involved. His only signed piece was his report of the education debate: 'Rudeness has a function . . . if it expresses legitimate disillusion with the plethora of stale jokes, bad arguments and juvenile antics that stud a debate.'[50]

The next *Isis* carried a fascinating article by Potter, opening with his summer job working at a branch of W. H. Smith and taking all the first column to get to his subject, women's magazines, in the light of the previous month's launch of *Woman's Realm*: 'the *total* absence of social reality or personal truth is astounding . . . Ah, yes: the dear, sweet decorative vessels are there for us [he is addressing a male readership] . . . Women are not *people* – certainly not citizens.' He got in a lethal thrust at a prominent member of the hated Liberal Party: 'Mrs Ludovic Kennedy, it must be remembered, charmingly confessed an ignorance of politics almost as profound as her equally charming husband.'[51]. Elsewhere, the magazine carried its customary announcement of the appointment of next term's editor: Dennis Potter.

Rudd's last issue was full of Potterana. The editorial, signed D.C.G.P., reports that the H-bomb petition, elevated to a 'referendum', 'has achieved its main object magnificently, that of provoking people to think and talk with a sudden urgency about nuclear armaments, and people like myself who opposed it in favour of the more orthodox and

more uncompromising petition have been proved totally wrong ...
if our generation has one claim, it is *the right to be taken seriously.*'
(Potter's italics)[52]

There was a Potter paean to pubs and, in a further article, he
roundly declared: 'I have never been ashamed to admit that I
want to make a career in politics ...' even in '... our pin-striped
Labour Party, stinking as it does with the air of suburban houses
and well-mannered conversation over garden fences'.[53] He would
modulate the admission, not least in his first book, *The Glittering
Coffin*: 'One of my deeply felt ambitions in life is to become a
competent Labour Member of Parliament.'[54]

Thirty years later, Potter told Alan Yentob in an interview for *Arena*:
'I had thought that I was going to be a politician, I'd thought ... that
the instinct that I knew I had, and didn't understand what that instinct
was, was going to lead me into politics because that seemed to be the
access to what it was I wanted to say. In fact it isn't and wasn't.'[55]

His Oxford contemporaries take widely different views of what
might have been. Roger Smith, who was to be Potter's first story
editor, says: 'Perhaps I regret now that I started him writing plays.
He'd have been a wonderful political leader. That's what he should
have done.'[56]

Ken Trodd's belief is that ambiguities were bedded in early. 'By the
time even when he wrote *The Glittering Coffin*, what comes off that is
either someone who in a very shysterish way is going to be a politician
or someone who absolutely is *not* going to be that. Because the
position of that book is very much the young disillusioned visionary.
And writer. It isn't someone who could seriously expect to conquer
the Labour Party. But perhaps he did think he would give it a go.'[57]

My own view is that Dennis Potter, though highly erudite and fired
by great mental capacity, was not a natural intellectual and his politics
were not those of the analyst. Rather, he was someone politicised by
the experiences of his life, so that he felt his politics in the gut. He
could argue a case with great penetration and ingenuity but the cutting
edge of his politics was an emotional commitment.

In our highly structured parliamentary system, the politics of the
head rules the politics of the heart. With few exceptions, the skills
of politicking will outmanoeuvre the passion of causes. For all the
machiavellian talent that Trodd alluded to, it is hard to picture Potter
steeling himself to long years of not rocking the boat as a 'competent
Labour Member of Parliament', harder still to see him subscribing to
a front-bench ethos of collective responsibility. He found it hard to
suffer fools gladly and to make the ameliorating noises. You can
readily project the political obituary that might have been, of the

only (junior) member of the Wilson government to resign over *In Place of Strife* in 1968.

Brian Walden supported this reading: 'I think many people took the view of Dennis that he would calm down, that he obviously had the amazing talent and that in time he would become a Nye* figure. After all, Nye was very flamboyant when young. Dennis would become a wise figure and hold great jobs. Maybe. If his illness hadn't afflicted him, that might have happened but I somehow doubt it. I think he was inherently unclubbable. And consistency may be the hobgoblin of small minds†, but in politics they like a bit of steadiness. For instance, you get pacifists in the Labour Party who won't vote for the defence estimates. The whips say, "That's all right, Charlie's always held that point of view." And Dennis wasn't like that. He changed his mind a lot. In a sense the illness did him a favour in taking him away from the possibility of having to tramp through the bloody lobbies for all sorts of measures he didn't agree with. There are lots of MPs but you don't get many playwrights like Potter.'58

The new *Isis* editor duly took over. The advertisement‡ was banished from the cover of his first issue in favour of a table of contents that included Ken Trodd's 'Smoke Gets in Your Eyes', a dense show of knowledge about thirties dance-band music with a bow to Hoggart. Trodd was politics editor, a new post, and Roger Smith assistant news editor. The editorial was a sardonic piece on 'the shabby little band of so-called journalists' who had taken to hanging around Oxford to be fed what Potter saw as a campaign of vilification and innuendo on the H-bomb.59

But his next piece of writing was for the *New Statesman*, then thriving under Kingsley Martin's thirty-year editorship. It was a colourful and very personal article on 'Welfare State Oxford' and the working-class student's sense of dislocation:

> a coalminer's son, whippet-fancying and bitter by descent as it were, set down among the dreaming spires ... At home my parents grew away as I grew up; not their fault or mine ... My father is forced to communicate with me, much of the time, with an edgy kind of shyness, possibly tinged with contempt as well as admiration, rarely flashing into the real stuff except when one of

---

* Like Potter in his writings, Walden doesn't deem it necessary to reveal Nye as Aneurin Bevan, the inspirational leader of the Labour Party's left wing in the 1950s and early 1960s.

† 'A foolish consistency is the hobgoblin of little minds.' Ralph Waldo Emerson, 'Self-Reliance', *Essays*, 1841.

‡ The magazine was stiff with adverts, especially for cigarettes such as a brand endorsed by Lady Isobel Barnett and another to which Sir Laurence Olivier literally gave his name.

us is angry or inebriated . . . When my girl first came up to Oxford
to meet some of my friends, it was something of a strain for both,
and almost with guilt only I could see how or why fully. She must
have felt like I once felt as a private in the officers' mess.[60]

This remarkable baring of the soul provoked a lively correspondence.

'My girl' was a factory typist called Margaret Morgan whom Potter
had met at a Saturday night dance in Lydney at the other end of
the Forest of Dean. In *The Changing Forest*, he writes a masterly
impressionistic account of such a dance, intercut with overheard
remarks, snatches of song lyrics and advertising copy.

His frequent allusions to marriage suggest that commitment was
soon in Potter's mind. Roger Smith gives an entertaining account of
'an extremely beautiful upper-class girl [who] took a shine to him.
And he was terrified. He was always such a terrible puritan.'[61] This
siren, elsewhere accounted 'Miss Journalism 1957', worked on *Isis*
during Potter's editorship. She was, according to Jonathan Cecil, 'a
great beauty and a great friend of Kathleen Tynan so they made an
incredibly glamorous pair'.*[62]

Potter now played a leading role in a new controversy. As a result
of Special Branch inquiries (prompted, it was said, by a member of
the right-wing Oxford and Cambridge Club in London happening
upon the H-bomb issue of *Isis*), two students, William Miller and Paul
Thompson, were arrested. Both Labour Party members who had been
on the Russian course and worked at the Admiralty, they were charged
with a breach of the Official Secrets Act by supplying information for
the H-bomb issue.

Potter's inevitable editorial, brief, stark and surrounded by thick
white margins, was necessarily cryptic but a Miller–Thompson defence
fund was evidently being set up. In successive issues, he editorially
tweaked the noses of Tory opponents and was then obliged abjectly
to withdraw some of this knockabout. The letters poured in. 'We are
glad that our readers are not satisfied'[63] is the rather splendid riposte
to one published selection.

Another provocation was Trodd's assault, both waspish and florid,
on the monarchy ('the numen around the Royal syllables is potent').
The magazine's proprietors, Holywell Press, insisted that Potter print a
black-edged note dissociating them from Trodd's views. 'We welcome
literate comments,' it says.[64]

---

* Tynan died in 1994; her friend has lived on an ashram for many years so I have not
troubled her for her own version.

Jonathan Cecil, recalling Potter's advocacy of abolition of the aristocracy, adds: 'Not the Royal family, funnily enough. He thought they were good for the nation. He had a great traditionalist streak.'[65]

Meanwhile Potter, not content with one power base, found time to run for and win the chairmanship of the Labour Club, saying, 'I'd rather ruin the Labour Club in an exciting way, than carry on yawning.'[66]

The last *Isis* of Hilary term 1958 provides another drama. Potter is no longer editor. A declaration signed by 'The Proprietors' claims that recent issues constituted 'as choice an exhibition of bad manners that has ever (dis)graced the pages of any "intellectual" magazine. And we solemnly confide ... that the editor dismissed himself by the well-tried method of "staging a walk-out" ... we were assured that the whole staff "think as I do and agree with everything I do."'[67] There is more in this vein, including the specious but pre-emptive line that recent 'attacks' on the 'traditional' institutions of both university and nation justified breaking with the traditional freedom of the *Isis* editor to edit.

Nevill Coghill, Andrew Quicke and Alan Coren were among those who turned in material for the interregnum and Stephen Hugh-Jones was allowed a right of reply on behalf of the toppled regime. He wrote that the proprietors made it known that '*no* nominee [Potter] put forward would be accepted and that no member of the present staff would be re-employed'.[68] Hugh-Jones alluded to some none-too-subtle interventions in the affair by one of the most towering figures at Oxford, Hugh Trevor-Roper, Regius Professor of Modern History (now Lord Dacre). The professor was smarting under Potter's so-called 'offensive attacks',[69] specifically the allegation that he was looking to corral *Isis* into the Tory fold. It was surely Trevor-Roper lurking under this allusion in the proprietors' editorial: 'We were told by well-informed persons that "*Isis* is now definitely left-wing and will inevitably remain so"',[70] which was why they intervened in the handing-on of the editor's post.

The *Express* reckoned Potter was on three successive days hauled up before the proctors (the university judicature) and told to apologise or be sent down. Despite mischievous support from A. J. P. Taylor, he wrote the professor a letter of regret. Roger Smith says, 'I think he was pissed at the time. Trevor-Roper represented everything that Dennis despised.'[71]

Having addressed a national readership once already, Potter made his broad case from the same platform, though the *New Statesman* miscredits him 'Denis' Potter: 'Somewhere lurks that growing fear of vigour and rebellion that is coming to stain this sterile, conformist society of ours.' He gives a Pottered history of the changing political stance of *Isis* and contends that 'with Brize Norton bombers carrying H-bombs flying over the changing Oxford skyline, and the hideous new Woolworths squatting like an overgrown jukebox in the Cornmarket, *Isis* was not out of tone'.[72]

John Bowen, who edited the magazine in 1952, offers a more prosaic but credible reading of Potter's fall, citing themed issues and his distaste for advertising. He allows that the owners 'must have been outraged by Dennis's politics but more important the advertisers would tend to fall away. My own politics were left of centre as they are now but I didn't regard it as a political magazine, more a fun magazine with a bit of the literary. If you preserved an eclecticism, you kept readers who might then read the book reviews. This is the theory of writing for the television audience, after all. If you specialise, the readers who aren't specialist stay away.'[73] This is an image of the unaccommodating Potter as sketched by Brian Walden.

As the long vacation arrived, Potter was still only two years into his university course. But he had been noticed by influential people far beyond the dreaming spires and, by the time he returned for the Michaelmas term, he was no longer just a student.

At Oxford, he was an undoubted celebrity, viewed with something like awe by younger and less meteoric men. Norman Willis, later TUC General Secretary, arrived at Oriel from Ruskin College and met him 'in somebody's room talking – quite an occasion it was felt to be. I recall his general demeanour as being identical to his last television interview. He did not accord me any special status by virtue of me being from a manual worker's family (which did happen quite a lot, I'm afraid). When I told him I'd worked for the TGWU he just said, "You could do good work there." I felt *very* pleased.'[74]

Both Willis and Jonathan Cecil were immediately struck by what the latter calls 'his bright red hair and a dead pale face. He looked a very romantic poet type and he was holding forth about the iniquity of the Government, liberal socialism and how we should abolish the aristocracy. I thought, "My God, here's a man actually talking like the character in *Look Back in Anger*." Because Dennis used to talk in tirades in a way that I've never heard anyone else do.'

Cecil, scion of a great family that rose under Elizabeth I and son of the legendary Lord David Cecil who taught at New College, was the antithesis of the Ruskin boy, Willis. 'It wasn't until I'd left the room,' he continues, 'that somebody said to Dennis "Do you realise that's a member of the Cecil family, an aristocrat?" And I was rather touched because apparently he was very impressed. He thought I would cry "How dare you, you cad!" But instead I listened very carefully because

I'd reacted violently against my Eton background, I had all my options open and I was all for change and prepared to embrace a left-wing creed. Still am.'

So Dennis was a star then? 'Oh, *absolutely!* Ten or twelve years before I came up there was Ken Tynan and I think you could probably say that Dennis Potter was the next big star after Tynan. In a totally different way. He was a very passionate man indeed. When he'd had a drink in the pub, he was not above the possibility of fisticuffs. He wasn't a great joiner but he'd come out to eat and argue strenuously but always stimulatingly. I liked him greatly.'⁷⁵

4

I've Got the World on a String

'We're on the telly now!'
Jack Black, *Follow the Yellow Brick Road*[1]

Two days after the first Dennis Potter article appeared in the *New Statesman* on 3 May 1958, a telegram for its author arrived at the magazine's office in Great Turnstile. The sender was a producer in the BBC's current affairs department, Television Talks as it was then called. His name was Jack Ashley and he invited the student journalist to call him back.

It must be assumed that Potter did indeed phone Ashley but of course the BBC's Written Archive, which logs the telegram, has no record of the call. Ashley would no doubt have arranged a meeting with Potter and with his BBC collaborator, Christopher Mayhew. What they would have explained to the student star was their plan for a five-part summer series entitled *Does Class Matter?*, which Mayhew would write and present for a half-hour mid-evening slot. And they would have proposed to interview Potter for the series.

There are two versions of the script (one headed '1st cockshy script') before Potter appears in the third.[2] The files show evidence that Ashley had been seeking a student spokesman for some time and had enlisted the help of Noël Annan and others at Cambridge in the search. Whichever of them noticed the *Statesman* article had found their man.

Save for a brief trade union job, Jack Ashley, now Baron Ashley of Stoke, had been at the BBC since graduating from Cambridge in 1951. A specialist in industrial programmes, he took the chance offered by the redoubtable Assistant Head of Talks, Grace Wyndham Goldie, to do the series on class. 'With my working-class background I was naturally very interested. Chris and I didn't see eye-to-eye all

65

that much on the issues and the way of doing it but we worked things out.'[3]

He was at once struck by the just-turning-23-year-old. 'There was an unspoken rapport, we knew each other on sight. Chris is more of a public school boy. I was very fond of Dennis. But we never pursued the friendship – he was doing his thing and I was doing mine.'

Christopher Mayhew, now Baron Mayhew of Wimbledon, found Potter 'brilliant, intellectually brilliant, not an easy man perhaps, but very clever, ambitious of course, an extremely interesting fellow. What he said was always worth listening to but, dammit, I didn't meet him very often.'[4]

Time was pressing so it was not many days later when A. A. 'Tubby' Englander set up his film camera in Potter's room at New College and shot his responses to Mayhew's questions. Potter spoke about his embarrassment at his scout* calling him 'sir': 'I wanted him to think in fact that I was not from the working classes.' And he elaborated on the awkwardness with his family: 'My father is forced to communicate with me almost as it were with a kind of contempt . . . he is likely to ask me a question through my mother . . . I have a row with my sister inevitably over whether we should have something like *Life with the Lyons*† on . . . I never talk about Oxford at home . . . because somehow one would be using a qualitative kind of language. One would be saying that Oxford was better or something.'[5]

The pain in this odd mix of inhibition and trivia must have seemed the more pointed by Mayhew's portentous introduction over a self-conscious shot of Potter striding across the New quad: 'One of the undergraduates is a miner's son from the Forest of Dean, Mr Dennis Potter. In Mr Potter's life, we see the problem of social class in its modern setting.'[6]

Jack Ashley was pleased. 'I was very impressed with his contribution, very perspicacious and perceptive and strong.' Could he come across as pretentious? 'I think the problem there,' says Ashley wryly, 'is that I was rather pretentious myself, or at least cocky and tough and full of myself. So Dennis and I got on like a house on fire.'[7] Potter received the standard fee of three guineas;‡ Richard Hoggart, who also appeared in the programme, was paid eight guineas but he had to come to the studio at Ealing.

---

* College servant, usually old enough to be the student's father; called 'gyp' at Cambridge.
† Bland wireless sitcom, supposedly reflecting the lives of American movie stars Ben Lyon and Bebe Daniels Lyon (as she was always billed) and their actual children who had all settled in London. It ran for over a decade on the Light Programme and made a character star of Molly Weir as the housekeeper, Aggie.
‡ Approximately £3.15.

So far so good. The series was scheduled for August. Then a reporter from the Sunday newspaper *Reynolds News*, perhaps one of Potter's 'shabby little band' shadowing his every move, phoned and asked to see a transcript of the programme. Rather rashly, Ashley supplied an unedited script.

The paper played it big: MINER'S SON AT OXFORD FELT ASHAMED OF HOME: THE BOY WHO KEPT HIS FATHER SECRET yelled the headline. The reporter sketched some of Potter's celebrated college career and announced importantly: 'I have seen the script.' He flourished highlights: '[Potter] says that when Margaret Morgan came to see him at Oxford he was torn between talking in the language she understood and that of his fellow undergraduates.' And he purported to quote Ashley, damagingly: 'Potter should not have tried to conceal his background. I made it clear at Cambridge that I was not ashamed of my origins. They made me president of the Union.'

Worse, he quoted Margaret as saying: 'Dennis is very sincere. I'm a socialist like he is, though I'm not sure that it would be a good idea to have one of his Oxford friends as best man at our wedding. He wouldn't be quite in place down here.'

The reporter had even managed to rout out Walter Potter: 'There's no snobbery in Dennis. I don't think he has grown apart any more than any son does who is away for a few years. He's still got the old forest twang and he plays in the rugby team when he comes home.'[8]

An ambivalent essay in a political weekly might catch a BBC eye but headlines in a leftish popular daily must have hit a modest family in a West Country village like an earthquake. Potter wrote later: 'I shall never forget the moment when I came down the stairs in stockinged feet that Sunday morning to hear my mother read out that headline to the assembled household, or the momentary bewilderment on my father's face as he turned to me.'[9]

The text of an anguished telegram is on file at the BBC. It is from Mayhew to Potter, care of Spoincop (*sic*): 'Jack Ashley and I share your strong resentment *Reynolds* article and deny remarks atributed [*sic*] to us stop consider article will be completely discredited when actual interview shown stop protesting to editor'.[10] Simultaneously, Ashley telegrammed Potter to call him at home and reverse the charges. 'I do not recall receiving a response from him,' Ashley says; Potter always seems to have been selective in responding to contact.

The programme went out on 25 August. Introducing the series in *Radio Times*, Mayhew asked: 'Where in the social hierarchy do we place a miner's son studying at New College, Oxford? A blacksmith who has won a football pool? A wealthy businessman's daughter, obliged to run a sweet-shop in a working-class area of

South London?'[11] The edition, like the series, seems to have been tolerably well received, with an above-average score on the Reaction Index measured by the BBC.

Some sense of Potter's bruised feelings over the episode can be gleaned from his issuing of a writ against *Reynolds News*. A record of a meeting between the respective solicitors of the BBC and the newspaper notes that, off the record, the latter had conceded that the headline at least was likely to be defamatory and that Jack Ashley had complained of being misquoted.[12] The outcome is not recorded but Potter reported that 'the paper later apologised, and with an immediate generosity'.[13]

Nevertheless, Potter had done himself considerable good. Dealing with both a present Labour MP (Mayhew) and a future one (Ashley) is always useful if you have similar aspirations. I asked if either man had found Potter at all overawed by the episode. Lord Ashley reckoned him 'never overawed by anybody. He was down-to-earth with a sparkling sense of humour, in a way self-mocking: not unpleasant, rather endearing.'[14]

Lord Mayhew perceived him differently: 'He was enormously wrought-up before meeting a VIP, very sensitive, very self-conscious but interested. I think even then his artistic temperament shone out, but his prose writing didn't impress me. It was his conversation that was very original. I didn't see him as a writer. But he was an extremely unusual, sensitive, clever man with all kinds of vulnerabilities and a strong feeling of not being part of the gang.'[15]

Mayhew had an opportunity to consider Potter's prose writing because between the Oxford shoot and transmission the two had discussed and begun to collaborate on the book of the series. By 15 July he could write to Philip Unwin of publishers George Allen & Unwin that 'the book is going well and I have every hope that we shall finish it by the end of September – Dennis Potter is putting a tremendous amount of work into it.'[16]

Six weeks later, the tone was very different: 'I am sorry to say that work on the book is progressing terribly slowly. Dennis Potter is sending me stuff pretty regularly; but it will need a lot of work doing on it . . . At the same time, my ideas for the book are getting rather more ambitious.'

In October, Mayhew returned from a trip to Japan to find 'my desk piled high with envelopes from you', as he told Potter in a letter. And something else had developed:

> I knew that the BBC were going to offer you a job. If you have
> not already heard – the Director-General [Sir Ian Jacob] rang up

himself immediately after your interview with me was broadcast and made the suggestion that you might be taken on the staff! . . . As you already know perfectly well, it is a hard job in every sense, TV broadcasting. But if you have something to say, there is simply nothing to compare with it – neither writing, sound radio, public speaking, nor anything else.

By this time, Potter had run up a 50,000-word manuscript and this was in addition to the text of *The Glittering Coffin* which he had been writing for delivery to Gollancz by the end of the year. You begin to understand what Ken Trodd means when he says of Potter's energy that 'the amount of target-setting and target-achieving went on every second and if it ever slackened he resorted to ingenuities which made sure that the slackening was circumvented.'[17]

Given the prodigious effort, it is natural that, in a handwritten letter dated 30 November, Potter 'cannot hide the fact that I was terribly disappointed and rather bewildered to find that you are thinking of abandoning your book . . . perhaps you have been too kind to say that the stuff I sent you was either not good enough or completely out of tune with what you wanted . . . I would gladly rewrite the whole lot for you if necessary – you only have to say so, and I won't mind.'[18]

So the book on class never got written and no doubt Potter recycled at least some of it into both *The Glittering Coffin* and *The Changing Forest*. Mayhew sums up thus: 'Honourably enough, I think he just wanted to get his own views about class off his chest. I vaguely remember getting large quantities of neatly-written manuscript which bore no relation at all to the TV series. I was desperately busy at the time and had to call the book off. With hindsight, I should have taken on a hack writer, but admired Dennis and wanted to help him. At least I seem to have got him a job in BBC TV (I was on close and friendly terms with Ian Jacob) which is something.'[19]

For some of Potter's fellow students, class as a crusade was wearing thin. Lewis Rudd observed that 'his working-class background was not as unique as he liked to make out. Even the middle-class trogs* like myself who'd been to a day school in London weren't used to drinking sherry and being waited on by manservants, oddly enough. I should think about one per cent of undergraduates got that at home and Dennis made rather a lot of capital out of *not* being used to that. He was always The Only Person With a Humble Background at Oxford. But that didn't stop him being extremely likeable.'[20]

---

* Oxford parlance for grammar-school boys.

Potter returned to Oxford for his finals year with a book to finish, a marriage to anticipate and a BBC career for the taking. Not content with this load, he took on the editorship of the university Labour Club magazine, *The Clarion*, and ran for a return to the chair of the club, a post he had lost the term before, as well as for membership of the Union Standing Committee and Union Librarian. The first two campaigns were successful.

The proprietors' choice having resigned after one day, Potter's nominee for *Isis* editor, Nicholas Deakin, succeeded him after all. As a result the magazine, its definite article restored, remained open to his journalism. He took full advantage. A pre-Potter tradition revived was the weekly 'idol' profile, the first of which would be of the retiring editor by the new one. Deakin's is a shrewd assessment:

> He clings to a rather anarchistic code of political and personal loyalties with a tenacity surprising to those who mistake for opportunism his surface diffidence and militant rejection of the conventionally 'earnest' façade expected of serious public figures.
>
> The main weakness of his belief is an infuriating inability to see that others are motivated by different, if not always baser, standards. He never bothers with people he hates, and combines an (apparent) callousness with a charmingly guileless refusal to realise why his actions are often disastrously misunderstood.

As well as this anatomising of the Oxford celebrity, there are some piquant reflections on the private man:

> He still plays in the local rugby side, is popular with friends who left school at fifteen, always longs for the end of term with furious irritation and in vacations nothing will entice him from Gloucestershire ... He confesses to being, as he puts it, 'right-wing about sex' and his veneration of monogamy and the family *almost* led him to Catholicism when in the Army ... His money-sense is dangerously lacking, and he would prefer to become a key spokesman for our confused, fragmented generation.[21]

Elsewhere the old editorial row was wrapped up, with some scoffing at the 'bold suggestion' in *Time & Tide* that *The Isis* is 'exactly the kind of magazine which must be produced at Moscow University'.[22] After three months in jail, most of it served on remand, the two students

Miller and Thompson were freed and able to thank the magazine for its support and the fund's contribution of £541 to their defence costs. And Potter's *Clarion* was commended: 'It's good. It's *very* good. It's only sixpence.'[23]

A year earlier, Potter and Nadia Edelman had co-edited *The Clarion*, doubling sales and making £13 profit, but no copy survives in the Bodleian Library's patchy bundle. Two of the Michaelmas 1958 issues do, the first flagged 'No. 1 New Series'. It is printed by The Forest of Dean Newspapers Ltd at Coleford an arrangement continued long after Potter's graduation.

A long editorial, unsigned but unmistakable, heralded the magazine's availability at universities beyond Oxford and appealed to the Labour Party not to be 'embarrassed . . . none of us have [sic] any ears for the jargon and callous dishonesty of the Communists'. The writer develops a fine flow of rhetoric, ending appropriately enough in a clarion call: 'We have the job of remaining young and hopeful where there is no youth and precious little hope, of remaining patriots when our national identity is dwindling away in a steady capitulation before the New World on the one hand, and a militarily dangerous, criminal nostalgia for the supposed glories of the past on the other. And, of course, it can be done.'[24]

Potter's finest hour in Union debate now arrived, moving the motion 'That this House has no confidence in HM Government'. His guest speaker was Labour MP and later Prime Minister, James Callaghan. The guest supporting his opponent, Alan Haselhurst*, was then Minister of Labour and National Service, Iain Macleod. Among floor speakers supporting the Tories were Tony Newton and Philip Whitehead who, interestingly, was to become a distinguished current affairs producer in ITV, then a Labour MP and MEP.

Potter won a rave review from the *Isis* correspondent, Peter Jay, later Callaghan's son-in-law, ambassador in Washington and senior broadcaster:

> Dennis Potter spoke with a devastating combination of conviction and information. Sweeping aside outdated dreams about national prestige, he insisted that the Government had only replenished the gold reserves at the expense of bankrupting the primary producing countries which would turn Communist as a result. In a slashing peroration, he denounced the Tory chrome-plated coffee-bar civilisation; and with withering irony he juxtaposed the opportunity-state's values of efficiency

---

* Now a 'knight of the shires' on the Tory backbenches.

and liberty-to-be-imposed-upon-by-advertisers with the appalling realities of old-age poverty, stagnation, unemployment,
emigration, boredom, ITV and Selwyn Lloyd.* He was received
with a great ovation.[25]

Nevertheless, 'despite vigorous protest from your correspondent,
the motion was defeated by 296 votes to 209'. The performance can
have done no harm to Potter's campaign to recapture the Labour Club
chairmanship, however. An *Isis* report observed: 'Potter's greatest
enemies . . . are likely to be his lack of tact and his own energy. The
vigour of his opinions is believed mainly to have lost him this term's
chairmanship . . . It is generally accepted that if the Labour Club were
a finishing school, he'd never be head girl.'[26] And he was returned to
the Chair.

And so to the last of the public rows that punctuated Potter's Oxford
career: at his instigation, the Labour Club Executive Committee agreed
to attempt a drama production the following term. They settled on
Brecht's *The Caucasian Chalk Circle*, a commendably challenging
choice. Potter was to play Azdak, variously described as 'the judge'
and 'the village recorder', Margaret Forster (later a successful novelist)
was cast as Grusha the kitchenmaid and Natella, the governor's wife,
was given to Julia Gaitskell. 'The production will take place in the
Town Hall in seventh week,' the chairman-elect told *Cherwell*. 'This
means a clash with the OUDS [Dramatic Society] major, but I think
we'll survive.'[27]

Miss Gaitskell's participation would be full of resonance for Potter.
Her father Hugh, an old New College man, was the present Labour
Party leader, then living in uneasy peace with Bevan and the
parliamentary left. His nuclear 'fight and fight and fight again' speech
to Conference was almost two years and a general election ahead.

For the Labour Club to put on a play was unprecedented. Roger
Smith, who was also in the cast, had first encountered Potter at
Cuppers, the annual one-act play competition, at which New had
offered Ionesco's *The Shepherd's Chameleon*. 'He played the author
figure and I was one of three bird-like creatures who attack him. It
was quite surprising that he was an actor. He rather fancied himself
on-stage but felt guilty about it in a puritanical way. I understand that
because a side of me felt the same.

'It was unheard of to get the Labour Club to believe that drama
could have something to do with politics and be part of the battle.
We felt it was the Club's responsibility not to be its usual philistine

---

* Then Foreign Secretary, as he had been during the Suez débâcle.

self but actually put on what was considered to be one of the major radical left-wing writers. So it was really an experiment. I don't think they ever repeated it. They sort of died of shock.'[28]

Even before rehearsals began, the proctors weighed in. It was the lack of precedent for a political club branching out that caught their eye and they overruled the Club's resolution. Potter fired off one of his handwritten letters, a long and scrupulously argued appeal that described the proctorial ruling as 'an unfortunate error of judgement'.[29] But once again it was a face-off interrupted by the end of term.

Dennis and Margaret were married during the Christmas vacation – a full white wedding at Christchurch Parish Church in Berry Hill where Potter had been baptised. Despite being 'one of his Oxford friends', Roger Smith was the best man. In Oxford, the lads had been sharing 'dreary' digs in Divinity Road, aptly named for a tenant with a sacerdotal side. Now the new Mr & Mrs Potter moved up the hill and Smith went too, to live downstairs from the couple.

Everybody speaks well of Margaret. Jonathan Cecil recalls her 'coming up for some of the bottle parties we had in those days – they were then affianced as P. G. Wodehouse would put it – and she was awfully nice, I remember thinking, very much the girl next door.'[30]

Potter was straight back in the fray as soon as Hilary term began. The proctors had had second thoughts about the Brecht and decided that a fine of £10 for 'irregularities' would be more appropriate than an outright ban but demanded that the club's constitution be rewritten to exclude the possibility of future productions.

Under an illiterate headline, *Cherwell* reported: 'Stormy scenes arose at the Labour Club's policy meeting on Monday over the proctors' £10 fine . . . General support greeted a resolution proposed from the floor that the fine should not be paid.'[31] However, Treasurer Ron Owen's caution prevailed and the fine was finally accepted. Potter observed: 'We regard it as a fee for changing the proctors' minds.'[32]

Once again he was at the eye of a storm that raged across a wide terrain. A good and lively debate ensued in the press, particularly the *Oxford Mail*, and, as so often, the Forest of Dean scholar had sounded a trump that threatened to blow down some old walls. Fundamental issues of discipline and control were addressed.

He was now so celebrated that *The Isis* could account a great figure such as the then socialist Paul Johnson 'a more refined-looking version of Dennis Potter'.[33] A student Caesar, he did 'bestride the narrow world / Like a Colossus'.[34] One day he was disputing with a delegation from the Marxist–Leninists, Tony Cliff and Gerry Healy; another, he was invited to give a talk to the Liberal Party Group; another still, he was approaching the Soviet Embassy to offer *The Caucasian Chalk Circle* production as a gesture towards Prime Minister Macmillan's mooted 'cultural exchange' and the Arts Council for support in this mission.

And he was accorded his own regular column in *The Isis* with a legend-enhancing byline: a standing strip featuring his piercing eyes and the name Potter recurring, the fifth time bled off the end of the strip. He would never be packaged quite so becomingly on Fleet Street.

The six columns run the gamut of Potterian preoccupations: love of place and the past; advertising and admass culture; the new classlessness and the old privet hedges; youth and university; and the past again, quoting perhaps the finest thinker in Potter's pantheon, Raymond Williams, whose seminal book *Culture and Society* had recently been published.[35]

The most provocative of these pieces is 'And Bow Twice . . . ', an account of being summoned before the proctors: 'The room is sealed, but the distant hum of Broad Street traffic reminds you that this *is* the twentieth century . . . It is something of a surprise when they start speaking in English.' After a few more jocund thoughts, he stops short: 'I will not write more in this vein, since the proprietors of this magazine, enjoying the undoubted freedom of ownership – our basic Western privilege – managed to tamper with my column last week, which was good of them. So many kind people nowadays try and save you from the follies of free expression. Quite right, too. There is no place for radicalism in University life.'[36]

He still spoke regularly in the Union for he had decided to seek the highest office and pass his final term as president. But it was not to be: he ran fourth in a field of five with 147 votes, the working-class Tory Tony Newton prevailing. Potter did top the poll with 316 votes for the Standing Committee, however. As finals loomed, he wound down his activities, reviewing a few plays with wolfish glee and, in 'positively the last article I shall write for *Isis*', asking rhetorically: 'When does love and respect shade into a kind of benevolent condescension, when does self-deception or even blatant hypocrisy begin to flood into the consciousness of the well-meaning and so-called "committed" individual?'[37]

Dennis Potter left New College, Oxford, with a class II pass in PPE. This was the least of what he took with him.

5

Won't You Join the Dance?

'I have always been convinced that one hour of *Panorama* comes across as at least two in real time.'

Dennis Potter[1]

Dennis Potter left Oxford with the rosiest prospects of any graduate of his generation. He was headed for Television Talks at the BBC, 'which at that particular stage in television's development was very much a place that people wanted to come to', according to its then head, Leonard Miall. 'He was very bright but of course he knew nothing about the technique of television.'[2] It was not to turn out quite as it had promised.

Potter began his BBC contract, as already noted, on 6 July 1959. 'As a general trainee, I went first into radio, Bush House and all that', he was to tell Roy Plomley on *Desert Island Discs* eighteen years later. 'So you were thrust in front of a microphone almost straight away doing little talks about football and – I don't know, goodness knows what – to an unknown and probably non-existent audience. And then to Lime Grove and I worked briefly on *Panorama* and *Tonight*.'[3]

The 'goodness knows what' cryptogram is a throwaway in an unusually airy performance that reflects years of anticipation: 'I yearn to fulfil one last, hopeless, eye-smarting ambition,' he wrote in 1968. 'Will someone, somewhere, sometime *please* ask me what eight records I would play over and over again on that no longer frequented desert island on the fourth floor of Broadcasting House?'[4]

To apply for the privilege of indulging this pleasant and widely imagined fantasy quite so earnestly and publicly is gauche. But another hare is set running in his sketch of his traineeship and it is the single word *Tonight*.

Other than the *Discs* transcript, I have encountered no reference to *Tonight* in the literature. It was Alasdair Milne, the programme's deputy editor at the time, who set me seeking Potter's involvement. 'Cliff Michelmore was here to lunch yesterday,' he told me the day I visited, 'and he agreed with me that he thought Dennis came to us first. He was with us about three months and it didn't work for him. Daily journalism was not his game. But Grace Goldie took a fancy to him and I'm pretty certain she moved him on to *Panorama*'.[5]

Everyone else I consulted (Leonard Miall, Cynthia Judah, Liz Cowley, Jan Fairer, Anthony de Lotbinière) was adamant that Potter was never on the *Tonight* team, save Margaret Douglas who was uncertain. On the other hand, what else was Potter doing before he turns up in the *Panorama* files in November of 1959?

'He arrived, very much out of place really, on *Panorama*,' says Michael Peacock. 'I was on my second stint as editor and I was kind of tougher. He might have lived to tell the tale had he joined a few years earlier.'[6]

On Tuesdays, the day after transmission, there would be a team meeting. Potter first appears on the minutes circulation list on 10 November, along with Peacock, associate producer David Wheeler, Jack Ashley, Jeremy Murray-Brown, David Webster, Keith Latham, Jim Tobin and Susan Harper.[7] By the next meeting, he had been assigned to two items for the edition of 23 November and had already got in his bid to do 'Closing of Pits in the Forest of Dean' on 30 November.

Of the two items, one was a mere ruffling of feathers. A Mr Ivor George had unguardedly been allowed on to the previous edition of the BBC's stately flagship to inveigh against the depredations inflicted on innocent racing pigeons by the peregrine falcon and to propose that the notorious bird of prey be removed from the Protected Birds List. James Robertson Justice had been, as legendary presenter Richard Dimbleby's introduction genially remarked, 'burning up the trunk lines to Lime Grove ever since last Monday evening'[8] and, though Peacock had been fending him off with letters describing falconry as 'a somewhat obscure sport', the massy and vehement actor was not to be gainsaid.

Justice was unleashed for three long minutes upon the loyal and blameless *Panorama* audience to put the case against, and the green trainee was assigned to supervise him. Beguiling images come to mind. The text is not on file but there is an exchange of letters, of mounting bad temper and hilarity, with one J. Selby-Thomas FFCS of Gloucester, secretary of The Confederation of Long Distance Racing Pigeon Unions of Great Britain ('founded 1958', an announcement somehow lacking the requisite grandeur on a missive dated 1959) which 'represents some 120,000 *bona fide* racing pigeon fanciers, which include Her Majesty Queen Elizabeth the Second who does maintain a loft of pigeons at Sandringham'.[9] Peacock, a wily bird, eventually proffered a masterly dose of BBC emollient.

Potter's other task was, at least in theory, more serious. The Lord Chief Justice had advocated the return of corporal punishment, commonly known as 'the birch', the Home Secretary (R. A. Butler) had demurred, and the makings of an archetypal television debate were in place. On file is a letter from Potter to Jacobs, Young & Westbury Ltd of Borough High Street, London SE1, confirming a telephone order for a birch. Its specifications are: 'overall length – 40 inches; length of handle – 15 inches; approx. circumference of spray – 4–6 inches'.[10] It would be a splendid souvenir of his traineeship.

The item followed a routine studio format, with the prop, graphics and a Dimbleby recitation of facts and figures followed by a discussion between stalwart right-wing MP Cyril Osborne and civil servant Kenneth Younger. Chairing the discussion was Robin Day for whom this *Panorama* debut was, according to Peacock's candid memo to Huw Wheldon, 'not a startling one'. The unit was 'short of two producers. There was no one apart from a trainee with precisely seven days' experience of television available to work with Day on the item.'[11] This reference further undermines the Potter-at-*Tonight* theory.

In his memoirs, Sir Robin recalls the 'fearsome birch' and the 'red-haired young man'[12] but, so he told me, he mentioned Potter 'only in passing, by way of name-dropping!'[13]

The Forest of Dean report was more ambitious. Potter, producer David Wheeler and reporter James Mossman checked into Speech House Hotel in Coleford to make a thirteen-minute film, the most substantial item in the edition.* It focused on the forest's historic dependence on a declining coal industry, interviewing a former miner angry at the false expectations of continuity encouraged by the National Coal Board and at the union which he felt had let him down. Younger people were planning to move away, but he spurned quitting 'a little country on its own'. This witness was Walter Potter. A local headmaster spoke of the 'very strong community spirit' but a former colliery manager, accurately predicting the death of the whole industry, averred: 'My advice to the young generation is to get out.'[14] Michael Peacock says he found the piece 'very interesting, good social colour but nothing that made me feel that Dennis was a

---

* The programme included a discussion marking Churchill's 85th birthday but the reaction to Potter's role from one of the participants, Professor Hugh Trevor-Roper, is not recorded.

potential producer nor did he have a particular feel for what we now call television journalism'.[15] The report prompted complaints from the NCB, magisterially slapped down by Peacock, and from the Forest of Dean Development Association.

After this effort, Potter goes to ground until Christmas week, when he researched a thirteen-minute film report on 'Paperbacks', fronted by Robert Kee, for a rather self-consciously festive edition that attracted fierce disdain from the Controller of Programmes, Kenneth Adam. Item producer Jack Ashley says he can remember nothing of it but the file shows that Richard Hoggart came down from Leicester University to take part. Doubtless the trainee's idea, Hoggart's contribution was the last mark Potter made on current affairs programmes.

Michael Peacock says, 'I recollect I spent too much time trying to persuade him that we didn't really want to do an item about the evils of advertising, in the sense that it sets out to mislead or offer a very partial view of the world. I couldn't in the end make much of him, so I fielded him back to Grace [Goldie] who had sponsored him in the first place. He was clearly intelligent, clearly had something going for him, but he was not a journalist. A nicer class of person altogether.'[16]

Potter retained an admiration for Peacock's leadership skills and, when he was appointed Controller to launch BBC2, wrote that Peacock 'is not the kind of person to bungle such an opportunity'.[17] But he seems to have taken against *Panorama* for, during his reviewing years, there were few programmes he sniped at so often or so churlishly, calling it 'the fat old bore' and mocking 'this week's characteristically ridiculous question'.[18] He saved his loftiest scorn for Richard Dimbleby, referred to in most quarters in the same reverential tones that the broadcaster himself deployed on state occasions. A typical Potter thrust would be: 'Richard Dimbleby had less time to pontificate than usual. He must remember that *The Epilogue* is scheduled for a later hour.'[19]

What could Grace Wyndham Goldie do with her protégé who was 'not a journalist'? She came up with a brilliant solution. One of her producers, no more of a journalist than Potter but a true artist, was presently in editing, a period when concentrated work is done while simultaneously a broadening view is being developed in a measured way. So Potter was attached for a valuable few weeks to the great Denis Mitchell, then cutting his wonderful African trilogy, *The Wind of Change*. What I would give to have been a fly on the wall when these two giants of the medium met and talked: the old maestro then 48, epoch-making documentary poetry like *Night in the City*, *Morning in the Streets* and *A Soho Story* under his belt, much more scattered and frustrating patterns ahead of him; and the young crusader, heading for 25, seeking the role that will make him the greatest individual exponent in the medium's history.

It was a time that would reverberate for Potter: Mitchell was chafing at his BBC contract, considering offers from outside and stirrings of co-production possibilities. The BBC bureaucracy squirmed, aware of his high standing, reluctant in those days to make allowances for any individual, however exalted.

Potter must have watched the innovator at his meticulous work with wide-eyed eagerness. Certainly he was very taken with the older Denis and wrote of him later as 'the one man in British television who is indisputably a film-maker of brilliance';[20] and of a re-run of *Night in the City*: 'he coaxes drama and poetry from cold and lonely streets'.[21]

And of course they would have chewed over Potter's ideas. Clearly the Mossman–Wheeler film for *Panorama* had not quenched his desire to come to grips with his roots, face to face as well as from the safety of his writing desk. Potter was already working on an idea for a longer film report about the changing forest and now he had a champion for it. He told Philip Purser: 'Denis persuaded them to let me make the film about the Forest of Dean.'[22] And there is a veiled reference to Mitchell in the project's title. That incantation the silicotic miner had given him provided the raw material: 'Blessed is the land between the two rivers'. The last of Mitchell's African trilogy, *Between Two Worlds*, gave him the edited essence. Potter called his project *Between Two Rivers*.

He drew up a 'brief preliminary statement of aims: The intention would be to give an essentially personal view of the feel and tempo of a small but very distinct region of England, and of how its people are reacting to the drift, pressures and opportunities of our new, fairly prosperous "admass" society.' After citing 'the emergence of status-seeking in what was predominantly a one-class society', he continued: 'I would want to make it clear that . . . I began to reject this fabric, with its essentially working-class and non-metropolitan connotations, but . . . have found personal equilibrium . . . by coming to terms with it . . . finding for myself the validity and vitality of this community.'[23]

Four days later, he was putting flesh on these bones with a list of suggested ingredients and characters and with further observations: 'Why do I sense falsehood and commercial deception – or, even more strikingly, a decline in personal dignity – beneath the attractive gloss and the neon-lit optimism?'[24] You can hear in this the tones of the earnest young socialist arguing with the sceptical editor of *Panorama*.

Grace Wyndham Goldie liked the sound of the proposal and passed it to one of her film-makers, A. C. J. de Lotbinière, known as Tony. 'She said to me "He's got ideas, would you take him on,"' recalls de Lotbinière. 'Though I'd been to Cambridge and in the army, I was absolutely the antithesis of everything he was.' In the mellifluous tones of the patrician class, he adds good-humouredly: 'My voice wasn't exactly his voice. But we worked together very well and we remained friends. When he and Margaret were living in south London, I used to go and see them.'25*

As was then the way, the programme was accepted and in pre-production within days. Filming resources were allocated to begin on 15 February for a shoot until 2 March. 'I went down on a recce to plan the film and make contact with the people we were going to interview. Of course we didn't have researchers in those days, you did the whole thing yourself so you became wholly involved.'

This was when de Lotbinière stayed at Spion Kop. 'I got on frightfully well with his father and with his sister and I think Dennis might have been slightly fed up that I got on so well. For his theme, he was having to show them in two lights, one from his Oxford perspective when he rather despised them, the other from coming back when he realised their full value. So all this had to be done in the film. I found it fractionally distasteful, simply because I'd become great friends with the mother and father. Dennis was slightly narked. He was terribly class-conscious.

'I suppose I stayed a week at Spion Kop. For the filming, the crew and I were based at a nice little inn, plumb in the middle of the forest. You made a film like that with a vehicle the size of a London bus to do the sound and a vast Mitchell camera and lights everywhere, so how could anyone be remotely natural? I had a very good cameraman who would even do hand-held. In those early days, you usually had to beat the cameraman over the head to do that.'26

Back at Lime Grove, a stream of bumf was being generated by a bureaucratic process which, needless to say, did not fit Potter's circumstances. First there was the etiquette of his status in the 'training reserve' and the implications for his 'normal duties' of such personal involvement in a project. Then there was the growing realisation that the tyro intended actually to appear on camera. These weighty issues occupied such great minds – and great names, a BBC characteristic in those days – as M. Kinchin Smith and C. J. Pennethorne Hughes, even unto Leonard Miall, until it was understood that no appearance fee was being sought, at which point Grace Goldie's usually peremptory command deserted her in a memo to de Lotbinière: 'I think it would

* Three months after talking to me, Tony de Lotbinière died, aged 70.

80

be wise to have a talk with the West Region expert on the Forest of Dean.'[27] This is just the kind of institutional shuffle that would drive Potter – or any serious programme-maker – crazy.

Despite the red tape, the film got made. The opening image is a threat: a garage hand's transistor radio blares as he goes to attend to a car, twin enemies to village peace. We see Dennis and Margaret at the Christchurch baptism of Jane, his mother and father behind, Walter with his head bowed. 'It's a story of my discovery of things here to respect,' says Dennis's commentary.[28]

The film touches all aspects of old Berry Hill life: the mines and the cottages, the chapel and the working men's club, the silver band and the rugby match. Children are read to by an old lady in a felt hat. Dennis's mum hits 'Walkin' My Baby Back Home' on the club joanna. Walter and friends strike up 'Painting the Clouds with Sunshine' in the parlour. The preacher shows off the Salem banner. The bandmaster gamely urges his musicians to the Italianate essence of a tune. It's an iconography of a Forest of Dean childhood, lovingly displayed, then scorned, then re-embraced.

The highpoint of scorn is rather searing: Walter tucking into his tea at the parlour table, Margaret keeping a weather-eye on his needs through the kitchen doorway and Dennis's strained voice-over – 'even at home with my own parents I felt a shame-faced irritation with the tempo of a pickle-jar style of living' – a line which on paper looks hung about with proviso but which in the ear sounds like conviction, sentence and excommunication all in one moment.

While much of Potter's commentary is callow and overwrought, de Lotbinière utters his own overstatement in the section depicting the author's disenchantment. There is a montage of garrulous faces over a speeded-up babble track, a sequence laughable in the wrong way. And grim-faced concentration on dominoes is undercut by a honeyed voice reciting Byron, a comment utterly changed by time.

But for most of its length it is an honourable visual essay, lively in the cutting, full of movement and detail in the camerawork. Potter marks the change of gear with a level-gazed address to camera, confident in his coat and pullover and swept-back hair, breath showing in the crisp air. He has come back and made his peace with his roots. Now he wants to save them from 'the synthetic and canned . . . a dazzling but somehow superficial way of life'. The key image is the jukebox, an image of the consumerism and processed culture which 'seem to crumble away the individuality of the people I know'. It is a process most of his audience would have recognised wherever they lived and it has of course continued. What can Potter have made of the 1990s version, with the Forest Tandoori and the Coleford Movie Mart?

'From that basic film,' de Lotbinière says, 'stems almost everything he ever did.' Rather it stands four-square on the road Potter had already taken and would pursue. It is unarguably a writer's film. Its director points out that it is a precursor of a well-liked BBC2 series, *One Pair of Eyes*, which followed the pattern of *Between Two Rivers* quite closely and ran from 1967 until well into the 1970s. De Lotbinière, who made sixteen of the films and was executive producer on many more, says 'they always used to get good notices'.

There was less good notice for the Forest of Dean film in a zinging memo from Controller of Programmes Kenneth Adam to Leonard Miall:

> Tony de Lotbinière's production was masterly in the main, although there were some curiously fierce cuts – ['What did he know about it?' interjected the director when I read it to him] – and he is surely to be congratulated on the naturalness of the amateur 'cast'. But I was thoroughly disappointed by the quality of Potter's thought; there was nothing original about it at all; thousands of young men who are deracinated in this way could have provided the same kind of commentary. It was currently 'cross' but I did not believe in the anguish. I felt it was a whipped-up *espresso* emotion. And I am getting very tired indeed of protests against mass media, exposures of teenagers and All That.

He ended by calling it 'a curiously jejune film'.[29]

Leonard Miall, amused to be reminded, expounded his law of BBC memos: 'They're not always designed to tell you what happened. They're sometimes designed to protect the person writing them.'[30]

De Lotbinière has a happier memory: 'I got a fan letter from David Niven – I didn't know him, it came out of the blue – who said, "I was making *The Guns of Navarone* and I came back home and saw *Between Two Rivers* and I must congratulate you. I thought it was absolutely wonderful."'[31]

So here was Potter with a Hollywood fan and a 'personal view' programme on his CV. But was he happy? It may have been the film's commentary to which Potter was alluding in a later aside: 'The temptations of the shrill voice are very strong for me.'[32] And it may be that *Between Two Rivers* later embarrassed him; at any rate, he never made another programme like it.

The grave, wistful youth shown in the *Radio Times* billing with an inevitable cigarette was now a published author. Gollancz brought out *The Glittering Coffin* in February 1960 and shortly afterwards a second impression (flagged 'They've sat up!') which allowed him to add a postscript on the general election of 8 October 1959 in which the Conservatives won an unprecedented third-in-a-row victory of a hundred seats. Potter's sour anatomising of Labour's 'bright, up-to-date picture of a moderate, sensible, progressive Party, where progressive means the ability to provide more consumer goods and more self-deception'[33] could have been written this week.

The book gets patted on the head, even now, as a 'youthful polemic' but it deserves better. Drawing heavily on his collected student journalism, it is much more than the sum of such parts, building a long essay in *engagé* journalism that would not disgrace James Cameron. Potter adumbrates with quite uncanny acumen. He foresees that 'posters and faces and jingles will matter more . . . and policy less',[34] that the past will become 'packaged' as 'our heritage' and that the Party will suffer a similar fate,[35] that localities will look identical, regional distinctions be flattened out and politics become 'a fringe activity',[36] that 'in the event of . . . continued Socialist electoral defeat, the monolithic nature of the Labour Party will be split beyond repair'[37] and, in a personal message to Tony Blair, he avers that 'the collective ownership of the means of production . . . must remain the essential criterion for a Socialist party'.[38]

There is plenty more on familiar Potter matters: class, childhood, Oxford, advertising, the Bomb, England, popular culture, jukeboxes and privet hedges. But the Labour Party is the big target in the book's sights and (Ken Trodd is right) there is little to gladden either the sixties apparatchiks of Transport House or indeed the nineties demographagogues of Walworth Road. It shows a certain brazen courage to write: 'To the young worker, the Labour Party is as remote and as puzzling as any other British institution, distant from his interests and not a part of his problems. To the young intellectual, the Labour Party is part of the Establishment against which one reacts, not a weapon one uses in the fight'[39] and then blithely to embark on the search for a candidacy for the next election. This, though, is where Potter's thoughts were turning.

The Glittering Coffin got some good reviews and was able to trumpet its second impression as 'a challenge to every smug convention. It recreates a vision, which is the desperate need of the hour.'[40] The *New Statesman*, usually Potter's friend, was less sure and its complaints of untidiness and lack of discipline and generalisation, if a touch carping, are not unfounded. The conclusion, though, is all wrong: 'Mr Potter's future is . . . bleak. I fear that he will achieve his ambition'[41] which, of course, was to become 'a competent Labour MP'.

These glimpses of fame fed each other. Potter began to be invited on to television and radio. A notable coup was to appear on *The*

Brains' Trust, which had been a Home Service institution for twenty years. There were special circumstances: the Easter Day edition was dedicated to youth and all the participants were under thirty. Shirley Williams took the chair.

Meanwhile, another new role was shaping up for Potter, one which would help him towards his true destiny. And another row was brewing, one much less clear-cut than the glorious incursions at Oxford and much more elusive in the records.

6

Close as Pages in a Book

'An adaptation . . . must be an act of loving criticism as
well as vandalising bravado.'

Dennis Potter[1]

For some time, there had been agitation within the BBC for a series
about books, not least from Controller of Programmes Kenneth
Adam, and not least because the urbane Corporation mandarins were
continuously twitchy about the decent fortnightly series on ABC, an
upstart ITV station, called *The Bookman*. 'I am determined we will
have a programme sooner rather than later,' thundered Adam in a
memo to Head of Talks Leonard Miall. 'Our prestige in the publishing
world is very low. Review books are now a mere trickle. They all go
to ITV. This is a challenge which *must* be met.'[2]

As 1960 began, pilots were in preparation by as many as three
producers. A fourth, Stephen Hearst, fortuitously spoke of books in an
unrelated meeting with Adam and was duly drafted in. Miall's deputy,
Grace Wyndham Goldie, noted in a memo to him marking Hearst's
involvement: 'I have simultaneously been discussing some ideas with
Dennis Potter and it seemed to me that these might have something
very valuable to contribute . . . His notions were primarily concerned
with a book programme of a non-intellectual kind which would hit
the kind of young audience which reads, on the whole, paperbacks
rather than "hardback" books.'[3]

With nothing yet formulated, the project was abruptly required to
be up and running. Hearst learned by a roundabout route in June
that a fortnightly Sunday-afternoon slot of 45 minutes in October
had been booked and that each edition was now budgeted at
£650. Though away on location, he gamely addressed his thoughts

to the matter, arguing for an anchorman, a feature that had not been thought necessary for the 30-minute programme everyone had been anticipating.

A long memo from Goldie to Adam in September reveals that, like *Panorama*, the still-untitled books programme was relying on trainees to keep it going: 'In Hearst's and Burstall's absence on leave, a plan for the first set of programmes has been drawn up very considerably by Dennis Potter, who is working very well on the series, and a trainee, Ian Martin,* who shows considerable practical promise.'⁴ Matters were not helped by the Potters' recent move to St Paul's Mansions, Hammersmith, where the phone was yet to be installed.

Once Hearst was back in the office, pre-production gathered pace. Potter was assigned to three functions: script outlines, 'ideas', and final content of scripts. It had always been part of the thinking that there would be dramatised scenes from books in the programme and these in particular fell to the Script Associate, as he was dubbed. John McGrath, an Oxford contemporary of Potter's, was to direct the dramas.

At Goldie's suggestion, a young QC and defeated Labour candidate for Putney, Dick Taverne, was approached to present the show. Kenneth Adam breathed fire: 'I was told that we were not having an anchorman and bought the format on this specific understanding. I must know about this.'⁵ His memo bore a red star sticker marked 'urgent'. Goldie made the requisite pacifying noises.

Meanwhile, Burstall wrote to Richard Hoggart (indicating existing friendship), inviting him to watch and comment on the programme. He referred to Potter 'who resigned from the BBC' and was 'writing for the programme on a freelance basis . . . Dennis asks me to send you his regards.' Hoggart did respond at length, praising the dramatisations and other ingredients.⁶

The reference to resignation raises an elusive controversy over Potter's relations with the BBC. Preparing the ground for the comprehensive and invaluable interview published as *Potter on Potter*, editor Graham Fuller wrote of this period that 'his forthright articles in the political press [were] disapproved of by the BBC'.⁷ It may be that this inconclusive formulation has been over-interpreted. Projected as, for instance: 'He fell out very soon over his writing for the left-wing *New Statesman* and departed the BBC',⁸ it makes a nonsense because Potter would not write again for the *Statesman* until 1967.

If there was disapproval or a falling-out, Leonard Miall would have

---

* Christopher Burstall, one of the pilot producers, was now the series director. Ian Martin went on to be Current Affairs Controller at Thames Television.

been party to it. He will have none of it. 'It certainly was the case that if you were working in my department you could not write for *any* newspaper or magazine, whatever its politics were. So there'd be nothing particular about the *New Statesman* or the left at all. That was a general ruling at the BBC, that people on the staff could not also write for newspapers.'9

It had occurred to me that this might be a touch of myth-making on Potter's part, adding a *bouquet garni* of martyred radical to the *ragoût* of his thirty-five-year wrangle with the BBC. Did Miall think he was romancing? 'Absolutely. Totally.'

Later Jack Ashley, determined to stand for Parliament, went straight to his selection conference in Stoke from being told by Kenneth Adam that, as a candidate, he could not stay at the BBC. He transferred to *Tomorrow's World* for the duration and was given a celebratory lunch at the BBC on his election. If Ashley could hang on, why would a mere trainee feel so compromised that he was impelled to leave?10

The official record shows that Potter's resignation took effect from 30 September 1960. But it shows too that he was re-contracted from 22 September for twelve weeks, later renewed twice, for 'research and script-writing for *Bookstand*' on a salary of £16 10s 0d per week, rising within the month to £22 because the programme was requiring him 'a full ten days instead of the anticipated five' on each fortnightly edition.

A handwritten note, undated, unsigned and declaring no recipient, says that 'this trainee will not be retained by Tel[evision] Estab[lishment] because he is publishing [a] book in December with political bias' and goes on to discuss the subtle distinction between being retained on an in-house contract and being a freelance contributor. There is a reference to 'this problem child'. No such book existed, however. *The Changing Forest* was not written until 1961 and was published on 9 April 1962.11

My own conclusion is that Potter's political writings are a red herring. He had been a trainee almost fifteen months. He had no prospect of a producing post and had not thrived on any existing programme. Going freelance to do regular BBC work allowed him to negotiate better money than a trainee would receive and to make appearances, if the opportunity arose, and be paid extra.

The first edition of *Bookstand* went out at 16.10 on Sunday 16 October, billed in *Radio Times* as 'a kaleidoscope from the world of books with Dick Taverne'. Goldie, no less, wrote the *Radio Times* introduction, an indication of how much store the BBC management set by the show, but it is a stilted piece: 'It will set out not to give criticism of books but rather to produce a slight flavour of a few of them . . . These impressions . . . are being presented in a mass medium which is very much part of the contemporary world.'[12]

Potter's contributions enjoyed a handsome showcase in the inaugural edition. He dramatised extracts from four contemporary novels: Iris Murdoch's *Under the Net*, Kingsley Amis's *That Uncertain Feeling*, John Wain's *Hurry on Down* and Stan Barstow's *A Kind of Loving*. Among the studio guests was Roger Smith giving his views on the Murdoch title.

The Duty Clerk reported 'eight calls of congratulation on this programme, all very enthusiastic about it. All suggested there was perhaps a little too much talk on each book and that they would have preferred longer "drama" episodes from each book.'[13] Kenneth Adam's memo next day to Leonard Miall proposes an item for – but says nothing about – the show.

The first series of *Bookstand* ran to eighteen editions, taking it to June 1961. Potter's dramatised extracts ranged across Henry James, Albert Camus, Aldous Huxley, Raymond Williams, Colin MacInnes, Dashiell Hammett and Elinor Glyn and were acted by, among others, Michael Caine, Terence Stamp, Frank Finlay, Prunella Scales, Peter Bowles and Vernon Dobtcheff. Guests in the studio included Richard Hoggart, Raymond Williams, Paul Johnson, Leonard Miall (who was not paid, of course!) and Potter's old tutor Anthony Quinton. In addition, Potter interviewed a number of writers, among them Francis Chichester in Plymouth, and talked on westerns ('These are the classic scenes of the Out West story, the traditional settings which were often drab, boring, suburban. Towns where you could safely take snaps'[14]), jazz and novels including one about Oxford, *A Middle-Class Education*. He must have relished every moment.

The programme was well received and Hearst claimed an audience beating that for *The Bookman* by up to eight-to-one. This was despite some chopping and changing over its length, eventually fixed at half an hour.

But an alarm bell rang in February 1961. Adam memoed Miall: 'DG* told me on Wednesday he had gone on to read *The Outsider* [of Camus] after seeing last week's dramatised excerpt on *Bookstand*. He thought the excerpt "quite unworthy" of the book and it reinforced his dislike of this method of treatment.'[15] This incident is a significant marking of the programme's card.

In April, Hearst memoed Goldie on Potter: 'He is original, he is extremely well-read and has a far greater interest in books and the book world than his political leanings indicate. There are, however,

---

* Sir Hugh Carleton Greene was the BBC's combative Director-General at this time.

the summer months when the programme rests and unless some other work can be found for him he may be forced to take a full-time job with the *Daily Herald*.'[16]

Hearst was not to know that his concern was academic. Adam was moving up to Director of Television and, in a memo to his successor, Stuart Hood, he wrote: 'Commenting on last Sunday's *Bookstand* and in particular on the dramatised episode in it, DG said yesterday that it was clear to him that his visit to the [Television] Centre* to discuss the programme and its content had been a waste of time since his special criticism, of dramatisation, had been wholly ignored ... I think, as does he, the programme should stop, and be restarted under different auspices.'[17] This stance rather confirms Malcolm Muggeridge's crack that Adam was 'a man of straw, dear boy'.[18]

Dismally, Hood showed no more independent thought: 'I must entirely agree with DG's strictures ... The filmed and dramatised inserts are a waste of time and money.'[19] In fact, the scene in the edition cited was uniquely not by Potter.

Hearst went on nudging fellow producers to seize the imminently available Potter. But seventeen days before the first series ended, he found himself fighting a last-ditch battle to cling to 'some of the original objectives of the programme'.[20] He had been told that it would go mid-week late-evening from October and that dramatised scenes were to end. To ensure the latter eventuality, the edition budget had been slashed to £400, two months after Hearst had been agitating for an increase to £900. But there was no remorse on the sixth floor of Television Centre and, inevitably but with immense dignity, Hearst asked to be relieved of the responsibility of producing the programme. Burstall took over but it was a poisoned chalice: the late-evening slot turned out to be a regional opt-out which meant the programme was never simultaneously networked. Those not taking it immediately were obliged to run it on Sunday afternoon, thus denying the programme the new freedom it might have enjoyed after the 21.00 watershed.

On 2 October, in what he once called 'the temporary safety of a letter',[21] Potter wrote to Burstall apologising 'for Friday', spoiled because he had 'a series' to do for the *Daily Herald* 'and I couldn't get away from one of those tedious "statement of aims" conferences which feature here as well as at Lime Grove'.[22] Evidently Potter was commissioned to write items for the second series, the last favour Hearst had been able to show him. But none got into the programmes.

* Directors-General were and still are based at Broadcasting House.

'Carleton Greene always had this reputation for being liberal and opening all the doors,' Stephen Hearst told me, 'but my experience of him was not that. We weren't told directly "don't do dramatisations", we were just given less money so that they were impossible. So I resigned and it became a literary programme for the middle class.'

Hearst contends that the Director-General's wife, Elaine Greene, a literary agent who died in 1995, complained that *Bookstand* 'brought literary criticism into disrepute' and that this was the source of the moves against it. Whatever, he now thinks 'We were a happy lot who learned a good deal from each other. Obviously Dennis learned greatly about the power of writing by tackling small items. He would work at home and then turn up on the recording day. We got on well. We met privately and I liked his wife enormously. But he undoubtedly had a tremendous distrust of anyone who was in charge. Conspiracy theory was always quickly in his mind.

'Because we worked in different spheres, I did not meet Dennis for a quarter of a century. It was in the Grosvenor House loo, at an awards ceremony. By then he was famous and constantly suffering with his hunched hands a visible martyrdom. But he was very warm.'[23]

Happily Hearst's career did not suffer from the *Bookstand débâcle*; he eventually rose high in BBC management and still works as an independent producer. Dick Taverne, who did become a Labour MP and later enjoyed fifteen minutes of intense fame by resigning the whip to stand successfully as an independent, is now an economic consultant. He thinks of *Bookstand* as 'a curious programme, which was never wholly successful but we were determined that it would be accessible to people who didn't read many books, hence the dramatised excerpts to bring books alive. Grace Wyndham Goldie was our friend. But the BBC high-ups really didn't like us and of course they thought it was really their territory. Admittedly we did strain too hard but we felt we were beginning to get it right when they abolished us. I think both the literary and the intellectual quality of the programme were unchallengeable.

'There was a certain amount of political undercurrent because John McGrath was very much of the left and Dennis was still full of rebellious *Glittering Coffin* thoughts and wanted to make heavy sociological statements all the time. I was regarded as a rather suspect Gaitskellite to some extent by Dennis and very much by John McGrath. But I think we worked together very amicably.'[24]

With the end of *Bookstand* Mark 1, Hearst, Taverne, McGrath, Martin and Potter all left. For the first time, Potter was to make his living in the private sector, having set up his escape route in plenty of time. Not, of course, that he and the BBC would be strangers. While he was staff number 24163, Potter had done something few Corporation staffers would dream of doing at any stage of their careers, let alone during the first year. He had published a book in which he grandly lectured his employer. The BBC, he had written, 'must learn how to speak to the people without indulging in its own, self-defeating polarisation, as seen in the careful segregation of programmes on sound radio, where the listener to the Light Programme is well protected from anything that could remotely suggest a little difficulty or a potential obscurity'.[25] It was a philosophy that had sat comfortably with that of *Bookstand* and it would continue to inform his thinking about the medium.

It's Only a Paper Moon

'I was drowning on the *Daily Herald*.'

Dennis Potter[1]

Calling itself 'the paper that cares',* the *Daily Herald* was what passed for a left-of-centre broadsheet in the Fleet Street of the early 1960s. At 3d, it was half the price of *Isis*, running to twelve or so pages and retaining such notable journalists as Geoffrey Goodman and Jon Akass. Many of them went on to careers in television, particularly the soccer correspondents (John Bromley, Peter Lorenzo, Sam Leitch). Anthony Carthew became ITN's long-serving court correspondent.

Celebrity columnists came and went – Alma Birk, Michael Foot, Dee Wells, that old turncoat Desmond Donnelly, Graham Hill, even Frankie Vaughan. The William Hickey-style gossip column was 'Henry Fielding' ('Mrs Thatcher, 36 next week, is certainly the most attractive woman in the House').

On the arts beat, music was covered by Richard Last, later the television critic of the *Daily Telegraph*. Theatre reviews and general arts reporting ('Brando to play Lawrence of Arabia') was by David Nathan. Television was reviewed by Phil Diack and reported by Philip Phillips whom Dennis Potter had twitted in *The Glittering Coffin*.[2]

Though the paper would be clearly in favour of the Labour Party at elections and other pivotal events, its general tenor was mainstream and conservative with a small 'c'. While it obviously played the big stories properly big (the Profumo scandal, the defection of Philby, the Great Train Robbery) and minutely charted the terminal illnesses of

---

* The slogan was dropped in 1961. One front page declared: 'There is something every day in the *Daily Herald* for people whose minds work.'

Bevan, Gaitskell, Pope John XXIII and the Macmillan government, there was nothing that occupied its front pages more extensively (even stretching to colour pictures) than royal and semi-royal family events: Princess Margaret's wedding, Prince Andrew's birth, Countess Mountbatten's death. In their very different ways, the *Morning Star* and the *Independent* in its early manifestation were much more robust over presumed popular sentiment.

There is nothing in Potter's writing to date that might suggest the *Herald* as a natural home for him; there again, an opportunist move in a young and ambitious person only becomes deplorable in proportion to that young person's expressed high-mindedness.

'He was an unusual creature to meet in Fleet Street in those days,' says David Nathan, for many years the theatre critic of the *Jewish Chronicle*. 'Because he never fitted in with daily paper life, he wasn't what you'd call a born journalist. He was liked but he was distant from the others. He'd had a different kind of experience.'[3]

Potter's first byline had appeared while he was working for *Bookstand*, in a run of guest columnists under the 'As I See It' rubric, along with a beady-eyed mug shot. The piece was another jig on the grave of Oxford, though done in a breezily mordant style for his new, non-academic readership and embracing other favoured themes such as 'the droves of bitterly disappointed Americans who descend upon "Axfard England" each summer. They are upset because the medievalism is not everywhere apparent, except maybe in their hotel bedrooms, and are in danger of mistaking the city's glistening new Woolworth's for Balliol College.' He comes to his own kind of upbeat conclusion: 'The process of rejection, the discovery of what a sterile thing "Tradition" can be, was, maybe, worth half the money the state spent on me.'[4] The last is a new allusion, suggesting that to a degree Potter saw himself as a bondsman obligated to repay the public's investment through the diversion he could provide.

The following week, the front page trailed what proved to be a damp squib called 'Group 60 Reports': 'A team of Oxford graduates are touring Britain looking at the social scene with the candid eye of youth'.[5] The group comprised Robin Blackburn, Perry Anderson, Nigelfred Young, Trodd, Smith and Potter. Perhaps the BBC had got wind of this scheme and assumed that its outcome would be a book 'with political bias'.

But only one report ever appeared, an unexceptionable piece on the decline of football, its falling gates and lack of glamour. Roger Smith smiles at the 'Group 60' episode. 'We set out to interview youth. We *shlepped* all round the country and sent the stuff back to the *Herald*. We must have been the only people who went in and out of Liverpool and never discovered the Beatles playing at the Cavern. That shows how eagle-eyed we were at examining youth.'[6]

Potter's *Herald* career proper began in August 1961, six weeks after the expiry of his *Bookstand* contract. For nine months he had a roving brief and his work appeared more irregularly than any of the other feature writers. 'I don't think they knew how to use him properly,' says Nathan, confirming my own feeling. 'They wanted him for the big series but these take time to prepare. On a paper, then as now, if you didn't fit clearly into the formula you didn't get used a lot. I had a definite beat, Dennis didn't.'[7]

The Potter essays, mostly on the leader page, comprise think pieces, topical arguments, reports based on somewhat loose and arbitrary inquiry and sundry book reviews. They range over popular pursuits, working-class conditions and routine thrusts at Oxford, with a couple of interviews thrown in. Often the evidential material is no less personal than that so often called in for Potter's student journalism. Thus: 'Our second baby was born one warm night in July . . . while a grotesque new machine was dropping concrete girders into position with all the gentility of a front-row Rugby forward bearing down on a tiny full-back.' This occurs in a vintage piece of overkill about the building of the Hammersmith flyover, which he reckons to find 'a beautiful thing, a cross between a Roman aqueduct and a Hollywood epic, soaring over earth-bound streets in an ecstasy of concrete, cable and sheer bravado.'

At the time, the Potters were living 'on the top floor of a block of flats on a bloodshot-eye level to the thing'.[8] St Paul's Mansions must be one of the buildings he is thinking of when he quips, of Michael Flanders: 'Even the doorman admires him – and a prophet is usually without honour in his own block of flats.'[9]

Though light, these are defining moments in Potter's journalism, demonstrating how he could never have been a real reporter and how, even as a critic, he is really a playwright marking time. The fact is that he is never objective. There are many columnists – *Private Eye* presently keeps a tally – who use the word 'I' far more extensively than Potter ever did. But many of those are simply lazy writers. In Potter's case, he is never detached or analytical. Rather, his own presence is ever palpable in his own observations. The circumstances of the gleaning of experiences and the body's very sensations in the course of that gleaning are always to the fore in his professional journalism.

One of the more remarkable examples of Potter's surroundings weighing heavier than the true task in hand comes much later, in a television review for the *Sunday Times*:

I do not think I have ever felt quite so low-spirited as I did on Monday night when reduced to watching *Panorama* in a hotel room in London while cold rain splattered on the smeared glazing which separated my few cubic inches of stale air from the dirty and darkened streets of what is now apparently the capital city of the damned. Two or three boisterous Arabs in the adjoining room were thumping and banging on the thin walls and the urgent klaxons of several police cars ooh-ah-ed in urban alarm beyond the windows as I sprawled morosely on the narrow bed to watch grave David Dimbleby and three painfully solemn journalists question the smiling Prime Minister.[10]

The editor of *Panorama* would be entitled to argue that, as a television review, this evocation of a place, of a mood, of a moment would, with some work, make a perfectly usable passage in a contemporary novel.

Of the *Herald* essays, in some ways the most surprising is a piece covering (or rather failing to cover) the Lincoln by-election. Instead of getting stuck into anything pertinent to party or topical politics, Potter takes the opportunity to play a variation on another favourite theme: 'The easiest way to map England is still by listening. Accents, like hills and rivers, are good landmarks. In Lincoln, the talk is reticent, flat, but with the rounded stealth of the old Poacher County. A nice sound. They are quiet people in these parts.'[11] This is attractive enough but why hang it on a by-election? The only candidate Potter speaks to is an Independent who inevitably will lose his deposit and the quote he uses is dispensable. The Labour winner, with the constituency's highest ever majority, is none other than Dick Taverne.

If Potter's eye was not on the ball in Lincoln, it should not be wondered at. While he was staying in the town, he began to have a disturbing sensation, a feeling 'that there was a sea-change going on within me'. There were odd manifestations. 'My nails were pitted. I couldn't sleep. I was pale and losing weight.' But he seems to have attempted to ride out these disagreeable ailments.

Later that month, he was sent to observe a gathering of Young Conservatives at Friends' House in the Euston Road. Attempting to stand up to leave the press table, he found himself balked. 'My knees were locked and one of them was swelling up. I could see it growing under my trousers. When I was crossing the road outside, my legs locked again. I was sweating with panic. They took me into hospital and there were red rings round my neck and spots on my legs.'[12]

His condition puzzled the doctors. Most alarming was the speed with which it 'just invaded every joint – bang! My jaws, fingers, knees, hips, ankles, toes. And paralysis became more than a metaphor for how I felt about my job. It was actually sitting in me; that's what it felt like.'

He woke one morning soon after to find his skin beginning to break up. 'It was like one of the plagues of Egypt! With one hundred per cent psoriasis you lose control of your body temperature. You semi-hallucinate. You're in danger of septicæmia, and therefore you're in danger of dying . . . You can't find a point of normal skin. Your pores, your whole face, your eyelids, everything is caked and cracked and bleeding, to such a degree that without drugs you could not possibly survive. It was physically like a visitation, and it was a crisis point . . . either you give in, or you survive and create something out of this bomb-site which you've become.'[13]

The condition was psoriatic arthropathy: literally, skin-and-joints disease. It is both uncommon and hereditary. Potter's was much the most virulent case known in his family history where otherwise only the psoriasis element seems to have surfaced. His mother Margaret remembers that Dennis 'first had a little patch on his back when he was in the army but it must have quietened down. I get it on my head and a bit on my legs. I've got an idea that my paternal grandfather had it. My father didn't but he had very dry skin which would powder. Thank goodness my daughter is unaffected and so are the grandchildren.'[14]

This 'visitation' never left him. For the rest of his life, Potter was on a regime of medication, varying considerably as new drugs came on the market and the condition swung through cycles of remission and renewal. The drugs too, of course, had side-effects and eventually a carcinogenic pay-off. So the disease and its treatment proved fatal, as Potter knew it would, but it required thirty-two years to do so. He could and would build on his bomb-site.

There was a penalty in heart and mind and spirit too. He undoubtedly weathered periods of bitterness, of depression, of despair. Those further visitations, that cross he perforce bore, inevitably informed his work, as Potter could be candid enough to accept. Writing after the Birmingham pub bombs of 1974, he let loose a poleaxing piece of invective – indeed, a true hellfire sermon – at the bearer of the message:

The bright box in the corner of the room can turn itself within minutes into a hell-hole: there, where the dancers cavort and pop singers clean their teeth with the microphone, where lewd comedians snigger and magical detergents remove impossible stains, there, inches above the carpet, is a chopped, edited, summarised version of a few of the terrors and miseries and endless conflicts which afflict our kind . . . We can look down and see the world boiling, and then we can go and put the cat out . . . How is it that we can walk about without being sick on the streets, perhaps the only meaningful sacrament left to man? *He that increaseth knowledge increaseth sorrow*: surely no rational mind in our scientific century could ever accept such Old Testament tosh, but . . . (Potter's italics and dots)[15]

Four years on, in an introduction to the stage version of *Brimstone and Treacle*, he recalled the time when he was writing the teleplay. The years of illness

had not only taken their toll in physical damage but had also, and perhaps inevitably, mediated my view of the world and the people in it. I recall writing (and the words now make me shudder) that the only meaningful sacrament left to human beings was for them to gather in the streets in order to be sick together, splashing vomit on the paving stones as the final and most eloquent plea to an apparently deaf, dumb and blind God. I sensed at that time, and can see much more clearly in retrospect, that I was engaged in an extremely severe struggle not so much against the dull grind of a painful and debilitating illness but with unresolved, almost unacknowledged, 'spiritual' questions . . . I concentrated most of my energies into work, work, work: the guarantee, or so it seemed, of my personal dignity and an affirmation of things within me which I mistakenly thought my illness could not reach.[16]

The capacity to shudder had receded again by 1984 when Potter reluctantly turned out an introduction to the three plays published as *Waiting for the Boat*, an essay which is surely the most vacillating and incoherent he ever perpetrated. In discussing his fine script *Joe's Ark*, he wrote: 'The resolution makes more than a wry nod at possibilities which can comprehend pain, or disgust or the implacable presence of death itself. The viewer was not left with the thought that the only possible sacrament these characters could possibly celebrate was one which involves standing together on the nearest intersection of the dirtiest possible thoroughfare in order, collectively, to be physically sick.'[17]

And yet again, this time in (I would argue) his very best and most decisive essay (delivered as an Edinburgh Festival lecture in memory of his old mentor James MacTaggart):

Chemotherapy lifted the bondage, providing a large degree of emancipation as the price of intermittent liver biopsies and a regular up-chuck time that seemed entirely fitting for one who had for too long, and with a dangerously religious temperament, felt that the only truly meaningful sacrament left was for people to gather at the muddied and unlit crossroads at eventide in order to vomit. Collectively. – [then softened with] – All right. This is getting too extreme.[18]

It is striking how Potter cleaves to images over long periods – as though they might indeed have a sacramental significance for him – even while there are adjustments (and sometimes seismic shifts) within the thoughts that those images serve to dramatise and make concrete.

From his earliest work, he had been given to remarking upon expectorational and other bodily evacuations. Illness now spoke to this predilection and gave the work a heightened, indeed an unrivalled sensitivity to human function and malfunction. The phlegm he saw on the grate was now his own.

During his absence from the office, the *Daily Herald* ran a thin, fairly enthusiastic review of his second book, *The Changing Forest*, by the then Labour MP for Gloucester. Potter must have loathed the piece, especially having it called 'a very nostalgic book – part travelogue, part social enquiry'.[19]

But he took up the offer of a week as holiday relief to the paper's television critic, Alan Dick, who had succeeded Phil Diack, and filed his first piece (on a favourite theme, westerns) on 7 May 1962. These six reviews set out Potter's stall most effectively, immediately demonstrating a style that oddly combines the rococo with the chatty and establishing his biases, enthusiasms and priorities. And of course, the quality of thought and expression must have been far beyond the expectations of all but his most optimistic readers.

After a further two-month absence, he returned as the *Herald*'s regular television critic. He was to fulfil this role for twenty-seven months, the longest continuous commitment of his working life. Space was tight and the pieces were rarely more than 150 words, occasionally dropping to almost fifty (the varying lengths probably indicate that he would have been cut to fit the available space, sometimes harshly). Generally they ran shorter than and in a secondary position on the page to David Nathan's theatre reviews, surely a reflection of the abiding belief among the Establishment (of which newspapers were very much a part) that the box was culturally inferior to the stage, rather than of any pecking order among the critics themselves.

The *Herald* reviews rank low in the canon. Some of them are awful – slackly written, glib, inattentive and hung with swags of purple piffle. The reviewer soon picked up on the prevailing popular press lingo and adopted such all-purpose shorthand as 'rhythmic' for anything about popular music, 'electronic' for the output of the medium, 'kaleidoscope' for anything multifaceted and so on. The style survives in the *Evening Standard* columns of Milton Shulman.

Being Potter, however, some of the clichés were minted for his own use. On separate occasions, both Tony Hancock and Sid James had 'boiled cabbage' faces. A West Country accent was customarily 'buttery'. And no reviewer ever used the word 'sick' with quite so many shades of implication (or so often).

His kind words could alight on the unlikeliest people and programmes: *The Black and White Minstrel Show*, Pat Boone, *Hugh and I*, Tommy Steele and, after a war of attrition, *The Lucy Show*. While he certainly had his special hates and berated them without mercy, his line was that all manner of idiocies were redeemed if he could adjudge the programme 'entertaining' or even if it 'kept us awake'. His similes, many of them outlandishly inappropriate, often concerned religion, medicine or drink. Though so lately married, he took the view that screen women were frankly to be ogled (for example, on *Stars and Garters*: 'this make-believe alcohol is translated into genuinely tipsy exuberance. And I'd rather have a beautiful phoney as barmaid than an old fat one who's real.')[20]

But there is a case for the defence. He has an excuse in that his deadline for phoning in copy meant he could review nothing transmitted after 22.00 hours and he was probably briefed to ignore anything before evening peak. Much more significant, he overrode the restrictions and bloomed into the medium's champion. Despite periodic assurances that most television is 'junk', more often than not he wrote with high enthusiasm.

It must be remembered that Potter did not grow up with television.* His parents first had a set in 1957 when he was at Oxford. Access to the medium came on his London sojourn. 'I first saw television when I was in my late teens. It made my heart *pound*. Here was a medium of great

---

* Potter's formative influence was the wireless. In the same superb Edinburgh Television Festival lecture (shamefully credited by the lecture's publisher, Faber, as the *Film* Festival) quoted above, Potter recalled that 'more than the coming of the bus and the train, or even the daily newspaper, it was the voices out of the air which, as though by magic, pushed out those constricting boundaries. You could hear a play that made the back of your neck tingle as well as a dance band that made your foot tap, a brow-furrowing talk about something I'd never heard of, as well as an I say-I say-I say music-hall routine, or even (and how bizarre) a ventriloquist's dummy [Archie Andrews, with Peter Brough] as well as a not wholly dissimilar newsreader. And none of it was trying to sell you anything. Maybe.'[21]

power, of potentially wondrous delights, that could slice through all the tedious hierarchies of the printed word and help to emancipate us from many of the stifling tyrannies of class and status and gutter-press ignorance . . . Switch on, tune in and *grow*.'[22]

Before returning to Hammersmith as a journalist, Potter would have had relatively few opportunities to consume television as a viewer (viewing was considered *infra dig* at Oxford; and people who actually work in the medium are notoriously almost as ill-informed about what it is actually broadcasting as politicians). So the *Herald* afforded him a crash course. Confined to the house, he could graze at his leisure and absorb the lessons.

After a couple of months, Potter persuaded the paper to allow him more space in the less-pressurised Saturday edition and there he established a column called In My View. What he noted most keenly and what most developed his critical stance was television drama. In a dry run ahead of In My View, Potter stood back to note: 'In the abuse we need to throw back at the little grey-faced monster squatting in our living rooms . . . we sometimes fail to notice the growth of the medium into something which attracts and holds creative writers and talented performers . . . who do not get enough credit for what could yet turn out to be the most significant cultural revolution of our times'[23] and he goes on to cite Denis Mitchell, Alun Owen, current affairs generally and (again!) *The Black and White Minstrel Show*. The phrase that leaps out is 'creative writers', partly because reviewers in the popular press didn't use offensive language like that, partly because of what is to come for Potter himself.

The inaugural In My View brings news of 'constant turmoil' in 'the overworked drama departments of both channels . . . On one side there are those who want to be cautious and take plays and ideas direct from the theatre. On the other are the revolutionaries who want to shake things up a bit. They are eager to inject new forms, fresh techniques, bolder themes into the TV play.'[24] There is no doubt to which camp Potter inclines.

A yet more significant portent lurks in Potter's gleeful reaction to Granada's *War and Peace* in March 1963: 'surely the most exciting evening that TV has ever given us'.[25] This was the famed Piscator stage dramatisation, televisualised by Robert David MacDonald and directed by Silvio Narizzano, with a cast headed by Kenneth Griffith as Napoleon, Daniel Massey as Prince Andrei and Nicol Williamson as Besukhov. It was shown either side of the 15-minute ITN News from 20.00 to 23.00, 'the first time that a play of this magnitude has been shown on British TV in one evening'[26] as *TV Times* genuflected.

Magnitude, however, is no guarantee of anything. Resuming on the Saturday, Potter was on to other aspects. There was a narrator stepping out of the action to address the camera, 'more than the chain yoking the fragments together . . . He made sense of it all. Even more important, the part of the narrator in this superb production showed convincingly that the simple, naturalistic, tediously "authentic" drama is not the only way of liberating the TV play . . . Granada's tele-marathon was more than just a thrilling experience. It must also be the launching pad for a great deal more thought about the uses and possibilities of good television drama.'[27]

The evidence of Potter's own teleplays is that he himself leapt off that launching pad, taking a Piscatoresque parachute with him. As he glided through the air, he looked down on something of a wasteland for, as he noted in the critical bouquets he dished out at the end of that year, 'one-shot plays were often snivelling, sour-minded disappointments'.[28] There was a job to be done.

By now Potter had started writing for television, but not plays. At Lime Grove, the search had been on for a different kind of topical comment programme and, in February 1962, a proposal for *Saturday Night*, 'a late-night programme with a satirical approach',[29] was submitted by one of the producers in the *Tonight* unit, Ned Sherrin. The proposal was accepted and in June, Sherrin recorded his pilot. Controller of Programmes Stuart Hood approved a second pilot in August, though with the usual shoddy BBC calculations in mind: 'the competitor is going to attempt a light-hearted review of the week every Thursday in the autumn quarter.'[30]

At the *Herald*, David Nathan had been tinkering with a notion for a television serial about students but 'the unfortunate thing was that I hadn't been to university so I didn't have any background'. So he tried it out on the new guy a desk or two away: Potter before his 'visitation'. 'We just started; drawing on Dennis's experience of Oxford, and we tried but it didn't work. But he did say "you can write dialogue."' [31]

Sherrin's new show was unveiled on 24 November 1962, with a title John Bird had coined, *That Was the Week That Was*. In a news report, Potter attempted an ungainly definition of satire as 'how to laugh when something is gripping your throat and trying to shake you to death' and essayed that *TW3*, as it came to be known, was 'written by a variety of people with chips rather than pips on their shoulders'.[32]

David Nathan promptly went to interview Sherrin and anchorman David Frost for the *Herald*. 'On the way there I saw something in the paper which struck me as worth a comment. I mentioned it to Ned and he said "Yes, write it." Well, I hadn't done anything like that before but I did and they used it the following week. Then I got another idea and

I wrote that. And then Ned asked if I knew Dennis and he suggested that as a lot of people writing for the show seemed to operate best in pairs we might do the same. Dennis thought it was a good idea. We were both desperately short of money at the time – the *Herald* didn't pay very well.

'So we started writing sketches. We would meet every week, sometimes at his place, sometimes where I lived in Wembley Park. It's difficult to say how we operated. I tended to do the ones that required research into the files like the Attlee sketch.' This one was in fact their first joint credit, going out on 5 January. Their second credit was a month later and thereafter there were few editions to which they did not contribute.

One of the best-remembered of *TW3* sketches is by Nathan and Potter, officially entitled 'Mother's Day' but popularly known by its opening line: 'What is a Mum?' A nicely savage litany of advertising images aimed at housewives, it draws on slogans of the time: 'She thinks every wash-day is a miracle. And since she adds the extra egg to everything except the bacon, she is probably constipated as well.'[33]

'Well, that was mainly Dennis,' says Nathan unsurprisingly. 'Very much Dennis. Originally Jack Rosenthal had sent the idea to Ned who didn't tell us it was Jack's, he just rang me and said "Would you like to have a go at this?" I was busy doing something and Dennis took it over and read it back to me on the phone. I thought it sounded fine. I think I contributed one line. We pushed it in and it was quite a success, that one.' It was even repeated.

For their sketches, the pair usually received 15 guineas each. Others featured a spokesman for the South African government fielding questions with smooth cynicism; a trawl through the records 'proving' that the Tories favoured nationalisation; a piece of mischief using the songs of Adam Faith; a paste-together of Crossbencher's failed predictions in the *Sunday Express*; a wicked routine joshing the doings of the CND-supporting Canon Collins; a reckless joke about Hugh Carleton Greene and many more.

TW3 may now look like a refugee from the tamer end of the Edinburgh Festival fringe but in its heyday it represented a necessary blast of fresh air. And it was a huge success, building its audience from 3.5 million for its opener to an almost unheard-of 10 million for a near-midnight slot by the end of its first run in April 1963. The show returned in September but was abruptly and controversially cancelled at the year's end, ostensibly because 1964 would be an election year.

'Dennis once said that *That Was the Week* and I were a lifeline,' Nathan recalled. 'That was presumably when he was drowning. But it was a very important move for me and I think for Dennis too at the time. There was a great sense of excitement about being part of it. It does help when your name pops up. They didn't always know what you'd written. That also helps.' But important people wanted to know. Cecil Madden, then Assistant to the Controller of Programmes, sent a memo to Ned Sherrin, the entire contents of which were: 'I saw David Nathan and Dennis Potter had a writing credit. What did they do for you?'[34]

What *TW3* did for Potter was put a bit of welcome spending money in his pocket. It enabled the Potters to leave Hammersmith for Fairway Avenue, Kingsbury, round the corner from David and Norma Nathan. A touching indication of the humdrum side of a writer's life lies in the *TW3* contracts file: a letter in Potter's fastidious hand apologising for being 'a nuisance' but asking for help because 'I have not got a complete set of records for the tax man'; and a genial reply from the Assistant Head of Copyright: 'To date there have been over 150 contributors to *That Was the Week That Was*. Let us hope they do not all have similar tax problems!'[35]

8

Painting the Clouds with Sunshine

'God knows, elections are dull enough anyway. If you start dragging *honesty* in as well, then *everybody* will stay at home and watch the wrestling.'

Jack Hay, *Vote, Vote, Vote for Nigel Barton*[1]

Nineteen sixty-four was indeed election year and Labour was expected to win. Since leaving university, Dennis Potter had been steadily applying for Labour candidacies, including at Epping where he was short-listed but lost out to Stan Newens. At last, early in 1962, he won the nomination for Hertfordshire East, a dormitory area due north of London and a safe Conservative fiefdom.

When his 'visitation' struck, Potter might reasonably have given up the impossible task. On the other hand, the sitting Member was a tempting target for the aggressive son of a coal-miner: a baronet and junior minister in his mid-fifties who had addressed Oxford students in Potter's time, the Rt Hon. Sir Derek Walker-Smith Bt TD QC. Even the Liberal candidate was a Lieutenant Commander. It would be *fun*.

And 'the electors were in for a treat', according to the constituency Labour Party agent, Ron Brewer. 'His election pamphlet was exquisitely written (it is the only one I have kept from more than thirty years of electioneering). His thoughtful speeches sparkled. They were made without notes and, though they lacked rhetorical flourish, caught his audience by their sheer honesty, language and wit. He gave no sign that a few minutes before he entered the hall he had taken a trip round the back where he could ease the nausea and vomiting caused by his medication.'[2]

Though he could only walk with a stick, Potter played out the allotted role. Old mates like Roger Smith canvassed. Dick Taverne

MP came to speak for him. 'He was a most eloquent candidate,' says Taverne. 'We had lunch in the House of Commons afterwards. He wanted to discuss whether he should continue as a candidate. He asked whether politics was corrupting. My view was: yes, in a way. The way I saw it as corrupting was in the party system. Party discipline and party advantage eat into your soul.'[3]

Labour won the general election and Harold Wilson formed his first government. Sir Derek* held Hertfordshire East with a comfortable majority of nearly 8000, down from 10,181 in 1959. Had Potter been returned, he would have been part of a new Labour intake that included Shirley Williams, Peter Shore, Stan Newens, Eric Heffer, Roy Hattersley, Ivor Richard, Norman Buchan, Renee Short, Joel Barnett, Hugh Jenkins, Sam Silkin, Shirley Summerskill, Norman Atkinson, Stan Orme, Anne Kerr, David Ennals, Eric Varley, Captain Robert Maxwell and Brian Walden (Birmingham All Saints).

By election day, Potter had grown so disenchanted with the political role he had long planned that (so he claimed) he didn't even vote for himself. 'When I went canvassing with my political agent . . . they would start discussing things like "What are you going to do about all the blacks?" Well, I would attempt to engage and get a sharp kick on the ankle, which was fair enough, because his job was to get the vote out and mine was to realise that I was in the wrong trade . . . I felt that very strong streak of charlatanry in me . . . I would probably be leader of the Labour Party by now [laughing] if I hadn't been ill – in other words, I could have been that kind of sub-criminal [deadly serious].'[4]

A year on from the election, he told reporter Barry Norman with the arrogance of youth: 'I won't stand for Parliament again. I've got four offers, actually, to have my name put forward but I haven't even replied to them.'[5] The only pre-election reference to his political role in his journalism was a characteristic bite at the hand of the party that fed his ambitions. Wearing his television critic's hat, he could not forbear an expression of his now well-attested loathing for party political broadcasts: 'As a prospective Labour candidate myself, I nevertheless watched this Labour Party propaganda with distaste. Because it was boring. Because it was amateurish. Because it was *compulsory.*'[†6] (Potter's italics)

In September 1964 the *Daily Herald* metamorphosed into *The Sun*, under the ownership of Mirror Newspapers. Potter gave up

---

* When he eventually left the Commons, Walker-Smith took the title Baron Broxbourne.
† At this time, all channels were obliged by the regulations to broadcast PPBs simultaneously.

his reviewing* and for a short period – the election was imminent – wrote leaders. As these are by nature anonymous, one must look for his signature in the style and concerns rather than in a byline.

'Colourful posters in the modern mood are beginning to appear on church noticeboards. You can feel a little holier each day, with fabulous pink angels ... As churchmen have the right to ask: "Why should the Devil have all the best billboards?"'7 Surely this is Mr Leader-Writer Potter in *TW3* mode.

After the election, Potter wrote (I surmise) one more leader and then severed his link with the paper. He did so with few regrets, observing drily on a later occasion that he 'had joined on the mistaken assumption that it was a Socialist newspaper. I was doing my usual sort of do-barmaids-eat-their-young? pieces.'8 This tends both to sensationalise and to undervalue the work he had done for the *Herald*.

The end of these two roads, career journalism and career politics, did not leave him high and dry. For he was already engaged upon a furious regime of writing television plays.

As far back as June, Potter had slipped the following aside into a review, the burden of which was a consideration of the blurring of drama's edges, the mixing of fact with fiction: 'Although I cannot give details, I know of a new young dramatist who is writing a play for the BBC which uses speeches from Nye Bevan and Sir Oswald Mosley.'9 Only a select few could know then, as we can know now with hindsight, that the 'new young dramatist' was Potter himself and the play was *Vote, Vote, Vote for Nigel Barton*. Anyone who ever felt Potter to be incapable of archness will be sadly disabused by this absurd performance.

What is so revealing, however, is the date. The election was not until 15 October. Far from writing this play about an uncomfortable Labour candidate in an unwinnable seat as a piece of emotion recollected in tranquillity, Potter was well stuck into it – for the use of newsreel is hardly central to the story – months before the campaign proper even began.

The daily reviews also reveal (by their nature) what Potter had been watching. In May 1963 he noticed a play by Arden Winch, *Return to the Regiment*, which by his account chimes intriguingly with the climax of *Vote, Vote, Vote*: 'During the stiffly informal dinner, the general ... rises to make his proud and patriotic response. But the young writer ... who has been soaking up whisky all evening is provoked into

---

* The poet Adrian Mitchell, a marvellous choice, succeeded him in a more prominent and regular space than Potter ever enjoyed.

an angrily drunken interruption. He flings back the bloody record of a meaningless advance which made more widows than inches of ground gained. Unfortunately, such a confrontation, valid in so many ways, was too melodramatic, too dependent on whisky.'[10] Potter learned well from these perceived errors.

Towards the end of the same year, Alun Owen's *A Local Boy* was broadcast, a play about a Labour selection process, 'a splendidly accomplished piece of venom, rhetoric and humour'[11] which was exactly the commentators' view of *Vote, Vote, Vote*.*

No imputation of plagiarism is intended. Potter said that 'almost everything I see is, if not material for writing, it's material for living, which is the same thing to me'[12] and, though he was then referring to *events* that he witnessed, he would inevitably draw material from the 'grey-faced little screen', as he so often chaffingly called it, which he watched daily for his work. He was consciously studying television drama. Of course plays that preceded his own informed his writing.

For years Potter numbered *Vote* his first teleplay – he does so in the introduction to the published text of the two *Nigel Barton* plays. This is a moot point, however. *Vote* was commissioned by the BBC on 23 June 1964, four days before the allusion to it in his review. But by then he had already delivered another play to the BBC. There are two possible explanations for this discrepancy in the account. One is that *Vote* was begun first but set aside – perhaps to accommodate the material Potter anticipated gathering from the election campaign.

I prefer my other theory, though it is less comfortable and more convoluted. The introduction to the *Nigel Barton* plays gives no indication that this 'first' play was actually transmitted fourth, rather implying that *Vote* was preceded only by its companion piece *Stand Up, Nigel Barton*, the events of which take chronological precedence. But Potter's first play transmitted was the first he delivered: *The Confidence Course*. And betweentimes there was *Alice*.

My own view is that Potter rewrote history – or allowed a rewrite to be assumed – so that his play-writing career appeared to open with the flourish of the *Barton* pair. And I call as a witness Stanley Baxter. The comedy star, now retired, appeared in *The Confidence Course*, 'the only completely straight part I ever did on television'. He says: 'I think he couldn't have been totally happy with what we did because he didn't use to list it as his first play. It's been dropped.'†[13]

We shall not drop it, however. It concerns the operation of a

---

* Potter also covered, in November 1962, *Don Juan in Hell* on ITV which, it could be argued, bears at least a superficial resemblance to his most Shavian play, *The Confidence Course*.
† *The Confidence Course* and *Alice* are among thirteen works not included in Potter's *Who's Who* entry.

public seminar by an evangelistic organisation, designed to persuade members of the public to part with their money in the belief that they have learned something to their advantage about their fears and insecurities. Various fragments allow us to piece together the genesis of this strange, original and *quondam* outcast play. First is a memo from the producer of the four plays in question, James MacTaggart. Dated 8 March 1965, it states: 'Some time ago Potter, as a freelance journalist and broadcaster, was commissioned by the sound programme *Ten O'Clock* to do a report on such courses. He attended a demonstration by the Dale Carnegie organisation. In the event the report was not broadcast.'[14]

'Some time ago' is infuriating but proximity to the event renders it compelling. Potter's own account of covering Carnegie for his newspaper might be less than accurate after almost three decades. However, he offers a specific detail that could not have applied to the BBC: 'The *Herald* wouldn't use the article because Dale Carnegie was advertising in the paper.'[15]

David Nathan sheds further light: 'After *That Was the Week*, Dennis was intent on more interesting work and he started to write a play called *The Confidence Course*. He intended we should write it together, operating as we had with the sketches. So I was at the typewriter, because I typed faster than Dennis, and he walked up and down and we wrote dialogue between us. But every line I contributed the first week was taken out the second. I hadn't been on this Pelmanism* course that he'd investigated for the *Herald* so I didn't have much to say about it. So I said "Come on, Dennis, this is your play, why don't you go away and write it." And that was more or less that. We saw each other from time to time afterwards.'[17]

A third source is Roger Smith. He was now at the BBC, as Potter had told his readers in a February 1964 piece about the BBC's eight-year ratings low and the 'relative unpopularity of the plays' which was being put about as an explanation.

This week two young men took over the responsibility for the next series of 'First Nights',† the weekend plays which have taken the brunt of criticism. They are James McTaggart [*sic*],

---

* 'A system of mind and memory training originated by W. J. Ennever in the closing years of the nineteenth century' which employed 'very extensive advertising'.[16]
† First Night, produced by John Elliot, was Sydney Newman's first (and largely unsuccessful) attempt to reproduce his ABC success at the BBC. It ran for one season, 1963–4, and included new plays by Alun Owen, Nigel Kneale, Arnold Wesker, Simon Raven and Terence Frisby. The error was to run it slap against Armchair Theatre. MacTaggart dropped First Night for The Wednesday Play.

as executive producer,* and Roger Smith, as script editor . . .
McTaggart thinks 'naturalism' – the kind of dreary authenticity
which duplicates the very grease on the fish-and-chip paper –
has had its day. Smith, who has to find the plays, said: 'We're
talking with a lot of writers to see what can be done about
changing the form and the contents of the TV play . . . We're
going out for a big audience and this can be done only by being
adventurous.[18]

It is forgivably disingenuous that, on this occasion, Potter is not
jumping up and down in the background of the piece, yelling 'look
at me, Ma'. After all, only four days earlier, Smith had commissioned
The Confidence Course.

'I came into the drama department as a scriptwriter/adapter,' Smith
recalls. 'When we started to plan The Wednesday Play, I went to see
Dennis. What *didn't* happen was that he said "I understand you're
working for the BBC now and here's a play"! *I* said "Why on earth
don't you write a play? This is a great opportunity. I don't know
how long I'll be here but at the moment they're saying "Go and
find playwrights" and I'm finding people who *aren't* playwrights.
Haven't you got any ideas?" He started talking about the notion that
became *The Confidence Course* so I commissioned him to write it. I
just believed he could do it. I wanted people who'd never written for
television before. I'd go to novelists and journalists. It was strange that
he hadn't thought of it for television.[†] The idea that television was just
waiting for Dennis Potter to happen is a myth. In a way, television
was the enemy.'[19]

There is one more inspirational source but it must wait until the play
itself has been considered. *The Confidence Course* takes place entirely
in a hotel suite where the director of the course (played by Dennis
Price) and his henchmen have set up shop. The director is discovered
going through his lines; the first we hear is: 'Perhaps once, and ONCE
ONLY, in your life, Opportunity comes – and with it, Redemption'.[20]
This is a highly significant beginning.

An unseen, unidentified narrator sets the scene: one of the henchmen, Jones (Artro Morris), 'worries about his conscience almost as
much as he does about his dandruff. Both can be very embarrassing.'
At last a customer appears, Mr Thomas (John Moore), whom they
quickly smother with disorientation techniques. Thomas ('I'm so sorry,

---

* In fact MacTaggart never used this title.
† The official version (*Potter on Potter*, p. 3) is that he was originally writing *The Confidence Course* as a novel.

so terribly sorry. It – well, it *is* raining outside, you see, and – I'm so sorry') speaks exactly like Francis Francis, the milksop in *Lipstick on Your Collar*, nearly thirty years later.

More people venture in, 'each one looking for something purchasable called CONFIDENCE, knowing themselves failures of one sort or another, but unwilling to acknowledge the need for a psychiatrist'. In the corridor lurks a mysterious stranger who, when Jones approaches him, says he has seen the course advertisement 'but it didn't look out of place amongst the striped toothpaste and coloured toilet rolls'. To Jones's inquiry after his name, he calls it 'an administrative and occasionally religious device that has nothing in particular to do with one's identity. I'm Hazlitt actually, 1778–1965.'

In the hall, the director is speaking. 'Every phrase has been considered . . . It might almost be a party political broadcast.' He plays his audience, a little boost here, a little humiliation there. 'Hazlitt' begins to lob incendiary observations into the gathering. The director, inviting sympathy by isolating the seditionist, conducts an elaborate memory demonstration, then begins to pluck people from the audience.

Rosalind (Yootha Joyce), whom the narrator identifies as a 'spinster', lives in Fulham, 'almost in Chelsea'. The director goads her into an outburst against her boss ('a pig!') and the girls in the typing pool: 'Just tarts they are, clopping in on their high heels. All lipstick and powder. They don't even know how to spell, except s-e-x.' For the first time, she gives vent to resentment and the director accepts the credit.

Bloom (John Quentin), who has 'a secretary willing to have her bottom pinched', suffers from stuttering. Mocking without mercy, the director rouses him until he achieves the 'Peter Piper' tongue-twister. In a Max Miller-ish turn, Greenway (John Blythe) tells how he was saved by the course. Provoked beyond endurance, 'Hazlitt' launches a diatribe against the 'gigantic conspiracy' of advertising: 'an arbitrarily defined Perfection assails us *all the time*. Even a pimple on a young girl's face can become a symbol of sin and depravity . . . My doctor cannot help me because he does not look like Dr Kildare . . . It's all a jingle jangle, a jangle jingle jungle . . .'

The director soothes with smooth words, resumes his demonstrations, then samples another textbook customer, Mrs Wallace (Joan Sanderson), who believes her husband is lacking. The director tells her she should offer him 'a pink glow of soft, submissive femininity'. 'Hazlitt' intervenes brutally, describing the death of the real Hazlitt from stomach cancer and accusing the course of missing the crucial ingredient: 'a happy life'. The director accuses him of madness but he embarks upon a substantial passage from the actual essays of Hazlitt:

'People walk along the streets the day after our deaths just as they did before, and the crowd is not diminished . . . The million are devoid of sentiment, and care as little for you or me as if we belonged to the moon.'*[21]

Instructing his men to eject 'Hazlitt', thereby prompting an unseemly scramble, the director loses his composure and inadvertently betrays his contempt for the customers. They get the message and he loses the confidence of the meeting. The narrator underlines that 'the weak have become strong and the strong weak' as they straggle out, disdaining the course.

So *The Confidence Course* is a moral fable and a social comedy, lifted into originality by its use of an intruder passing as a supernatural being, in this case a ghost. It has its indigestible aspects – the narrator must be a vestige of its life as a novel – and, as is apt to occur in highly coloured writing, the depiction of the plausible shark is so relished and sure-footed that he is in danger of carrying the day. But it certainly announces a writer to be reckoned with.

Stanley Baxter, who played 'Hazlitt', 'loved the play. It certainly didn't strike me as apprentice work. I jumped at the chance to play it. It was all part of his grand theme about how people manipulate: the Murdochs, the charlatans of this world. I so agreed with everything he felt about the tabloids. And that last interview he did with [Melvyn] Bragg was so moving. He called his cancer Rupert. I loved that.'

Baxter recalls the ubiquitous posters on the Underground at the time of the production: 'Come to the Caxton Hall, Cure Your Blushing' and similar such claims. He had read Hazlitt's essays at school. Had he thought that at any level Potter meant the character to be literally Hazlitt? 'I simply didn't know and I felt it must remain a mystery. I played him in a kind of raincoat, shuffling in. I think most probably he was a tortured soul who'd been through those treadmills of hypocrisy and the way the world fucked him up and now he wasn't going to let this man fuck anybody else up and had come to spike his guns. That's how I looked at it.'[22]

The participation of Stanley Baxter in Potter's 'first' play is of abiding significance because, as we shall see, Potter grew particularly to favour actors with a comedy background, an important indication of how he, unlike some of his critics, perceived his work.

Gilchrist Calder, who directed the play, told Potter at their first meeting that 'as far as I was concerned at that stage it was a radio play. There wasn't a lot of "vision" in it. We had to make a few adjustments to get it into a television state. He had a brain

---

* The actor Peter Jeffrey read very finely from this essay at Potter's memorial service.

so he'd ask "why"? quite a lot but he was very affable about it. I didn't find it a particularly difficult piece to do. I directed some of Johnny Speight's first work and that was far more way out than any of Dennis's early plays. It was the quality of the writing that attracted me straight away.'[23]

The production was budgeted at £4000 of which its author received £600. It was recorded in studio 4 on 10 February 1965 and transmitted a fortnight later. Neither the telerecording nor any copy is known to survive.

Some reviews are collected in a BBC envelope crediting the play to 'Simon Potter'. Adrian Mitchell called it 'a powerful parable'.[24] In the *Daily Mirror*, Richard Sear nicely evoked that power: 'one of those wordy, idealistic plays which are an outcry against life itself – but end up a small voice in the mass of television . . . he crammed three or four plays into one, filling the screen with telling phrases and rich prose . . . my set began to quiver from the strain.'[25]

The Dale Carnegie Course made representations about the play which the BBC properly rejected: 'In writing his play the author did not have any particular Course in mind. You yourself have pointed out that there were differences between the demonstration shown and the one which you run.'[26]

No doubt Potter drew on his observation of both Pelmanism and the Carnegie Course in the play but, as no journalism resulted, this does not help us with a writing chronology. Nor does that striking use of a character representing William Hazlitt, except to date the conception of the play later than spring 1962. For Potter only discovered Hazlitt during his first stay in hospital, when he 'seemed to me at least as emancipating as a mouthful of steroids'.[27] It was a new love-affair that lasted the rest of his life, informing Potter's thought extensively and allowing him in this play to filter himself through a figure from history.

Hazlitt disturbed people and can still do so, very effectively. It was his intellectual distinction and social misfortune to have no time to spare for those 'who think by proxy and talk by rote' . . . And he could use invective with such viperish skill that his victims might well have examined themselves in a hand-mirror to see if the venomous prose had erupted into discoloured flesh or broken skin. A quirky, pungent, obsessive, honest and extremely forceful writer who alienated most of his friends, he exposed himself without mercy, and yet 'never gave the lie to his own soul'.[28]

This is Potter at his most limpidly autobiographical.

Virginia Woolf's view might have been expressed of Potter:

112

Hazlitt was not one of those non-committal writers who shuffle off in a mist and die of their own insignificance. His essays are emphatically himself. He has no reticence and he has no shame. He tells us exactly what he thinks, and he tells us – the confidence is less seductive – what he feels. As of all men he had the most intense consciousness of his own existence, since never a day passed without inflicting on him a pang of hate or of jealousy, some thrill of anger or pleasure, we cannot read him for long without coming in contact with a very singular character – ill-conditioned yet high-minded; mean yet noble; intensely egotistical yet inspired by the most genuine passion for the rights and liberties of mankind.[29]

Clearly it was the recognition of a kindred spirit and, perhaps, of a wise counsel that fired Potter. It is tempting to speculate that a reading of this lash across the back of Coleridge contributed decisively to his own sense of drowning at the *Herald*: 'Alas! Frailty, thy name is *Genius*! – What is become of all this mighty heap of hope, of thought, of learning and humanity? It has ended in swallowing doses of oblivion and in writing paragraphs in the *Courier*.'[30]

Potter seriously contemplated a life of Hazlitt: 'modern lit-biographies seize greedily upon the most trivial events or quirks of character or accidents of inheritance which make the man as opposed to the works. And in Hazlitt's case it is exceptionally difficult to separate the two: he used himself, used up himself, in so unique a fashion that it would even be perverse to attempt the exercise. The adder on the path has to be stepped on, or stepped over . . . He was the type of manic depressive who was able to use even the black moments to reach down into himself and find an extremity of meaning or experience which could be communicated to others. Hazlitt was one of those prickly, introspective radicals who have conservative tastes and a longing for the past which is too lyrical or too melancholic to be dismissed as mere nostalgia.'[31]

Hazlitt bestowed upon Potter a vehicle for articulating in a play the rage against admass that he was denied on *Panorama*. He was a mouthpiece. It was not a technique to which the rapidly-learning playwright would resort again because he found it too explicit. 'I don't like political drama,' he said in 1993, 'because I think the way to argue politics is through the essay or prose discourse. Obviously your feelings and aspirations – social, religious and political – inform what you write. But I don't think you should write on their behalf; you shouldn't fly those flags.'[32]

* * * *

Vote, Vote, Vote for Nigel Barton is not a political drama in the sense that no lead role represents a fixed position or a card of issues. The play follows the course of a by-election campaign from the death of the sitting Member (brought down while fox-hunting) to the eve of poll. Doubtless in a spirit of jocularity, the playwright implies a shaft of Trollopean comedy, for the constituency is given as West Barset. Nigel Barton (Keith Barron) was the heavily defeated Labour candidate in the October 1964 general election; it is now April 1965. He is a journalist, an Oxford graduate and the son of a coal-miner who 'could draw an apple on the white margins of a newspaper which was so good, so ripe, so perfectly rounded and shaded, that you *ached* to pluck it off the pages'.[33] He has a wife, Anne (Valerie Gearon), who was, as Nigel throws at her during a spat, 'brought up to assuage your guilt by smiling at the window-cleaner and over-tipping the dustman'.

But Nigel does not get to play all the best tunes; indeed Anne has the key speech: 'Yours is the worst form of betrayal. Your own memories tell you clearly enough what politics is about – and yet you sneer at ideas, you sneer at ideology, you sneer at theory – and reduce everything to petty little slogans for cheap party advantage.' So the play addresses the 'corrupting' effect of 'party discipline and party advantage' about which Dick Taverne had cautioned Potter. And, despite Anne's remark, almost her first in the play, that 'there's a little bit of the charlatan in you', Nigel will be, it may be surmised, 'happy to emerge as a fool rather than a charlatan', like Potter in the furore with Brian Walden at Oxford.

The play's most eye-catching character is the local agent, Jack Hay (played by John Bailey). At the end of his first scene, in which he is seen talking to Nigel on the phone, Jack startlingly winks at the camera. Henceforth, he is complicit with the audience. His is the voice of the professional, the machine politico, but he is cynical as well as realistic, crossing himself at the mention of 'old-age pensioners'. His detachment and pragmatism is set against the principles of both Anne and the members of the local party GMC.

The scenes with Anne and with Jack interleave action from the campaign, including a notably droll turn by a seen-it-all woman on her doorstep and an excruciating sequence in an 'old folks' home' where the bewildered old men ('I only want me leg!') are badgered in their different ways by the charge nurse, Jack and an embarrassed Nigel.

Nigel finally has his epiphany at the Barset Annual Council Dinner. The (none too young) Tory candidate (Cyril Luckham), complete with war ribbons, gives an archetypally seigneurial address ('the seditious television playwrights may snipe and jeer') which provokes Nigel into daring to discuss politics, especially class politics, and to make an angry denunciation of his opponent's complacency. He anatomises the 'dead ideas, dead thoughts, dead slogans, all of them sicked up on your own doorstep'. When the guests start beating time with the cutlery, Nigel favours his rival with a V-sign, a moment captured by the local paper's photographer.

Anne is delighted ('You know very well how the Labour Party loves a rebel') and begins to talk of how to build on the confrontation. Her words dissolve into those of Jack on how to claw his way back. But Nigel only has ashes in his mouth.

As a piece of play-making, *Vote* is a smashing success. It is funny, vital, pacy and contrives to suggest a canvas much broader and more peopled than it actually is. It presents a flawed (or at least a troubled and uncertain) protagonist without sacrificing sympathy and identification. And it assuredly tears up the rule book, primarily in the way Jack Hay uses access to the camera. In Potter's words, it was an attempt 'to use the familiar, party-political-broadcast technique of the direct, niggling narrative by a huge face into the camera . . . without allowing the audience the comfort of thinking that what was so obviously being shot right at them like a poisoned dart was objectively "true"'.[34]

To-camera address was not unknown in teledrama, as we know from Potter's report on the Piscator *War and Peace*. But in that case the device had been used to answer a need for compression. Here, as in *The Confidence Course* where it also featured briefly, it was organic.

'It was a time when people tended to say "Oh, you can't do that",' says director Gareth Davies. 'Your response, being young and arrogant, was "Yes I can" . . . Sometimes foolishly. All the address to the audience was in the script but it wasn't normally done in plays. Of course, it's done all the time in the theatre, which was my background. So I had no problem with it. We talked about how to distort it. Dennis was always very receptive to technical notions. We decided to ease in with the turret camera on a wide, 35-degree lens to distort the face gradually. Dennis never wanted realism.'[35]

In one of his later sorties against the 'necrotic' party political broadcast, Potter recalled: 'In a TV play I once wrote about the horrors of electioneering, I specified the use of the big close-up to set up a jarring dislocation between the calculated platitudes of the candidate and all those subtle betrayals or evasions mapped like tiny blood vessels on that mobile cartography between chin and forehead.'[36]

Jack Hay aside, the play is not without its own cynicism or at least a touch of *Weltschmerz*. Nigel gamely attempts a disquisition on 'The Origins of the Present Crisis' for the edification of a village Labour Women's Group. This is, at best, commendable ambition on Nigel's part; at worst it suggests Potter has forgotten that, were this Nigel's opening appearance on the stump, he might have been excused for a first-time offence of offering caviar to the general, but this is his *second* campaign. It is doubly unfortunate that the audience is a women's group, comfortably patronised in the portrayal and dismissed by Jack as 'frigid about ideology, too'.

The weakest element in the writing is the character of Anne. She functions broadly as Nigel's conscience but 'where she is coming from' has not been secured. Her views reflect the expediency not of a character who is seen as a smart operator but of a writer who needs a shifting sounding-board. Nigel resents her being 'all pure and disapproving' but her line 'I might feel differently if you had the faintest glimmer of a chance' is hardly an indication of purity. In another remark that unmistakably locates the play in a period when writers were gleefully discovering (or rediscovering) the metaphorical use of sex, Anne casually notes that 'this blasted by-election has made you impotent as well as crooked'. And in her final scene, she is obliged to perform an unwieldy contortion from dismay through admiration to connivance and politicking. It is a bewildering journey and it suggests that Potter was too diligent in his attempts to make her more than a mere 'position'.

The play went to studio on 12–14 April. Gareth Davies was allowed six cameras instead of the usual five. All went smoothly until a vengeful god intervened. As an engineer's memo explained: 'Every alternate roll [of film] suffered from a fault condition due to mis-registration of the film in the camera gate of FR 31. This was a mechanical failure which could not be foreseen or noticed during the time of recording and it was due to a small screw which had broken.'*37

Two more recording days were required and these could not be found before June so the play lost its late April slot and was rescheduled for transmission on 23 June. 'But by that time,' wrote Potter, 'a few highly-charged whispers about the "dangerous" nature of the play had begun to drift round and round the rubbery, anonymous and appropriately circular corridors of the hideous new

---

* The unexpected presence of film in the process indicates the primitive nature of what was called telerecording before the arrival of video recording. The studio pictures, captured by electronic cameras, were fed to the engine room of Television Centre where they were literally filmed as they arrived on a pair of fixed cameras, alternating rather as projectors alternate when films are screened. At the *Vote* recording, one of these film cameras generated visibly damaged footage, leaving half the telerecording unusable.

BBC Television Centre. One by one, BBC executives were called in to see the telerecording and were seen to emerge shaking their heads like nervous marionettes.'[38]

At 14.30 on the day of transmission, the decision to postpone the play was made known. No public statement was issued but the BBC press office was given a form of words with which to fend off inquiries, quoting Huw Wheldon, the recently appointed Controller of Programmes, as follows: 'Sydney Newman, who saw a pre-run of *Vote, Vote, Vote for Nigel Barton* yesterday, decided that the production as a whole was not yet ready for transmission. He asked me to see it. I did, and I agree with him. The play is therefore postponed ... When we transmit *Vote* ..., or whether we transmit it, will depend on further work and further consideration.'[39]

Reported *The Observer*:

It was a jocular remark on Tuesday afternoon that led to the withdrawal of [the play] ... James McTaggart [*sic*] told Michael Bakewell, head of plays, that the play 'had a go' at politicians. Bakewell thought that Sydney Newman, head of drama, should be warned. Newman, who has been making soothing noises in the clean-up TV direction, was alarmed and called in Paul Fox, head of current affairs. He took the line that politicians should not be mocked and that the play was too accurate ... Next to be consulted was Huw Wheldon ... He congratulated Newman for stepping in because of the play's political implications (pretty innocuous except to the politicians of Television Centre). And so to Kenneth Adam, director of BBC TV. He ordered the play off.[40]

This has all the hallmarks of a briefing from someone at no further remove from events than MacTaggart himself.

Fox's memo to Wheldon is on file. 'The play is very nearly a documentary,' he declared, immediately casting doubt upon his grasp on, well, *realism* if not indeed reality. Among other idiosyncratic objections, he notes that 'the Tory is on for about seven minutes – looking a buffoon – the Labour man is on for nearly sixty minutes: a bit starry-eyed, but basically the good guy.'[41] This is the reading of a parliamentary train-spotter. It is extraordinary that the fate of a play should hang on the opinion of an administrator illiterate about drama.

Potter raced to Television Centre only to be placated by Newman and persuaded not to go public. By his account: 'I was asked by one chief BBC executive whether or not I was "some kind of fascist" ...

it is felt to be obscure impertinence if a writer demonstrates that he has thought about his work or has a serious intention in mind. Cut out that crap, is the unspoken attitude, and let's talk about rewrites, old chap.'[42]

The 'executive' could hardly be Sydney Newman if 'cut out that crap' was unspoken. In an account on another occasion, Potter claimed that, at this interview, Newman demanded to know why he wanted 'to shit on the Queen'. Potter's gloss, polished with the hindsight of twenty-eight years of brooding, was that 'He must already have known that this is not a particularly easy thing to do from a kneeling position.'[43]

An on-air announcement 'hoped' that *Vote* would be transmitted 'at some future date'.[44] Roger Smith and his two assistants now handed in their resignations in protest. Newman refused to accept them. 'He said "What are you talking about? You're leaving anyway!"' says Smith. 'It was true. Twenty-six plays, one a week, was quite enough for me.'*[45]

Negotiations began in earnest about rewrites. Potter's agent, Roger Hancock, extracted some useful concessions from Newman, including: 'Should we feel upon having read all the press reports that our client's professional reputation as a playwright has suffered as a result of the cancellation of the transmission, you will issue a statement making it quite clear that the quality of his writing was not in question.'[46] In his reply, Newman remarked somewhat tartly but no doubt accurately: 'I don't think Dennis Potter has suffered even vaguely at the hands of the press.'[47] In the end, 'about one fifth of the play'[48] was rewritten, for which Potter was paid an additional £100.

'There was an argument about whether the end of the play would upset the political parties,' recalls Gareth Davies. 'It's true that I was approached by both a Labour and a Tory peer whom I knew, both of them claiming it was the buggers in the other party who were kicking up. They were both wrong. No pressure was brought to bear by the parties. It was a state of nerves on the BBC's part.'[49]

The lunacy of the BBC's search to justify its own timorousness is illustrated by one instruction Davies received, concerning a line that referred to 'a cross on a ballot paper'. He was told that 'cross' must be changed to 'X', 'because there are religious connotations'.

'It came down to pride and face-saving,' says Davies. 'It really couldn't have been more inept. I don't think we made very many alterations and I don't think it did any important damage to the piece,

---

* As a student of The Wednesday Play, I have always regarded Roger Smith as a hero; I hope this book renders him less of an unsung hero.

frankly.' One divergence between the telerecording and the published text is instructive: a reference to 'The Keep Television Clean Group' on paper becomes 'The Keep Bread Pure Group' on screen.

The need for a second partial reshoot sowed confusion in the BBC's housekeeping. Michael Peacock, now BBC1 Controller, sent Michael Bakewell a suitably headmasterly memo about the programme budget growing to 'the fantastic figure of £13,611. Pray, inform me whether you intend to absorb this cost within the average budget for the Wednesday Play.'[50] The original budget had been £6,250 19s 11d and one of the series' slots had to be sacrificed to accommodate the ballooning expense.

Gareth Davies reveals that 'somebody forgot to change the design budget so we had the same money for the reshoot as for the whole production first time. We built much bigger sets. The BBC was wonderfully inefficient in those days. You could drive a coach and horses through the bureaucracy which was what made television so exciting. Now you can't and it's boring. But I do remember we had to do some additional filming against evergreen trees to get round the continuity.'

Another budget finagle concerned Potter's 75-guinea fee for 'technical advice', justified by his election experience. Davies recalls no such advice: 'It was a device to get him a bit more money, I would say. But the standard contract gave the writer an allowance to come to first rehearsal and the run-through and nothing in between. That's rubbish, to me. It's *his* play. The writer is always welcome.'

As well as absorbing the cost of two plays, the revamped *Vote* exceeded the 75-minute limit for the Wednesday Play and MacTaggart, shrewdly exploiting the BBC's embarrassment, applied for and got dispensation for a slot of 78 minutes.

The Corporation was unmistakably discomposed. When a stringer on the *Sunday Telegraph* aimed a passing squib at the BBC bowing to 'campaigners', Huw Wheldon swept into print with a perfectly honourable but quite unnecessarily weighty reply. After all the agony, the BBC was left looking obdurate and confused when the play was received with great acclaim and won the SFTA Award, the forerunner of the BAFTA Award. But before that happened, two more Potter plays were ready for recording.

9

I'm Learning a Lot from You

'You got to bend at the knees, see. When you do hit the
ground. That's Rule Number One, that is.'

Peter, *Blue Remembered Hills*[1]

Happily, the two script assistants who took a stand along with Roger
Smith over the treatment of *Vote, Vote, Vote for Nigel Barton* did allow
themselves to be persuaded to rescind their resignations. Each went
on to change television drama in his own particular way.

One was Smith's ally from Oxford days, Kenneth Trodd. 'He was
coming back from teaching in a university in Africa so I said "Do
you want a job?"' is Smith's no-nonsense account. The other recruit
was Tony Garnett. 'He was an actor I'd seen in David Mercer's play,
A Climate of Fear. I wrote a play about my own marriage breaking
up and I asked Tony to play me, in effect, and I got to like him.'*[2]

A week after *Vote* was in studio for the first time, Garnett commissioned an untitled Potter play at 75 minutes. When *Vote* was
rescheduled for the second season and Smith was known to be
leaving, Garnett looked after the rewrites, taking a shared credit as
story editor. He also took over another Potter/Smith project, *Alice*,
which bears no editor's name.

Alice is about the relationship between Charles Lutwidge Dodgson
and Alice Liddell, the dearest to him of the children for whom he wrote
stories under the pseudonym Lewis Carroll. It begins with what would
become a familiar Potter setting, a train, but this one evokes the train

---

* Garnett went on to produce strongly political drama, notably *Cathy Come Home*, many
of the social-realist films directed by Ken Loach, and the serials *Days of Hope* and *Law
and Order*.

120

journey in the 'Looking-Glass Insects' chapter of Carroll's *Through the Looking-Glass and What Alice Found There*. The older Dodgson (he died at seventy-five in 1898) is assailed by a plummy-voiced couple who are travelling in the same carriage. The woman reveals herself as (or claims to be) one of the children to whom he once told stories: 'You asked me to consider myself your very special friend, Mr Dodgson.'[3] Hurt by their condescension, Dodgson (George Baker) becomes abrasive.

Memory carries him back to his days as a young Oxford don ('I'm late, I'm late'). He observes the indifference of the college gardener (Billy Russell) to the decaying of the roses and imagines him as a playing-card. The Liddell girls squabble in a well-bred fashion about correct forms of speech. Their mother (Rosalie Crutchley) talks about Dodgson who has been taking the children's pictures. 'As regards the photographic camera,' she says, 'he is becoming very distinguished.' The cool remark by Alice (Deborah Watling) that Dodgson 'loves me' visibly disturbs Mrs Liddell. Her husband (David Langton) is Dean of Christ Church where Dodgson has tenure. In a tutorial, Dodgson grows shyly cross with a student and sets him a logical conundrum.

The distaff Liddells take an excursion on the river with Dodgson and a fellow cleric as their guests. Alice holds his gaze daringly, then splashes water in his face for 'looking at me'. Mrs Liddell smooths over the moment.* Later, Dodgson reads stories that will join *Alice's Adventures in Wonderland*. One is enacted, 'A Mad Tea-Party', with Alice as her namesake.

In his college rooms Dodgson is beset by an oleaginous jeweller (John Moffatt) trying to sell him a music box that plays 'Twinkle Twinkle Little Star' ('we can supply all things today, sir, including magic'). But the magic is mechanical and contrived. Dodgson breaks from his defensive shell by spiralling into whimsical variations of the song, later to be put into the mouth of the Mad Hatter.

Mrs Liddell has a nameless dread of Dodgson's intentions but the Dean is more exercised by his perceived anti-progressive stance on college politics. Mrs Liddell destroys Dodgson's letters to Alice. Dodgson tries to photograph Alice but the child is skittish. He tells her of a treacle-mine in the Forest of Dean. 'The Mock Turtle's Story' is enacted. The first *Alice* book is now written: 'it really is, in most places, remarkably funny' its author tells himself.

The Liddells discuss Dodgson again. The Dean will not allow the book to be dedicated to Alice. His wife believes that Dodgson means to wait until he may marry Alice. 'You might as well wait for the

---

* Mrs Liddell's attendance on this trip is an addition of Potter's.

moon to turn to cheese,' scoffs the Dean, adding, as he returns to his breakfast: 'Or fried bacon.'

Interviewed by the publisher Alexander Macmillan (Maurice Hedley), Dodgson imagines himself mocked. 'Advice from a Caterpillar' is enacted. The real Alice is delighted with the 'Father William' poem but delivers a rebuff as cruel as a child alone can muster: 'It's only a book, isn't it.'

Switching between the heavy hand and the offhand, the Dean interviews an increasingly hysterical Dodgson, then demands to know from Alice whether she has been 'rude to Mr Dodgson, thoughtlessly unkind' or whether he has ever 'frightened' her. He counsels her, from Dodgson's prefatory verse, that she take the gift of the book 'with a gentle hand'. Later he says of Dodgson to a colleague: 'I get the impression that he's harbouring some great and secret disappointment.'

Six years on from the river trip and three from first publication, Dodgson takes a picnic with the Liddell women, a boy or two in tow. He cannot grasp the family dynamic. Mrs Liddell, more imperiously innocent than ever, proposes hide-and-seek: 'Let us not miss an opportunity to have some *fun.*' Alice is casually cruel about the book to which she gave her name but they allow Dodgson to read some Mock Turtle and then Alice's sister reads the haunting close of the book. Alice hugs Dodgson, who has been recalling all this on the train.

Carroll's stories were staple fare on television as far back as 1937, when versions of both *Wonderland* and *Looking Glass* were televised from Alexandra Palace. Potter's producer, James MacTaggart, made his own dramatisation of *Looking Glass* in 1973, using the then popular technique of Colour Separation Overlay which allowed figures to be electronically matted into two-dimensional 'sets'. The most celebrated production was Jonathan Miller's post-Freud film of *Wonderland*, the year after Potter's *Alice.* The least was an all-star Irwin Allen travesty for CBS (Carol Channing as the White Queen, Sammy Davis Jr as the Caterpillar, Telly Savalas as the Cheshire Cat . . .).

Portraits of Lewis Carroll are less common, though in 1994 the National Theatre mounted a play by Christopher Hampton and Martha Clarke, *Alice's Adventures Under Ground*, which explored the writer by dramatising his writings.

Carroll/Dodgson is the third tormented Potter protagonist but the first whose demons are more of psyche than of circumstance, more interior than exterior. The torment is unusually delicately handled but the exigencies of production have also muffled what might have been more explicit. Here is a case where the wider alternatives opened by the more painstaking process of film might have scored over recording 'as live' in the studio. At any rate Deborah Watling is too old and cannot help but be too knowing and so lacks ambiguity as the ten-year-old child. Happily, however, she is the dark girl of history rather than the fair of Tenniel and the butter blonde of Disney and other renderings.

Where he can, Potter underpins the story with intimations of mortality. The scenes from the book, enacted against Tennielesque line-drawn backgrounds, are played out largely by elderly but sportive actors (middle-aged John Bailey is the Mad Hatter). There is a plangent moment in a domestic evening scene when Mrs Liddell is distracted by the 'black' outside. On another occasion, she lectures Dodgson that 'nothing lasts for ever, not on this earth anyway', to which he replies: 'Ah, but it does, Mrs Liddell!'

Rosalie Crutchley recalls 'very clearly a rather shy young man with his red hair sitting at the side of the rehearsal room watching us. Of course we rehearsed then, we didn't just do it as you do now on film. I think I only spoke one or two words to him. In those days, one didn't march up and talk. We were much more introverted. But we all knew he was *on our side*, if you see what I mean. You didn't feel that always from a writer. He was obviously going to be a remarkable man.'[4]

George Baker got to know Potter rather better. 'Just after *Alice*, I was running the theatre in Bury St Edmunds and I tried to see if we could adapt the script for the stage. Dennis and I worked very hard at that. He would have loved it, I believe, but sadly I had insufficient grant and I couldn't raise the money outside so we had to part on that one. He didn't pursue it elsewhere.'[5]

During rehearsal, as Baker remembers it, 'Gareth Davies had Dennis and Tony Garnett there nearly all the time, so we discussed the sexuality of it a great deal. I love writers being around. Dodgson had seven sisters so his comfort in childhood must have been in small girls and their toys and in amusing them. The play is the beginning of Dennis's interest in that syndrome but I don't think it is a disturbing play and the obsession is not stated. It was just that we understood where we were with it.

'I asked Dennis if he thought Dodgson knew what he was and Dennis said no. At that time, he wouldn't have understood such a thing. I think he allowed himself to indulge those feelings and others allowed him to indulge them because nobody thought in those terms. He thought he was safe.'

The production required seven days of location filming at Christ Church, on Port Meadow and on the Thames. A Peacock memo instructed Michael Bakewell: 'The film effort request for *Alice* in the

Wednesday series appears to be well above the level we discussed at the Plays offers meeting (i.e. average four days shooting with ceiling of seven days). You will make sure that cuts are put in hand.'[6] In the studio, Davies asked for, and got, six cameras. 'It was a case of "Permission to use the spare at all times, sah!"' he laughs. 'We tended to ask for more than we thought they would give us.'[7]

MacTaggart decided to open the second run of the Wednesday Play with *Alice* on 13 October 1965. Sydney Newman watched off air. Next morning he fired off a memo to the benighted Bakewell:

> As I recall it, The Wednesday Play primarily was to do two jobs: 1) secure the biggest audience possible; 2) do plays that dramatise the turning-points in contemporary Britain. What audience was in mind when *Alice* was picked as an opener? Were the boys thinking of the eight million or so who had come to like the Wednesday Play or were they thinking of the critics, themselves or what?
>
> Even if there were good reasons for opening with *Alice*, how, after all the creative thinking and fine talk about 'getting them in the first 30 seconds',* could they have gone on and on for over ten minutes with what seemed to be like one teaser after another, each one duller than the other . . .
>
> I'm absolutely sick.[8]

Just over six million watched *Alice* and the Appreciation Index was a touch above average for the series. Descendants of both Dodgson and Macmillan the publisher wrote to complain about the respective portrayals. Potter went on *Points of View* to answer comments from viewers about the play, for which he earned eight guineas plus a further £5 15s 0d for the first-class return rail fare from Cromer, the Potters having recently moved into the Old Club House at Northrepps in Norfolk. The BBC appears not to possess a copy of *Alice*, but to the delight of Gareth Davies and George Baker there is a version telerecorded on to film at the British Film Institute.

Four months after Tony Garnett's commission, Potter handed in his hitherto untitled play. It was a second story about Nigel Barton, this time contrasting his boyhood attending a state primary school in a mining village with his (in Kenneth Adam's word) deracinated young manhood as an Oxford scholar.

The play opens with Nigel's father Harry (Jack Woolgar) walking up

---

* His favoured formulation was 'You gotta grab 'em by the balls in the first two minutes'.

the middle of the road to join the pit's evening shift while the student Nigel follows on the pavement. The relationship, swiftly sketched, is teasing, exasperated, belittling, profoundly emotional on both sides. A neighbour aims a jibe at Nigel: 'There's more things in heaven and earth than meets the eye. And they don't all come out of books!'9 It's a cunning line, suggesting no intended allusion on the character's part, yet attaching to Nigel by its source in *Hamlet* a hint of the indecisive prince.

We see him discomfited by his New College scout's embrace of hierarchy, then back at school where his cleverness isolates him from the likes of class daredevil Georgie Pringle (Johnny Wade). At an Oxford party peopled by braying *poseurs*, *Isis* reporter Nigel is cruelly presented to a spritzy woman as 'Peregrine Worsthorne'. She is a judge's daughter, Jill Blakeney* (Vickery Turner), and she frightens him away.

In the schoolroom, Miss Tillings (Janet Henfrey) wants 'a good boy [to] read a nice, clean, *respectable* bit from the Holy Bible'. And she gives the play its title with her command: '*Stand Up, Nigel Barton!*'

Stoned, Jill calls on Nigel in his rooms, piqued by his earnestness. He is defensive: 'The days of the kowtowing little runt of a scholarship boy, you know, they're over, they're finished.' Far away, Harry gently crosses swords with his wife (Katherine Parr) over Nigel's Oxford life: 'I bet he even picks his nose with his hanky.' In the school-yard, Nigel is viciously ragged as 'teacher's pet'.

Nigel gives a 'paper speech' in a Union debate, riding the interjections of the languid president (Charles Lewsen). This is intercut with the village working men's club where Nigel's grown-up classmates now congregate (Georgie is the club comic) and Harry fiercely protects Nigel from the snide provocations of his drinking chum Jordan (Peter Madden). After the debate, Nigel meets graduate Norman Conrad (Brian Hankins) who wants to interview him: 'I'm doing a telly programme about class in Britain in about a month's time. On the BBC of course!'

After 'The Old Rugged Cross' has been roared out in the club, Nigel is up before the proctors for singing the hymn 'when inebriated'. His defence – 'Why should God have all the best tunes?' – threatens to make the proctors smile.

Back in the schoolroom, Nigel has destroyed the class daffodil for revenge. When Miss Tillings' inquisition begins, he blames Georgie for the outrage. The lie spreads until the whole class has corroborated it. The interview under his belt, Nigel inveighs against admass to Jill,

---

* Blakeney is the name of a village on the western fringe of the Forest of Dean.

now his 'darling'. She notes pertinently: 'They've opened the door and let you in.' But Nigel feels that he betrayed his parents in the interview.

A *Globe* reporter (P. J. Kavanagh) seeks out the Bartons but Harry sends him packing with a silicotic flea in his ear. Nigel watches the broadcast with them. The thrust of it is that 'I don't feel I belong anywhere', either at Oxford or at home. Harry is hurt and angry, Nigel embarrassed and craven. His mother says: 'Pity we ever watched it, Nigel. We missed *No Hiding Place** and all.' Nigel follows Harry towards the club, his dad stubbornly stomping up the middle of the road.

The personal nature of so much poured into this piece will be evident from the events described in foregoing chapters. In the smallest details, Potter's own experience resounds. For instance, he has Nigel speak of 'a tightrope between two worlds', surely a nod to Denis Mitchell.[†]

In the published text, the rhythms and expressions of the mining village are clearly those of the Forest of Dean ('butty', 'ol'un' and so on) but Potter says unconvincingly in his opening stage direction that the play is set in 'probably South Nottinghamshire'. This is a rationalisation of the fact that all the village scenes were shot in the village of Bestwood and in the telerecording the language becomes a generalised north country ('ecky bloody thump').

Davies had been puzzling over how to give the working men's club scenes an authentic atmosphere, impossible in a Television Centre studio set with London extras. Film on location was out of the question, for such a complicated set-up would take way too long. But there was the multi-camera Outside Broadcast unit. OB had been called in for drama at Granada and BBC Wales, as Davies very well knew, but never by London planners. It was Tony Garnett's suggestion to record the scenes in an actual club.

'We rented the Bestwood club,' says Davies, 'and spent about £200 on beer, played bingo, sang songs and told filthy jokes till the members were really relaxed. The cameras were the size of a coffin but we took the lights off the front of them and played the scenes. It was very exciting. Nobody had done it quite like that before. Tony had a gift for setting other people's imaginations alight. It's a helluva trick.'[10]

The club scenes do come off the screen, as does the Union sequence

---

* A *bête noire* of Potter the critic, usually on the grounds that it appeared under-rehearsed because it was so prone to fluffs. Gareth Davies, who worked on the series several times as an actor, confirms that Potter's instinct was correct.

[†] Sadly, in the recording Keith Barron inadvertently kills the allusion to *Between Two Worlds* by giving the line as 'a tightrope between two different worlds'.

filmed on site. It is only the cutting between them which becomes predictable. Another challenge could only be met by a typical studio fudge. Says Davies: 'The documentary about class was meant to be on film but we had to make it with enormous difficulty in the studio, having got permission for a pre-recording with delivery in sequence. Keith had to do funny head movements to make it look as if cut on film.'*

Davies's work on the play enhances it greatly. A couple of swift montages give a strong sense of place. An occasional freeze-frame to link scenes has no smack of sixties modishness. The studio work is very lively and beautifully set by Richard Henry. The school-yard scene, for instance, looks like a location and is most convincingly lit for outdoors. Two chunks of Nigel and Jill's dialogue in the text are shed from the recording, quite rightly for they are needlessly explicit and explanatory.†

The structure of the play is very bold and for the most part successful. As can be seen from the rough synopsis above, Potter moves freely between past and present. The story in each time-scale is essentially linear but because of the economy of many of the scenes and the confident leaps forward, they do not *seem* linear. Though Potter never loses the thread, there is a (false) sensation that the perspective fans out in several directions.

Structure and style exist in a dynamic relationship. In his 1967 essay, Potter aired his

> attempt to illustrate the difficulties and complexities which can beset anyone moving across the minefields of class in this country. 'Environment' is here the crucial factor, but where [Nigel] has moved on and 'up', this becomes translated into 'memory' . . . The so-called flashback is the visual way of demonstrating how emotions, ideas or events from the past can impinge upon the present. But . . . [it] has degenerated into a stylistic cliché . . . I tried to get round the difficulties not by sacrificing any of the complexities of the character's often hypocritical and almost always ambiguous relationship with his working-class background – the 'past' – but by chipping the play up into swiftly moving fragments so that the 'present' was not the *norm* out of which one lurched cumbersomely back into previous times.[11]

---

* Multi-camera electronic recording is in sequence, cutting between cameras. Film is constructed in editing by taking footage out of sequence and cutting it together.
† A couple of cuts in Georgie's club routine would appear to be of a censorious nature: 'He couldn't tell his arse from his elbow' becomes 'his pen from his pencil' and the punch-line ('This is the shit house!') takes a sound drop and a distracting shot-change.

In his study of the medium, Potter picked up on television's account of itself – used of *Panorama* but applied across the medium – as 'a window on the world', which implied that reality was something brought by the medium to the viewer who only had to view in order to experience it. As a compulsively ambivalent consumer of commercials, Potter was just as aware of the power of non-naturalistic viewing.

He saw that naturalism was not how one marshalled thought processes or memories or emotion. So, to invade a prevailingly naturalistic medium with non-naturalistic devices was 'a way of making people put the lights out, draw the curtains, sit around and pay attention. If it fails, of course, it fails – abysmally. If it works, it works in a way that draws you right into that box, as opposed to standing looking through a window . . . Non-naturalism and its use of the inside of your head is more likely to remind you about the shreds of your own sovereignty.'[12] Structure and style, chicken and egg.

To-camera address is used again in *Stand Up* and more expressively than in *Vote*. In the first short scene in the schoolroom, both Nigel and Miss Tillings speak their thoughts aloud, address each other *and* address the camera, a giddy switch between levels of reality that yet works perfectly and establishes the conventions with admirable economy.

Nigel's intimations to the camera are the objective correlative of Potter's processing of his experiences in his mind and/or his journalism. To allow Miss Tillings (and Jack Hay in *Vote*) to share the 'access' to the audience is in a way a feint, a means of protecting the nakedness of Potter's self-exposure. He is already regarding his younger self with the 'tender contempt' of which he was to speak often in later years, memorably in his last interview.* With all deference to his righteous indignation at being taken for a mere autobiographer, the play cannot be cleanly separated out from a process of self-assessment. There is an echo of wish-fulfilment in Nigel throwing in his lot with the kind of classy Oxford siren who had terrified Dennis. Jill's twitting of him with 'You mean you actually *talk* like that!' is a shrugging defence mechanism on Potter's part. Her amusement at his earnestness is tenderish contempt. That she is in worse trouble herself, allows Potter to eat his cake and have it too.

A major Potter theme, budding in *Vote* and *Alice*, blooms fully in *Stand Up, Nigel Barton*. It is the intertwining of betrayal and

---

* 'I think we should always look back on our own past with a sort of tender contempt. As long as the tenderness is there, but also please let some of the contempt be there, because we know what we are like, we know how we hustle and bustle and shove and push.'[13]

June Thomas and Margaret Potter in Berry Hill, October 1994

Iris Hughes, October 1994

Salem Chapel, Berry Hill

Potter's cousin Dawn at the Salem Chapel organ, October 1994

Dennis and Margaret Potter, 1935

Dennis and Margaret Potter, 1955

Dennis and June Potter, 1939

Walter, Margaret, Dennis and June, 1940

Dennis Potter marries Margaret Morgan, 1958

Dennis and Margaret visit the *Pennies From Heaven* shoot, 1978

Martyrs to integrity:

Cyril Luckham, Keith Barron and Valerie Gearon in *Vote, Vote, Vote for Nigel Barton*

Colin Blakely as Christ in *Son of Man*

'Two Faces in Conflict':
Dan Jackson and Terence de Marney in *Emergency – Ward 9*

Joseph O'Conor and Patrick Magee in *Message for Posterity*

Man and beast:

Patrick Barr and Gina the bear in *A Beast with Two Backs*

Freddie Jones in his pet shop in *Joe's Ark*

Man and the elements:

Above
Colin Blakely obsessively asks 'Is it me?' in *Son of Man*

Alan Badel as Philip Gosse seeks God's guidance in *Where Adam Stood*

Madness behind the teacups:

Deborah Watling, John Saunders, Peter Bartlett and John Bailey in *Alice*

Denholm Elliott and Patricia Lawrence entertain a demon (Michael Kitchen) in *Brimstone and Treacle*

guilt. The scene where the Barton family views the bright son on television, publicly detaching himself from his background, is bound to suggest that the Potter of *Does Class Matter?* and *Between Two Rivers* is here castigating himself, for Nigel cannot emerge decently from the scene.

That this was an act of expiation is a matter about which Potter blew hot and cold over many years. A few days after transmission, he told a reporter: 'What I tried to do was to express what I meant in a less hurtful and perhaps more mature way than I did when I went on TV myself.'[14]

In 1978 he talked to Melvyn Bragg about the relationship between *Does Class Matter?* and *Stand Up*: 'I said things which I meant and were reflecting my experience in the room while I was talking but, when I stood back from them, I hadn't edited them, I hadn't filtered them through the love and respect and just sheer emotional gut feeling you have for your own parents . . . Although I wasn't present with them when they were watching it, I imagined how my father wouldn't have said anything, he would simply have looked at my mother when I said that on the actual programme. And from that you want to discharge the . . . [he peters out] . . . The truth is a very unadorned beast, you ought to provide it with a little bit more pasture . . . [He adds, riding over Bragg beginning his next question:] But I was also satirising that form of documentary at that time.'[15]

In 1987 Alan Yentob asked if, in *Does Class Matter?*, he felt he had betrayed his parents. Potter answered slowly, 'Yes. Yes. Yes. I did' and smiled ruefully. Yentob questioned whether *Nigel Barton* 'came out of that' and Potter referred to the broadcast scene: 'He appeared on television and had to watch it with his parents and . . . they didn't mind, they were proud of him, but he knew he'd been a shit and, *mea culpa*, yes.'[16]

In 1993, Graham Fuller asked if the play was 'to atone for *Between Two Rivers*'. Potter said: 'There is some truth in that, but it's also *not* the truth . . . [it was] as much about objecting to the way politics was presented on the screen as about my own discharging of guilts. Using the guilt as a dramatic device is not discharging it. There is no way you can discharge guilt. What is *is* . . . You cannot bend the knee and say *mea culpa* and ask for the past to be wiped away. But . . . you can live within it and *show* it, which is the only possible form of absolution.'[17]

In *Stand Up*, Potter very specifically locates betrayal in childhood with Nigel's lie about the despoiled daffodil. Here, and always when he writes about children, any idea that pre-pubescence is a pre-lapsarian idyll is rapidly snuffed out. If a 1975 article is to be believed, this was an intensely autobiographical scene:

> I made his motives clearer than mine had been when I did the same thing a few weeks before my ninth birthday . . .
> The teacher, in fact, had been young and gentle, the first love of my life, the emancipator. Nigel Barton was asked, in shocked tones, if he knew anything about it . . . so was Dennis Potter, betrayed by sudden crimson and a jerk of anxiety. Both boys stood up and immediately told a lie. Yes, I *did* know, Miss, but . . . Elaborate, plausibly detailed, a story came almost unbidden to my lips, garnished with a fine show of reluctance about giving up the name of the boy I had said had taken the flower . . .
> It worked quite well in the play . . . But it worked best of all back there in 1944. The class had picked up the possibilities of drama . . . The lie had so enveloped [the accused boy] that he saw no choice but to accept it as the truth, really the truth. And I discovered in one precocious leap, back there in childhood, what people are like when they sense drama in the air . . . I realised how a fiction generates its own heat, moves forward and compels belief. Plays and novels are accusations, their characters victims, their audiences or readers the witnesses.[18]

The notion of betrayal as a lifelong reflex is enhanced by the adult actor playing the child as well as the grown-up. 'Dennis called me,' says Gareth Davies, 'at four in the morning which he tended to do, to say "I don't want to use kids for the flashbacks because they can't act, they can't *comment*". We decided to use the same actors. There was a bit of a battle getting them to wear short trousers. But that's very Dennis, I think, trying to find a level of comment.'[19]

As a gambit, it was hardly revolutionary. Terry Scott, Beryl Reid, Benny Hill and Dick Emery were always getting into school gear and mimicking the verbal and physical convulsions of children. 'Of course,' says Davies, 'it was done all the time but we had to battle against a feeling that in the classical *theatah* you didn't do that. Why not? We thought you ought to be able to use any weapon.'

Alan Yentob asked Potter what he had learned from writing the *Nigel Barton* plays. 'I learned from it how far I had to go. But I also learned that you could do it . . . I thought "How is it that I am going to express . . . the excitement, the zest, the terror, the anxiety . . . between those children to an adult audience?" And the only way . . . was not to allow the audience, the adult to distance himself or herself by saying "Ahh! children!" . . . But at the same time using the adult body as a magnifying glass for the childhood, of physicality in childhood, emotion in childhood, restlessness, but using that as the reverse of the magnifying glass as well, to make you see how much of it was still in adult life.'[20]

In his introduction to the texts, Potter says that *Stand Up* benefited from the experience of *Vote*, that he had discovered 'that a movement is in some circumstances preferable to a line of dialogue and that a quick change of scene between one environment and another can do the work of a speech of careful explanation. I removed many more adjectives and deliberately left much more "unstated": better a sharp nudge in the ribs than a long, hot rant of indignant rhetoric, better meiosis than megaphones. But I cannot persuade myself that these two plays . . . represent anything more than my apprenticeship as a playwright.'[21] The disparager of Potter might argue that this claim to self-improvement demonstrated more of the pseudo-geusiatic than the meiotic.

What Potter really goes for in *Stand Up* is a double edge to the dialogue. Thus Nigel on Oxford: 'This place is utterly artificial and pretentious and I worked hard to get here.' Thus his mother: 'He'll always remember where he came from. You don't forget things like that.' This is still the Potter who wrote in *The Glittering Coffin*: 'Talking about class in highly personal terms is a shocking and embarrassing thing for an Englishman to do'[22] and there is a self-consciousness, a deliberation about the way in which some of the assertions he wants to make in the play are hung about with irony and detachment.

We should not forget that, perhaps dissatisfied with *The Confidence Course*, Potter was and would remain determined to avoid the overtly political play, the play with an agenda, as he makes clear in a review of *All Good Men* by Trevor Griffiths: 'I prefer to see plays in which "ideas" are not exposed on the surface like basking sharks (or, in some cases, stranded cod) but arise with the insistence of discovery out of the fumbling yearnings, uncertain liaisons and perilous stratagems we usually make out of life.'[23]

Because of the postponement of *Vote*, it was decided to put out the two *Barton* plays on successive Wednesdays just before Christmas 1965, with *Stand Up* going first as it constituted what was certainly not then called a 'prequel' to the by-election play. Potter went on BBC2's largely live arts review magazine, *Late Night Line-Up*, both weeks, first to anticipate, then to summarise, the broadcasts.

Writing in *Radio Times*, Tony Garnett described Nigel as 'part of the cream of the first Free Milk generation'.[24] The critics hit all kinds of notes. Derek Malcolm thought *Stand Up* 'ploughed through the old ground as if it had never been worked before';[25] Julian Holland quipped 'Unlucky Jim has found his Doom at the Top' but called Potter 'this exciting new playwright';[26] Philip Purser declared it 'obviously autobiographical'.[27] Maurice Richardson observed: 'If the BBC Wednesday Play series keeps up its standard of absurdity, I shall have to build a new wing on my *sottisier*.'*[28]

But it was Nancy Banks-Smith in *The Sun* who put her finger on a flaw that also affected *Vote* and would run right through Potter's work: 'The women were weird. The witch, a bitch and a fool. The schoolmistress was a nightmare to frighten little children with. The girlfriend a tart on tranquillisers. And Mum . . . well, Dennis Potter is the co-author of the satire "What is a Mum?" . . . and he hasn't changed his mind.'[29] Potter did not even think to distinguish the mother-figure with a first name: she is merely 'Mrs Barton'. And he makes her clueless; it cannot possibly be a portrait of his own mother.

Reviewing *Vote*, Adrian Mitchell (now at the *Sunday Times*) noted that 'Mr Edward Heath was unlucky enough to broadcast before [the play] and his smiling line "I think I know what makes Terriers† tick" might have come from the play.'[30]

Potter reckoned he 'spent some time on the telephone that day vainly trying to get the opening titles dropped so that we could go straight from Mr Heath's toothy valedictory smile into the play itself'.[31] He may have loathed party political broadcasts but they had a habit of co-operating with him: *The Confidence Course* was also preceded by a PPB. Writing of the play's cancellation, Banks-Smith in fact suggested 'my own pet theory . . . that the BBC feared some half-wit voter would take it for a party political broadcast.'[32]

The reception was rousing. It 'would make anybody wearing a hat in the sitting room hurl it in the air . . . An inspired piece which reeked of high experience and disillusion,' cried James Thomas.[33] 'One of the great TV spectacles . . . he changed from rip-roaring farce to deep human tragedy,' raved Kenneth Eastaugh.[34] But Mary Crozier found Nigel 'still a bore . . . Mr Potter makes everything a bit bigger or blacker or funnier than life . . . he came out last night as a political cartoonist.'[35]

Potter observed wryly: 'My agent wrote that I was the only candidate who turned his old speeches into plays.'[36] Ron Brewer was indeed amazed: 'Many of the scenes in *Vote* . . . had a basis in events during two years of campaigning. But I was shaken to see and hear a television character repeating episodes of my life which I

---

* An anthology of 'howlers' and other idiocies.
† The Territorial Army, locally-run volunteer troops, stood down two years later.

must have discussed with Potter. If that were not enough, my sly asides, more joky than cynical, were repeated in the play as a heavy sardonic approach. John Bailey . . . even used my gestures.'[37]

Stand Up attracted seven million viewers, *Vote* 8.75 million. The latter's Appreciation Rating was ten points above the Wednesday Play average. Awards and sales abroad followed.

So Potter had enjoyed a first year as a teledramatist of unrivalled incident, conspicuousness and encouragement, crowned at the end with glowing success. He had come in on the high tide of the single play. As he described it in 1993: 'Jimmy MacTaggart and his bushy-tailed acolytes used to sit around somewhere in the Fifth Circle* talking with a younger conviction about the evident iniquities of the BBC management, the tapeworm-length persistence of BBC cowardice, and the insufferable perversities of the BBC threat to the very existence of the single play. You can imagine how much greater our indignation would have been had we known at the time that we were sitting slap in the middle of what later observers were to call the Golden Age of television drama.'[38]

In many ways, the moment had already passed. Roger Smith was gone. After *Vote*, MacTaggart would only produce two more Wednesday Plays before switching full-time to direction. Between the respective transmissions of *Alice* and *Stand Up*, the particular character of the Tony Garnett influence on BBC play-making had made its presence felt with the Ken Loach/Nell Dunn film *Up the Junction*, a very different kind of drama from Potter's. If he was to capitalise on his brilliant start, Potter would need to forge some new alliances.

* The drama department is on the fifth floor of the circular Television Centre.

10

Ridin' High

'Watching *Emergency – Ward 10* while actually in hospital, as I did last night, is an uncanny situation.'

Dennis Potter[1]

When there's a new gunslinger in town, everybody in the saloon gets to hear about it and everybody wants to know how fast on the draw he is. So the challenges are thrown down from all sides. One of the first to come calling on Potter was the splashy BBC2 series, Theatre 625, whose producer Cedric Messina is now remembered for televising stage classics as Play of the Month. In June 1965, Messina's script editor James Brabazon commissioned a play called *Message for Posterity*. Potter's agent Roger Hancock offered the piece as 'the first of a trilogy'.[2] Potter's fee (for a 90-minute play) was now £850.

Before *Message* was ready in January 1966 (five weeks late), Tony Garnett had asked for another play at 75 minutes with a generous end-of-the-year deadline. So enticed, Potter would deliver the still untitled play six months early. On 11 January, following what must have been a hearty lunch with Potter and Hancock, Head of Plays Michael Bakewell booked three 75-minute plays (the so-called 'trilogy' perhaps) 'for transmission on either channel' with delivery spread over eighteen months.[3] Testament of faith though this was, another deal put in train that day was of far greater long-term significance, even though only for a single 30-minute play. For it was the formal commencement of the central working relationship of Potter's life. *Emergency – Ward 11* was ordered by Ken Trodd.

The BBC2 slot Thirty Minute Theatre was in its first season and would endure (with variations like the Birmingham-based Second City Firsts) well into the 1970s. Tricky though the short form undoubtedly was – often much more so than writers imagined when they first attempted it – the series was heavily used as a 'nursery slope' both for new writers and for new approaches. Potter's single piece at this length was in no sense a breakthrough, though in his own development it does herald the most detached, journalistic phase of his drama work, story-telling rather than self-exploration.

Emergency – Ward 9, as it was retitled, is Potter's report from the front, offered as a specific corrective to ATV's soap opera (twice a week from 1957 to 1967) *Emergency – Ward 10*, and also to other hospital-based entertainment like the American imports *Dr Kildare* and *Ben Casey*. The script[4] is noteworthy (and quoteworthy) for its stage directions. It is set in a 'ramshackle London hospital ... full of creaky, clatter-clop medical noises'. Three patients are particularly characterised. Flanders (Terence de Marney) is 'an old, working-class Londoner in for bronchitis ... a querulous, clapped-out Rumpelstiltskin'. Padstow (Tenniel Evans) has 'a big, wet, earnest schoolmaster's face'; he is the one who, according to Nurse Angela (Gillian Lewis), is 'jotting it all down': stowing it on his pad, you might say. And there is Adzola (Dan Jackson) who has 'something of the story-book chieftain about him'.

The ritual humiliations of being a patient are swiftly established, as is the sense of also being a supplicant. Angela watches Flanders coughing 'with the kind of amused distaste which passes in medical circles as "compassionate efficiency"'. When Adzola 'glides' by, Padstow incautiously remarks that 'Matron ought to pad behind him with a ceremonial fly-swat' but this triggers an outburst of racist comment from Flanders. When Padstow attempts liberal bromides, he cries "Ere! You ain't a preacher, are you?' Padstow is, as it happens, a lay preacher in the Free Church: 'Blackboard chalk for six days, rock of ages on the seventh.'

An old man is 'drifting into death, but not easily'. At night, Flanders uses a devious ruse to make him a forbidden cup of tea. The next night is the old man's crisis: while he dies curtained off from the ward, Flanders and Padstow discuss heaven. 'All them bleedin' harps,' grumbles Flanders. 'I'd rather hear one of the good old songs meself.' He pursues the notion of heaven until it begins to get surreal ('What about going to the lavatory, then? ... somebody'll have to make the paper, won't they? Or does it just fly into yer hand, like?'), and Padstow snaps: 'You blaspheme and you deny the brotherhood of man ... Hell-fire and damnation, that's what you'll get.' Later Flanders provokes Adzola by his offhand use of the term 'Sambo'. Staff intervene and Flanders shuffles back to bed bemused by the 'fuss ... Little Black Sambo, that's what it said on the wall at school ... I was only trying to be *good*.'

With Flanders mercifully asleep, Padstow unctuously apologises to Adzola who responds: 'He's no good. He's low-class, that man', not what Padstow had in mind. Privately he prays but is disturbed by the snivelling Flanders who fears he will never get to heaven because 'I've piddled in my bed'. When Padstow resumes prayers, he asks him to 'put in a word for me'.

What will be clear from this synopsis is that the play addresses working-class attitudes and beliefs quite as much as it seeks to redress the romanticised images of nurses as angels (the name Angela is an especially Potteresque joke) and patients as nobly suffering. The racist talk – too gross to merit illustration – is surely intended to be thought odious. (Trodd describes it as 'ironic, if not so well developed as with the Pakistani character in *The Singing Detective*').[5]

Adzola, however, hardly invites sympathy. He is decidedly imperious and unsociable (he demands Radio Caroline!) where illness is expected to be a leveller and a bonding experience. As the play has no time for the self-righteous liberal Christian, the conclusion must be that Potter intends Flanders to be seen as to some degree redeemed by his remorse.

Potter wrote candidly of his own racism. 'There are moments when I have to recognise it in myself,' he confided in 1968, 'a faint, mocking echo of the filth expressed by racialists everywhere. Alf Garnett* makes articulate the buried feelings we are ashamed to acknowledge as our own.'[6] Within three months of that piece of journalism, Enoch Powell excluded himself from the Conservative Shadow Cabinet of Edward Heath with a notorious speech about race relations in which he expressed himself 'filled with foreboding. Like the Roman, I seem to see the River Tiber foaming with much blood.'† Responding to this speech (and calling Powell 'the man with the box of matches . . . now he has turned into a Faust'), Potter declared: 'I, too, fear the stranger. Instinctively – and primitively – I do not "like" people with black skins . . . We are irrational creatures. Every cathedral has its hideous gargoyles. Within us, each of us, boil all sorts of primeval hatreds and violence.'[7] Such a passage must demonstrate some kind of total lack in Potter but each reader can fill in their own blank: lack of accommodation? of guile? of sensitivity? of circumspection? of hypocrisy? Whatever lack it is, it is certainly not lack of singularity. As the *Observer's*

---

* Working-class bigot and central figure in Johnny Speight's sitcom *Till Death Us Do Part*.
† As a fellow student of the classics, Potter will have recognised the reference to the Sibyl's prophecy in Virgil's *Aeneid, Book VI*.

media correspondent Richard Brooks once put it, 'he rejoices in being politically incorrect'.[8]

Potter retained a degree of admiration for Powell, referring to him often in his journalism simply as 'Enoch', assuming that the first name was as unmistakable as that of 'Nye'. He had met him a year before at his first appearance on the long-running radio programme, *Any Questions?*, and must have recognised a fellow maverick and anti-modernist.

That medical confinement brings out animosity in the sick was confirmed for Potter six years later: 'I spent the whole dreary summer on my back in a sprawling East End hospital where every other bed in the ward (including mine) seemed to be occupied by one or another sickly manifestation of Alf Garnett.'[9] He must have felt that his depiction of the ward as a crucible of enmity and fear was reinforced by experience. At any rate, he was to explore the theme at much greater depth in *The Singing Detective*.

Once again, direction fell to Gareth Davies: 'Casting a black actor who was prepared to take the part and *not* be nice was extremely difficult in those days. I had a long, long discussion with Johnny Sekka, the Senegalese actor, who simply would not do it because he said it reflected badly on black people. My argument was the easy one that in a grown-up world we all come from all over the spectrum and his reply was "It's easy for you to say that". To which there's no answer.'[10]

In the studio, multi-camera shooting of a single set posed its usual problem of keeping the shots clear, so nurses were forever swishing curtains around beds for no better reason than to mask the hardware. 'I do remember one actor who was supposed to have died gave his death a second time,' laughs Davies. 'He kept saying "I only want a cup of tea" and he gave us one too many. A classic rep situation.'

Conventional wisdom maintains that the play went out live and unrecorded. What this omits is its repeat fifteen months later. It was telerecorded; the recording was junked thereafter.

Gareth Davies reports: 'We'd do it live, record it off air and go for some pick-ups straight after for the repeat. There was a rule that you could do a maximum of five edits in a programme because editing tape was a major business – up in front of the Controller the following morning in your best interview suit for a "why-have-you-cut-the-tape?" session because it cost all of sixty quid, you know. Absolutely daft.'

Was it good working live? 'We spent all our time railing against it, not wanting to do it and making it more and more complicated. But there was a challenge about it. I'm torn, really. The worst part was that it stopped you using film technique. But I do sometimes miss the buzz. On the other hand, I used to think if you wanted that sort of buzz you should go and direct the air traffic at Heathrow.

'Dennis had a different view then, he was very pro studio and anti film. He didn't come to film till *much* later. His argument – which I then didn't agree with and now think he had a helluva point – was that a particular conjunction of events and people in that space can find a style and an atmosphere and a concentration you don't get anywhere else. And rehearsal brings a pace and rhythm that filming often doesn't.

'It's a vibrant place to be, a studio, when everything's going. We've lost it and we patronise it. But *Emergency – Ward 9* was an exciting play for television, the adrenalin flow was bloody enormous. I think the idea that we'll all be great artists if we make quickie films is rubbish. There should be room for both and we've thrown one out.'

The play went out on Easter Monday. Nancy Banks-Smith's review in *The Sun* reads like one of Potter's own: 'Thank goodness for Dennis Potter. A loaf of fresh bread in the stale wilderness of Bank Holiday Monday viewing . . . Easter diabetes. Sugar in the morning, sugar in the evening, sugar at suppertime. And BBC2 holding out alone against the sickly surrender . . . It made *Emergency – Ward 10* look like perjury, an offence against the whole truth . . . it doesn't sound entertaining? But you must believe me, it was. If living and dying and the bit between are entertainment.'[11]

From commission to transmission of *Emergency – Ward 9* was precisely three calendar months, unthinkable to a drama producer in the 1990s. During those three months, Potter received an intriguing (and possibly pioneering) commission jointly from the BBC and a company called Perdita Productions for a project that entailed both stage royalties and television rights. It must be presumed this came to nothing.

Message for Posterity was accepted 'subject to certain agreed revisions'[12] but it fell to new story editor Rosemary Hill to exemplify the artless nonchalance that held sway at the BBC in those days as she warned Potter of a production delay 'because Gareth [Davies] has to do a Play of the Month in a bit of a hurry . . . In the meantime Cedric [Messina] and I are both wondering whether you have any notions for another play as well as this one.' Potter also received his first half-payments for all three of Michael Bakewell's commissions, a cheque for the princely sum of £1,275.

At some point around this time, the Potter family left Norfolk, 'which neither his wife Margaret nor he could warm to'[13] (very flat, Norfolk), and returned to the Forest of Dean, taking a house in Allaston Road, Lydney.

In June 1966, Potter delivered two scripts. One, *See You in My Dreams*, was towards the Bakewell trio. Trodd (now styling himself Kenith), who made the official acceptance, thinks the title was a tribute to a Clive Exton play which Potter much admired, *Land of My Dreams*. The other was the play commissioned by Tony Garnett. But by now Garnett had been made up to producer and was embarked on the project that would establish his name and become the most famous Wednesday Play of all, *Cathy Come Home*. Trodd took over responsibility for the still untitled Potter script. A week later, it was known as *Where the Buffalo Roam*.

The play is a modern urban tragedy. Its hero is a Swansea teenager who spends much of his time in a fantasy of himself as an outlaw in the Old West. Willy Turner (Hywel Bennett) is on probation and attending remedial classes. He is not above threatening his mother (Megs Jenkins) with the bread-knife for neglecting to call him Shane ('I reckon it suits me, see').[14] Mrs Turner upbraids him harmlessly ('Late again, late again') but she is too weak to do other than defer to him and too careless to see what is brewing – it needs probation officer Jenkins (Glyn Houston) to tell her that Willy cannot read. 'He's one of the few adults left,' Jenkins observes sagely, 'who can look at a neon sign and think it beautiful.' But he calls the cowboy fixation 'too silly for words'.

Grandad (Aubrey Richards) also lives in the terraced house, grumbling about his wounded ear from the trenches and belittling the boy. Willy's father is dead but the man's brutality – he would beat the boy for stammering – comes back to haunt him, as do his humiliations at school. Jenkins is aghast at how dysfunctional this family is.

In town, Willy is abandoned by the slatternly Susan (Denise Buckley) when he persists in being a western movie plot-bore. He's laughed out of the class for demanding to be called Shane. Waiting for the cinema to open, Willy fritters away the chance to befriend Carol (Rhiann John) who is more desirable in every sense than Susan. In the crowded auditorium, Willy rounds on a woman rustling sweet wrappers but she gives better than she gets ('Go home and wash yourself') and the spat spreads. The cinema staff wrestle Willy up the aisle but are hilariously stopped dead by the end-of-screening anthem (*that* dates it!) and Willy escapes.

Rolling in at 1.00 a.m., Willy deflects his mother's concern but flares up when she abases herself. She finally finds the courage to slap his face and he is stunned. Her peace-offering is a western novelette, *Dead Man's Gulch*, to help him read. He is both pleased and crushed.

On his bed, he is tormented by the cruelties of childhood. He gets his gun – a real gun – and, adopting his Shane persona, kills Grandad. We do not see him shoot his mother, but BBC Wales news coverage next day tells us she is dead. That night Willy slays a genial policeman whom he pictures as a western lawman.

An extensive police stake-out ensues when Willy is cornered on the roof of a cold store. He exchanges fire with what he sees as the posse and he is hit. He dies, the words 'Geronimo' and 'Daddy' on his lips. His body is lowered to the street by a crane.

Where the Buffalo Roam is a post-Freudian, post-'kitchen sink'/Free Cinema play, embracing such disparate elements as high tragedy and *nouvelle vague* high jinks, fantasy and sexual repression, not to mention religious imagery. Keith Waterhouse and Willis Hall's *Billy Liar* is an obvious (though entirely comedic) forerunner and the domestic scenes bear a strong resemblance to Harold Pinter's 1960 teleplay *A Night Out*. That it works as well as it does is greatly to the credit of Gareth Davies' direction for Potter has laid out a minefield to negotiate.

Along with David Peters in *Moonlight on the Highway*, Willy Turner is Potter's most disturbed protagonist and it can be no accident that the name of each contains a slang word for penis (Peter; Willy). 'Turner' also implies instability. Early on, Potter gives him the kind of line ('Thursdays is a brown sort of colour') that conventionally indicates a poet and dreamer; later Willy sees the word 'it' as 'like a man standing outside a church'. But little else in the writing takes the boy for a fallen angel. He is simply seen as a victim with a dangerous fixation. It is Hywel Bennett's damaged-cherub looks, together with the daft pathos of cowboy language delivered in the wide-eyed accent of South Wales, that invest Willy with a glassy radiance and lift the tale into an eerie romance.

Elsewhere Davies manages to arm Willy with a 'real' gun and to gloss over the moment without its implausibility needlessly detaining us. He is less lucky with the entirely unreal and expedient figure of the probation officer, Jenkins. 'When in doubt trust to a reliable actor' is a fair maxim but Glyn Houston's solidity never looks likely to weigh the character down into the texture of the play. As the riverboat gambler whom Willy guns down in his fantasy, he is much more persuasive; the hint in his day clothes of a secret life of risk only muddies the water. The stodgiest scene has Jenkins bonding with Black the remedial teacher (Richard Davies) in sudden discovery of their own shared liking for westerns ('Knocks Robin Hood into a cocked hat as far as I'm concerned,' says the latter), allowing Potter once again to flourish his grasp on the genre and his abhorrence at the revisionism he perceives within it.

Potter offers a cunning psychological stroke: when we first see Willy imagining himself as a Jack Palance gunslinger in black – and later when he daydreams of being hunted – it is *himself* that Willy confronts and outdraws, both in his bedroom mirror and in a *Doppelgänger* dream-vision. Though he is assailed by images of his father and his Miss Tillings-like teacher, even having a kind of 'visitation' by the former before he finally snaps, his confrontations with figures of authority are 'real', only being cloaked in fantasy when they are already under way in his 'real' story.

In Willy's outpouring, prompted by the kindly-meant questions of Carol, Potter tellingly suggests that his dream is not of escapism in a generalised way but of particular wide-open-spaces escape,* of release from narrow-mindedness in narrow rooms. The play might equally well have been called *Don't Fence Me In*. It is about being denied a life. Even his crabby, cackling Grandad once got away: it was to the Great War and it is the only thing he can talk about. That is why Willy kills him first. Indeed, as we never see him kill his mother – it is off-stage and so a notional murder – it might be said that Willy kills only the person who did once escape.

While the story is linear, with memory stylised in the mind's eye (as it were) rather than casting us back in time, Potter does require leaps into fantasy in mid-movement and this is done in the edit with great bravado and skill by Howard Billingham. Davies tops it with a striking image of a sheet of newspaper skittering in the breeze down an urban hill, apparently jerking to gunshots, and tails it with one of the great teledrama set pieces in the stake-out, Willy's death under water cascading from a burst tank and the crucifixion image of his corpse being swung upright through the night sky by a crane. Like all the outdoor scenes, it was recorded by OB cameras in Swansea. This is location work of a high order.

'It was written to be played in London,' says Davies, 'but I thought the language could be freed up if we went to Wales. Not because I'm Welsh particularly, though I obviously am. But it's like watching Jimmy McGovern's work [*Cracker; Priest*] which is the nearest thing now to the Wednesday Play. They only *seem* naturalistic, they're really these mythic characters talking poetry. And Dennis wasn't really familiar with London in writing terms. Though he always used to profess to hate the Welsh, if you come from the Forest of Dean you're just over the road anyway and the culture and background are very similar, chapel and pits and close communities. All the energy comes from the

---

* See 'Escapism' in *The Dictionary of Diseased English* by Kenneth Hudson (Macmillan, 1977).

west, not from the east, in that part of the world. So he was very happy to agree to it. Hywel Bennett was Welsh-speaking Welsh. He'd made *The Family Way** but it hadn't come out yet so he was an unknown really. An amazing technical actor at the age of twenty-three.'[15]

Getting OB meant an extended bout of office politics. One intriguing ingredient is a Trodd memo (on behalf of producer Lionel Harris) to new Head of Plays Gerald Savory which, given Trodd's subsequent championing of film, might look an artful piece of dissimulation. Arbitrating between options (a ten-day film shoot in London with three days in Television Centre or a six-day OB operation in Swansea with two days in a Cardiff studio), Trodd argued strongly for the latter.[16] What clinched it was continuity of style instead of the hated film/tape mix.

But there was much head-shaking, mostly from Cardiff bureaucrats who felt, conceivably with justice, that it was 'a great pity that so little notice was given for a request for major facilities'.[17] The same teleprint (the fax of its day) listed the conflicting requirements of *Grandstand* (sports programming always assumes precedence at the BBC), regretted the prior commitments of requested design, wardrobe and make-up personnel and added, rather ruefully, 'I understand that you do not want Wales supporting production staff.'

In the end *Grandstand* did surrender its OB unit booking and took its coverage via London (presumably at some expense). Design staff, schedules and costs were jiggled to dovetail with the visitors. It has to be said that London requirements always *did* presume upon BBC regions' autonomy. Gareth Davies was relieved: 'I've always thought it was a good idea to get away from the Centre. But then I'm a dedicated provincial.'

Potter himself had remarked on the possibilities of electronic cameras on location when his mentor Denis Mitchell made use of them for a series of programmes for Granada in 1964 of which *The Entertainers* drew Potter's attention by getting itself postponed by the ITA because of the participation of strippers. Potter, evidently shown a sneak preview by Mitchell (a technique he would adapt himself), called it 'the first full-scale attempt to make a "film" using mobile video-tape machines . . . Think of ordinary sound tape recorders and you can imagine the potential of this new method, which opens vast new worlds for the little screen.'[18]

Buffalo was a complex and ambitious production. The armourer's list alone covered sixteen separate items. Production assistant John

---

* Popular but inauthentic and now forgotten Boulting Brothers film of a Bill Naughton play.

Glenister had to write innumerable letters seeking location and facility permissions, including asking the supplier of a horse if he himself could ride it for the recording and 'make the horse rear in that "Roy Rogers" way'. The reply could not 'guarantee' the rearing as 'this is normally considered a bad habit and is not a normal trick to teach' but he would see what he could do.[19] No Trigger-like rearing occurs in any of Willy's fantasies.

In the shoot-out, Davies used a hand-held camera. 'It was the size of a bazooka. You needed to be about six foot four to carry it. And a trolley went with it – that needed another man. That was what we called hand-held. They were running around on a glass rooftop – it was fairly hairy.' For the crowd scenes, 'we put in the local papers that the BBC would be in town and recorded the crowds who turned up. We just broke every rule in the book.'

On a big production budget of some £12,000, producer Lionel Harris was soon looking at a projected overspend of £500. In a cogent memo to him, Davies argued passionately against cuts: 'As with any drama production, it would be possible to save this £500 but the resulting play would not do justice to the author's original intentions, the director's interpretation of those intentions and the general standards of the BBC Drama Department.'[20] Harris's response is not recorded but BBC1 Controller Peacock did eventually agree the revised budget. Recording overran in the studio, though by how much was disputed. Evidently the London interlopers felt that Cardiff crews were not up to scratch.

Once a rough telerecording was viewed, the misgivings began. Gerald Savory announced: 'Even though "bloody" is used as an everyday adjective, no exception can legitimately be taken to the play, which is honest, absorbing and dramatic.'[21] Huw Wheldon recommended an on-air warning, 'not because I am persuaded that I should have any anxiety about it, but simply because it seems not unlikely that it might cause a certain amount of fuss'.[22]

By 24 October, another concern had arisen. As Savory put it to Peacock: 'Because of the Aberfan disaster,* I thought it might be advisable to postpone transmission of [*Buffalo*] which has a Swansea setting and a final scene of the youth's burial [*sic*]. I spoke to C.P.Tel [Wheldon] about it and his advice was to be prepared to replace it with *The Mayfly and the Frog*,† which we will now rush to completion.'[23]

In the event, *Buffalo* kept its 2 November transmission but it may be

---

* On 21 October the mid-Glamorgan village of Aberfan was engulfed by a slurry tip undermined by rain. 144 lost their lives including 116 schoolchildren.
† May/December romantic comedy by Jack Russell, starring Felicity Kendal and John Gielgud.

imagined that the playwright shared the sensitivity on this matter. Soon after he resumed reviewing in *The Sun*, an episode of *Softly Softly*, the successor to *Z Cars*, took an emergency similar to that at Aberfan as its subject. Potter rose up in anguish: 'I do not live very far from that miserable village and was there soon after the disaster. The sight of those poor, suffering, tormented parents queuing ankle-deep in slime outside the chapel will stay with me for ever . . . No, no, in the name of all compassion, this is too soon, too glib, too easy.'[24] The reader must make her own judgement as to the nature of the impulse that made Potter dash to the site of the catastrophe, whether he was witnessing or wallowing, whether he could consider himself the servant of the maimed or of the muse.

In an exchange of memos, Savory had started to question other elements: the scuffle at the picture-house ('this would never happen except as an episode in a Marx Brothers film'), the climactic sequence ('no artistic reason to prolong it') and the use of the song 'Laredo' over the closing image.[25] Davies briskly despatched these points. Both cinema and rooftop sequences were in rough-assembly state and earmarked for shortening but he tartly defended the former as 'scripted and approved at every stage' and necessary 'to relieve the tension before building to the climax'. The author's instructions say of this scene 'All the timing is for comedy'.[26] 'Laredo' is used on the track throughout the finished version but had only been dubbed in at the end on the rough.

Fears allayed, Potter again opened the Wednesday Play season, *Buffalo* being seen by an audience of around 8.25 million and scoring an Appreciation Rating 11 per cent higher than the series average. In his *Sunday Times* review, Maurice Wiggin got it in one: '[Potter] is a moralist and he wants to change us. He wants us to be more unselfish, gentle and compassionate. He wants us to bear more guilt than we can comfortably carry. He is not only on the side of the angels, he wants us to behave like angels. He is a polemical writer; or, to put it in an old-fashioned way, there is a religious basis to his work. For this I respect him.'[27] As far as I am aware, Wiggin, who alone noted the crucifixion allusion at the end of the play, was the first writer to record this as a serious perception about Potter.

Opinions divided. Peter Black, also catching a sacerdotal echo, called it 'a strong and controversial sermon' weakened by 'stridency and exaggeration . . . a straight and implacable reconstruction of an actual case would have suited his purpose better',[28] which begged the question whether he correctly perceived the purpose. By contrast, S.R.C. (Sylvia Clayton?) in the *Daily Telegraph* thought Willy 'a diagram from a psychological textbook rather than a person'.[29] Even Nancy

Banks-Smith found 'there were some lumps of uncooked psychology ... which made it too much like a classic case history'[30] and there was a sour, niggly notice from Philip Purser. But Jimmy Thomas in the *Express* hailed 'a classic example of how TV has escaped at last from the conventional confines of the theatre and begun to create real drama for itself'.[31] The *Mirror*'s Kenneth Eastaugh was 'left questioning present-day values with a mind full of uneasy thoughts. And that's good.'[32]

Reviewing its first repeat, Stanley Reynolds pictured a different playwright altogether: 'The man of mystery is beyond a doubt Dennis Potter. True enough Potter writes television criticism almost every week in the rear end of the *New Statesman* but in those expansive surroundings he seems to give even less of himself away than he does in his television plays ... a rare television talent who creates credible characters in absorbing plots, and yet always seems to fall short of telling his true feelings. Who, who, who is Dennis Potter?'[33] It is tempting to respond: 'Pay, pay, pay attention, Stanley Reynolds' but happily he will atone for this lapse later.

Where the Buffalo Roam won no awards but it marks a high-water mark in Potter's relations with the BBC. Unusually, at his quarterly meeting with the BBC board, Director of Television Kenneth Adam went out of his way to note that 'the play has been warmly commended'.[34] The Corporation has screened the recording on four occasions to date. I am happy to be challenged but I believe this to be a record only equalled by *Cathy Come Home* and Peter McDougall's *Just Another Saturday*,* although, of course, compared with the number of times supposedly favourite movies like *The Great Escape* and *El Cid* are trotted out, it is chicken-feed.

* Play for Today of 1975 shot on film in Glasgow by director John MacKenzie, concerning the pressures on the young drum major of an Orange Lodge marching band.

11

The Honeymoon is Over

'The stories we read in childhood have a potency that
cannot be destroyed, not even by the nostalgia which
is normally the most powerful disinfectant known to
man'.

Dennis Potter[1]

On 22 August 1966, Dennis Potter signed up to deliver a 75-minute
play for story editor Kenith Trodd. 'Potter is having to write it to a very
specific and early deadline,' Trodd explained in his commissioning
notes. 'The notion is an experimental one and does not, as far as we
are concerned, come within the agreed programme of his three-play
contract. I suggest we therefore treat it separately.'[2]

The reason for the precipitateness was a startling one: 'This is to be
our Christmas show . . . [It] will be a version of the fairy tale, probably
set in a contemporary princeling state (such as Monaco).' So Potter
went into a brown study in Lydney to write *Almost Cinderella*.

The subsequent sequence of events is listed in a letter to Potter from
Trodd: 'You delivered the script to me on October 17th. The next day
Gareth Davies (the prospective director) and I gave you our detailed
first reactions to the script by telephone. About October 20th it became
clear that the play would not as hoped now be recorded on December
10th. On October 26th you met Lionel Harris about the play.'[3]

By the time of Trodd's letter, the problem over the script had
reached the public prints. Huw Wheldon asked Gerald Savory for
'background' on behalf of Kenneth Adam. Savory explained that
Potter 'was commissioned to write a modern version of *Cinderella*,
to be transmitted either the Wednesday before or the Wednesday
after Christmas. He was paid his half fee of £425. When it was

delivered, the producer – Lionel Harris – had grave doubts as to its suitability as Christmas fare and referred to me. My dislike of it went further than Lionel Harris's and I immediately decided against doing it. Ultimately I agreed that Potter should be told that in our opinion so much work needed doing on it that it could not possibly be ready for this Christmas. I shall be meeting with Potter shortly, and will then decide whether to have him try again, or to abandon it. He has been paid the remainder of his fee.'[4]

In Trodd's chronology, 'on October 30th the *Sunday Times* ran their story'. This was an Atticus column item by Hunter Davies based on what Savory reckoned was a 'pure chance' meeting with Potter at TC, resulting in a 90-minute briefing. Savory concluded: 'My personal view is that Potter feels that the only way his two *Barton* plays got on to the screen was by yelling to the press and that it might work again'.

The Atticus article is accompanied by an outrageously staged photograph of Potter, respectable in jacket and tie, reading (from a fairy story, we imagine) to his wife and three good and attentive children curled up on the window-seat.

Hunter Davies takes an amused line with all parties. His gloss on the plot goes: 'Prince Charming turns out to be a sexual degenerate who on the stroke of midnight does something rather nasty to Cinderella. Other festive bits include a TV broadcast by the Prime Minister on the economic freeze in which he attacks a certain family for spending a lot of money on a big ball. The King and Queen are watching and argue about who should turn it off . . . there is a scene with Prince Charming and a prostitute on a gravestone.'

He says Potter 'believes that as fairy tales can worry children, adult versions of them should as well' and quotes him: 'As you bring in real things and people when you're reading a fairy story to your child, like saying "that house is just like Aunt So and So's", so you should with a grown-up story.'[5] It hardly seems much of a case to carry away from an hour and a half's interrogation.

Trodd's chronology continues: 'On November 30th the play was discussed at your meeting with Gerald Savory. On December 6th to 8th there was extensive press comment about the play. I very much regret that the statement in *The Stage* for December 15th says that you have been sent a list of suggested alterations to the play if, in fact, this is not so.'

Savory reported on the meeting to Huw Wheldon. 'I said that I found the satire heavy-handed and the humour rather "sniggering" and that the piece contained so many styles as to make it very difficult for the viewer to know how to take it. I said that to my mind the character of the miniskirted Cinderella was by far the best characterisation and that it was in this style that I had imagined the play to be written when I countersigned the commission note. Also, I felt it a pity that Cinderella had been reduced to a small part. Potter said that he considered Prince Charming the leading character and I said I found the scene in the graveyard where he meets a promiscuous girl hard to take. I assured him I had no quarrel with the content, that I was not a Monarchist, nor a purist, nor prurient . . .

'He told me what he was trying to get at in the play but I told him that, in my view, he hadn't written what he really intended . . . He thought it was his best play to date and that he had not been able to work since . . . I proposed that I should read *Almost Cinderella* a third time in the light of our conversation . . . My impression is that Potter himself went to the press.'[6]

On the day of this memo, Savory received a telegram: 'Warmest congratulations on decision not to film *Cinderella*. Strongest objection to public money being spent twisting the magic stories of childhood into perverted fantacies [sic] of sexual behaviour'.[7] Savory's new fan was someone whose very existence the BBC Director-General would not acknowledge: the President of the National Viewers and Listeners Association, Mary Whitehouse. At support from such a quarter, a letter from the Manchester Humanist Society sneered: 'How can you look your colleagues in the face?'[8]

For his part, as it happens, Potter tended to be rather sympathetically disposed towards the NVLA. Meeting him some years later, Stanley Reynolds found that he 'loves the idea of Mrs Whitehouse. He sees her as standing up for all the people with ducks on their walls who have been laughed at and treated like rubbish by the sophisticated metropolitan minority.'[9]

On this same December day, Potter was quoted in *all* the newspapers, a separate quote for each one. This is what Trodd delicately referred to as 'extensive press comment'. The formulation for the *Daily Mail* had it as his intention 'to bring out the impact of the story on adults rather than retell it as they saw it when they were children at the pantomime'.[10]

To the *Daily Sketch* he said: 'I now feel that, if I could arrange my career so that I never have to write for BBC Television again, I intend to do so.'[11] There remains some doubt as to whether Potter had correctly judged the public mood to be in his favour, however. Of the substantial correspondence generated and kept on file, precious little supports the castigating viewer who told Savory, 'We are not prepared to be treated like children, you know.'[12]

Parliamentarians weighed in. Labour MP William Hamling tabled a question to the Postmaster-General about 'the new approach to pantomime by television producers', calling on him to direct the BBC governors 'to preserve the romance and humour'. A veteran BBC-baiting Tory, James Dance, put down a motion attacking it for 'altering traditional children's stories' and introducing 'perversion and violence'.[13] Potter was a little unlucky in that Jonathan Miller's version of *Alice in Wonderland*, due for transmission on 28 December, was already the subject of wild speculation and, though greatly admired when it did go out, nevertheless sparked an ill-tempered and ill-informed storm in the Commons.

Early in 1967, Savory sent Potter a lengthy and considered reaction to *Almost Cinderella*, thereby lifting the curtain a little more on a work that is lost until Potter's estate decides to make it available:

Sometimes the method is pure pantomime, sometimes realistic and on occasion the actors step out of character to address the audience . . . I *still* find the satire a bit heavy-handed – especially the Prime Minister's broadcast (difficult to do because the real thing so often seems satirical in itself). I'm also wondering whether the 'in' jokes about television would really work. There's no doubt that the graveyard scene is controversial but I can't honestly say that I myself object to it strongly. The ballroom finale is, as you say, the glossy Hollywood musical and is in yet another convention. Can you find a way satisfactory to you whereby your intentions could be made somewhat clearer and presented on fewer different levels? Of course, I know you *can* do it; what I really mean is – do you feel *inclined* to?[14]

Evidently Potter did not, for the play drops out of the official record. Savory could turn his mind to a nicely simmering row about the changes he wanted in a drama-documentary about the assassination of Rasputin. But *Almost Cinderella* remained an especially tender spot for the most sensitive-skinned of writers. As he told Philip Purser six years later: 'Tinkering with a fairy story is a worse blasphemy to [the BBC] than tinkering with the Bible.'[15]

As Hunter Davies's report revealed, 'The BBC have been very clever. While flattening him with one hand, they've produced a goody from behind their backs with the other. This is a Potter play called *Message for Posterity* which they've been sitting on for a year.' He quoted Potter: '"They now intend to put that on at Christmas-time instead, which keeps me happy and reduces my manoeuvrability in criticising them".'[16]

As it turned out, Potter had to wait a further five months for the transmission of *Message*. Even so – and despite his continuing threats to sever his BBC ties ('If it's shelved for good, I just won't bother to send them any more,' he told Hunter Davies; and it was) – he went on negotiating new commissions with Trodd.

The reason for delay on *Message* was casting. Production was postponed, first because one of the two leads had a heart attack, then because of difficulty recasting. It seems clear that many actors of the generation required for the two leads were reluctant to take on what they perceived – quite correctly – as a savage caricature of Winston Churchill.

Message for Posterity begins with the *TW3* comedy of a parliamentary committee negotiating a becoming gesture to an elderly Tory former Prime Minister. They light on a portrait. The commissioned artist is James Player (Patrick Magee), equally elderly anarch and voluptuary, who enjoys running rings round the journalists drawn by his startling commission. Player's main sounding-board is his daughter Gillian (Patricia Lawrence). The sitter, Sir David Browning (Joseph O'Conor), drifts in and out of his past, both political and cultural. Player comes to Browning's country estate and the two old lions circle each other growling, while generations of natural and acquired cubs frolic in the background: Browning's son Richard (Geoffrey Chater), granddaughter Clara (Anna Calder-Marshall) and political secretary Hawkins (Donald Hewlett).

Player seems to believe that in this portrait he can wreak political revenge on Browning for sins that can be traced back to the General Strike. He will depict 'little pink and blue veins all broken, like an ordnance survey map, on his beady, bird-eyed, anteater snout. Flesh the colour of old putty. Pink rims to his little pig eyes. Oh, poor old devil, rotting away.'[17] Then he becomes aware that this is also self-portraiture.

The sittings allow points to be scored until Browning apparently collapses and expires. Effectively dancing on his grave, Player props him up to allow the painting to continue, then runs amuck smashing things when Browning revives. He is led away and Browning is pampered by his ranks-closing family in his hospital suite: 'We always win in the end.'

Potter's original ending had the elder statesman 'delighted, ecstatic even' at the portrait: 'He believes that the canvas has given history the most striking proof yet of his greatness' whereas Player's sense of it is that 'the painting shows the grotesque evil of power . . . and represents the most terrifying, brilliant indictment yet of the guilty', fulfilling his 'divine mission to tear away all the layers of camouflage and habit which protect all the things he wants to paint'. While the retinue look at the picture aghast, the pair are united in their delight.[18] As a theory of history, this is fair enough, though the choice of language suggests that Potter would have been unlikely to present it in as disinterested a way as the thesis might intend. The denouement he plumped for is more jaundiced and partial. It fails to rescue a poor play, however.

The barely disguised source is the painting of Churchill by Graham Sutherland as a retirement gift from the House of Commons. The Great Man put a wry spin on his acceptance of 'a remarkable example of modern art'. Legend has it that Churchill's wife ordered the portrait to be destroyed. But with none of Sutherland's urbanity, Player is more an Augustus John figure. Browning is distinguished from his model by the inclusion of reference to Churchill in the lines, an expedient reportedly pressed on Potter.[19] Real-world allusions embrace Robin Day, Bernard Levin, A. J. Munnings, the *New Statesman* and *The Black and White Minstrel Show*. Browning even lives at Eastrepps, perhaps next door to Potter's Norfolk fastness of Northrepps.

'It's like *The Dresser* which was inspired by Wolfit* but really nothing like him,' says Joseph O'Conor who finally played Browning. 'You could say the character was wittily senile. I remember particularly how delighted I was with the wit and the strenuous strength of the writing which was rare in a new play. The dialogue was a joy to speak.'[20]

But Potter gets distracted by his own fundamental discomfort with the contemporary world. His instinct may have been to present his protagonists as mutually and sympathetically out of sorts with 'the age of the little man', as Browning calls it, but it never fully reveals itself as his intent.

Potter surely felt this, however. He might have rewritten the opening line of one of his favourite novels, L. P. Hartley's *The Go-Between*, as 'the *present* is a foreign country; they do things differently there'.[21] In a resonant little scene, cut from the 1967 recording, Clara Browning avers crossly: 'The past is past. The past is dead.' Her German lover shakes his head: 'You English. You just don't want to know.'

Clara seems to embody all the brutality of youth, specifically of youth in the make-it-new sixties. As it turns out, it is her kiss-of-life that revives her grandfather: 'new life from the young' as her father observes sagely. His own *Realpolitik* is quite the most brutish of all but Potter has the family united against the foe at the end. As a study of the ability of old money and old power to learn quickly how to speculate in new markets, *Message for Posterity* does not hold a candle

---

* Ronald Harwood's 1980 play, later filmed, drew on his own period as dresser to old-school actor-manager Sir Donald Wolfit but made neither 'Sir' a full portrait of Wolfit nor the eponym a self-portrait.

to Trevor Griffiths's play *Country** or such works of David Mercer as *The Parachute* and *The Cellar and the Almond Tree.*†

The view, dimly recalled from 1967, that the play's schema overshadowed its execution was only confirmed by a revival of the play in a new production directed by David Jones and screened four and a half months after Potter's death. Instead of Patrick Magee's Irish-irascible as Player, it brandished Eric Porter's Welsh-irascible. John Neville played Browning, both actors bringing a sense of the intermittent visibility of their own careers to a long-unavailable play (the 1967 telerecording was another not archived by the BBC).

Its first director, Gareth Davies, confesses: 'I never liked it. Nothing against the actors involved who were very good, but for whatever reason it never sprang into life. I'm surprised it's one they decided to do again. The original spark was fine, a good intellectual idea, looking for a metaphor in that painting. But I don't think Dennis ever developed it, it wasn't really there. It was more like a French piece playing hunt-the-thimble.'[22] Joseph O'Conor says, 'I thought it worked better then than as a revival. It may have dated, of course.' He remembers Potter being 'pretty furious because they cut the slot from an hour and a half to an hour and a quarter at no sort of notice which meant that the German lover vanished entirely.'

The official record suggests that the play was ordered at 75 minutes and ran for over 80 in the studio so cuts were forced upon it. It was allowed to transmit at 79 minutes. Breaching 80 would have triggered additional acting payments. At least the BBC did well by Potter in the sense that, yet again, one of his political plays went out straight after a PPB.

The audience was below 3.5 million and appreciation his lowest since *The Confidence Course.* In a long and judicious article, T. C. Worsley pinpointed all its faults including its 'reliance on caricature'.‡ But he averred long-term support: 'I am severe towards Mr Potter's work only because I am so sure that his real gifts will one day flower into something remarkable . . . Bright ideas are the first thing and these he has. Technical virtuosity is the next and this he commands.'[23] Sadly, Worsley did not live to see the full flowering.

Ahead of transmission, Gerald Savory sent Potter a nice note including the thought, blandly expressed in BBC-speak but probably

---

* Directed by Richard Eyre and shown on BBC1 in 1981, this was the first – and the only one made – of a projected series of six plays called Tory Stories.
† The former was produced by Tony Garnett for Play of the Month in 1967 with a cast directed by Anthony Page and led by John Osborne; the latter was a Wednesday Play of 1970, directed by Alan Bridges and produced by Graeme McDonald.
‡ Potter's true gift as a caricaturist is continually downgraded.

earnestly meant: 'I do hope you will be doing another for us before long.'[24] The BBC would not want to lose its leading writer. But the collapse of *Almost Cinderella* and the poor reception accorded to *Message for Posterity* after all its delays (it had been scheduled four times) rather took the shine off Potter's star. Three weeks after *Message* went out, Trodd rejected the second instalment of his triple commission, a play called *By the Rivers of Babylon*.

That month the Potters finally settled at Morecambe Lodge in Ross-on-Wye. Dennis's sister June tells the story: 'My husband was the first there. He was working on the telephone exchanges and he was in rooms there with two workmates. The owner was a divorcee who let the top floor. After we married we lived there together. The house had been for sale for two years. It was going for £5900 and the average house price was £2000. So it was expensive.

'I was doing a little bit of work for Dennis and he came over and he said "Oh, we'll have this, then." Frightened Margaret to death, you know! So they bought it and that's how they came to live at Ross.'[25]

Potter may have settled domestically – he and Margaret lived at Morecambe Lodge until their deaths – but he was about to make a career move that would prove much less decisive. He was to go to ITV.

I Get Along Without You Very Well

'Why can't we both get out of the house now and
again?'

Mrs Bates, *Brimstone and Treacle*[1]

'I think . . . there was some peevishness going on somewhere'[2] was
Potter's laconic explanation for his departure from the BBC and into
the arms of, successively, Rediffusion and LWT in 1967–8. The
respective results were a seminal miscalculation and a negligible
divertissement.

The Bonegrinder would not detain us long but that it marks a
far-reaching new development in Potter's work. American tourist Sam
Adams (Weston Gavin) picks an argument with city types watching
the Trooping of the Colour. Over breakfast, George and Gladys King
(George Baker, Margaret Tyzack) share spluttering outrage at Britain's
decline ('Do your duty these days,' he cries, 'and you're treated like
some kind of halfwit'[3]) as well as a loveless marriage.

George lip-smackingly deplores photographs of women in the
newspaper and joins his neighbour Lapwell (Brian Oulton) for
a morning routine of walking to the Underground transfixed by
miniskirts ('Young girls nowadays . . .'). Having chatted up a woman
in Trafalgar Square, Sam uses and abuses a prostitute (Linda Marlowe).
Gladys is left to stew at home and worry for her sick sister. 'Nothing
ever happens to me, George,' she says aloud. 'I wish you'd break
your neck.'

At the bank, George ogles a secretary and defers to his boss (Arthur
Cox). Sam clashes with a park-keeper and a policeman on his way to
a louche pub, the Duke of Clarence. George arrives there too and so
'Uncle Sam meets King George', as Sam announces (in case we missed

it). George is soon terrorised, then drunk. Meanwhile Gladys's sister dies while Gladys reads from *The Rime of the Ancient Mariner*.

Later, when the sister has been buried, George, now a wreck, contrives to hit Gladys on the head with his rolled newspaper. He weeps and tells her a doctored version of his meeting with Sam. Gladys decides that Sam is blackmailing him. He is certainly stalking the house and inveigles his way in. They watch news of the Vietnam War on television, then Sam throws his weight about: 'Try to look on me as your bad, bad, little boy,' he tells Gladys. She is more concerned with George's cringeing.

Sam takes over, ever more obnoxious. Computerisation at the bank has rendered George redundant. ('Poor old George,' muses his boss. 'Poor creepy old Georgie.') Gladys steels him to fight back: 'We've always paid our bills and kept the hedge cut,' she declares. George stalks his prey with the coal hammer but is only provoked to the deed when Sam recites 'Fee Fi Fo Fum'. Gladys then shops him to the police because he 'let the side down'.

There are three main grounds for the claim that *The Bonegrinder* is a pivotal piece in the Potter canon. First, it demonstrates more vividly than any other work the crass and raucous comedy that Potter favoured and – most significant – the fact that this outlandish style could yet be entirely misread and misunderstood. Second, it demonstrates more vividly than any other work how buoyantly hidebound and chauvinistic Potter could be. Finally, it heralds a major theme that is generally held to announce itself rather later in Potter's work, the so-called 'visitation' motif.

To begin with the humour, Stanley Reynolds, castigated earlier for getting it wrong, is singing from Sankey on this matter: 'Sometimes . . . I get thinking that I am the only one in the country who realises Potter's stuff is comedy. I asked him about this and he said he always made sure to write "a comedy" under the title of all his plays except *Son of Man*.'[4] In the same piece, Reynolds disclosed that for *The Bonegrinder* 'Potter got his idea from a crazy Canadian sailor in a pub one afternoon in Ladbroke Grove'.

From the account above of the business of *The Bonegrinder*, its comic nature might appear obvious. Veteran director Joan Kemp-Welch had other ideas. 'Joan didn't ever think it was a comedy,' says George Baker. 'She saw nothing funny in it at all. I thought it was the most wonderful play. I took Maggie Tyzack aside and I said, "Maggie, there's laughs in this, it's a contentious piece of literature, it's the dying of England." But it was a very hard uphill struggle to do anything with it. Joan insisted on doing it absolutely straightforward. It was very badly received. But the *script* works. So it was heartbreak, actually.'[5]

Shuddering through the heavy weather that Kemp-Welch made of it, one can see that the play needs the touch of a director who has no difficulty uttering truly low knockabout. The profoundly shallow is a fiercely strong instinct in Potter and the director who ignores it misses the heart of his work by a clear mile. 'There is a deep capacity for uninhibited enjoyment buried under the placid and hag-ridden exterior of the British male,' Potter announced in his first piece of regular professional journalism.[6] And during his famously self-exposing stint as a *Sun* columnist (when *The Bonegrinder* was transmitted) he described himself in terms which only those convinced that he was a vaudevillean at heart can recognise: 'Regular readers of this nervy little patch will know by now that I have a terrible weakness for disastrous puns and really bad jokes.'[7] In fact, Michael Billington in his *Guardian* theatre reviews (with his beloved *can belto* singers) or Philip French covering movies for *The Observer* will perpetrate more shameless wordplay in a fortnight than Potter essayed in his entire critical career. But the *thought* was there.

Potter did write comedies. But they were not ingratiating or attitudinising. They were his own somewhat crazed versions of pub routines and seaside-postcard rudery, trundled through the ghost-train ride of his psyche. George King in *The Bonegrinder* might almost be played as the hero of Alan Bennett's *The Madness of George III*, Sam Adams with the threateningly antisocial and astringent contempt of a W. C. Fields.

The abhorrence of American culture and, by projection, of American life is epidemic in Potter's early work. The 'dying of England' is consequent upon the thriving of the States in Potter's demonology. Here is an enumeration of evils sparked by the CBS drama series about social work, *East Side*, *West Side*: 'From chewing-gum and neon, broken noses and jukeboxes, canned imports and noisy drama, delinquent mothers and sobbing saxophones, Good Lord Deliver Us.'[8] On the other hand, as with domestic *mores*, it was the erosion of old ways that he most deplored, so that even American traditions gained a patina of charm and authenticity over time. Hence, in revisionist series like Warner's *Harry O* and CBS's *Cannon*, 'the evocative conventions of the gangster film slip and slide away into the adulterated mush which American TV writers make of almost all American experience'.[9]

But what most got his dander up was the spectacle of the solidity of his England being patronised by the flightiness of passing New World trade. Of an NBC documentary shot in 'Strat-Ferd, England', saucily shown by the BBC on St George's Day, Potter observed drily: 'Perhaps it is time we stood back a little and examined the claims of our own culture, before it becomes yet another quaint symbol for tourist brochures.'[10]

The attitude to Americana that he presents is as wild and primitive as anything in Dickens and the latter had the rationale of satirical intent based on first-hand experience. It would be another ten years before Potter set wary foot on American soil.

That he might dismiss it as a 'shoddy, unthinking piece' twenty-five years later[11] was hardly in Potter's mind at *The Bonegrinder*'s transmission. That morning, his *Sun* column evinced high anticipation, masquerading as self-depreciation:

> Tonight between 8.30 and 10.00 o'clock it will be my limbs on the rack. And when (no, if) you initially jab the button to change channels, the bonegrinding will really start to get personal. Come what may, though, I shall stay with the play until the bitter end . . . I simply chain-smoke and tremble at the back of the kneecaps, listening to the dialogue and pretending not to know what is going to happen next . . .
>
> Millions of viewers, yes. But I can't see them or touch them, hidden away under their aerials. A colossal audience fragmented into hundreds of thousands of private rooms. A huge throng broken down into small family units, swamping the set in a tide of domestic chatter or a cataract of boiling kettles and flushing cisterns.[12]

Hold that thought, the one about the set swamped in chatter and kettles and cisterns. In *The Bonegrinder*, as well as addressing the horror of rampant, gum-chewing imperialism, Potter is again excoriating the culture of suburban England that he sees as costive, thin-blooded and repressed (sexual repression standing in for every kind of bridled instinct). It is the culture of always having 'paid our bills and kept the hedge cut'. Ah, those privet hedges! If he invoked them once to stand for regimented England, he invoked them a thousand times. Interestingly enough, it was Enoch Powell of all people who actually challenged the image.

The two men met on *Any Questions* – in January 1967. Potter was as keen to appear as he was about *Desert Island Discs*. When producer Michael Bowen sent an invitation so very BBC in its cool understatement ('It's usually quite entertaining'[13]), Potter wrote back with alacrity, 'happy' to accept 'and [I] must confess – without the usual whine of the freelance! – that I have often wanted to take part'[14].

The programme came from the Community College at Chepstow, just down the A48 and over the Wye from Lydney where Potter was then living. It began with a question concerning the urge to 'live with danger' in the light of the death of speed-driver Donald Campbell. Going first, Powell immediately quoted the Bible. Potter's opening gambit was 'I think there is a very real form of death behind privet hedges and cups of tea and that really man's need is to live with endeavour rather than danger.'15

After the others had spoken, Powell came back at Potter: 'I was much alarmed by the references to the cups of tea and puzzled by the privet hedges'. Potter explained: 'Well, the privet hedge is my private emblem perhaps, my personal shorthand for the kind of death which seems most to afflict this country, which are rows and rows of suburban houses surrounded by neatly cut privet hedge, in which people quietly die, as I see it.'*

In *The Bonegrinder* George and Gladys King are the quietly dying. Potter's device to shake them up is to introduce into their protected world a disruptive visitor. It is the main thrust of those aforementioned 'visitation' plays but of course the disruptive visitor can be traced right back to 'Hazlitt' in *The Confidence Course* and to Nigel Barton canvassing on the doorstep.

My own theory about this quintessential figure in Potter's work is that he (it is always a man or a man-boy) is meant to stand for Potter himself, for Potter as a playwright visiting the nation through the 'little screen'. His perceived audience is this very swathe of Britons lurking behind their hedges and watching 'the play' with a cup of tea. They are not the decision-makers and adventurers, the movers and shakers who lead a full life and are 'too busy' to watch the telly. They are the women who stay home and dream of romance and the men whose working lives are spent upon a metaphorical treadmill. Their minds are warped by nameless dread and narrow experience and cultural sterility. These are the domestic chatterers, the kettle-boilers and the cistern-flushers whom Potter pictures half-watching the box. So his *plays* are the interlopers – the pushy Americans and would-be angels and prodigal sons and spiv salesmen and insinuating devils – who wheedle their way through those suburban front-doors and sweet-talk the vulnerable housewives and undermine the desperate husbands. His plays carry the promise of experience and balm and 'miracle' cures and eroticism and spirituality, carry that promise right into your living room where you live and are most vulnerable, but it is a false promise because the visitor is only a play, not a first-hand, personal experience. 'Rise,' Potter's plays shout, 'take up thy bed and walk.'16

If *The Bonegrinder* had been directed by Gareth Davies or Barry

---

* Potter would make four more appearances on the programme.

Davis (who handled the later plays with the 'visitation' theme) it could have worked. It might be posited that the theme could have been brought off if made at Ealing Studios or even by the Boulting Brothers, but my argument is that it is their essential domestic consumption that defines these works.

Certainly this play came a critical cropper. In the *Telegraph*, Séan Day-Lewis backhandedly dubbed it 'as watchable as a street accident'.[17] The *Mail*'s Peter Black called Potter's world-view 'as queer and unbalanced as Malcolm Muggeridge's and, like it, it seems to be based upon a picture of Britain as presented in the Sunday papers'.*[18] Nancy Banks-Smith had the unenviable task of reviewing it for *The Sun* and carried it off with aplomb: 'I allow nobody, but nobody, to be nasty to Dennis Potter, except me.'[19] A chastened playwright slunk back into print:

> The TV critics savaged my play on ITV last week. Their scornful unanimity was so appalling that I hardly dare to look in the shaving mirror in case some gibbering monster spits back at its own hideous reflection . . . I was so badly shaken by the reviews that I examined my conscience and scraped fearfully at what is left of my soul . . . Reluctantly I have to acknowledge complete and utter failure. I was deeply ashamed of the play and therefore ashamed of myself. The sense of failure is one of those emotions which can cripple a human being, be he a carpenter or a cobbler or a writer.[20]

His column in *The Sun* followed a six-week stint as guest television critic at the beginning of 1968. 'Nancy Banks-Smith, firing on all three barrels, has long been one of my pleasures, too,' he wrote in response to a 'bring back Nancy' letter. 'One sad thing about scribbling these reviews is that I could then read only myself in this spot instead of her.'[21]

He was not always well-disposed to fellow critics. 'There is very little written about television,' he observed in 1984, 'which does not eventually betray condescension or a rather less culpable unease.'[22] Back in 1970, he tried to articulate the experience for a critic of being criticised himself: 'As a writer, it still affects me inasmuch as I don't like bad criticism. I take it personally. Of course whether I take it seriously is another point. But at least it does give you, as a writer, a background against which to react.'[23]

Potter had returned to journalism in July 1967 with some television

---

* At this time the *Mail on Sunday* was still in the future.

reviews for the *New Statesman*, beginning with the advent of colour on BBC2: 'So the grass at Wimbledon is *green* . . .'[24] At the time, Paul Johnson was editor and Ken Trodd was doing occasional reviews of novels. Potter's delivery was fitful, however, for his illness had begun to bite deeper. By September he gave up the attempt, but the following month he began occasional book reviews for *The Times*, perhaps in the belief that default was not so damaging in the less date-tied area of literary notices.

What would Hazlitt have said? The paper was a pet target: 'Let the mob shout, let the city roar, and the voice of *The Times* is heard above them all, with outrageous deafening clamour; but let the vulgar hubbub cease, and no whisper, no echo of it is ever heard of in *The Times*.'[25] Potter reviewed non-fiction, especially literary biographies, for the paper, though not often those in which the subject had fallen into 'the whorish clutches of incompetent biographers'.[26]

Even as he contemplated the lives of others filtered through the sensibilities of yet others, Potter's own life-story as ever insisted on bleeding in. The following is from his (ultimately enthusiastic) review of Michael Meyer's definitive *Henrik Ibsen: The Making of a Dramatist 1828–1864*:

> There have been some studies of famous writers and artists which read a little like out-patient dossiers – lending support to the mechanistic but degenerate thesis that 'creativity' itself is but kindred to, say, a raw psoriatic rash which itches deep into infancy, bits of the bleeding flesh of childhood caught under hard adult fingernails. In such dreary circumstances Biography can become a gargoyled extension to the path-lab rather than the last legitimate sanctuary for 'great men'.[27]

Again, writing of the collected essays of Orwell, a writer to whom Potter is often compared, he contends that 'pessimism and persistent ill-health are much more likely than the conviction of a faith or the vagaries of a conscience to give a writer a reputation for honesty . . . Illness will eventually corrode even the most resilient of spirits.'[28]

Illness must now have been uppermost in Potter's mind. The arthritic element was torturing each of his hands into the shapes that would always be described in terms of aggression, even by sympathisers: as claws, as the clenched fists of a pugilist. Potter described himself as 'a writer who needs to clutch his pen as though it were a lifebelt'.[29] His penchant for longhand now proved fortuitous for he could not have used a keyboard if he had wished to.

Many visiting journalists fell rather hungrily on Potter's condition as 'good copy'. There are too many highly detailed descriptions to choose from. Philip Purser's has the merit of being exhaustive:

> Potter might be the survivor of some grim inquisition, his painful limp a legacy of The Boot, his fingers twisted and the nails blunted an opaque yellow by screwed instruments . . . Potter says it's the biblical leprosy and that both troubles are classic stress illnesses . . . when [it] is at its worst, he cannot even eat, for his jaw muscles seize; he cannot read, for the psoriasis gums up his eyelids. In periods of remission he is gay and fiercely hopeful.[30]

Potter and Purser dine together, the former explaining that he must choose meat or wine, his regime of steroids prohibiting both at once. Later in the encounter he is 'back in bed with a regression of the illness. His face and arms are aflame. He winces as his joints scrape and click. He sips milk laced with whisky and chain-smokes Player's Gold Leaf.' This is the daily reality out of which Potter writes *The Bonegrinder* and *Shaggy Dog* and his *Times* book reviews. If they exhibit a degree of asperity, is it to be wondered at?

This is not to say that artists require allowance to be made. The physical ordeal is not an excuse. It is merely a fact. In reality, the remarkable aspect is not the evident pain, it is the evident stoicism. In that way, Potter was an archetypal English hero. He was patient under fire. He was possessed of the great English virtue of forbearance.

But he did not forbear in silence. For the English, their illnesses take precedence. Potter was not exactly an illness bore but he was very happy to share the details. His family cannot have benefited from much more detail of his progress than did the readers of *The Sun* during the summer of 1968. On the fateful morning of the transmission of *The Bonegrinder*, he had medical progress to report:

> Suddenly, gloriously, incredibly and (to others) quite incomprehensibly, I have been given back my health. On Thursday a specialist in Birmingham acknowledged that something peculiar had happened. Something psychogenic, as he put it. Or mind over body, joy over pain, defiance over despair. All at once I stopped taking such a heavy daily dose of steroids that I might have, should have, collapsed. It was stupid and arrogant. But worked! . . . I no longer get a hot stab of pain when I turn my head. I am filled with big bright bubbles of exuberance and gratitude.[31]

Three months later, however, he was 'back with a walking stick, tip-tapping out a tiny route with my swollen toes. And waiting with an ill temper to go back into hospital. The night the Soviet tanks rolled into Prague, the world slid back into the ice-age of cold war and – But the same night, in the same small hours, I could feel the hot fluid pumping into my fingers again. Pessimism sits on my mind like an old black crow on a shrivelled tree . . . George Orwell was dying when he wrote *1984*, hawking up political despair. Hope, you see, is a function of healthy minds.'[32]

After his next column, he missed three in a row when he took a further turn for the worse. As soon as he could, he enlightened his readers: 'I am glad to be back again, even though still on my back again. Tomorrow I begin my fourth week in this huge, trolley-clanking hospital. But now there is a light at the end of the tunnel as I sing the praises of a biliously yellow little tablet called Methotrexate.* Until the last few days, the most burning issue in my mind has undoubtedly been whether to turn over in bed or not.'[33]

In this piece, he gave some sense of what a cussed patient he was: 'A formidable nurse descended upon me like Joshua upon Jericho and began massaging some foul slop into my scalp . . . tonight, in the small hours, when all the lights are out, I am very carefully, very deliberately, going to burn a small black hole in the sheets with my cigarette . . . such primitive defiance [will] make me feel good, hitting back at the huge white figures towering over my bed'. He would only manage one more *Sun* column but he kept going in *The Times* where he described himself as 'a manic-depressive getting through the day on steroids and librium, the night on sodium amytal'.

Yet his spirits remained high: 'After a particularly harrowing year of physical illness and mental self-exploration, I clutch at the realisation – call it intolerable arrogance if you like – that I might one day write something which will "survive".'[34]

Shaggy Dog has not survived in either sense. The LWT recording was wiped and the play has barely kept a toehold in even the fullest accounts of Potter's career. He was working on it at the time of the rebuff over *The Bonegrinder* and the decline in his health and he suspected that 'the stress will spill out on the page, insufficiently controlled'.[35] The play was written for a repertory group of actors, The Company of Five, set up to supply the new ITV company by producer Stella Richman and actor John Neville. The other players involved were Gwen Watford (who did not appear in *Shaggy Dog*), Ann Bell, Cyril

---

* Methotrexate is a hepatotoxin, which is to say it is destructive to the liver.

Luckham and Ray Smith. Other plays commissioned were by Alun Owen, Leon Griffiths, C. P. Taylor, Roy Minton and Julian Bond.

Neville plays Wilkie, a cranky City gent, going for an interview ('If I don't walk on the cracks, I'll get the job').[36] James (Luckham) regrets the aim 'to deliberately hurt, embarrass and humiliate a man, a man of our own class, a man who simply wants a job with the RestAwhile Organisation'. He and Johnson (Smith) are joined by Parker (Derek Godfrey), 'the stress bod with all the latest psychological mumbo-jumbo in his briefcase'. The mumbo-jumbo is no more than such anomalous appurtenances as clown-nose and blonde wig.

Made to wait, Wilkie studies the legs of the receptionist (Bell) and starts a joke which is interrupted by his summons. Ignoring Parker's disconcerting tactics, he acquits himself well, grows erratic, starts his joke, then pulls a gun. 'You make a sense of humour sound like a physical attribute,' he tells James. 'Like knock knees . . . or carbuncles or bunyans [*sic*!]' He delivers a diatribe on the state of industry, then restarts his joke. Looking in on the interview, Johnson assumes it's all part of the experiment. When he and the receptionist hear shots, he merely says, 'Let them get on with it'. The receptionist finds Parker and James slain and she faints. Wilkie carries her to the window, completes his elaborate joke and jumps.

Shaggy Dog resembles *The Confidence Course* in style and effect, though it is clearly much broader and larkier. It also sounds a little like a John Bowen play, *A Case of Character*, which Potter reviewed in 1964: 'Plays that prowl around inside the head can be even more exciting than those which deal only with external actions and physical dangers.'[37] As before, no imputation is made against Potter, only that ideas go round and round the business. Bowen says that his own play was anyway a reworking of an uncredited writer's idea.

It hardly seems to matter whether we can believe that Wilkie has held down a successful career in 'cucumber-flavoured crisps' or whether we take him for a lunatic posing as a businessman. Unfortunately, the supposed 'psychological tests' have not exercised Potter's ingenuity in sufficient depth, coming across as mere pranks (on the page at least).

Again Gareth Davies directed but he spares it few words: 'A sad piece about a madman applying for a job. Not a great play. A sort of sour joke.'[38] Michael Billington agreed in *The Times*: 'It seemed like a mere sketch for the play Mr Potter could write about life at executive level.'[39] Yet Peter Black thought it 'his best play for some time'.[40]

Both these ITV plays were dropped from Potter's *Who's Who* entry, along with *Message for Posterity* and *Emergency – Ward 9*. If Potter really flounced out of the BBC to teach them a lesson, the gesture backfired. But it was not like that. Ken Trodd observes: 'He just took those commissions. He hadn't really gone at all. Just as later there was a presumption in the press that he'd left England for Hollywood which he never did.'[41] Ten days after *Shaggy Dog* went out, he was back at the BBC with a vengeance.

13

Man, Beast and Virtue

'Feminism's all very well, but in this business somebody
always gets the girl.'

Narrator, *Blackeyes*[1]

All the time that Potter was apparently playing away with upstart ITV
companies, he was fulfilling old commissions and accepting new ones
from the BBC. There was so much toing and froing that it became quite
a muddle, known to the BBC Copyright Department as 'The Dennis
Potter Problem'.

The source of the problem appears to be the cavalier commissions
by Michael Bakewell. Moving over as Wednesday Play producer
from Thirty Minute Theatre, Graeme McDonald inherited these
commissions. He also inherited Trodd as script editor. 'I walked into
Kenith's room,' he recalls, 'and he seemed to be covering somebody
up with newspaper. That was Dennis Potter, whom I'd never met and
whom he obviously wanted to hide from me.'[2]

Like any self-respecting and ambitious producer, McDonald set
about adding to the list. *The Blue Remembered Hills* was to be the
first of 'two companion plays – one about childhood and one about
old age. The first will be the third of his three-play contract . . . the
second will require a new commission.'[3] The latter was subsequently
announced as *Tell Me Not Here*, both titles taken from the poet A. E.
Housman.

Well ahead of delivery date, Potter decided the linked plays
were beyond him. He had already delivered *A Beast with Two
Backs* which he wanted Trodd and McDonald to accept as a new
commission. 'We are not disposed to do this,'[4] Trodd informed the
Copyright Department. *Beast* was paid for as a substitute for *The Blue
Remembered Hills*, a title which Potter laid aside for future use.

165

His agent Roger Hancock was keen to keep open the option of eventually delivering the linked plays and tried to persuade the BBC to accept an open-ended contract. The BBC would have none of it. Around this time, Potter had also been commissioned to supply a play to the National Theatre, a deal which never bore fruit.

Before long, McDonald had commissioned another Potter play. *Take This Water* was to be the 'story of a religious revolutionary . . . we are anxious to encourage Dennis Potter to begin writing this new play immediately. Hopefully [*sic*] for a transmission at Easter.'[5] This play would metamorphose into *Son of Man*.

Meanwhile, Potter switched agents from Hancock to Clive Goodwin. Two women who worked successively at the Goodwin agency, Ann Scott and Margaret Hare (who later reverted to her unmarried name of Matheson), would go on to script-edit Potter plays.

Out of this frenzy of commission and submission, *A Beast with Two Backs* emerged triumphant and went into production. It was to be the first of his works substantially shot on film and the filming was done where it was set, in the Forest of Dean. For the play deals with the forest's past.

There are many versions of the tale of the bear that the foresters killed. One of the most durable bases it on the village of Ruardean, a few miles north-east of Berry Hill. According to this account, there were four Frenchmen who brought two dancing bears through the area. When gossip spread the notion that one of the creatures had attacked a child in Cinderford with fatal consequences, a group of villagers set upon the small party, felling one of the bears and cutting its throat. The other bear lumbered into the village where someone killed it with a shotgun. The men fled, two of them having sustained a bloody beating.

The television telling is centred on Lower Lydbrook between Berry Hill and Ruardean and features one dancer (played by a brown bear answering to the name of Gina) and one man, an Italian called Joe (Patrick Barr). Initially they are a welcome novelty to the local children: 'You do talk funny . . . Bis thou from Gloucester?'[6] At the time of this couple's innocent progress through the forest, a married man, Micky Teague (Laurence Carter), is canoodling among the ferns with a raven-haired temptress called Rebecca (Geraldine Newman). When she reveals (or claims) that she is 'three weeks past me time', he staves in her head with a rock.

Two scapegoats present themselves: Rufus (Christian Rodska) is a simpleton, the butt of much sport among the local lads. His guardian, the fire-and-brimstone preacher Ebenezer (Denis Carey), is quick to detect failings in all man's actions and sin in all such failings. When

Rufus, having been tied to his bed, escapes over the roof and flees to the forest, he discovers Rebecca. Ebenezer finds him whimpering over the stricken woman – not quite dead – and finishes her off, believing Rufus responsible for the attack.

The other creature capable of killing but not of protestations of innocence is Gina. Led by the pathologically malicious Will (Terence Sewards), the lads turn the fickle crowd against Joe and Gina, who are easy to characterise as alien and hence as a threat. They are run out of the village.

A police inspector (Basil Henson) comes asking questions. He plays Will shrewdly and gets him to put the finger on Micky, whose affair with Rebecca is widely known. Word of the crime quickly spreads. When interrogated, Micky's wife Joan (Madeleine Newbury) stalwartly stands by him: 'Oh, I know all about that, sir. 'Twere nothing. Only there are some evil tongues in this place.'

Ebenezer tries to seduce a confession from Rufus: 'Did 'er tempt 'ee with 'er womanly wiles? You've got the body if not the mind and soul of a man.' He tries to smother Rufus with a pillow but cannot finish it. 'God is more cruel than I be.'

In a packed Zion chapel, Ebenezer evokes 'Satan hisself . . . stalking our steep green hill'. His gruesome account of the rankness of the deed withers the villagers' highly receptive souls and, when he addresses 'the beast within', they miss the metaphor, seize on the idea of the beast, rise up into a lynch-mob and rush out in search of Gina.

Joe has evidently had better luck in another forest community so Gina has a honey-pot. The village lads appear on the hill and, formal in their Sunday best, shy rocks at the bear. Rufus finds Ebenezer hanging in the bell-tower. Gina is dead and Joe cannot grasp what has happened. 'A man shouldn't cry like that,' says Jack (Roger Gartland) wonderingly. He is the only one among the lads with the potential for reflection. 'It's only an animal' is kindly meant but his offer of a shilling makes Joe mad. Joe is left to mourn.

Straggling home, the lads meet a demented Rufus running across the bridge, 'as though the devil hisself were on his tail,' says Harry (Anthony Andrews).

A Beast with Two Backs is a story of the transference of guilt, a wholesale progress from Micky to Rufus to Ebenezer to Gina and, by the moral, to Will and Harry and Jack and the whole community. But Potter's Old Testament soul leaves no doubt that the process starts with the transaction between Rebecca and Micky: she gave him of the tree, and he did eat.

In summary, the play may seem a departure. But it is of a piece with what had gone before. Joe is the stranger whose unheralded visit unlocks repressed force, in particular sexual appetite and guilt. The inexorable momentum of tragedy had been tried out in the urban canyons of *Where the Buffalo Roam*. And the theme of man's fall and woman's continuing guilt has become an unmissable thread right through the work. Again and again, women are perceived and condemned as the source of carnality. Defilement is not of women by men but of men by women. It is rampant in the workplace, as we learn from Rosalind, the pent-up secretary, lashing the 'tarts' she works with in *The Confidence Course*, from George King in *The Bonegrinder*, accounting a secretary a 'flighty little tart – needs her bottom tanned', and from Wilkie in *Shaggy Dog*, who 'droolingly' eyes a woman in a lift, tells himself 'Miniskirts? I'd bloody well miniskirt her' and calls Parker the business consultant 'a whore among men'.

Defilement is also implicit in marriage, for Willy Turner's father went with 'sluts', as the grandad unanswerably avers in *Buffalo*. In Nigel Barton's union, there is a strong whiff of disappointment that perhaps Anne has not bitten deep enough into the apple, as suggested in such of his shafts as 'prissy little cow' and 'your condescending Hampstead Socialism collapses at the first belch of wind from a navvy's guts', an image of distinct physicality as well as of class alienation. The Oxford Nigel is immediately attracted to Jill, described by a fellow student as the 'biggest whore since Messalina',* the same man warning her (does Potter imply: 'with justice'?) that 'these sons of workers . . . like their women to be very prim and proper or on their backs with their mouths shut'.

James Player in *Message for Posterity* suggests that his 'nasty little bitch' of a daughter Gillian was the outcome of whoring and explains her face as 'post-coital sadness'. Willy Turner dismisses the patently nice girl Carol as a 'silly bitch'. And Ebenezer roars at the doomed Rebecca stretched out among the ferns: 'Slut, slut, slut.'

'The most offensive group of words applied to the female population,' Germaine Greer wrote, 'are those which bear the weight of neurotic male disgust for illicit or casual sex.'[7] Such words and/or the accompanying neurosis seem to come most readily to men of Potter's class born before the Second World War. Richard Hoggart, elsewhere so meticulous in his objectivity, assumes a distinctly strident and puritanical tone in accounts of men's 'speaking of their sexual adventures and plans; you are likely to feel smothered by the boring animality, the mongrel-dogs-rutting-in-alleyways quality . . . To each class its own forms of cruelty and dirt; that of working-class people is sometimes of a gratuitously debasing coarseness.'[8]

* Wife of the Roman Emperor Claudius.

The locution 'you are likely to feel' patently assumes that the reader is as fastidious. Even more indicative of Hoggart's condescension is his pen portrait – it is avowedly admiring – of a charwoman: 'She had the spirits, and I say this with no intention of disparaging her, of a mongrel bitch.'9

Gareth Davies remembers tackling Potter: '"All these women you write," I said, "they're always somebody's mother or somebody's wife or somebody's mistress, that's all they're there for, to serve some sort of male." "That's right," he said. "All my own fantasies."'

Davies laughs, partly to convey Potter's own laughter. 'He wasn't interested in women in plays. "Boring characters," he said. "They don't *work*"* – this was the sixties, remember. "I find them rather dull," he said. I thought it was a shame but it wasn't his nature so he never did write women properly. I would have found it a problem if I'd done his later work. I'd have found *Blackeyes* a problem.'

Davies did some preparation on *A Beast with Two Backs.* 'It was originally based on something he'd seen on television. Someone who had attacked and sexually assaulted a child was hurried into a magistrates' court with a blanket over his head and there were a lot of screaming people, mostly women, hurling abuse and sometimes stones at this figure. Dennis was shocked by that and interested in the duality of people attacking the man as violent and being violent themselves.

'He described the play he wanted to write and I thought it sounded very powerful but I personally couldn't direct it, on the grounds that nobody knows how powerful television is and Dennis would have to get right inside the mind of a man who did that and if we in any way triggered just one thing by doing it, none of us could live with ourselves. Dennis said that was rubbish, it was all right in the theatre and in a novel. So we had an argument about censorship and self-censorship. Right or wrong, that was my view at the time.

'After a while, he came up with a completely different play. It was based on a story which I'd been told too by my father in South Wales. I suspect it might have been one of those stories that surface everywhere, like the one about the dead granny on the roof-rack in Spain. For my money it was more powerful because the metaphor takes the heat out of it. But I'll never know if I was right. And I didn't direct the play anyway because I wasn't available. I'd like to have made it because I did a lot of wandering about the Forest of Dean thinking about it. But I thought it was very well done.'10

'Lionel Harris had been looking after the slot,' says Graeme

---

* Potter meant this in the sense of having jobs.

McDonald who produced *Beast*, 'and eventually he directed it. I think that was a mutual idea. He had good and positive feelings about the play.'[11] Harris filmed at Lydbrook Baptist Church, Goodrich Castle and the Old Oak Quarry on Speech House Road as well as all over the village. The Berry Hill Silver Prize Band was hired at a fee of 60 guineas to render 'Early One Morning', 'Widdecombe Fair' and 'The Soldier's Song' from *Faust*. Local children 'with authentic accents'[12] were rounded up. McDonald fretted at an overspend of £2828 'and we have no cover story at all'.[13] Gerald Savory appealed on their behalf: 'It is a play on a large scale but, in my opinion, something quite exceptional.'[14]

Harris used the forest well, shooting from trees and ditches. There are many striking images, none more convincingly distant than that of Joe striding and Gina waddling upright between rows of stone cottages, pursued by children in pinafore dresses and floppy caps. Monochrome may help to make it seem a fragment from a lost world but largely it is that dead and innocent sense that anything out of the ordinary was a great spectacle. Potter would later write: 'When television drama calls back yesterday, the problem is often seen mainly as a matter of set design, costume fittings and a swift raid upon the dubbing studio for a few standard noises off, such as the clop-clop of horse and carriage for anything earlier than Henry Ford's first incarnation'.[15] There is none of that mere dressing-up in *Beast*.

The dialogue is clodded with ancient concerns, beast and earth images, god-fearing reference. 'Ta-Ra-Ra Boom-De-Ay!', an American music-hall song unveiled at the Oxford Music Hall in 1892, is doing yeoman's service in the village alehouse (the play is set a little before the turn of the century).

Making Joe what the kids call a 'dirty Eytalian' resonates with the prisoners of war of Potter's childhood. An odder echo is the chime of Joan's forgiving support of the faithless Micky and something Potter told a journalist in 1993 which she used in an obituary notice: 'He was quite convinced that he was in love with the *Blackeyes* actress Gina Bellman. "And you know what my wife said? She said, 'Dennis, don't be such a silly old bugger' – and she was right, that's what I am".'[16]

Above eight million watched the play and gave it strong appreciation. Stanley Reynolds was not impressed: 'A little way into this period piece ... I stopped puzzling over the title to wonder why he bothered to write the play at all'.[17] I have always understood the title to be a traditional image of the missionary position, in which case it underlines the sense that the 'beast in man' is his lust.* However,

* The earliest example of the image that I can locate is in Book 1, chapter three of *Gargantua* by François Rabelais.

Shaun MacLoughlin, who had taken over script-editing duty from Trodd, wrote in *Radio Times*: 'There is – as the title suggests – more than one candidate for blame'.[18] Doubtless Potter found the title useful for its multiple suggestiveness.

Maurice Wiggin argued powerfully that

> what distinguishes Mr Potter from the run of writers, even 'serious' writers, is his *sæva indignatio*,* a terrible anger which far transcends mere impatience with the mechanics of any 'system'. It is a radical wrath, Swiftian in its ferocity. Mr Potter wants to reform God and man. But I doubt if he allows himself much hope: he seems to be developing into a pessimist on the grand scale, not exactly a Manichee† but a blood brother to Inge, Orwell and Wells . . . one day he will touch off the big explosion.'[19]

A week after *Beast* was transmitted, Potter had his first taste of the theatre. For Anthony Tuckey at the Bristol Old Vic, he fused the two Barton scripts into a single theatre piece under the title *Vote, Vote, Vote for Nigel Barton*. Among a cast of twenty, Frank Barrie played Nigel, Martin Friend (later a teledrama director) was Jack Hay and Janet Henfrey reprised Miss Tillings. The production ran for the four weeks to Christmas.

With Ken Trodd leaving the BBC to set up the production company Kestrel‡ with Tony Garnett and Ken Loach, Graeme McDonald and Shaun MacLoughlin were keen not to lose their star writer so, in February 1969, they commissioned two more of Potter's projects that would never see the light of day. The working title of one was *Condescension*, an exploration of 'the attitudes of the middle-aged of condescenions [*sic*] towards the very old and the very young'. The fee for this was reduced by a previous commission remaining unfulfilled. The other was *Prostitute Reformer* and it aimed to be a 'modern parallel, in the form probably of a non-conformist minister, to Gladstone's attempts to reform prostitutes'.[29] Potter's fee was now up to £1250.

None too catchy though the latter title might be, it gives an indication of a gathering preoccupation in Potter's work, present if inchoate at the outset, which was to run on through the rest of his career.

It is an inquiry for another occasion whether Paddington chose

---

* Dean Swift's self-penned epitaph, carved on his tomb in Dublin, is *'Ubi sæva indignatio ulterius cor lacerare nequit'* ('Where fierce indignation can no more lacerate the heart').
† Mani claimed to be the paraclete sent to re-establish the true distinction between chaos and light, as first expounded before Christ. Wiggin is contributing to the Old Testament image that lightly adheres to Potter.
‡ Named for the haunting little Loach/Garnett/Barry Hines feature film *Kes*, the company's *raison d'être* was to provide one-off drama (not necessarily telemovies) for the new ITV company LWT formed by, among others, Michael Peacock.

Potter or Potter chose Paddington. Russell Twisk was one of many interviewers who could report: 'I met Dennis Potter at a hotel above Paddington Station; he rather dislikes coming to London and stays as close to getaway point, the railways, as he can.'[21] As in many conurbations, the area adjacent to the station was, and is, a well-established red-light district. Potter's preoccupation with prostitutes was fed by his Paddington peripatetics.

To what extent and in what manner he studied his subject is for others to determine, though part of that process will doubtless embrace the much-rehearsed adventure with the policeman who required to be kneed when he shone a presumptuous torch into a basement.

Concern with prostitutes also informs the play Potter sold to Ken Trodd at Kestrel. *Moonlight on the Highway* is a strange, transitional work, full of unresolved pain, guilt and resentment drawing on psychological damage that its author may or may not have himself sustained. An earlier version under the title *By the Rivers of Babylon* was rejected by Trodd back at the BBC. 'It contained a form of that confession that the character makes in *Moonlight on the Highway*,' says Trodd, 'but very raw and not well worked, a very tortured version, itchy – which was a word Clive Goodwin used about some of Dennis's work at this period.'[22] The confession was made (or 'tried out') in life by Potter on various old chums in those maudlin moments when booze segues from stimulant to narcotic. But in his novel *Hide and Seek*, the author warns against setting any store by such confessions: 'This is the way one over-embroiders invention when playing complicated games of intellectual hide and seek with one's closest friends.'[23]

Moonlight is apt to make the flesh crawl. David Peters (Ian Holm) is waiting to see the psychiatrist at a large NHS hospital. He is drawn into a laborious misunderstanding with an old Londoner (Wally Patch) about the identity of the singer who accompanies all the pain in Peters's head: Al Bowlly.* Also in his head is a vivid memory of the spiky-haired man who abused him at ten. The day before, Peters was playing the Bowlly disc 'Lover Come Back to Me' in his room when he received a visit from a miniskirted blonde, Marie Holdsworth (Deborah Grant). She said she was researching a television programme on Bowlly. As editor

---

* Half Greek, half Lebanese, Bowlly was born in 1898 and brought up in South Africa where he became a musician. He turned to singing for an engagement at Raffles Hotel in Singapore, then settled in London where he recorded and toured, mostly with the Roy Fox and Ray Noble dance bands. He was killed in a London air raid in April 1941. In 1968 Potter wrote: 'Whenever the cold winds blow too bleakly through my mind I like to listen to some elderly and rather scratchy recordings of Al Bowlly . . . the big crooning swoon on the wireless round about the time I was cutting my first milk teeth. So for me his throatily-velvety version of "You May Not Be an Angel" has the lingering flavours of chewy rusks, cod-liver oil and National Dried Milk.'[24]

of *The Al Bowlly Tapestry*, Peters was delighted and, unperturbed by her apparent air-headedness and her use of expressions like 'Groovy!', he made ham-fisted advances. Understandably this drove her away.

Fired up as he enters the clinic, Peters turns his aggression on 'the vulgarity of the age'[25] of which the music of Bowlly represents a repudiation. He is soon free-associating about the abuse at harrowing and emotional length, to the constant accompaniment of Bowlly; also about the deaths of both his father and Bowlly by wartime bombs. His mother, who has died only recently, lost her foot in an explosion. The psychiatrist Dr Chilton (Anthony Bate) sends him away with a prescription – he must not take the pills with alcohol or cheese – and then asks his students for their diagnoses: 'Pretend I'm Joan Bakewell'.

It is the thirty-fifth annual meeting of the Al Bowlly Appreciation Society. Conducting a double-act with his sound man Gerald (Frederick Peisley), the society's president (Robin Wentworth) fusses over the arrangements. His address, largely a tirade against contemporary culture, might have been written by Peters (or as an essay by Potter): 'The immortal Al Bowlly will go on throughout the years when the sickening sixties and the grubby, long-haired, dirty-mouthed, so-called pop singers of today are happily gone and forgotten'. While Peters sifts images of the Second World War, Chilton is making a conventional analysis of Peters's guilt complex and pronouncing on the appeal of singers like Bowlly: 'He makes sex sound simple, he makes sex sound lovely. Not a bit like sex at all, in fact.'

Heedless of Chilton's warning, Peters mixes pills and drink so that when the time comes for his report to the meeting, he is near-incoherent. He tries to say something true about Bowlly: 'All the songs are about love, never about *making* love, never about – copulation.' This has an impact similar to Nigel Barton at a political meeting wondering aloud if his flies are open. The abuser is in his mind again and, against a rising hubbub, he suddenly makes his grand confession: 'I have slept with 136 women. Prostitutes . . . You can't buy love. I know I'm wicked. Don't you realise I've repented?' Gerald puts on 'Moonlight on the Highway' while the president restores order. Peters flees, ecstatic: 'I've said it! Good old Al.'

Was it Potter's purpose in this broken-backed play to provide himself with a platform upon which to articulate this tawdry revelation? Such a possibility must be considered, for not only had he done so in the rejected BBC script, he repeated the exercise in *Hide and Seek*. Writing in near first-person of his *alter ego* figure Daniel Miller, Potter noted his 'admission that in his first thirty-five years he had achieved little

more than the black art to dispense a several sin to every sense.* 156
prostitutes and a wife with lucid green eyes sobbing on a settee with
a stinging red weal on half her once gentle face. 156 whores and a
bottle of pretty capsules which do not mix with cheese.'[26]

The strongest argument that this is a public shriving is contained
in those last lines Potter gave to Peters: 'I know I'm wicked. Don't
you realise I've repented? . . . I've said it!' Repentance – but more
important, redemption – is taking its place as the major theme of
Potter's work.

It will be seen that redemption has always been lurking near the
centre of Potter's concerns. At the very beginning of *The Confidence
Course* it is there: 'Opportunity comes – and with it Redemption.' From
here on it will sit on the shoulder of all Potter's heroes, a promise and a
guardian as they struggle against whatever the writer calls in to torture
them. But, provided they confess and repent – like David Peters and
Daniel Miller (and Dennis Potter; how these three names refract light
from each other) – they will be redeemed.

Not that he was ever to make redemption easy. He might have said
with Golgo Brone: 'I'm awkward at Redemption – a beginner; / My
method is to crucify the sinner.'[27] Or perhaps he had it in mind to
refute C. S. Lewis's dictum: 'Here comes the catch. Only a bad person
needs to repent: only a good person can repent perfectly. The worse
you are the more you need it and the less you can do it.'[28]

Potter sought to create very bad persons – bad *men*, of course –
who yet repent perfectly. Or, as in Peters' case, men troubled with
secret guilt that required exorcism. What he would increasingly say
of his work was something damnably difficult to grasp unless the
absolute preoccupation with redemption is noted: that the work was
essentially religious. I have not come across any instance of Potter
accounting *Moonlight* a religious play† but it is the type of work that
subsequently he did so describe. At this point such a description might
have seemed presumptuous; or he might simply have feared yet more
critical scorn.

'We're all creatures of the prevailing moral discourse all the time,
you know,' Potter told John Wyver in 1978, 'but perhaps it takes
something to happen to you personally to make it seem important
to orientate yourself in this way. I don't know whether – had it not

---

* 'The black art to dispense / A several sin to every sense' is one of many quotations dispersed
in the novel from *The Retreat* by the seventeenth-century religious poet, Henry Vaughan.
† Stanley Reynolds claimed that 'Potter got this idea from Nichol [sic] Williamson who has
a thing about Al Bowlly and who at a party suddenly said: "I can sing just like Al Bowlly"
and sat down at the piano and did.'[29] In his (perfectly honourable) pursuit of the comedic
Potter, Reynolds would believe anything.

been for illness and that kind of anxiety, which really is personal in structure, about yourself and the people around you and the world – whether I would have turned quite so firmly in this way.'[30]

This firm turn to religion may seem to be travelling in disguise in much of Potter's later work. But there is no mistaking the religious context of his next play or its significance in his development. 'I regard it as the end of my apprenticeship as a dramatist,' the playwright averred, 'the first play I am pleased with.'[31]

14

I'm Beginning to See the Light

'That's what it's like on a voyage, old son. *The* voyage.
We don't necessarily know exactly where we are going.
Mind you, it would be a pity if we did.'

Jack, *Sufficient Carbohydrate*[1]

Son of Man is a paradox. We might dub it 'Potter's Apocrypha'. It is a
religious play only insofar as it is a version of Christ's return from the
wilderness and the events leading to his death. But it is not of itself
especially religious; certainly it is not devotional. It is a play that marks
the end of Potter's agnosticism rather than the beginning of his belief.
Or, as Potter told Graham Fuller: '"Agnosticism" is the closest word
to what was going on when I wrote that play, but probably a better
description of my state would be some kind of yearning, as well as a
certain amount of anger at the milk-and-water Christ, the Holman Hunt
Light of the World Christ, or the Catholic Christ, the supra-mystical,
risen-from-the-dead Christ, which is something else.'*[2]

At the time of the play, Potter was still routinely perceived in the
press as 'a confirmed atheist'.[3] His position was never as bald as that,
however. As far back as 1963, he wrote, pretty conclusively: 'Anyone
who claims to be totally uninterested in any sort of spiritual response
to the ache of life is little more than a narrow-headed thug.'[4]

And his reviews were full of religious allusion, even when used as
a handy means of deflation, indeed dragged in somewhat gratuitously:

---

* Nine years later, Lew Grade financed a god-awful all-star made-for-television *Jesus of
Nazareth* scripted by no less than Anthony Burgess. At a reception at the Italian Embassy, I
asked its director Franco Zeffirelli why he had cast Robert Powell (whom Grade reportedly
made marry his live-in girlfriend) as a conventional Holman Hunt Christ. Zeffirelli evaded the
question, insisting that 'the public' would accept no other kind (for 'public' read 'money').

'Good jazz . . . is mounted on the small screen about as frequently as Elizabeth Taylor is pictured in the *Church Times*.'[5] Or 'Is it true that Mr [Jimmy] Savile was discovered, fully grown, in the bulrushes?'[6]

Mary Craig, who interviewed Potter for the Radio 4 programme *Sunday* in 1976, drew on his remarks in a profile for the *Catholic Herald*:

> After *Son of Man*, he began to change. He wrote that play in a mood of belligerence, out of a desire to strike back at his chapel childhood . . . But the writing of it turned him back towards the parables, 'into the challenge and beauty, the glory and pain and sometimes shoddiness of the New Testament. A sense of tension, of wonder and gratitude and bewilderment began to grow in me.' He has arrived at the point where he can no longer live without some idea of a loving God.[7]

Besides a mood of belligerence, sickness attended the work. 'I wrote most of the play in six weeks, in hospital in Birmingham . . . Physically it was difficult. The pen had to be strapped to my hand because I couldn't hold it. The paper got sploshed with the steroid grease they were putting on my skin. In other ways it was easy. I wrote it easier than any other play. I finished it at two o'clock in the morning – the BBC had someone waiting to take it away to be typed.'[8]

His is a vernacular Christ. The indelible image from the production is of Colin Blakely, beefy and hairy, huddled in the desert in the *snow*, retching up anguish and doubt: 'Is it *me*?'[9] But the times are propitious. 'I didn't want to be chosen either,' Christ tells Peter and Andrew (Brian Blessed, Gawn Grainger), 'but the kingdom of Heaven is at hand.' Ripeness is all and the people are eager to be led. Once he has accepted the messianic role, he brings to them a deeply revolutionary message: 'Love your enemy . . . What I'm saying to you now hasn't been said since the world began.' And 'Turn the other cheek . . . do you *want* me to tell you easy things?'

Pilate (Robert Hardy) is portrayed as a skilful, modern governor, tetchy and shrewd and physically loose. At a barefist bout, laid on as supper entertainment, he is roused, wanting blood and death. Procla his wife (Patricia Lawrence) reproves him indulgently: 'Such violence cannot be good for the digestion'. He snaps back: 'Violence is what makes a man, so an army, so an empire.' He gladly subscribes to the military instinct to control the restive people with despatch. 'There are more miracles in these few sour acres than there are flies in my larder,' he grumbles but he likes the commander's (Godfrey Quigley) answer: 'Quite so, sir. Swat them before they lay their eggs.'

In fact Potter eschews miracles of a 'magic' kind, merely showing Christ in a humane act of quelling fear by force of character, just the kind of inspirational behaviour that will grow into supernatural power in the fevered talk of idolaters. The clerical establishment needs only to make stick charges of blasphemy or agitation against prelatic authority to quell any incipient messiah. Caiaphas (Bernard Hepton) represents this interest, a man grown sleek in power and contemptuous of civil authority: he says Pilate has 'the manners of a carpenter and the intellect of a wood beetle'.

Pilate has the measure of Caiaphas, though: 'What priest ever wanted his religion to be taken too seriously?' But he is rattled when a servant girl Ruth (Wendy Allnutt) will not deny Christ even as she is flogged to death for showing spirit. 'Ideas are what we fear, sir,' he tells his commander. 'Ideas . . . This is the one they have been waiting for.'

Christ is betrayed by a weak and easily manipulated Judas (Edward Hardwicke) but successively defies Caiaphas and Pilate with silence and a beatific smile. Pilate momentarily mistakes him for a halfwit – 'I find no fault in him' – but becomes unnerved and strikes him. Aghast at both the act and his own unmanned reaction to it, he nevertheless apologises. Christ says, 'Don't be afraid.' That does it. Pilate watches grimly as he is flogged, then crowned with thorns. Nailed to the Cross, Christ cries out in the tone of a stuck pig: 'Why have you forsaken me?'

Message for Posterity is conventionally seen as Potter's last 'public' play, tangling with political power as reflected on the front pages. But *Son of Man* deals very directly with power and protest, statecraft and sedition, highly pertinent material in the late 1960s. Christ's message is portrayed as a threat to good order and a challenge to pragmatic rule in both Church and State.

That is why it is central to Potter's purpose to present him primarily as a man and only in parentheses as a divine.* His Christ subscribes to a religion more reminiscent of that of Blake: 'Thou art a Man, God is no more, / Thine own humanity learn to adore.'[10] So he is a figure of inspiration and vigour, not afraid to make a strapping stranger bristle by telling him: 'I love you, Peter.'

The idiom is neutral and informal, attempting neither self-conscious archaisms nor a strenuous modernity. As working men, the disciples (or their spokesmen Peter and Andrew) talk a rough-hewn language. They first imagine Christ 'a loony, a nutcase'. Later, Peter quaffs water and belches companionably: 'Beats fishing, eh?' The preaching is

---

* It says much about BBC executives' capacity to misperceive their artists (or simply their inability to attend) that Alasdair Milne should think the title of the play was *Son of God*.[11]

something of a turn; indeed rhetorical effects are brilliantly turned, the genial and wry abruptly abrasive and direct. Familiar texts (the Beatitudes, say) are punctuated by the emphatically colloquial: 'Shut up', 'Use your flaming heads'.

For some, this sits uncomfortably but one of several rewards is Christ's truly persuasive reaction on encountering an example of the Cross routinely raised to implement the execution of Jerusalem's trouble-makers: 'It's good timber, this. Hewed with the grain from the heart of the tree. I could fill a room with tables and chairs with wood like this.' This Christ is his father's (as opposed to his Father's) son.

And Potter, writing out of his own Passion, can find the words for an experience that is simultaneously psychological, spiritual and physical: 'He burns inside me. He tears at my chest. He lights up my eyes. He tugs at my clothes. Oh God, Holy Father, you have hunted me down. You have opened the top of my head. And I have heard you, I have seen you.'

To ask that such a play be encompassed in a studio was the BBC at its most insensate. Gareth Davies 'tried to get it done as a big-scale production with other countries so we could share locations and extras and feed in our own Jesuses but that never took off. Too early for that. The irony is it won the European Broadcasting Union Play of the Year Award.'[12]

With a cast of over ninety, seventeen items of livestock, a twenty-six-strong boys' choir, water-tank and flaming torches, a supplementary studio was corralled. Poor old *Play School* had to postpone recording for two days. 'I remember some of their people coming into the gallery by mistake and being surprised to find us doing a Roman orgy,' laughs Davies. 'The vision-mixer had brought her knitting. I said "I think you'll find you can put that away." Even *Play School* couldn't match big, black, bare-fist boxers.'

A delightful memo from Davies' assistant to Artists' Bookings reassures that for 'people involved in crucifixtion [sic] sequences . . . no special insurance will be needed'.[13] But much that was special was required. Davies asked for two hand-held cameras, making eight in all (one of the cameramen was the aforementioned Geoff Feld). He used them well, exploring the enticingly chaotic atmosphere of the scenes where the centurions break up the crowd. The studio teems with life – a deceptive sense of numbers – and thrills with the alien sound of women keening. Where the studio is heavily populated, the camerawork is effectively documentary, snatching shots on the wing, so that the scene can be played for its own energy instead of for nicely-framed pictures. This is not what you see in a studio production.

Of course there are great limitations, though even a somewhat rickety wilderness is enhanced by the monochrome studio lighting which makes the perspective unfathomable and so apparently limitless. Only the water-tank fails seriously to make its weight: there is no illusion that the fishermen might ever catch anything.

'The studio was a helluva problem,' says Davies. 'I think we did bite off more than we could chew technically. We had huge wind machines that we couldn't use because they interfered with the sound. The electricians worked till midnight, well past any official time. They didn't pull the plugs until we'd achieved the apotheosis – we'd got him up on the Cross. But we still had to come back for an extra day.'

So it was a stupendous over-run. 'We always knew it was inevitable. The idea was to go in and fail and make them realise the impossibility of the way things were scheduled. But Gerald Savory was absolutely marvellous.' However difficult it was to achieve and however rough-and-ready the result, there was a tremendous build-up of anticipation, especially when the play was abruptly pulled from the schedule by Huw Wheldon and the new BBC1 Controller Paul Fox. 'Their reasons were undoubtedly the wrong ones,' Potter told *The Times*, 'but the decision coincided with my own feelings. I did not want the play shown in what is still called Holy Week, and coated over with the sickly piety of a religious offering for Easter.'[14]

The world only had to wait a fortnight. As ever, the reception was very mixed. Sylvia Clayton found Potter's Christ 'a harsh, hectoring figure, who made the Beatitudes more like a party political broadcast'[15] (*that* must have stung him!). Julian Critchley in *The Times* noted: 'A carpenter's view of the Cross, a disputatious, radical, vivid human being whose message – if not his divinity – came over with a considerable force'.[16]

Son of Man did rather poorly in the ratings, attracting 4.5 million viewers. The BBC thought it should do better and scheduled an unprecedentedly early repeat in June. The Church Assembly dignified the play with a debate on its merits. The industry also blessed it with the Writers' Guild Award and an Allied Craft Award from SFTA who also honoured Colin Blakely.

This must have pleased Potter who had spotted the actor as Brother Martin in *Saint Joan*: 'He had a marvellous pent-up hatred . . . It was the pent-up quality that I wanted.'[17] Did he cast the actress who played Ruth? A year before he had sent her a love-letter in print: 'Wendy Allnutt is paralysingly beautiful, with huge, dark eyes which suddenly flood with warmth or freeze into an icy indifference. She can also act, an accomplishment which is not entirely irrelevant.'[18]

Robin Midgley, director of the Phoenix Theatre in Leicester, contacted Potter with the suggestion that the play might have a stage life. Potter must have gone to work with a will for the result was on the stage after six months and later had a London run at the Roundhouse.* Frank Finlay played Christ, the first stage assumption since the end of censorship by the Lord Chamberlain. Joseph O'Conor, who was Pilate, found it 'very rewarding. It's a beautiful play, I think. Dennis came up for it and he was extremely *simpatico* with the performers. He thought of himself as a performer.'[19]

Soon after *Son of Man*, Potter had a new commission from a BBC producer he had not worked with before, Mark Shivas. The project was a 90-minute BBC2 special; its title was *The Last Nazi* and its subject the incarceration of Rudolf Hess in Spandau prison. Whether the script was delivered and rejected or never delivered goes unrecorded in the BBC Written Archive which is not accessible after the turn of the 1970s.

Where *Son of Man* looks forward spiritually, Potter's next play, *Lay Down Your Arms*, looks back emotionally. Its main setting is the War Office a little after the period when Potter himself reported there as a language clerk on the Russian course, which is the fate of Private Bob Hawk (Nikolas Simmonds). The laid-back officers in mufti kill the time slowly as with the heavily drawn out 'willy' joke of wastrel-in-chief Major Hisscock (Peter Cellier). But the work is earnest: 'You might say we are the eyes, ears and nose of our country,' says Lieutenant Colonel Bateman (Leonard Trolley).[20]

Major Wilson (John Warner) tests Hawk's Russian and finds it accomplished: 'Why are you still a Private?' Hawk is grammar school, Oxford, son of a Yorkshire coal-miner. 'Speak Russian, does he?' sneers Wilson. Hawk thinks of his father (Joby Blanshard), volatile, reactionary, mocking the boy for reading Lenin. Haunted by taunts from the office – 'What do you do, play with yourself?' – Hawk goes to see a production of Chekhov's *The Seagull* ('lifeless, bitter and gloomy' is a remarked line) but is all too aware of the couples in the audience. Walking through Soho, he is offered a 'nice time' by a tart (Renny Lister) and goes with her for thirty shillings. Her mocking voice and his father's – 'You've never been underground, deep down' – resound in his head as he sits at his desk.

Back home, Hawk is quizzed by his mother (Julia Jones) about his London life. He dresses it up but she knows he is lying. When he returns, the Suez balloon goes up, allowing the officers to revel in their xenophobic narrowness.

---

* The most striking aspect of the event was that we did not applaud but filed out in silence.

In a pub Hawk gradually convinces a group of football loudmouths that he is the Russian national goalkeeper, an act only spoiled through the appearance and unwitting betrayal by his old friend Pete (Michael Cashman). Sporting a black eye at the office, Hawk recklessly tries to get at his colleagues with an oblique fancy. Pete despairs of Hawk's fantasising; the latter is gauche with Pete's girl Pat (Therese McMurray). Madly, Hawk determines to steal a classified document to show Pete how 'important' he is at the War Office.

Working on intercepted mail, he is moved by a Russian soldier's thoughts about breaking with his father. He speaks out of turn and is disciplined for gross insubordination. He has a tiny triumph in that he leaves Corporal May (George Layton) smiling. When Pete doesn't show up, Hawk dumps the purloined document in the lake.

Lay Down Your Arms is one of Potter's plays that delivers less than it seems, touching momentous events without illuminating them (as well as the unexplored issue of Suez, there are some self-conscious references to Kim Philby about whom he may already have decided to write at length) and presenting the officer class in what now looks a stereotyped and somewhat demeaning way. He may have deplored the 'agenda' drama of a Trevor Griffiths or a David Edgar but at least those writers allow their class and other enemies a degree of stature as individuals and integrity within their belief systems, however misguided. The silly and mindlessly racist toffs here come from the pen of the *TW3* sketch-writer, the caricaturist.

The central theme – or the most heartfelt material in the play – is Hawk's sexual isolation. In any other writer's work, the prevarication by Hawk would provoke questions about repressed or secretive homosexuality. No suggestion of the kind arises here. The beginning and end of it seems to be the agony of spermy youth, muzzled and misemployed.

Christopher Morahan, who directed *Lay Down Your Arms* with great sympathy and delicacy for Ken Trodd's Kestrel quota at LWT, fondly recalls 'that lovely sequence where he falls deeply in love with the girl playing Nina in *The Seagull*. It's to do with growing up and that marvellous romanticism you have at eighteen or nineteen. Hawk's feelings also had to do with studying Russian. Some of those National Servicemen who undertook the Russian course went on to do great things with the language, like Michael Frayn's Chekhov adaptations.

'I was particularly pleased with the performances in the War Office. They did it with great truth and a dry deadpan sense of humour, no overstating of the case. Of course people like John Warner and Peter Cellier were nearly the generation they were playing. We'd all done National Service. Those characters were part of our direct experience, just slightly exaggerated but affectionately. It needed to be accurate. A younger generation's reference is to other performances.

'Taken within the whole canon, it isn't a significant piece. I'd call it autobiographically informed by a fair irony about the middle class. I find it very pleasing. But it isn't a *painful* piece, apart from the pain of being nineteen.'

Almost everything in the play would be reworked twenty-three years later in *Lipstick on Your Collar*. 'I had a slight sense of *déjà vu*,' says Morahan with a deft *soupçon* of barb, 'notwithstanding the vigour of the songs which were terrific fun. But he took the sexual anguish much further with the bewildering lust for the girl upstairs and so forth. It became rather mannered. It moved into a different world, more like [something made by] Francis Ford Coppola's Zoetrope [company]. I couldn't make up my mind if that street was real or "made".'[21]

Looking at the play now, it is hard to imagine it giving much in the way of offence or causing misgivings at London Weekend but the papers always found something succulent in the prospect of a new Potter. The *Daily Sketch* reported the company sending their star writer a letter: 'We really don't think we can include the word "******!" but, if you have no objection, we would be prepared to replace it with a "*-*-*!"' Potter is quoted as saying: 'I suppose it's quite possible that some viewers will be upset. But, if they are, they ought to be upset by the British Army for I'm merely presenting a diluted version of life as I found it during my National Service.'[22]

The sort of viewers who got upset wrote to the *Sunday Telegraph*: 'I suspect that I speak for most ordinary non-intellectuals who resent having such muck served to us as family entertainment. With seven years' Army service and twenty years with a rugger club, I don't regard myself as particularly prudish!' thundered J. Temple-Griffiths of Coldwaltham, Sussex.[23] If it was merely 'muck' that Potter dumped on Whitehall (and the play did contain a telling post-Trooping the Colour shot of a man shovelling up horse-shit), how much more unpalatable that he was about to begin depositing it right into the suburban viewer's living-room.

15

Who's That Knockin' at My Door?

'Home is the girl's prison and the woman's workhouse.'
Bernard Shaw[1]

At the end of 1969, Potter delivered instead of *Condescension* a very different work. It is the first of the three plays primarily embraced by the sobriquet 'visitation plays' and although they are spread across six years I shall consider them as a group.

Angels Are So Few has, as a superscription, verse ii of chapter 13 of Paul's Epistle to the Hebrews* 'Be not forgetful to entertain strangers: / For thereby some have entertained angels unawares.'[2] Michael Biddle (Tom Bell) is 'marching up to Zion' in his sandals through a wilderness of suburbia. When he offers a dead leaf ('God made it') to a postman (Godfrey James) and proclaims himself an angel, the latter speeds away in his van, turning it over and killing himself. Michael observes bitterly: 'The dog has turned to his own vomit again.'†

Cynthia Nicholls (Christine Hargreaves) is a housewife oppressed by everything, including her small son. Together they are transfixed by a macabre fairy story read on television. Michael presses the doorbell. 'I have come to tell you a beautiful thing,' he announces. He is insinuating and confuses her by weaving the sexual with the religious. As it is cold and 'seeing as you're not selling anything', she weakens and admits him. He taps into conventional childhood memories: 'There's more in your head than you'd get in a million books'. When he tells her that he is an angel, her abrupt laugh freezes. He grows menacing, has an image of her across a bed, in abandon or

---

* Oddly it is given in the caption as Hebrews 13:i.
† 'As a dog returneth to his vomit, so a fool returneth to his folly', Proverbs 26:xi.

perhaps dead. 'Are you lost in this prison of a kitchen?' he asks, before leaving with the promise/threat to return. He becomes exultant in the street to the 'Hallelujah Chorus'.

That evening, Cynthia and her husband Richard (Barry Cookson) are transfixed by a sublimely stolid telereport on the porn industry. When the presenter (Kenneth Ives) interviews a Danish 'girl' (Denise Buckley) who hymns sexual licence, Richard is apoplectic ('bloody little slut!') and snaps the set off. 'A straightforward incitement to perversion and immorality,' he calls it. Cynthia feels resentful and patronised – 'You don't know why I get het-up about *anything*' – and hits him with a litany of housewifery. She works up to a fine climax: 'If the milkman didn't have dirty teeth and a wart on the side of his nose, I'd let him screw me rigid.' He stomps up to bed, an ashtray flung after him.

Switching back on, Cynthia catches the *Epilogue* clergyman (John Glyn Jones) pontificating about angels: 'They are the messengers of God . . . they were also sent to warn of death'. Richard comes down in his khaki pajamas and she is contrite.

Next day, Michael is at the home of an old couple, the Cawsers, he (Erik Chitty) amused, she (Susan Richards) warm about angels: 'she's Welsh, you see,' he explains. When she tells him about a remembered Victorian picture of an angel, Michael reckons it would be 'my mate, Freddie'. Mrs Cawser protests that it was 'a lady angel' and he's mortified: 'You mean, with *tits?*' His outpouring of horror about sex disturbs the couple and Mr Cawser tells him to leave. Michael turns nasty, precipitating the old boy's collapse and death.

Ecstatic, Michael runs back to Cynthia's letter-box. She sees him and, in her housecoat and with her son at his gran's, she has the devil in her. So he is soon in the kitchen expounding hobgoblins. There is an undertone to the notion of spirits 'invading you' as the power-balance shifts towards what she wants, which is what he dreads. He follows her fearfully upstairs, ostensibly to get socks for his cold feet. 'And I'd like you to show me your wings,' she says.

As he perches terrified on the unmade bed, Cynthia takes off his sandals and caresses his feet. Reverting to a disturbed boy, Michael strips to show his wings. She strokes his (bare) back, holds him as he weeps and takes him to bed ('I need a *real* angel'). It's quickly over and he dresses, abusing her: 'Dirty bitch . . . Satan's harlot'. She tells him to fly away, he throws open the window but he cannot jump: 'Got no wings'. She watches him run down the street but he soon perks up again and strides forward purposefully to Al Bowlly singing 'I'll String Along with You'.

Schmoedipus bears no superscription although if it did it would surely be the allegedly time-honoured Yiddish joke, 'Oedipus Schmoedipus, what does it matter as long as a boy loves his mother?', which gives Potter his title. The play begins with an electric train set, operated by middle-aged Tom Carter (John Carson). His wife Elizabeth (Anna Cropper) mocks him ('chuff chuff') over the breakfast table and asks, with some edge: 'Are you building a new layout upstairs?'[3] He goes to work and she looks in the mirror: 'Tick-tock'.

Warned by her friend Dorothy (Carol Macready), Elizabeth sees a young man (Tim Curry) watching outside. He rings the doorbell. She is disturbed to find he knows a lot about her – indeed, he claims to be 'your baby boy, Momma dear', the issue of her teenage pregnancy. She is suffused with emotions.

In a cab, Tom's colleague Ronnie (John Horsley) lusts after a woman glimpsed on Blackfriars Bridge: 'All in the mind, Ronnie' – 'Can't say it's anywhere else, worse luck.' Both sublimate sexuality in model trains.

Elizabeth is remembering her teenaged self as 'a very frightened little creature in a bottle-green gymslip with an overbearing father, a dimwit mother and a cow of a headmistress'. Glen – whom she would have called Adrian – is well ensconced. He says his foster-parents in Canada died in a fire and allows an innuendo that he was responsible. He mocks Elizabeth's style: 'At school in geography, they told me the Pennines were the backbone of England. They didn't say anything about ladies with sherry and ding-dong doorbells.'

Tom works in food processing, a field evidently dedicated to regimenting natural things and bombarding them with chemicals. Younger and coarser than him, Tom's boss Blake (Bob Hoskins) disadvantages him and he is unguardedly caustic. In the corridor he bucks himself up by imitating a train. Elizabeth is now loosened by sherry. Glen dips in and out of infantilism: 'Most grown-ups try to recapture their childhoods one way or another'. She accuses him of playing games. In the pub, Tom and Ronnie grow misty about boyhood. 'You can't expect wives to understand these things, can you,' says Tom. Ronnie notes that men recreate childhood much more than women.

By now Glen has found the train set and delights in crashing the trains. Elizabeth distracts him into serenading her with the ineffable vaudeville number 'M-O-T-H-E-R'. He leaves her transported. She comes to, throws up in the kitchen sink, summons Dorothy, hears a baby's cries while she waits. We see the destroyed train set. Elizabeth pours out to Dorothy how she fell to the dodgems man to the tune of 'When the Red Red Robin'.

When Tom returns from work Elizabeth seems to be confessing that she smothered Adrian at two days old. He is only concerned about his train set and rushes upstairs. He returns to chide her: everything's fine. It seems to be an old routine and he starts to play at being her baby which gives Dorothy the creeps. 'You really must not involve other people,' he scolds when she has gone. Elizabeth warns: 'He's bound to come back.' Then he becomes the overbearing father and she the naughty child. Alone, she is a picture of contentment.

Brimstone and Treacle has two superscriptions: 'There resides infinitely more good in the demonic man than in the trivial man' (Kierkegaard) and 'A spoonful of sugar helps the medicine go down' (Andrews*). Martin Taylor (Michael Kitchen) deliberately collides with a businessman in the street and tries unsuccessfully to engage him. He fares better with his second victim, Mr Bates (Denholm Elliott), who embarrassedly plays along with the notion that they have met before and inadvertently discloses a deal of information about his home, including that his daughter Pattie is 'just a vegetable'[4] after a car accident glimpsed in flashback. By faking a collapse, Martin gets hold of Bates's wallet so that when Bates, pretending to fetch the car, makes good his escape, Martin can still trace him.

With involuntary gurgles from Pattie (Michelle Newell) as chorus, Bates and his wife (Patricia Lawrence) worry away at their circumstances. She, a sunny stoic tied to the house, still clings to hope of Pattie's gradual recovery. He, a sour fatalist out in a world he loathes, scorns such hope: 'There is no god and there are no miracles'. His shame and guilt does get to her: 'All I know is we need something or someone to save us or I shall . . .' and the doorbell interrupts.

Martin is all pious concern over Pattie and quotes Bishop Henry King's poem 'The Exequy' (a great favourite of Potter's). Mrs Bates is very moved and Martin plays her emotion against Bates's preoccupation with his wallet returned by the 'innocent' visitor but shy £40. Martin presents the perfect guest: 'I love housework . . . such a peaceful act.' Claiming he had hoped to marry Pattie before her accident (which a supposed long trip to the US in an attempt to forget her prevented him from discovering), Martin now proposes to dedicate himself to her service. 'You could be . . . the devil himself for all we know,' protests Bates but he is easily circumvented by the obvious need to relieve his wife's regime of care. 'We live in the shadows, Mr Taylor, and we can see no light.' It's settled. Mrs Bates finds herself called 'Mumsy' and Martin gets to sleep in Pattie's former

---

* Presumably the attribution to 'Andrews' (i.e. Julie) is thought to work better as a joke, but it is a bizarre kind of joke for a writer to make, like crediting 'Good timber, this' to 'Blakely'. The correct attribution is Sherman, as in Richard M. and Robert B. Sherman who wrote the score for the film musical *Mary Poppins* from which the quotation comes.

room preserved like a shrine with its Mick Jagger pin-up in devil mode. To 'That Old Black Magic', he explores, particularly taken with her bra. A diabolic dream takes in the car accident.

In the morning, with Bates gone to work, Martin talks Mrs Bates into going out for a shampoo and set ('Don't dilly-dally now, duckie'). Alone with Pattie, he feeds her, whirls her around and then makes love to/rapes her. On her return, Mrs Bates notes 'a light in her eyes'. They talk of prayer and he agrees to instruct her. The prayers are a mixture of satanic invocation and rabble-rousing evangelism with a touch of *Carmina Burana* but Mrs Bates seems pleased enough and her emotion breaks in tears.

Bates is reluctantly appreciative of Martin's cooking but disturbed at the implications of him caring for Pattie: 'Her brain may be damaged but her body is that of an attractive young woman'. He is caught on the horns of a dilemma, his justifiable suspicions easily characterised as churlishness. Mention of Pattie's friend who played a prostitute in the amateur dramatics – 'a tall, dark girl,' Mrs Bates recalls, 'with lovely white teeth' – causes Bates ill-disguised anguish. 'She was a slut. You just take my word for it,' he blurts out. He turns his guilt on his wife, absurdly accusing her of 'killing' Pattie.

Martin smoothes things over ('It's difficult to be a father nowadays') and draws out Bates's pet hates – black people, decimalisation, fluoridisation – testing the logic of his National Front support. Bates is crestfallen: 'I simply want the world to stop where it is, and go back a bit'.

That night, Martin revisits Pattie: 'I reckon you enjoy this as much as I do, you greedy little girl'. This time she screams. The Bateses run down in time to see Martin slip out of the front door. Pattie sits up: 'What happened, Daddy?' A fast flashback sequence shows her running from her father's adultery with her friend into the path of a car. Fleeing down the road, Martin bumps into a man. And it begins again . . .

Though they have become bracketed, the points of divergence between these plays are more notable than their similarities: the suburban setting, the power of memory and visitation itself.

Even though it is Michael in *Angels* who observes, 'Memory, memory, memory, now that's an unearthly thing if you like', this play is the least concerned with it. Both Tom Carter in *Schmoedipus* and Mr Bates in *Brimstone* dwell on the past, the former surrounding himself with its emblems, the latter longing for his memory's version of it. Potter wrote and talked about his own past increasingly and, as he did so, considered the powerful ambiguity of how we process what has gone. 'Memory is always a great problem for the dramatist,' he had suggested in 1968. 'We carry it around with us as a raw, insistent, perpetually challenging burden. But to translate it into dramatic terms on the television screen one needs more than an off-screen voice, a dissonant chord of music or a dip in the lighting.'[5]

Potter spoke in 1980 of the way we try to relate to our own childhoods: 'By that usual process in England of accident and examination, you journey from it before you are old enough really to understand it and therefore a large part of your adult life is inevitably tinged with that dead emotion which is nostalgia.' There were more 'valuable' emotions: 'a genuine regret that you cannot actually be part of it and a genuine relief that you're not part of it'.[6]

Nostalgia was to be rooted out: 'Viewers are by now quite prepared to find themselves awash in the middle of an old tune or paddling about between the soggy banks of yesterday's carefully gathered future. Nostalgia has left more than a grubby little tidemark along our embattled shores, for now it runs free in the broken gutters, overflows the cracked drains and gurgles up in a choking swirl as high as the open mouth.'[7]

It was the revisionism of nostalgia that Potter deplored. Both Carter and Bates illustrate his view that 'we constantly rewrite our past to fit the moods or prejudices or even the hopes of our present'.[8] Childhood recreated as infantilism is the very stuff of *Schmoedipus*, so that Glen comes to stand for both Elizabeth's and Tom's lost childhoods and – a separate issue – lost innocence. The two later plays sharply identify infantilism with sexuality. In *Schmoedipus*, the preoccupation with toys that seems to be a sexual turn-off at the outset has become game-playing as an integral part of sex by the end. The scenes between Glen and Elizabeth are highly charged erotically, a sense made explicit by a kiss that moves towards seduction and resolves as affection. In *Brimstone*, Martin plays the adopted son with Mrs Bates and uses baby-talk to seduce her chastely and Pattie wantonly.

Glen and Martin are very different intruders but each has an intended appeal for the audience while Michael has none. They momentarily address the camera, which Michael never does, and they are depicted as roguish, seductive and clever. Michael is inescapably strange, held at arm's length. Martin and Michael both have supernatural powers. In a simple convention, they can make the lighting change at will. But Michael is not presented consistently and, in that sense, *Angels* is a failed piece because it is not so much ambiguous as unclear. Martin, a much more successful character, is specifically a demon – we see his alien feet – and always able to manipulate. This is a great deal of what makes *Brimstone* a comedy.

But Mrs Bates is also an inconsistent character. It is rather as though

Potter wanted to make her merely a simple-minded lump, a happy pig to set beside her husband's unhappy Socrates, then thought better of it and gave her a few lines ('I feel as though I were scraping my nails on the lid . . . of my coffin') more characteristic of her husband.

By contrast the housewives are the central figures of the first two plays and Elizabeth Carter may be the most complex woman Potter ever created. *Schmoedipus* works so well – it is certainly the best of the three, perfectly poised equidistantly between Pinter and Orton – because, although the perspective may change and the ground remain uncertain, the fantasy (if such it is) is always, and clearly, Elizabeth's. There is no extraneous supernatural mischief in this play so that, with one unnerving exception, you can at least believe your *eyes* even while the reliability of appearance is in question. (The exception is the pan across the wrecked train set which, if we are to believe Tom, must be something *we* imagined or – a tricky concept this – something in the imagination of Elizabeth who is not in the room; the alternative reading is that Tom accepts Elizabeth's destruction of his hobby as part of their sex-play but this undermines far too thoroughly his previous behaviour.)

What is not in doubt about *Schmoedipus* and *Brimstone* is that they are comedies as outrageous and black as the English uniquely know how to write. Only a writer with Potter's confidence would dare to orchestrate the incoherent noises of a brain-damaged character as a running commentary on the action.* Each play allows the intruder to do a turn, Martin performing his pious/pagan prayers (one of Potter's more wicked jokes), Glen giving his sentimental song. For this, Tim Curry slips into Jolson's tones as a kitschy arrangement sneaks in under the piano but the triumph is by director Barry Davis who shows fine judgement in resisting the manifest temptation to overstate it. The set piece stays within bounds, still believably the daydream of a suburban housewife.

No such high comedy graces *Angels*, only the parenthetical satire of the television programmes watched by Cynthia and Richard Nicholls.† Maybe director Gareth Davies could have made it funnier although this would have required a playing against the lines that does not arise in the other plays. 'There was no violent split,' he says, 'but this is where Dennis and I began to come adrift. *Angels* was associated with another play called *Only Make Believe* and I felt the two together made one good play, a stronger and much more dense piece, and I still

---

* 'Ts ka ka kh yop . . . Yamyamyamyamyap ooo . . . Cock! . . . Deeeeeiseeeee! . . . Yap eee yop' are among the observations carefully prescribed for Pattie in the published stage text.[9]'
† Though *Angels Are So Few*, made for the first season of Play for Today, was Potter's first work in colour, the Nichollses' viewing is in monochrome.

maintain that. Dennis said I hadn't done it well and I think he was right because I didn't know *how* to do it well. I didn't find myself believing in it. That was my fault.' I told him it is the only pre-1980s Potter play never repeated. He laughed. 'Quite right.'[10]

Potter told *Radio Times* that the play 'isn't just some sort of ha-ha comedy illusion. The man sincerely believes he is an angel and this fantasy is the total justification for his behaviour and his being . . . In a sense the play is about the way we manipulate our fantasies to protect ourselves and what happens to us when they are ripped away. A lot of people do have their wings pulled off in life, after all.'[11]

It was Potter's own illusion to anticipate being discounted as a comedy, at least by the godfearing burghers of Strathclyde:

Bishopbriggs Town Council last night agreed that Mr James Proctor, the Provost, should write to 'the highest possible authority' complaining about the standard of BBC television programmes in general and Thursday night's play *Angels Are So Few* by Dennis Potter in particular. At the meeting, Mr Proctor said, "I am a fairly broad-minded person and we in Bishopbriggs are building a good, clean, honest borough but last Thursday night a play about "Angels", which was splashed into people's living-rooms, must have shocked many people.'[12]

It was the ninth and last 'splash' of Potter's that Gareth Davies directed. The writer would never again benefit from such continuity, though *Schmoedipus* and *Brimstone* were among three directed by the late Barry Davis. '*Brimstone and Treacle* I thought was very good,' says Davies. 'That seems to me to be an intellectual exercise. There's no danger of stirring up primeval emotions in people.' But *Brimstone* was the cause of the most public dispute in Potter's career, a row which will be considered in a later chapter.

We Open in Venice

'Whose memories are these?'
Hide and Seek[1]

The next three works to appear all drew on real lives, though only the third did so formally. The first, *Paper Roses*, was written for Ken Trodd and put into production through Granada, Potter's only experience with the Manchester-based company.

Like his previous ITV play, this delved back into Potter's young manhood (he was now thirty-six). Its setting is a Fleet Street newspaper office unmistakably based on that of the *Daily Herald* and its informal source was a *Herald* veteran called Maurice Fagence. 'He was a great reporter,' says Potter's old friend on the paper, David Nathan. 'He covered the Israeli War of Independence in 1948 and allegedly brought back an Israeli girl as a kind of helpmeet. Then suddenly there was a change of regime and this fine old reporter, who'd risked his life for the paper, was being sent out on rubbishy jobs, the kind of stuff he wouldn't have done in forty years, doorstepping.'[2]

The play is subtitled *A Tabloid Story*. In fact the *Herald* was never a tabloid but, had it survived, it would undoubtedly have become one, like every other down- and mid-market paper. The Fagence character is named Clarence Hubbard, conveniently allowing fellow hacks to dismiss him as 'Old Mother' and Potter to echo a situation from the nursery rhyme. Hubbard (Bill Maynard) is not taking his humiliation at all heroically, rather driving the others (Desmond Perry, William Simons) mad with maunderings about the years when he 'always used to be out on a job'.[3]

The slow day is intercut with snatches of home life (wherein he vents his frustration on his wife), and of the younger Hubbard phoning in trivial stories with great relish. Editor Joe (John Carson) intends to pension Hubbard off even though he recognises the man's record. He and Chart (Donald Gee), one of the younger hacks who have to listen to the old josser, share a leer at Joe's secretary. Back home, Hubbard has locked his wife (Aimee Delamain) in the understairs cupboard.

Hubbard has all his cuttings dug out from the library. He and the messenger (Joe Gladwin) are like old soldiers drawn together by reminiscence. Meanwhile, his wife is found unconscious. Recovered, she loyally tells the brutally casual police that she locked herself in the cupboard.

To Hubbard's outrage, Joe offers him horoscope duty. He expresses his displeasure by giving Chart a Thesaurus-worth of synonyms for the word 'erosion'. Then he tosses all his cuttings from a high window. Finally, he lays into the broken lift, then plunges down the lift shaft.

Paper Roses has many echoes. The office scenes are much like – though somewhat sourer than – those in Michael Frayn's definitive Fleet Street novel of four years earlier, *Towards the End of the Morning*. Hubbard's mysterious and emblematic use of the word 'roses' evokes the 'rosebud' of another bloated old newspaperman, Citizen Kane. The 'old campaign' encounter between Hubbard and feisty little Joe Gladwin's messenger is like Falstaff with Justice Shallow. There is something of Archie Rice in Hubbard too, suggesting the tones and concerns that Potter's writing frequently shares with that of John Osborne.

The presentation of the scenes brings in another school of drama altogether: it is positively Brechtian. Apart from bursts of pointedly chosen popular song, the characters are introduced with tabloidese pen-portraits over freeze-frames, the action is punctuated by trios of wry headlines and the whole proceedings are being viewed on a television set by the paper's tetchily wool-gathering television critic (Dudley Jones, mischievously got up to bear more than a passing resemblance to the *Herald*'s Phil Diack), who needless to say gives the play the thumbs-down at the end.

We do not need to feel pre-empted by Potter: his critic's review is not far off the mark: while the play has much to divert in its trappings and its central performance and Barry Davis's lively direction, it is not worth much more than a 'basement par' on an inside page.

Ken Trodd recalls that 'when Dennis delivered *Paper Roses* to me, I was outraged because it didn't seem to be an all-out attack on tabloid journalists. It seemed just to be dealing with this old boy. And yet of course it was, in its way. It was acclaimed by all the ex-tabloid journalists I knew, like those at *World in Action*, as totally accurate and devastating but it didn't approach it in that way and he never did overtly attack public themes again. Part of that was a sort of revolt against Loachery and filming in the streets.'⁴

The men of the fourth estate also appear in the next BBC play, *Traitor*, but this is a weightier affair altogether. It portrays a man who 'had to turn my back on all that I had been brought up to love'. It is about Kim Philby. In the course of his extended interview with Graham Fuller in *Potter on Potter*, the playwright is more instructive on this play and its later companion, *Blade on the Feather*, than about any other. 'I was exploring the long, deep rhythm of an English native,' he says. 'What interested me was the misstatement that someone could politically betray their country and be presumed not to love it . . . Strip away things like nationalism and militarism and Empire . . . and you're still left with a considerable body of *something* to which, not uncritically, God forbid, you emotionally respond, in the same way as you acknowledge your own parents.'⁵

Adrian Harris (John Le Mesurier) restlessly awaits the world's press in his Moscow flat. His head buzzes with his childhood and the obsessional interest of his father Sir Arthur (Lyndon Brook) in Camelot and the king for whom he is named. Sir Arthur reads to the boy Adrian (Sean Maddox) from Tennyson's *Idylls of the King*. He bends the ear of a house-guest: 'At England's hour of need, he will return.'⁶

'Clubs on the left, brothels on the right, Kremlin in the middle,' observes Simpson (Vincent Ball) as his colleagues gaze across Moscow while toiling up the stairs of Harris's block of flats. Harris welcomes them sardonically: 'the gentlemen of the press – the curious appellation you even more curiously prefer'. He immediately wants to know where James (Jack Hedley), their smooth spokesman, went to school. The 'gentlemen' take his lofty scorn of the capitalist press with fair grace.

From Eton and Oxford to 'this rather sparse little room', James wonders if he can be happy. Harris declines to be judged by a materialist measure and gets stuck into the scotch. He compares them to Blake's 'invisible worm' and begins to describe the country against which he rebelled, 'all the festering hypocrisies of English ruling families'.

In his mind, he is back at prep school, being shamed by his Hazlitt-quoting schoolmaster (John Saunders) for his supposed inferiority to his father and for stuttering over Blake. With a wild indecency, he takes reckless revenge and has his face slapped. The slap triggers images of the poverty of the thirties set to Blake's *Jerusalem*. His mother, Lady Emma (Diana Fairfax), worries about his unhappiness away at school. Sir Arthur is more concerned about the effect of the General Strike on his archaeological dig: 'Life today's been reduced to a question of pounds, shillings and pence. Nobody seems to lift up their heads any more, no pride, no vision, no sense of magic.' He does not lift his head to the opulence around him.

James bandies words with Harris about Stalin. 'Once and for all, I am what I am and I did what I did because of what I believe,' Harris cries, scorning James as a Wykehamist on a tabloid. Cameraman Thomas (Jon Laurimore) sneaks a shot of him taking a drink – 'no pictures' had been agreed – and Harris sees a flash of an assassination. To the suggestion that his portrait be captioned 'The Traitor', Harris responds with a long panegyric to 'the England of the watermill and the cricket field . . . I always stutter when I get pretentious'.

The atmosphere deteriorates when thrusts over Vietnam and Czechoslovakia are exchanged with the American, Blake* (Neil McCallum): 'I haven't got your sort of conscience,' Harris slurs, 'the dribbling, snivelling kind.' Slithering to the floor, he relives the events leading up to the previously subliminal hit: languid discussion with his FO colleague Craig (John Quentin) – 'My God, Adrian, talk about pennies from heaven', 'Roubles, at any rate' – and a clear sense that Harris has an asylum-seeker taken out by a hit man to protect his own cover.

Falling down drunk, Harris stumbles over the lines from Blake that had defeated him as a child and James teases out the memory of thirties poverty. The set-up to the journalists' arrival is re-run with a significant addition: while they are climbing the stairs, Harris locates a bugging device in the flat. As he greets them, he tells himself: 'For God's sake, remember the microphone.'

This fascinating play embodies Potter's ambiguities about his heritage in the widest sense, the educational, socio-political and literary traditions of England. Class betrayal was much in his thoughts for, like so many instinctively left-leaning but 'upwardly-mobile' parents, the Potters had felt the need to bite the educational bullet and, with a great show of squirming, enrol their children in private schools ('I feel both anger and shame';[7] it 'makes them feel a bit guilty'[8]).

The Oxford élite he had despised or affected to disdain had begun to look less alien: 'There are those who hate Oxford because they never went there, and those who loathe it because they did,' he wrote in the context of the Queen's Silver Jubilee. 'When I came down eighteen years ago I was decidedly in the latter category, but time has mellowed my feelings into something more ambivalent.'[9] Later, when his children did not follow him to college, he was cast

* No connection with the poet appears to be intended by naming the character so. We must conclude that Potter was inattentive.

down: 'Even though I'd been publicly despising, I wanted that for them. Every parent starts wanting something for their offspring. It amounts to impressing other people.'[10]

The love of English literature glows strong in *Traitor* as it informs several plays. Of Tennyson, Potter said: 'To us perhaps it is the quality of the doubt which catches hold.'[11] The remark derives from another BBC Radio invitation Potter was to accept with great pleasure six years later, the presentation of favourite extracts in *With Great Pleasure*. His selection embraces Chekhov and Chandler, Crompton and Eliot, Grossmith and Grimm, Newbolt and *The Exequy* and, of course, the Bible and Hazlitt, but, forever fugitive, he quotes Ruskin's 'Tell me what you like and I'll tell you what you are' only to refute it: 'Sometimes I want the printed word to console me, sometimes to amuse, or challenge or even frighten me – so many demands – and then, of course, there are occasions when I get pleasure from the succulent adjectives on the side of a sauce bottle . . . No, you cannot diagnose me by what I have read and liked, only by what I have read and forgotten, or even by what I have read and then eaten.'[12]

In *Traitor* Potter crucially distinguishes between Adrian's overt stumble over the challenge of Blake and Sir Arthur's complacent embrace of Camelot, couched in terms that might just as well be a yearning for the return of Oswald Mosley. His revolt against that Avalonian mistiness drove Harris into the oblivion of another equally pious dream, that of unreconstructed Communism. *Radio Times* quoted Potter: 'It takes a kind of courage but the final treachery is to hold on to an ideal which has been proved invalid. It may be brave, but it is still treachery. You have to be clear-eyed. The worst traitors are the dogmatists who think it is weakness to change their minds.'[13] The analysis, as far as it goes, is interesting and so are the accoutrements from Philby's life with which he endows Harris – notably the late alcoholism of a man who in youth barely took a glass – but the character is at heart quite as much a self-portrait. And therein lies the play's mesmerising quality and its astonishing emotional impact.

To Mark Shivas, the producer who had fruitlessly commissioned *The Last Nazi*, went the historic task of producing Potter's first serial; and what a work it is! One of the books sent by *The Times* to Potter for review was a new translation of the *Mémoires* of Giacomo Casanova. The reviewer had barely glanced at the cover before he was putting the tome aside and setting off on his own projection of the life – and especially the interior life – of the proverbial libertine, eighteenth-century Venice's answer to Don Juan. The resulting six-parter is in no sense an adaptation; indeed *Casanova* could claim to be the first original personal drama serial of significance.*

At the outset, an apparently pious Casanova (Frank Finlay) gaily throws off prayerfulness and leaps into bed with the voluptuous Barberina (Christine Noonan). But Messer Grande (Victor Baring) bursts in to charge him with 'impiousness, fraud and fornication'. He is incarcerated with the taunting jailer Lorenzo (Norman Rossington), temporarily sharing his cell with the overbearing, frightened Schalon (Patrick Newell), falling greedily on Virgil when he is allowed books and finally getting out after five years. In prison, memory takes him back over various sexual conquests, told with a certain nod to *Il Decamerone*.

With a country maiden Christina (Zienia Merton) and her cleric uncle (George Benson), Casanova shares a gondola and then a room, flirting through his claimed need for a wife. He is frustrated until morning when the uncle is gone and Christina welcoming. But when she expects his hand he gives her to another and weeps at the wedding.

Staying in Grenoble, Casanova follows his own version of the advice proffered by his sottish friend Valenglart (David Swift), only to seduce the caretaker's daughters (Julia Cornelius, Brigid Erin Bates) and their cousin (Caroline Dowdeswell) 'one at a time',[14] by playing them off against each other.

Back in Italy, he flees from a fracas at the *commedia dell'arte*, but in seeking refuge he causes the collapse of elderly Capitani (Frederick Peisley). With fancy footwork, Casanova is soon perceived as a benefactor to both his host and the man's daughter Genoveffa (Lyn Yeldham). When he tries to dupe them with a cod invocation of magic that takes advantage of her virginity, the elements intervene to the wonder of father and daughter and the terror of Casanova.

He roisters again in Grenoble with Valenglart, spotting the latter's god-daughter Anne (Ania Marson) at a concert. Overcoming her piety, he possesses her by feigning faintness and taking advantage of her concern. Afterwards, he is baffled by her resentment and remorse. We learn that later she becomes the king's mistress.

In England, Casanova imagines that his fellow-traveller Mr Hart (Rossington) is his old jailer. Schalon, met in a coffee-shop, alerts him to English hypocrisy. When he tries to take advantage of a married woman, Pauline (Valerie Gearon), he falters and affects shame – or perhaps it is genuine.

* John Hopkins's ground-breaking four-part serial *Talking to a Stranger* (1966), directed by Christoper Morahan, hardly suits the form's later description as the television novel.

At the end of his life, he is in the employ of a German count as librarian, conducting a running battle with the major-domo, Feldkirchner (Graham Crowden), who accuses him of harassing the cook. Casanova is working on his memoirs and so spends much time in memory. Feldkirchner takes vengeance by destroying some of his notes, then repents. Casanova's health is failing and Dr Rasp (John Ringham) prescribes female company. The patient barters with Caroline (Gillian Hills) over a last favour which she finally grants. The young Casanova blows kisses to the sky.

The sentiment providing the most apt epigraph for *Casanova* is uttered not by the hero but by an unnamed man on a coach: 'Memory, that's what life's for. Building your own little store, eh?' For the serial is a disquisition on imprisonment in all its manifestations and on the fine line between freedom and licence. The body and its appetites are just as incarcerating as the walls of a dungeon. The 'little store' which enables the prisoner either of compulsion or of the state to endure is the stuff of his mind: memory, fantasy, dream, imagination, repentance and so redemption and release. For Potter, more imprisoned than ever by his illness in his Ross-on-Wye fastness, no consideration could be more vital. *Casanova* is at the heart of his work, a pivotal piece.

Early in the first episode, the conditions of his incarceration are dwelt upon, both for their value (lighting and sound in both location shoot and studio recording are of the highest order) and to underline his plight. Casanova comes to recognise his sexual appetite as 'a disease, a fever' and feels the need to 'escape from myself'. In his younger days he is cavalier: 'You are a virtuous maiden, I like that. Please bolt the door'. Even in the late episode in England, his demeanour is at first casually goatish: 'There's not a woman in the place. It's like eggs without salt'. But his easy professions of love, initially a show of skill, begin to require annotation: 'I may not mean it the way other men mean it, but I mean it all the same.' By the time he fervently protests his love for Pauline ('Dear God, I mean it'), his multitudinous declarations have come to haunt him and even he no longer knows what he means or wants.

Seduction scenes are men's fantasies. Those Potter offers – initially not entirely without wish-fulfilment (or luxuriation in their own skill) – are themselves soon deepened to serve a serious purpose. Alongside is a poignant, personal sub-theme on the impediments to Casanova's writing; his contrivance of ink from mulberry juice is very moving.

Potter's Casanova is unique among his driven characters in not being racked by guilt. His sense of being the prisoner of his appetite is accepted with a fatalistic stoicism. He is a man who can pray in seeming earnest only to blow it with a raspberry. Valenglart, who as his candid friend comes nearest to being his conscience, declares: 'You damage people . . . full of sweet words and foul cruelty.' Casanova resents this but only momentarily; he remembers watching from a window a man being hanged, drawn and quartered while a matron in the party was (not very discreetly) taken from behind. The world is as it is.

Production assistant on *Where the Buffalo Roam*, John Glenister was now a director and, having won his spurs on *The Six Wives of Henry VIII* and (most pertinently) *The Canterbury Tales*, he was offered episodes one, two and four of *Casanova* (Mark Cullingham handled the rest). 'I saw the original script as delivered by Dennis,' he says, 'and the thing that gob-smacked me was that it was all written out in his extraordinary copperplate hand. The other thing that struck me was the immense amount of direction detail in the text. I was fairly green then and I didn't take offence which I would now because the director doesn't want to be led by the writer.

'But I realised that he was having almost to storyboard it because he wasn't going to be able to come on location and discuss it with the crew. At first, we sat with the cast and read the scripts for three or four days and we'd find speeches that were difficult or didn't seem to work and, as Dennis was too ill to be contacted, we had to play around with them but we found we could never do anything that worked better. Once you had confidence in it, you realised it was a watertight script, that he'd thought it through deeper and further than you ever could on your shooting schedule.

'He'd also worked out as a theme running right through the use of Vivaldi's *Four Seasons*, nothing like as well-known a piece as it is now. He'd actually picked out every phrase. He'd choreographed the whole play. And we absolutely abided by it because he was right.

'The structure was something we had never encountered before. Casanova's life is told in a linear way but with his past always informing his future so, although it goes from A to Z, as you get to M, so B, C and D are beginning to push behind. In many ways, his use of different time-scales has been the hallmark of his work, I think. Casanova never goes back into his past, the past comes up to him.'[15]

Sadly the BBC decided that, for repeat and especially for export purposes, six 55-minute episodes were not commercial so it was recut into two parts of 96 and 99 minutes respectively. The two-parter begins with Casanova in old age, then fans out in an entirely unchronological way. The largest single sacrifice is the greater part of the material detailing the jail years so that Lorenzo, originally billed second, becomes little more than a cameo. Potter restructured the scripts as a guide to the re-edit and, although the form is imposed rather than organic, he must have learned from the process for thereafter he moved increasingly towards a freer structure in his work.

Both the directors had an initial shoot in and near Venice (a medieval town sixty miles away standing in for Grenoble) before recording most of the story in the studio. 'Dennis had never seen Venice,' says Glenister, 'he'd never been out of England, so his whole sense of it was based on Canaletto and Guardi. I realised when I got there that Canaletto and Guardi had been dead a long time. We had enormous problems working round the modernisations. But we also found Casanova is still a dirty name there. He's no son of Venice, they want to disown him. In the end we changed the slateboard to *Canova* and said we were making a documentary about the sculptor.'

Pious Venetians may disown Casanova but Potter's intent, could they perceive it, might reassure them. Interviewing him for the 'God slot' programme, *Anno Domini*, in 1977, Colin Morris unguardedly called *Son of Man* 'your best-known play'. Potter hotly demurred: 'I would say my best-known play was *Casanova*, and I would say that *Casanova* was more religious than *Son of Man* . . . nothing could be easier than to write a humanistic, I think rather evasive picture . . . of Jesus, in which really many of the central claims were evaded. *Casanova* . . . finishes with his desire to escape from his appetites, from his flesh, from his particular obsessions and compulsions and yet enjoy them to the full, which seems a very human and necessary and perpetual dilemma . . . That is exactly what the God slot does, you see. It makes you look for religion in the obvious places. No critics picked up in *Follow the Yellow Brick Road* that it was essentially and passionately a religious play.'[16] Thus forearmed, we shall consider this play in the next chapter.

Says Who? Says You, Says I!

'Perhaps the most disconcerting thing a character in a
novel can do is to announce that he is indeed a character
in a novel.'

Hide and Seek[1]

By the time of *Casanova*'s transmission, Potter's psoriatic arthropathy
was making further inroads into his joints and in the first half of
1972 he went through a prolonged period of torture. As the medical
correspondent of the *Sunday Times* Oliver Gillie describes it, 'His
spine became affected and he had to lie flat in bed; he could not
move his right arm. His fingers curled inwards towards his palms.
The only way he could continue writing was to convert his hand
into a kind of vice and force a pen into it.'[2]

By Potter's own account, 'The skin closed around my fist. I could
only move my left arm. I was clad in clothes which continually itched.
I had gone into a fever and was suffering from a steroid reaction.
I was under an illusion that there was a cat in the bed and that
it was eating my ankles. I thought "It can't be, you silly bugger"
but I still believed it. I was in such hellish pain that I couldn't
tell which limb was which.'[3] The Methotrexate treatment had been
harsh, its hepatotoxicity requiring him to write off two days each
week to diarrhoea and nausea. On top of topical and intralesional
corticosteroids, tar solution baths, gold injections and ferocious doses
of aspirin, it made for quite a regime.

When his play *Follow the Yellow Brick Road* went out, he was
'in bed at the London Hospital, unable to move much else besides
my left arm and maybe my penis, in an occasional erection which
imperiously seemed to take no account of my collapsed hands, caked

and cracked skin and feverishly swollen joints'.[4] Accordingly, his thoughts turned to mastery of his skills and authorship of his fate. The writer/performer as protagonist came to the fore in a group of works of which *Yellow Brick Road* was the first, the most incisive and the easiest to live with.

Jack Black (Denholm Elliott) is an actor jobbing in advertisements. To psychiatrist Dr Whitman (Richard Vernon), he exhibits paranoia and obsessional neurosis, a hatred of the teleplays he never gets cast in and the 'Trotskyites' who make them: 'They turn gold into hay, these people. Virgins into whores,* love into a sticky slime and Jesus Christ into an imbecile bleeding and screaming meaninglessly on a cross.'[5] He cleaves to a childhood sensation of 'radiance . . . God was too near' but he angrily and unconvincingly denies the deity now, for the only word sent to answer his prayer was 'slime'.

His estranged wife Judy (Billie Whitelaw) collects him from the hospital, endures his abuse and is contrite about her adultery, 'the only time'. It seems that his 'slime' obsession has undermined Jack's sex drive. She concedes that she slept with his agent Colin Sands too. He knocks her down, kicks her, threatens to jump in the Thames and drives the car at her.

By her account, Sands (Bernard Hepton) came on to her strongly while the coast was clear (his 'child bride' Veronica was out of town buying a poodle). Judy was drinking recklessly and soon blabbing about the collapse of sex with Jack and his being '*transfigured* with disgust'. As practised at seduction as at the roasting of a quail that he tossed off while talking, Sands easily bagged her.

Jack calls at Colin's but only finds Veronica (Michele Dotrice) and her puppy. He recalls how 'pure' and 'still' he first found her but is aware that, as with 'love', he uses such words in an 'antique' way. He pours out his heart, confesses he wrote letters to her that he then destroyed. 'All right,' she says. 'We've got an hour.' He is appalled.

Jack is irritated to find Whitman's 'stooge' Dr Bilson (Dennis Waterman) on duty at the surgery. After a fractious interview he accepts the new medication Bilson eagerly advocates. Jack's next job (in reality or imagination) is fronting a presentation of the drug with St Paul's words: 'Whatsoever things are true, whatsoever things are honest, whatsoever things are just . . .'[6]

The play began 'a particular sequence of work and thought which was taking me clear of an in-turned spiritual nihilism and on towards a new and (for me) startling but exhilarating trust in the order of things,' Potter wrote six years later. 'I wanted, half-mockingly . . . to show how

---

* Elliott gives the phrase thus but Potter's text reads 'angels into whores'.

the human dream for *some* concept of "perfection", some Zion or Eden or Golden City, will surface and take hold of whatever circumstances are at hand – no matter how ludicrous.'[7] Some fell on stony ground. It is perhaps surprising that critics missed Potter's religious intent for there is much talk of God, both mocked and revealed, in the play.

At the outset, Jack's discomfort is presented (with a brilliant display by Potter and great skill by director Alan Bridges) as a consciousness of being watched. He is, he perceives, appearing in a play where there is 'not much bloody action, hardly any dialogue at all, just background noises'.

He addresses a woman (Ruth Dunning) in the hospital waiting room as if she were an extra in the continuing drama of his own existence: 'You haven't got many lines. You're not very important.' He shoos away the camera he feels is on him. He is foisted with lines he would sooner not speak: 'Load of old tat. Dirty too. Obscene. I don't want to be in this play.'

Jack is 'in denial', so that whatever he blusters against reveals what he craves. In denying God, he is telling his psychiatrist that his core belief is that God is the author of his lines, of his existence. In a characteristic Potter quibble, Jack's grim grasp on faith is set against Judy being faithless with the shifting Sands.

The ambivalences in Jack and in the play are so very suggestive of Potter's purchase on his particular *milieu*. A parasitical agent also looms over the novel *Hide and Seek**. The *mores* of teledrama producers are again scorned in *Only Make Believe* and depicted in *Double Dare*. Potter bites hard on the hand that helps him.

Clive Goodwin, then managing his interests, was an agent of high profile and influence, rivalled only by the legendary Peggy Ramsay. He embodied everything at that time described (and derided and feared) as 'trendy'. His Cromwell Road flat operated as a media and political salon where he played host to fashionable writers, directors, producers and intellectuals who subscribed to the day's quasi-revolutionary agitations. Trevor Griffiths's *The Party* is based on just such an event.

Potter reserved some of his most splenetic invective for what he observed at Goodwin gatherings. A reception for the French student leader Daniel Cohn-Bendit ('Danny le Rouge') was 'a bit like a benefit concert for clapped-out seaside donkeys' at which

---

* The conjunction of the names 'Goodwin' and 'Sands' can hardly be accidental. Clive Goodwin, who died in 1977, was my own agent in the early 1970s. When, as one does, I was having a phase of feeling ill-served by him, he showed me a draft of the sequence in *Hide and Seek* in which The Author quotes and derides his agent. He clearly thought he was its inspiration.

'the impotent, squawking, posturing, finger-jabbing nincompoops' with 'public school voices' were spouting 'horsehair'. Most ideologically unsound of all, 'even the booze ran out a couple of hours too soon'.[8]

On a more reflective occasion, he conceded that at such events 'I listened and felt very lonely and out of it. The same old hates, the same old dogma, the same belief that if only the systems of the world could be changed everyone would be happy. No concern for the sick and the bereft and the lonely and the suffocating. Jesus was *their* man.'[9]

Jack Black certainly feels 'out of it' in the world in which he moves (or would like to move). He feels out of it because he has a notion that it is an uproariously promiscuous world from which he is excluded. Whether his distaste excludes him or his exclusion is rationalised as distaste is moot. Insofar as Sands is predatory and Veronica casually available, Jack's image of this world appears to be justified. But the Sands scene is reported by Judy (perhaps 'visualised' by Jack) and the Veronica scene may equally be objective or a projection. In any event, it makes for a rich mixture and the production serves it full-heartedly.

As with *Shaggy Dog*, *Yellow Brick Road* was slotted into a run acted by a small repertory company of actors, named for the purpose The Sextet. Producing the collection, Roderick Graham had a 'chicken-and-egg problem: should I commission writers not knowing who the actors are, because I wouldn't get actors of the calibre I wanted without scripts?'

This he did and one who was asked to work blind was Potter. The brief was to write for two actors above the age of fifty, two below forty and two in their forties. The deal was brokered by script editor Margaret Hare and the commission was sealed by Graham on the phone. 'He wanted to write a play about a young man coming to London and being enraptured by the beauty of women in the lingerie and swimsuit posters. He falls in love with them, then discovers the reality of the model industry and this destroys his innocence and his belief in the purity of women. I said "Please write this play". Off he went and of course he wrote something entirely different but equally wonderful.

'I sent the first three scripts to a number of actors including Denholm Elliott who rang from a Turkish bath to say that on the strength of reading the Potter he already wanted to join. The rest of the series fell into place round that.' In the first of three dazzling depictions of Potteresque ambiguity, Elliott exactly captures the simultaneously sheepish and self-righteous in this floundering man.

'Dennis then proceeded to cause us all terrible trouble,' continues Graham. 'Without consulting him, Margaret and I had decided that his script was to be performed intact, that any attempt to alter a word would result in our withdrawing the play. In this mood, we marched in to see the Head of Plays, Gerald Savory. He liked the play as much as we did and wanted to do it as written so the wind fell out of our sails. It was quite disappointing. Dennis then wrote an article saying that all his work had caused panic and palpitations at Television Centre and his latest was being passed hand-to-hand by the white-faced censors of the sixth floor, which he couldn't understand because he'd written about the purity of God.

'If the old bugger had kept quiet it would have been perfectly all right, but the result of his article was that Huw Wheldon rang me next morning saying "Send me a script of this terrible Potter play." Dennis was just stirring his own stew because it had all been far too nice for him. It all came to nothing and the play was done exactly as he wrote it with the exception that the recording ran three and a half minutes over its allocated slot. I had to ring Dennis and say we ought to cut this particular scene and he said "Oh, I never liked it anyway, I didn't think it took us anywhere." Once again I had the wind taken out of my sails.

'Of course, the whole thing was done between us on a basis of trust and lack of fear, allowing people to take risks and so to do extraordinary things and to *improve*. That simply doesn't exist now. The checks and balances today are contrary to the creative impulse.'[10]

The next play touched at least one nerve, as Stanley Reynolds reported:

> Outraged Mrs Whitehouse leapt from the chair she sat in the other night and telephoned the BBC and the Press Association to tell them that this was it. It had finally happened ... Mrs Whitehouse's last straw was Dennis Potter's strange little play *Only Make Believe* on BBC1. I can't figure out what offended Mrs W in the play. And Dennis Potter can't either. 'I can see why she didn't like *Casanova*,' he said, 'but I cannot see what she found objectionable in this last play which, if anything, is a religious play.'[11]

That even a righteous woman like Mary Whitehouse missed the religious aspect might have given Potter pause. Many other women must have found a more secular objection to the portrayal of what they would deem sexual harassment, practised by a powerful man against a subordinate woman, without any sense that the sympathy of the play swung against him.

Christopher Hudson (Keith Barron) is writing a play for the BBC, specifically *Angels Are So Few*, from which scenes are recreated involving Michael the angel (Alun Armstrong), Cynthia the housewife (Rowena Cooper), Richard her husband (Geoffrey Palmer) and the elderly couple, the Cawsers (Susan Richards, George Howe). Having deliberately plunged his right palm on to the red-hot electric ring, Hudson cannot physically write, so he has hired typist Sandra George (Georgina Hale) from an agency.

For Sandra, it is a job to be done. For Hudson, she is privy to his vocation and he is both self-protective ('I've never dictated my work before. I don't know whether I can do it, you see. It's rather like asking you to share my fantasies, like inviting you to clomp up and down inside my head'[12]) and sarcastic ('You make my words come alive', when she flatly reads it back).

Hudson indulges the intellectual bullying and competitive erudition that never appeared to abash Potter himself. Sandra is expected to intuit when he is dictating and when free-wheeling and to soothe his self-pity over his failed marriage in face of his pitiless belittling of her own personality. In anyone's politics, his is repellent behaviour.

The fictional playwright is no less scathing about the field in which he works: 'a Play for Today – lasts just a bit longer than a bag of crisps and has the same sort of taste'. Though he accepts the commission, there are levels Hudson would not stoop to: 'I'm not writing *The Forsyte Saga* or crap like that'. When Sandra declines his plea to stay, he snarls after her: 'Cold little bitch. Make a good story editor.'

Another day, Hudson lets slip an unexpected Potter admission: 'I've never really written a convincing woman's part before. I've got to get this Cynthia right.' However, Potter assumes a lot when he has Hudson cry sardonically: 'Oh, Sandra, you are marvellous. Disgustingly like a real person.' He may have intended Sandra as a portrait based on a woman he had met* but it would be difficult to sustain an argument that Potter understood her in any important way or succeeded in making her 'real' (Georgina Hale carries her off with great aplomb but there is a sharp sense of bricks-without-straw as she covers lacunae in the character by playing mood-swings).

What escapes the writing, whether 'religious' or not, is a moral dimension in human interrelation. Returning to his own writing, Hudson says bitterly of the fictional Cynthia: 'She's the one woman I can do what I like with.' The thought is grotesque with its implications of compulsion and subjugation, but the play's sympathy is unmistakably with this sentiment.

* Séan Day-Lewis reported that *Only Make Believe* 'was created with an amanuensis but that was a play about writing a play with [an] amanuensis'.[13]

That Sandra is a malleable male fantasy is overt not just in her eventual submission to cradling him on the floor (how much 'further' it goes is unclear because the montage of angel statuary that succeeds the clinch is from *Angels Are So Few*) but in her earlier, overly sporting attitude to his overbearing advances: ''S'all right. You're entitled to try, I suppose.' The assumption of such 'entitlement' was antediluvian even in 1973. Submission comes after he has retreated into himself, after the references back to Salem and the hymns of Sankey have slipped down to childhood dread and the ache to be told 'it's only a dream'. But 'only God himself' can do that 'and he won't'.

An intriguing scene has Hudson's doctor (Laurence Hardy) advocating analysis. 'This is my dream palace, my dream furnace up here,' cries Hudson, tapping his head, 'my fantasy, my machinery, my capital, my raw material ... I won't go spilling that valuable material out to some – some quack on the far side of a walnut desk.' Sadly, the imagination factory was on short time when this play was on the stocks.

Producer Graeme McDonald does not noticeably leap to the play's defence. 'It's funny,' he observes drily, 'how the salient point in it is the self-inflicting of the wound.' Asked whether Potter would be commissioned in the usual way, he replies: '*Nothing* was in the usual way. One of the angels plays was commissioned as something happening on an airliner. He never liked or needed the hierarchy of the BBC, script editors, producers and so on. He was much easier to converse with on his home ground so one went and saw him there. Margaret was always very welcoming. He was a very private man so one was constantly surprised by him as a result. Dennis was one of two or three writers (Simon Gray was another) who contributed to the Play for Today slot almost by right. Our position was that we were eager to have their next work.'[14]*

The text of *Follow the Yellow Brick Road* was now selected by Billie Whitelaw's dramatist husband Robert Muller to join plays by John Bowen, Leo Lehman, Peter Nichols and Jack Rosenthal in a collection entitled *The Television Dramatist*.

Also published in 1973 was Potter's first novel, *Hide and Seek*, a post-structuralist exercise sold, at least in paperback, as a piece of Paddington news-stand sex-trash (those buying it as a masturbatory stimulant must have been sorely tried). The book exhibits in abundance what Potter described in other novelists' work as 'a twitchy anxiety to make absolutely sure that the poor, befuddled reader does indeed understand, my God yes, that *this is a novel he is reading*'[16]

---

* This contrasts with the petulant observation in *Hide and Seek*; 'It is, of course, the fate of all the truly talented to collect rejection slips from Philistines and cretins.'[15]

(his italics). And suspicion grows that the work is a mad parody of such novels.

At dull issue in the book is the not unduly elusive question of who is speaking, whose is the narrative voice, through whose eyes do we witness the traffic of the story – a question which Potter believed had become the major subject of contemporary fiction and was also the bacterium in its gut which was slowly killing it. Leaving aside doubt about the accuracy of this analysis, it is frankly perverse to diagnose a fatal condition in the novel and then embark upon an example of one of the most advanced cases of the syndrome.

What sits so well in *Follow the Yellow Brick Road* – the character at war with the world/work into which he was born – grinds weary and increasingly redundant in *Hide and Seek*. Daniel Miller flees to his native Forest of Dean from his wife ('Bitch! Dirty fucking whore!') and his 'decade of pain'. He is troubled by familiarly dismaying transformations in the world that presses in on him: 'Gold into hay. Angels into whores. Love into sticky slime. Gentle Jesus meek and mild into an imbecile bleeding and screaming on a cross.' Images from childhood crash in, not least the memory of being raped in the forest by an Italian POW with spiky hair and eyes the colour of phlegm. As an adult, Miller has ungovernable erections. And he has a history of whores that haunts him.

But the monkey on his shoulder itself shoulders into the narrative: 'I can emerge from behind the misleading radiance of third-person omnipotence and begin to address you, the reader, more directly.' This is The Author and, after ritual denials of autobiographical intent, he proceeds to air the preoccupations of the unrelated writer Dennis Potter. Increasingly, The Author forgets 'my running man, my guilty cripple' ('he is not my brother but I *am* his keeper') and, after a good long Hazlittesque rage against literary London, writes of 'his own' forays with, and fantasies of, prostitutes.

In this 'task', he (The Author) feels he must 'communicate the true nature of my attitude or (more important) my actual behaviour towards women'. The arrogance of 'The Author' invites the severest test of his 'task'. A deconstructionist thrust *en passant* is as much as it merits. The author (that is to say, The Author) refers to the 'foul abomination' of 'putting his penis in a prostitute's dribbling mouth'. The location of the adjective 'dribbling', attached to the mouth rather than to the penis, says more than may otherwise be decently contemplated about both the attitude and the behaviour of The Author towards women.

How the 1976 teleplay *Double Dare* came to be written sheds a further light on Potter's treatment of women. Suffering the condition popularly known as writer's block, he had completed no new play for some eighteen months. He overcame it by asking Ken Trodd to arrange for him to see an actress. By a process that remains unclear, Potter fashioned a work from the encounter. In the play, a television dramatist who has been ill is staying at a London hotel and periodically phoning his wife for reassuring if not entirely candid conversations. He is Martin Ellis (Alan Dobie). Though he has dreamed that his hands were 'all twisted and buckled',[17] the problem has been more of a 'nervous' kind. He, too, is assailed by writer's block and, to help him, his producer (whose name is Ben) has arranged for him to meet an actress called Helen (Kika Markham). She duly comes to the hotel.

Though they have met before, the encounter is awkward. She asks, 'Is it true that you haven't been outside your home for a year?' and he tells of his drug regime and its effect on his work. He is trying to write about 'the tension between a man and a girl' and wants to explore how to do this without being too explicit. Could she play a prostitute? 'Up to what point' would she be prepared to go in representing sex in a performance? And why had she appeared in a suggestive confectionery commercial?

Ellis admires a sex scene Helen played in a film – he pictures the scene with her wearing her crucifix – but she dismisses it as 'sentimental'. Of their respective crafts, she says, 'It's as though we both fall headlong into other people's dreams.' He is disturbed: he wrote this very sentence that morning. He is filled with foreboding: 'Jesus Christ, somebody's going to get hurt. There's violence in the air.' And he anticipates the message of regret she was writing before trying to slip away.

Ben (Joe Melia) arrives and contrives to avoid buying a drink. When Ellis goes to the bar, the producer asks Helen, 'Is he trying to get you into bed? . . . You'll get a good part out of it.' She calls him a pimp, he prefers 'handmaiden to art'. When she complains about the way actresses are exploited, he says, 'I didn't cut off your penis, darling. A joke.' When Ben goes, Ellis resumes probing what Helen would be willing to do in a role. He imagines that the explicitness of *Deep Throat* will be mainstream entertainment 'in ten, fifteen years from now'. He is distracted by 'something just beyond reach . . . the overwhelming feeling that I know what's going to happen.'

Meanwhile, a businessman (Malcolm Ferris) has hired Carol (Markham) from an escort agency and she comes to his hotel. He is too fast for her and she fends him off with the agency rules but in the dining-room they conduct a negotiation. In his room, she affects to admire the decor: 'I've just got to look at the ceiling, haven't I.' Humiliated in bed, the businessman rounds on her ('stinking whore').

Listening at the wall of his adjoining room, Ellis says, 'I knew how it would end. There's always blood on the grass behind the door.' When he sees Helen lying strangled in his bed, he screams silently. The businessman comes to see if all is well but Ellis sends him away and tries to phone. He can only reach the escort agency.

Laying sexual politics aside, *Double Dare* is a fascinating exploration of the way in which fantasising can penetrate human congress, both in the execution and in the germination of the play, for the actress Potter asked to meet was Kika Markham.

Director John MacKenzie knew this when he offered Markham the role. 'It seemed right,' he says. 'She wanted to know what happened to the play for which Dennis had interviewed her, she read it and wanted to do it, however much it might be based on actual events. There were things that puzzled me and I felt it could be interpreted in several different ways but Dennis didn't want to talk about it, he kept saying "Just do it your way." He came up to see a rehearsal and he said "that's fine" and practically nothing else. I tried to tell him what I was doing with it and he said "I leave it to you".

'I thought I could put a strong thriller element into *Double Dare* and build up that tension. There was this voyeuristic Potter element which is so *him*. It was a sort of play about himself and I liked the idea of that but it was a bit of a mess and I did a lot of rearranging which directors didn't usually do with his scripts so that's why I wanted his reaction.

'What also enticed me was that they agreed to do it all on film. I'd done the grab-it-on-the-street, wobblyscope stuff so this had great appeal, something more formal. There were a couple of street shots, then it was in the hotel which was built on the stage at Ealing. I think it was the first time an entire film got made there since the Ealing Studios days.

'I'd always fancied myself at a thriller so when Dennis said "Do it your way", I began to go for it. He was going through one of his bad phases and was really quite ill but I had to get him up to look at it. I thought he would explode but he didn't. Ken used to treat him so abominably. He didn't even send taxis for him, he was so mean. You can put that on the record. It was unbelievable. And Dennis didn't complain. They had their roles into which they fitted. The second time he came up, I did insist he was met by a car at the station. I thought he should be driven up from Ross really. He was having his liver treatment, it was awful.'

MacKenzie conducted an unusual read-through which clearly he would not have done had the author been available. 'Dennis over-writes and it was *filled* with purple passages in the stage directions.

You know: "her lips quiver, she pales before him" and on and on like that. So I said "Let's get this out of our system and do it as he says we should." And it was *hilarious*. We all went to town on it and it became a farce. We were so doubled-up, we could hardly get to the end. But we got the curse off it. The fact is, he gives you so much that you've got to throw a lot of it out.'[18]

If the structure (MacKenzie's imposed on Potter's) is too non-linear and sophisticated to suggest a mainstream film, the style and look nevertheless imitate a studio movie-making which had died in Hollywood about a decade earlier. *Double Dare* has a feel of late Hitchcock – 'one of my heroes,' says MacKenzie – and Potter might easily have written *Vertigo*.

Indeed Hitchcock's major themes all touch hands with Potter's: invasions into normalcy; guilt and its tranference; mistaken, disguised and doubled identity; betrayal; sexual repression and fear; voyeurism and obsessional love; psychoanalysis; woman as Madonna and whore and object. In Hitchcock the objectified woman is hot and energetic and blonde; in Potter cool and passive and raven. Hitchcock's Jesuit guilt buried itself in the mordant practical joke of murder and suspense. Potter's Chapel guilt swarmed through his body and bled into his work. But killing, fitful in early Potter, will proliferate as his sensibility moves nearer to Hitchcock's.

Potter later thought *Double Dare* 'very political because it was about what we expect of entertainments, what is writing about. I went over the edge into a kind of sickness myself in doing it because I was the actress and the writer in the hotel. He was seeking to draw from certain forms that we've now come to accept as entertainment a personal access to her dream out of assumptions about acting, actresses, women, women seen through ads and through the extracts I put in from a sort of banal play . . . I fell, I think, into the trap of doing it like *The People* . . . "Isn't this shocking?" and then every detail. The danger of that play was always that I would go over the line . . . A lot of our entertainment gives us tension and anxiety that is displaced from – it really is opium, you know, because it doesn't take you anywhere, except you know, sort of masturbation – it doesn't allow you to develop anything except second-hand lust.'[19]

Ahead of its transmission, he was stirring the pot and obliging every journalist looking for a headline. 'There is nakedness in it and very explicit sex scenes,' he told a slavering *Daily Express*. 'It examines the position of the actress as a whore figure. The way things are going, in a few years' time actresses will be required to copulate on-stage. The play deals with the social, moral and ethical questions involved and the BBC appear to have no objections to that.'[20]

Mary Whitehouse, evidently an *Express* reader, told the *Evening Standard* that she was applying to the Director of Public Prosecutions: 'The blasphemy and, in Potter's own words, "the very explicit sex scenes" in the play are a measure of the way in which the BBC is enthralled by the moral vandals of our time'.[21] No more was heard of this action; it was overtaken by the unholier row over *Brimstone and Treacle*, transmission of which *Double Dare* was brought forward to replace.

18

Sit Down, You're Rockin' the Boat

'How can he say anything if he's got that dummy stuck in
his gob?'
Cilla Black of a toddler in her show *Cilla*, quoted by
Dennis Potter in 'A Note from Mr Milne'[1]

'That's the one I was most proud of, I think,' says Graeme McDonald[2]
of the sixth and last of his Potter productions, *Joe's Ark*.* It is a tiny gem,
a contained and universally personal drama in a superbly controlled
studio set with a few jangling intrusions from another world, some
of which the author dropped when the text was published ten
years later.

The play considers the effect of imminent death and Potter 'chose
a beautiful young girl, rather than an ugly old man with warts on his
nose, to lay my small blooms at the feet of the dark angel'.[4] Lucy
(Angharad Rees) is in the terminal stages of osteogenic carcinoma
– cancer in the bone. Bitter against God, her widowed father Joe
(Freddie Jones) waits below in his pet shop in a village, Welsh but
familiar for wandering sheep and Sankey-singing chapels. Joe has
already 'lost' a child; his son Bobby (Dennis Waterman) is on the
road in a bad club act with a showgirl, Sally (Patricia Franklin).

Unwelcome visitors come to the shop. The Zion Chapel preacher
Dan Watkins (Edward Evans), whose sermon ('What is the long-range
weather forecast, brethren?'[5]) drove Joe noisily out of the chapel the
previous Sunday, is concerned that he is estranged from God, who
'calls the good to Himself'. Joe finds this insufficient and, in his shop

---

* Odd then that the BBC's two-year copyright on the script was allowed to expire and had
to be renewed before the play could be produced.[3]

where he can play God with the creatures, cannot accept the beauty of creation that Watkins reckons to see in a tankful of neon tetras. But alone he does pray: 'Take me instead.' Lucy perceives that 'his Christianity survived the death of my mother and the defection of my brother, but not this, I think'.

Lucy says this to Joe's other intruder, John (Christopher Guard). He is a fellow student at Oxford ('she seemed to glow there') who has hitched down in the torrential rain protesting his love. Joe is sceptical as he feeds baby alligators ('the world is full of maggots') but he lets him go up to Lucy's room.

John prattles awkwardly and has brought a fanatical biography, Thompson's life of Wordsworth, which she will clearly never open. She is aware only of essentials ('the way carrots taste different from cabbage') and finds gallows humour easier to bear than he. He agrees to write to her brother for her. Then she tires (of him) and shoos him away.

Joe is unhappy about the letter ('we don't go poking our noses into family') but it is too late. On receiving it, Bobby vents his grief by abusing a waiter in a café. He and Sally drive into the smokestack-pitted valleys. He delivers a tirade about how cancer is taboo in the comedy business, then asks her earnestly to marry him.

Lucy's doctor (Clive Graham) evades her question about 'the moment of death': 'Every doctor eventually expects his patient to collude with him, Lucy. Most real things are left unsaid.' Bobby arrives at the pet shop a moment too late. Meeting him on the stairs, Joe swiftly cradles his grief and mends his fences with a hoary Christian lie: 'She's with your Mam . . . she said she was going home.' The rain has stopped.

In a *Guardian* review, Peter Fiddick put well one aspect of this admired chamber piece: 'Calling it *Joe's Ark*, he summons as the central image the greatest crisis in that rich mythic Old Testament store – the moment when God, in effect, seems to reject his creatures and start again . . . He may be looking for the universalities, this Potter, but he looks in the earth where his roots are and the result is gripping and human.'[6]

The central concern of the play is Joe's bitter crisis of faith as he contemplates the deaths of his children (Bobby is 'dying' in the showbiz sense of the term). As the blessed and talented child leaves, called to the light that her name promises, the prodigal son returns and so, if only in the tones of conventional Chapel piety, does Joe's faith. The rain stops and the ark is grounded and at peace.

Freddie Jones remembers the final line about the rain stopping and reckons: 'I of course, pitifully grasping for every ounce of drama, did it with some force and Alan [Bridges, the director] said "I would like it to be dead. It's a state of shock." I suspect I cheated a bit. I'm such a *bastard* really, bloody old ham.'

By his account, the play insisted on being moving: 'The first morning, Alan Bridges said "You live it and I'll shoot it. Do what you want to do, make it your home." I put the script on the bed, not having learned the lines of course, and, when I'd come to the end of the speech about her little bit of blue ribbon, I caught a flash of white at the foot of the bed and turned to see this very distinguished director getting out his hanky. And he said "That's a bloody wrap, we'll go to the pub now."

'Dennis wanted to show premature death in the middle of life – puppies and kittens and parrots and fish – and upstairs this poor creature: one of the finest performances I've ever witnessed. If you deny an actress movement, variety of pitch, pace, facial movement, what is she left with? And yet she achieved that brilliantly, I thought.

'I think the most fearful phrase for me in the entire play was her saying to the boy "Go downstairs – I want to break wind." That was the most awful manifestation of what was happening. I don't know quite why. It was just that I felt you'd have to be dying to say it. It seemed to underpin the horror of the illness for me, a sort of summation. I'm sure that's why it's there.' It is, of course, characteristic of Potter that he should pinpoint the most physical awareness of the circumstances, like the old miner's sputum on the grate.

'Dennis only came to one rehearsal,' contines Jones, 'and I was appalled by the state of his hands. We went to the pub and he asked me to take a cigarette from between his fingers and put it out. He grasped his pint mug with his knuckles. I remember he once said he was afraid of losing pain altogether because he would query whether he'd be able to be creative any more. I don't remember that he talked much about Joe. Some writers are punctilious about every apostrophe and others are amazed and delighted with what the actor and director bring to them and I think he might have been the second.'

Potter's own account of the rehearsal he attended is rather different: 'Almost everyone concerned seemed intent upon excavating the solemnity rather than the intrinsic comedy of the piece, but I was at that time either too ill or too diffident to do anything much about it'. In the same essay, his introduction to the text, Potter also writes: 'The two intruders I especially did not want to come creeping up on me were Pathos and Sentimentality. I threw them out of the room several times, but, of course, they sneaked back in again, and I am unhappily aware of the sweet cloy of their breath upon the back of my neck as I re-read the play.'[8] All the more odd that he should excise leavening scenes of bawdy.

The consensus is against Potter on *Joe's Ark*. To find the solemnity – a less loaded word would be 'gravity' – rather than the comedy is no unworthy achievement; to be authentically moving is not merely to succumb to sentiment, however lavishly shed its director's tears.

Nevertheless, Potter told Melvyn Bragg the 'danger' for him was 'that it was sentimental and it was out of that that I decided to write *Brimstone and Treacle* which is turning it on its head, which is the girl who's inarticulate and instead of being surrounded by the good and concerned and compassionate, the agent for her channel to the world was evil'.[9]

Considered as a play in Chapter 15, *Brimstone and Treacle* was more famous as a *cause célèbre* though for scope and longevity the furore it caused pales beside the international sensation of Antony Thomas's documentary-drama *Death of a Princess* (ATV, 1980), the subject of a diplomatic incident between Britain and Saudi Arabia.

Brimstone had already been delayed inside the BBC before transmission was fixed for 6 April 1976, the first of three Potters in successive weeks: 'They have sat on the play for two years,' he told *The People*, 'but now they have suddenly taken courage.' The same report quoted Ken Trodd: 'It's true that the play's subject was a problem in the minds of some people in the drama department at first. But as soon as I read the script, I was keen to do it . . . I've no doubt the play will stir up a few arguments. But I think it's great.'[10]

In a panic almost nostalgically reminiscent of those of a decade earlier, *Brimstone* was pulled from the schedule eighteen days before transmission. The press reported 'an extraordinary scene at the Television Centre . . . it is understood BBC1 Controller Bryan Cowgill stormed out of a room in anger',[11] likening the play to 'a crash at Brands Hatch'.[12]

Potter was immediately on the phone to the papers. 'The scene satirises the trendy assumption that sex liberates and cures everything,' he told the *Guardian*. 'The opposite is often the case. The scene is intended to shock. I find it depressing, not that they find it shocking but that they cannot grasp that what they find shocking is precisely what really is shocking.'[13]

Cudgels were swiftly taken up. The BBC's statement argued that the play's 'central theme* . . . concerns the rape by the devil, in the

---

* It may be understandable that the BBC should egg its pudding but to account this incident 'the central theme' was more than mischievous, it was malicious.

guise of a young man, of a girl physically and mentally crippled by an accident' which was 'likely to outrage viewers to a degree that its importance as a play does not support'.[14] For a BBC handout to air the issue of artistic merit, as this implicitly does, was a new departure.

Though confined to bed, Potter explored the possibility of an injunction to prevent the substitution of *Double Dare* for *Brimstone* and the showing of *Where Adam Stood*, scheduled as the third play (though on BBC2). Cowgill rejoined tartly that the notion of the plays being intended for screening in a group had never been discussed, implying (surely correctly) that it was a new and convenient invention.* *Time Out* got sight of a letter sent to Potter by Alasdair Milne, Director of Programmes: 'I found the play brilliantly written and made, but nauseating. I believe that it is right in certain instances to outrage the viewers in order to get over a point of serious importance, but I am afraid that I believe in this case real outrage would be widely felt and that no such point would get across.'[15]

Solidarity with Potter, Trodd and director Barry Davis quickly spread through the BBC. The *Daily Mail* reported that 'Top producers . . . decided after an angry and sometimes emotional meeting this week to send a protest to Milne demanding urgent talks on what they called "the erosion of confidence in programme-makers"'.[16] But the Corporation held firm. Conflicting accounts began to appear, including that Cowgill had merely asked for 'a few minor changes . . . a slightly later starting time and heavy use of on-air presentation to warn viewers (always envisaged)' but that he also referred the play to Milne who hated it 'and Cowgill did an about-turn'.[17]

Returning to freelance directing after four years as BBC Head of Plays, Christopher Morahan delicately made his own view perfectly clear: 'The audience should be treated as a robust one, as mature people who can exercise their judgement. I would hope that a broadcasting organisation should not get in the position of being a guardian of the nation's morals. That is when I fear that responsibility goes over the borderline into paternalism.'[18]

According to another report, Potter 'is receiving quantities of outraged mail letters, some of them infinitely more obscene than *he* would know how to be'.[18] Meanwhile he dropped his injunction threat in the light of a rumoured reprieve that in the end took eleven years to materialise.

Potter set out his answer to Milne's 'brief and insolent letter' in a *New Statesman* article,[19] inevitably picking up on Milne's word 'nauseating'

---

* Only in their religious aspects (and, as Potter averred, *all* his work was religious now) were the three plays loosely relatable.

(wondering 'which passage of dialogue made him plunge retching to the sixth-floor lavatories at the Television Centre') and itemising the 'proven emetics' (*Jim'll Fix It*, the inevitable PPB) shown without concern. This being a piece of dialectic, he makes the incontestable point that 'it is right in certain instances to outrage the viewer in order to get over a point of no importance whatsoever'. Indeed one might develop his argument to refute strongly the mechanistic notion, common among executives and other commentators bred in journalism, that art is anything to do with 'getting over points' at all.

Milne ought to have taken seriously Potter's persuasive image of the BBC as 'an uneasy confederation of cunning groups, each pushing and concealing its product until the moment when it gets on the air . . . in the spaces between the words, so to speak, programmes get made'.* Just as awkward to contemplate would be the eleventh-hour nature of the concern, the play having been acquired by the BBC so long before.

In his memoirs, Alasdair Milne† draws a fine distinction: 'It has always seemed to me that it was the broadcaster's duty at times to shock, but that he must take care not to outrage his audience; otherwise the dialogue between them would become wholly one-sided. But outrage was, it seemed to me, what Dennis had achieved.'[20] Invited to expand on this argument, Milne now says: 'I've always believed that television should be in a position to shock people in the sense of stimulating them but not to the point of total outrage because then the screen comes between you and the viewer.

'I perhaps didn't make enough in my book of the climate at the time. [James] Callaghan was Home Secretary and he called in the Chairman [of the BBC, Sir Michael Swan] and [Charles] Curran who was then the Director-General. [The government] were very exercised about violence and sex – that goes on for ever of course – but they suddenly got very het-up about it.‡ As Director of Programmes I inherited from David Attenborough a ludicrous committee full of wise and wonderful men and women who would meet once a fortnight and pontificate about sex and violence. So the climate was

---

* I recall as a previewer being shown a Play for Today by Jim Allen, *The Spongers*, whose title shot was missing. Producer Tony Garnett explained with a discreet smile that the shot was still being processed; indeed it was not cut in until just before transmission. The full version showed just why: the title was superimposed on representations of the Queen and the Duke of Edinburgh. I also recall as a producer, not long after, soon falling into the language of 'getting away with' ideas and images. Dissembling was institutionalised at the BBC.
† Milne succeeded Sir Ian Trethowan as Director-General in 1981.
‡ In his memoirs, Curran (D-G 1969–77) writes: 'Drama in the permissive society offers an excellent opportunity for the moralising politician to beat his breast publicly for the sins and omissions of the broadcaster.'[21]

politically jumpy and to that extent it might have marginally coloured my judgement.'

To the suggestion that the concern was that of alienating the viewer and so bringing the BBC into disrepute, Milne says, 'That's a very good way of putting it. It would alienate the viewer to the point where he would take against the medium itself.' Asked whether the decision he had taken was an objective or a subjective one, he replies, 'Whether I was being more subjective than objective I couldn't be sure now. I probably wasn't sure at the time. It just seemed to me that it went altogether too far. You come to the point where the subjective approach to proper objectivity gets muddled. I was outraged by the play as Director of Programmes and therefore had to make a judgement about it.' And was he outraged as a *bloke* too? 'Both as a professional and as a bloke, yes.'

Potter's description of Milne as 'a puritanical Scot in a corner' makes him laugh. 'I don't think I'm all that puritanical really.' As to the lateness of the ban, he says, 'The business of referring up has its dangers. People disagree. If Ken Trodd, say, accepts a script and goes ahead and makes a play and somebody somewhere thinks "Well maybe we ought to check this with whoever's in charge" and the decision goes against it, I don't see how you can get round that, actually. The Director of Programmes manifestly can't read every script. Somewhere in the stream of programming, you have to believe that professionals roughly think alike. But they don't always.' So it is an implicit criticism of judgements made down the line? 'Yes. Absolutely. Without question.'

Of all adjectives, 'nauseating' could not help but be provocative to someone in Potter's situation, Milne owns – 'I do understand that, yes' – but he maintains that his own position was not grasped by the programme-makers. 'Certainly Chris [Morahan] and Ken couldn't understand why I found it nauseating. We were talking a different language. The fact was, I couldn't stand by it as a BBC executive. I don't think I was ever going to make Dennis understand that.'[22]

Potter himself naturally took every opportunity to refine his claim for *Brimstone*'s integrity. Invited by Mary Craig to expound what the play was 'trying to say', he offered: 'That people's lives have a shape and there is nothing more awesome than a man's, woman's, child's sense of that shape and of personal destiny; and that the moral choices open to us are based upon absolute freedom. It's a freedom which I can only approach by thinking of it as something given.

'A religion that doesn't go into the dark side, that isn't concerned with pain, that is something you put on Sunday-best clothes for is of no interest to me whatsoever: it's an insult to the central struggle of man to know or sometimes to reject, but at least to come to terms with religious experience.'[23]

And he told Melvyn Bragg: 'I do understand and conceive of the importance of what is called editorial responsibility and I do not underestimate the effect of television upon its viewers, because of the way it's received, the way it's distributed, the way you pick it up in your own home and without apparently the rational exercise of the same order of choice that you get when you buy a book, when you go to the cinema, when you go to the theatre . . . I don't for example join in the chorus of abuse about Mary Whitehouse because I think that at least she acknowledges the central moral importance of, to use the grandest word, art . . . People say the worst form of censorship is self-censorship. Well, I think that's the best form of censorship . . . Quite honestly, it took me six months between finishing *Brimstone and Treacle* and actually giving it into the hands of the BBC because I myself was worried about it . . . If you think at all about the reception of the play on a level other than the ideas within the play or the characters or the emotions, then I think you're well on the way to writing pap series . . . If you can't sometimes give alleged offence in order to open up something else, then drama itself is being asked to limp along on one leg and that's a great shame.'[24]

This last interview occurred at the time of the production of *Brimstone* on stage at the Open Space in London in February 1979, sixteen months after the play began a second life at the Crucible Theatre, Sheffield, when David Leland used it to launch a two-season run of new work. 'It was a good thing to get,' he says, 'because it had this mythological reputation attached to it as something the BBC wouldn't show. I negotiated through Judy Daish* and Dennis had nothing to do with the production except that he'd obviously given it his blessing. He came and saw it and that was all he did.

'He was intensely uncomfortable watching the play. In a paranoid way, I felt he simply didn't like the production. But all the actors in it were very good. We staged it in the studio which meant that the audience were on three sides so it was very intense from an audience point of view. People were riveted by it and there was the sensation of having your laugh frozen on your face. And the constant feature

---

* Potter's agent since the death of Clive Goodwin in 1977.

of this quite stunning young girl lying in bed and then being taken advantage of by this charming bastard was very disturbing: distressing and riveting at the same time.

'I got the sense from him of somebody being hypnotised by his own monster. He felt it was too explicit. In the theatre, the audience could choose to watch whatever they wanted, the whole picture was always available to them, whereas on television the camera chose what to look at.'[25]

The *Brimstone* material yielded two more versions before the premiere of the television original in 1987. One was a novelisation written by Potter's daughter Sarah (described as 'an adaptation of the screenplay by D. C. G. Potter') and published by Quartet in 1982. The other was the feature film of the same year, with Sting as Martin entertaining the neighbourhood with a rather too obviously intended hit-from-the-movie version of the sweet old Vivian Ellis number 'Spread a Little Happiness'. Denholm Elliott repeated his performance as Bates and Joan Plowright took over as his wife, her name changed from Amy to Norma, a gratuitous nod to Hitchcock's *Psycho*.

Richard Loncraine's direction pulled out all the stops, swathing the original sitcom-land setting in Hammer Films sensibility. What was thought to be gained by changing the inamorata of Bates, which so traumatised his daughter (Suzanna Hamilton), from a *Blackeyes* prototype to a middle-aged secretary is difficult to understand. It was, Loncraine says, 'a hard film to make. I hadn't seen the first version and truthfully I thought it was bloody awful when I did. Not to my credit but the film was a much better use of its theatricality. And Denholm and Joan together were more interesting but people don't agree with me on that.

'Dennis wasn't interested in being around. His attitude tended to be "If you don't like anything, fix it". I don't think he liked me very much. I probably stood up to him more than he liked. He was very abrasive and I'm abrasive too. He wasn't good at dealing with intelligent barrow-boys which is what people take me for though I'm really a cheap public school boy. So I was quite good at fazing him. I did develop the script a bit but I don't want to take away from what he wrote. He showed bursts of interest and then absolutely none and he never came on the set. A strange man.'[26]

In 1977 Potter took a course of new medication and was able to attend the Edinburgh International Television Festival, his first trip out of England as he delighted in telling me and no doubt everyone else. The Festival committee acquired the BBC recording of *Brimstone and*

Treacle for a screening* and Potter gave a sparky paper on 'Realism and Non-Naturalism'.

But there can be no doubt that the humiliation over the play set him back. It must have been with some gratitude that he took up the offer of a major dramatisation, that of Hardy's novel *The Mayor of Casterbridge*.

---

* The Festival is only open to industry professionals and no screenings are public.

Other People's Babies

'The simplicity of truth was not sufficient for me; I must needs embroider imagination upon it, and the folly, vanity and wickedness which disgraced my heart are more than I am able to express.'

Emily Gosse[1]

Dennis Potter had forthright views on the dramatising of prose fiction and memoir, or adaptation as he called it. In his reviewing, he followed the changing styles and techniques of the 'classic serial' tradition with a shrewd interest.

One production about which he was merciless was David Conroy's prestigious and expensive BBC *War and Peace* of 1972, a dramatisation in no less than twenty episodes by Jack Pulman, recorded in the studio and filmed on the plains of Yugoslavia. Alan Dobie, Anthony Hopkins, Morag Hood and Rupert Davies led the cast. Musing on its early stages, Potter wondered if 'it is the curse of television to reduce all its material into the same *kind* of experience' and he argued that, in tackling a dramatisation, '"why are we doing all this?" is *always* the first question to ask'.[2] In a later article, he advised that 'the adaptor must make his peace (a sort of armed truce) with his subject before he puts pen to paper, otherwise we shall go on being fobbed off with such failures as a *War and Peace* which is almost as good as *Crossroads*'.[3]

This is perhaps ungenerous to Jack Pulman, a fine craftsman who in his dramatisation of Robert Graves's *I, Claudius* four years later achieved more than mere craft (and was served by a master director in Herbert Wise instead of a journeyman). But of course Potter was still bewitched by the Granada production of the Piscator *War and Peace* of 1963.

Over the years, Potter tinkered with dramatisations of his own: numerous extracts for *Bookstand*, passing tales in *Alice* and *Casanova*, legend and anecdote in *A Beast with Two Backs*, *Son of Man* and *Traitor* and a short story for a many-handed series that will be considered later in the chapter. His first full-length dramatisation was of Angus Wilson's fifth novel, *Late Call* of 1964.

He was never an obvious choice. Wilson's is a beady and observational style. Far more appropriately than Potter (who used the name in *Vote, Vote, Vote for Nigel Barton*), Wilson could have set a work in West Barset. The Trollopean baton passed on by him came down not to Potter but to Alan Bennett.

Wilson's social comedy was anchored in fine detail of behaviour and interaction of character. He was infinitely subtle and almost entirely detached. He was also possessed, as far as the notion is meaningful, of a gay sensibility. Relations between men in his novels is coloured, most often in subterranean ways, by physical possibility.

Interaction of character was hardly a characteristic of Potter's work, save as between the ego and the id. Potter's people are marooned in their private dramas, making their own tragedies, hardly ever having them made by others. He never wrote about friendship. The marriages in his plays have always already turned sour, bad parodies of a union. His creations are lone killers, individualist exploiters, dreaming recluses. Potter's world is one of virtual reality, the opposite of Wilson's outpouring of tiny pinioned truths. And his worst enemy would not describe Dennis Potter as a subtle writer.

The novel of *Late Call* begins with an Edwardian idyll that darkens and then is left behind, unexplained (its main character not even identified as the child Sylvia), to hover over succeeding events, as remote as history. Typically, Potter haunts the adult Sylvia with it, playing it in whenever she has an opportunity to gaze into the middle distance. Although he does this diminishingly, so that by the fourth and last episode the past is forgotten, the effect is self-conscious and laboriously predictable. The rest of the story – of a woman of potential spirit and her disreputable, farty old husband adjusting to retirement with their self-important son and his recalcitrant children – is all laid out to be gazed upon with none of Wilson's depths and subtexts.

However unsympathetic Potter's handling, he did not deserve the obnoxiously incompetent production which the four-parter received. The direction is full of heavy-handed pointing and utterly without flair. The family-row scenes have no light and shade, degenerating into melodramatic posturing and yelling. The casting is inaccurate and much of the acting empty: Dandy Nichols and Leslie Dwyer as the lead couple are certainly excepted, Nichols especially being very splendid and, in the hotel scene, triumphantly showing miles of leg; but even Michael Bryant, the finest television actor of his generation, is left undirected as the pompous son.

And the Edwardian sequence, in brief launching each episode, is everything Potter set his face against, confirming his instincts about the use of child actors, suffusing the sequence with signals of 'nostalgia' (plinking piano, soft filters, vignetting) and contriving to be depersonalised (subjective camera – swirling, for instance – is only cut in for effect, the rest is conventionally objective in a way that memory is not). Unbelievably, not all the flashback is on film so that a sudden lurch to studio disorientates the viewer. Not only is this the least accomplished mounting which Potter's work ever received; the script is little better than a travesty of its source. Angus Wilson's asperity is nowhere in evidence. Troy Kennedy Martin's version of *The Old Men at the Zoo* (1983) and Andrew Davies's of *Anglo-Saxon Attitudes* (1992) are infinitely superior.

The third of the plays which Potter claimed were interconnected when *Brimstone and Treacle* was pulled from the schedule, *Where Adam Stood*, is not really a dramatisation at all. The film is flagged as 'based on *Father and Son* by Edmund Gosse'. Its broad situation and a brief though pivotal incident are taken from Gosse's memoir. The rest is Potter invention.

Philip and Emily Gosse were Plymouth Brethren, Edmund their only child. 'This, then, was the scene in which the soul of a little child was planted,' Edmund wrote, 'not in an ordinary open flower-border or carefully tended social *parterre*, but as on a ledge, split in the granite of some mountain.'[4] Edmund's mother died of breast cancer when he was eight. A Miss Marks was engaged as his governess. The threesome moved from Islington with its street theatre to Devon where the father pursued his work as a marine biologist. Edmund had been in awe of Gosse – 'my Mother always deferred to my Father, and in his absence spoke of him to me, as if he were all-wise. I confused him in some sense with God; at all events I believed that my Father knew everything and saw everything.'[5] But the compelling revelations of Charles Darwin began a 'two cultures' crisis in Gosse *père*: 'There is a peculiar agony in the paradox that truth has two forms, each of them indisputable, yet each antagonistic to the other'.[6]

While Gosse dominated the locality, Edmund grew away. At last he entered the secret world of fiction which Philip, who 'prided himself on never having read a page of Shakespeare', despised.[7] The boy's horizons widened through the exercise of imagination and, 'as I knelt, feeling very small, by the immense bulk of my Father, there gushed through my veins like a wine the determination to rebel'.[8] His own influences were in conflict: the Bible and secular writing, 'Jesus and Pan'.[9] By the age of seventeen, 'the dilemma was now before me that I must either deceive my Father . . . or paralyse my own character.'[10] He resolved to be his own man.

Father and Son is a masterpiece of the memoir form. That Edmund Gosse's boyhood touched hands in several particulars with that of William Hazlitt can only further have commended it to Potter: *Where Adam Stood* is in part an *hommage*.

In the film, Gosse (Alan Badel) and Edmund (Max Harris) are already ensconced in Devon. Philip is written and played stiff but kindly, warmer and more attentive than in the book. Unlike the real Gosse, this one neither seeks nor finds a second companion. Miss Marks (Heather Canning) is casting her cap at Gosse but she is as sinister as Daphne Du Maurier's Mrs Danvers.

Darwinism is represented by Brackley (Gareth Forwood), a fellow biologist, who envisages that in science 'there will soon be two camps and men will have to decide in which one to pitch their tents . . . There will be warfare and calumny, insult, scandal even.' 'Will my poor little sea anemones be safe, do you suppose?' Gosse inquires drily.[11]

But he is perturbed. Can it be that fossils demonstrate 'that the earth has been gradually modified, changed?' The boy, faith unshaken, reminds Gosse that the earth was made in six days. 'Some now read the rocks instead of the Book,' says Gosse. But the note of uncertainty unsettles Edmund. Gosse lays it before the Lord and is renewed. He tells his writer/cleric friend Charles Kingsley (Ronald Hines): 'Where Adam stood, he could see all around him the stigmata so to speak of a pre-existent existence, on the trunk of a tree, from his own stomach,* from the fossils that are in the rocks, that make them seem so very, very old, even to Adam himself'.

Edmund is troubled by dreams of an overbearing Christ. 'Too much that is restless in the soul' diagnoses his father. But he has unguardedly voiced the notion that prayers will be answered. Edmund has a devout wish: for a model sailing boat. With due solemnity, he tells Gosse that the Lord said he is to have the toy. Gosse is thrown by this challenge and Edmund, sensing the flaw in his father's philosophy, very deliberately jams a chair against his bedroom door. Brackley's voice expounds the theory of the survival of the fittest.

The exquisite sensibility of the book must needs slip past the camera. There are many small abominations, not least of language, for which one wants to castigate Potter. Somehow the depth of

---

* A reference to the famous conundrum of Adam's navel.

nineteenth-century conviction escapes the film: more persuasive would be an accomplished and precocious recitation of the gospels by Edmund than a halting one, a proclamation from memory rather than a reading of the same by Philip.

But on its own terms, *Where Adam Stood* is a fine piece. The greatest of its many liberties is the interpolation of an apocryphal madwoman Mary Teague (Jean Boht) who is apt to roll on the ground and fart ('All things show the glory of God,' preaches Gosse in an editorialising cut). In the film's most provocative stroke, Teague gigglingly drags Edmund into the woods, ostensibly to show him a jay's nest, and tries to assault him sexually. He hits her with a stone, apologises politely and runs. 'He'll blame you,' he rather knowingly tells the clucking Miss Marks, in whose safe-keeping he was supposed to be while his father talked to God on the beach.

Paradoxically, the introduction of a fictional incident of abuse into Gosse's actual childhood incurs a doubt as to whether the incident of abuse in Potter's own childhood was itself fictionally introduced. Is the spiky-haired man with eyes the colour of phlegm a piece of myth-making, an example of that 'apparent' autobiography that Potter enjoyed writing? Does the invention of a trauma invest with personal force and specificity that generalised priapic guilt that recurs at every level of Potter's work? His intention in placing the incident in *Where Adam Stood* is difficult to fathom. It has a reflexive appearance, as though to write about *any* boyhood had better embrace this critical moment, but at least he had the grace to change the title of his revisionist biography.

In *The Singing Detective*, Gibbon the psychiatrist will ask his writer-patient Marlow, 'Is it very likely that you would so exactly duplicate such a traumatic event in your life in the pages of a—?' and Marlow will interrupt, 'You just don't know writers. They'll use anything, anybody. They'll eat their own young.'[12] And so, of course, a little white lie, a striking invention, is an exploitation of quite a modest order.

But if Brian Gibson was not offended by it, perhaps we are not entitled to be either. He had just directed his first BBC drama, *Joey*, when Ken Trodd asked him to read *Where Adam Stood*. 'By coincidence my subject in Part Two of my degree was the reception of Darwin's *Origin of Species*. I had spent many, many months working on that so I was fascinated by the script. Dennis had already gone through the stage of taking what he wanted from the book so there was no need to go back to it. We all accepted as a given that the film would be a long way from the book. I had very few changes I wanted to ask for in the script so it was very much Dennis's vision. I liked what he brought to it. It was all good stuff.'

Shooting took place on the Devon coast near Torquay, 'not more than a few tens of miles from where Philip Gosse lived. Dennis came to the location just once. He was incredibly shy and reclusive. Really most of what I know about Dennis is through Ken rather than from him himself.'[13]

Back in 1973, before both *Late Call* and *Where Adam Stood*, Potter was asked to contribute to Wessex Tales, a series of dramatisations from among the many short stories by Thomas Hardy, not just those of his first collection whose title the series borrowed. Indeed, *A Tragedy of Two Ambitions* comes from the third collection, *Life's Little Ironies*. It is an unsettling fable of a drunken sot, his three bright children and the conspiracy between the two boys to prevent the old man ruining the daughter's chance of a very good marriage, even to the extent that the father loses his life. The boys take no pleasure in his death – both Hardy and Potter have the weaker son acknowledge that 'I see him every night'.

Directed by Michael Tuchner with an unavoidable degree of prettification, the 50-minute film stretches the material past its comfortable length but catches the remorseless quality of Hardy's vision. Potter is careful with Hardy's idiom and makes no important changes to the thrust or structure of the tale. It is a highly restrained, enabling job. He told Angela Carter: 'If you're tackling something of that stature, you feel some presence looking over your shoulder. And the more skilful the writer, the more difficult the adaptation.' In the same interview, Potter observes that 'Hardy's are the kind of stories that countrymen tell. Full of outlandish incident, of wild coincidences. But the extremes of melodrama encapsulate much of the English experience.'[14]

His purchase on the novelist and the landscape from which he sprang made Potter the precise choice for tackling one of the major novels, *The Mayor of Casterbridge*, first serialised in *The Graphic* in 1886. But as script editor Betty Willingale observes, 'A good idea like that seems so obvious afterwards but he'd not done a long dramatisation before.' In many ways, Potter's seven-parter improves on the original. The Hardy is one-paced (perhaps a function of its serial form) and its name character, Michael Henchard, is never deeply penetrated by the author but seen rather as from afar, ending as unknowable as he began. In that respect, it is one of the least of Hardy's eight great novels and so perhaps lends itself most readily to refashioning.

Willingale recalls inviting Potter to come in and meet her and the late producer Martin Lisemore. 'We didn't need a long conversation,' she remembers, 'because he so clearly understood about the book. Something tingled down my back when he said "Well, Henchard's a manic depressive, isn't he" and you just knew he'd got it. Without pushing it, Hardy's own neurosis probably added to the book in a way he wasn't aware of himself but Dennis was and he could bring it out through Henchard. So I think he improved it – like Dickens, there are acres of slack in Hardy, really.

'In those days we were doing an episode of one or other dramatisation *every week* and we had no leeway and no write-offs. I suppose if there had been a disaster the BBC2 Controller would have had to slip in a repeat. In such circumstances I usually kept in close touch with the writers and knew their thoughts. But Dennis just announced he wasn't going to send it in episode by episode. Martin went rather white but, all power to his elbow, he agreed.

'Dennis had six or seven months to do it and as the deadline approached I was getting fretful as you can imagine. The Friday came and nothing arrived and I was picturing us all being sacked. It was too horrible to contemplate. My telephone rang at about 5.30 and there was a very agitated Dennis, full of apologies – my heart was sinking like a stone – and it had been a very hot summer which was a great difficulty for his condition – I can't tell you how graciously he was apologising – but he had to come to London tomorrow and would it be all right if he left it in reception!

'I was filled with wonderment as I read it. His writing was somehow clearer than any typewriter and though I suppose current script editors and producers would just think we were lazy, it was all perfectly to length and, do you know?, not *one word* was changed. I kept those original scripts in my filing cabinet as a reminder for when anyone started moaning about being overworked. He was diligence itself. I gave him the scripts back when I retired.'[15]

Surveying the teleserial, Professor Christopher Ricks noted that 'a true dramatisation is one which has an ear for . . . dramatic ironies and can then refrain from dinning them into our ears . . . Mr Potter doesn't plod in the novelist's footsteps: he seizes the novel's lines of force, converging on the heart of the book, Henchard's relation to the "daughter" who does in a way become his daughter.'[16] The long scene in the first episode in which Henchard meets the young newcomer to the town and comes to believe that she is his daughter resounds hauntingly on the scene between mother and presumed son in Potter's own *Schmoedipus* of four years earlier. It leads to reconciliation with Henchard's wife and a brilliant episode end-line: 'Judge me by my future works'.[17]

The writing completed, Potter called it 'a general drama of pain . . . there were times, working on the dramatisation, when I did indeed feel a certain lowering of the spirits'.[18] But his work certainly bucked up his director, David Giles. 'I'd always had an allergy to Hardy since I was at school and we did *Under the Greenwood Tree*,' says Giles, 'and he was one of the authors who made my hand go into cramp when it reached up to the bookcase. I thought it was typical of the BBC to ask me to do Hardy when I knew they were going to do *Anna Karenina* at the same time and I *love* Tolstoy. But this was one of those occasions when I read the scripts before I read the book which was a wonderful way round to do it. They were his handwritten copies, a beautiful plain hand so good you forgot you were reading handwriting. I thought the scripts were just stunning and that he'd injected something into the ladies which isn't there in the book. He got inside Henchard, he *really* got inside Lucetta and he managed to introduce humour which made all the difference in the world.'[19] Hardy's Lucetta is 'full of little fidgets and flutters'[20] but Potter gives Anna Massey the lines to make her the flashing fire at the heart of Henchard's tragedy. Alan Bates has the 'rich *rouge et noir* of countenance'[21] that Hardy pictured for Henchard and finds an underpinning of innocence to the man's bluster.

The story speaks to Potter's own concerns with memory and buried guilt, identity and doubling. There is one eerily Potteresque image in the novel. Henchard intends to drown himself in the weir – drowning is an almost overused trope in late Potter – but he is stayed by seeing a floating body 'and then he perceived with a sense of horror that it was *himself*.[22] The humdrum, almost plausible explanation is that what he sees is an abandoned effigy of himself earlier used to mock him. But the image is a gift to the dramatist.

Once more Potter was involved in pioneering work, for *The Mayor of Casterbridge* was the first serial entirely shot by lightweight OB cameras. Alasdair Milne, then the Managing Director of Television, reckons that 'all the vans got bogged down in a field in Dorset for a whole weekend and the whole enterprise ground to a halt. I think there was some talk of it never being completed. Terrible shambles, it was. It didn't look too good either. The lighting was all wrong.'[23]

David Giles says, 'I come back at that. We were right on time and we were within fifty pence of the budget. So thank you, Alasdair Milne!' And Milne's appraisal of the look of it is also hard to sustain. In fact, it brought much credit to the OB department, especially in the exteriors in foul weather, thin light, dusk and even darkness, while the market-town scenes benefited from the immediacy of lighting that video captures rather than the embalming sheen of film.

Potter's Hardy was a welcome contribution to mainstream 'quality' television, a consolidation of his eminence and his professionalism. His next project was entirely his own inspiration, a piece that brought him much personal fame and the kind of popular audience that, even at the height of the 'talking point' appeal of the Wednesday Play, he could hardly have imagined.

20

You Can't Keep a Good Dreamer Down

'A popular song carries with it all the overtones of the period' James Player;
'"Aba-daba-daba-daba-daba-daba-daba said the monkey to the chimp"?'

Gillian Player, *Message for Posterity*[1]

'I feel a spring in my heel and a song in my heart,' Potter told Oliver Gillie in March 1977. Two months before, under the care of Guy's Hospital, he had become a guinea-pig in clinical trials for an anti-cancer treatment, Razoxin. The drug had been developed at the Imperial Cancer Research Laboratory in Lincoln's Inn Fields and, according to Gillie, 'it is probably the best-tolerated anti-cancer drug known'.[2]

Razoxin, like Methotrexate before it, was not used in this case to counteract cancer. 'Paradoxically,' as Gillie added, 'the Committee on Safety of Medicine says [it] must not be given to people with his condition.' Apart from Potter, it was prescribed only for terminal cases. But the great bonus was that its side-effects were nothing like as punitive as those of Methotrexate. For Potter, it 'really is a miracle'.

In an interview with Colin Morris he spoke of the psychology of being ill: 'There are characteristics in this condition of mine which match up with my deeper impulses and therefore it's dangerous, but I am by temperament reclusive. I am an extremely tense person, I prefer to live in tension and at the point of tension. These things together have made the illness seem to be almost an ally of certain things within me.'[3]

By April, he was so renewed that, as well as bursting with creative ideas, he resumed his reviewing. In December he could tell Roy Plomley: 'This is my year of miracles in terms of my personal life. The new cytotoxic drug that I'm taking in a clinical trial has brought me considerable, huge, tremendous, emancipating relief. In fact when I came out of hospital in March, I thought the whole world was washed clean, new, shining. It's a marvellous experience to . . . see what a joyous and gorgeous world we actually do live in.'*4

Out of the song in his heart came a major new piece. Choosing the Ambrose recording of 'The Clouds Will Soon Roll By' as one of his *Desert Island Discs*, Potter assumed playful sheepishness: 'Such a plangent, such a sweetly stupid, silly little song but it actually provokes something approaching genuine emotion in me. I would like to play this particularly when the light is fading and I'm getting a bit jumpy.' And he talked about the piece he was working on: 'I'm using up some of these peculiar obsessions that I have with that music, I'm trying to see what charge there is in it that I can use.'6

The story-line of the six-part, eight-hour *Pennies from Heaven* might have been written at any time in the fifty years preceding the Second World War. It touches hands with many works: for instance, Theodore Dreiser's great novel of 1900, *Sister Carrie*, (of which Potter would have been the ideal dramatiser), or (very different) Fritz Lang's 1937 movie *You Only Live Once* from the story by Gene Towne. As these references imply, the tale has an American rhythm to it. But the sensibility is pure nineteenth-century romanticism, the yen to live imaginatively.

It is 1935, the year of George V's silver jubilee: Potter was writing *Pennies* at the time of Elizabeth II's silver jubilee. Arthur Parker (Bob Hoskins) is a London sheet-music salesman, dreamer and opportunist, married to Joan (Gemma Craven), a *bourgeoise* with a thwarted desire for gracious living. The fault-line between them – class, propriety, reputation, money – is clearest 'in the bedroom',7 as Joan's gossip Irene (Jenny Logan) puts it. Arthur motors to Gloucester, pushing a new American number, 'Roll Along Prairie Moon', with little success. He has two encounters, one a fractious tumble in his car with a local woman (Rosemary Martin), the other a less perfunctory, more disturbing exchange with a derelict who plays the accordion (Kenneth Colley).

---

* Three years later, he surveyed how the drug had changed him: 'I experienced a state of total euphoria. There is damage done. My knees, hands and toes will never return to normal . . . There was one side-effect. [It] makes me infertile. At first I thought I was going to be impotent. I said "oh no, I would rather be sick." I also bruise very easily. But the relief is marvellous. Since then I have been going up to London much more. I am convivial again. I want to be much more concerned with my work.'5

In a music shop, he sees a young woman customer who stirs him deeply. He gives chase and watches her hand a coin to the Accordion Man (his 'Thangu ver' ver' much, ma'am' is his mantra). She is a Standard One teacher called Eileen Everson (Cheryl Campbell) and she lives with her widowed father (Michael Bilten) and squabbling brothers, Dave (Philip Jackson) and Maurice (Spencer Banks), in the Forest of Dean.

On a subsequent trip, Arthur seeks her out and sweet-talks all the Eversons into believing that he is a song-writer as well as a fancy Londoner with a *car*. At a guest-house, the coarse banter of fellow commercial travellers bruises his newly (re)discovered fine feelings. The Accordion Man busks in London; weirdly, Joan momentarily mistakes him for her errant husband. Arthur has turned Eileen's head ('You won't tell lies, will you, Arthur? . . . And you're not married, are you? Promise'). With an outrageous tale of his wife's accidental death, he makes love to her on the cottage floor.

Back home, he has murderous feelings towards Joan until he discovers the gesture she has made for him, at great cost to herself: rouging her nipples.* But he returns west, briefly distracted by a blind girl walking in a field. Eileen tells him she is pregnant but the sexual freedom each has discovered with the other brings them back together. To his genuine distress, Mr Warner the headmaster (Freddie Jones) must let her go. On his way home, Arthur is briefly detained by police to eliminate him from inquiries into the murder of a blind girl in a field. He returns to Joan full of indignation.

Eileen seeks her salvation in London. Soon pushed for cash, she allows herself to become obliged to a pimp called Tom (Hywel Bennett) who takes her in and procures an abortion. Joan reluctantly allows Arthur to invest 'Daddy's money' in a lock-up shop whence he tries to catch the trade in gramophone records but the only free-spending customer is the same Tom, at whose flat Arthur just misses bumping into Eileen. The first night Tom puts her on the game, Eileen runs into Arthur in the pub. They go to the shop, are seized with abandon, wreck the place and make love, then 'just go, just like that'.

Joan begs a police inspector (Dave King) to find her missing husband but the latter is appalled by the picture of unbridled lust she paints ('a man like that seems capable of anything') and begins to connect him with the blind girl's death. No one pays attention

* Alasdair Milne, then Managing Director of Television: 'The scene of the girl doing her nipples was referred to Bill Cotton as Controller BBC1. Bill's story is that he went in at 8.00 one morning to watch it and the cleaning lady [Milne roars] is in the room, hoovering about and looking. Bill's very funny about it.'[6]

to the Accordion Man's wish to confess to murder. So that she and Arthur can dine out, Eileen goes on the street and briefly encounters the Accordion Man who mistakes her for the blind girl. She lands a prominent politician (Ronald Fraser) but fails in her attempt to blackmail him. As Arthur's likeness appears as a wanted suspect, the Accordion Man drowns in the Thames.

Arthur and Eileen flee London. They lie low in a barn but when threatened by the farmer (Philip Locke), Eileen tricks him out of his shotgun and kills him. Arthur discovers the man was his captain in the army. They head back to London so that Eileen can earn but Arthur imagines he sees the Accordion Man and incriminates himself by fleeing helpful police.

Arthur goes on trial and all his lying catches up with him – even his war record is doubted. He is found guilty of murdering the blind girl and sentenced to death. Joan visits him in the condemned cell. His execution is swift. Then, reincarnated, he returns to Eileen on Hammersmith Bridge.

Four minutes into the opening scene of *Pennies from Heaven*, Arthur opens the bedroom curtains and stretches his arms towards the light flooding in as the soundtrack plays the Ambrose recording of 'The Clouds Will Soon Roll By'. When he turns towards the camera, he is seen to be full-heartedly miming to Elsie Carlisle's singing. The moment is a true turning-point: television will never be the same again. After this, all kinds of imaginative strokes are possible. The medium is freer, looser, more eclectic, less hidebound.

The serial encompasses many numbers, most of them (though by no means all) staged within the confines of the surrounding scene and with no more than a change of lighting and a magicked-up prop or two. As well as the main characters stepping into a new convention while yet remaining within the old, the dream or fantasy or spasm of spirits sweeps in all the players in the scene. As with the first number, the sex of the singer is immaterial to the mimer. It is the sentiment that signifies.

Piers Haggard was working at Thames Television when Ken Trodd rang to ask if he might be interested in directing the new Potter. He naturally asked what it was; Trodd said, 'I don't know really.'

'He did one of those Ken Trodd rambles,' says Haggard, 'but it seemed to be something about a salesman possibly and it might be the thirties or it might be now and it was based on a news clipping. There was absolutely no mention of music.

'Then it was January or so and I received the first script in a brown BBC envelope at the Taj Mahal Hotel in Bombay. We went down to the pool and I started to read. And this song comes up: he mimes a woman's voice. It was quite a shock. We got home and there was another script which I read. Dennis was on this new drug and he was writing very fast. Episodes two, three and four were written at about three-weekly intervals. The last took longer but it was a prodigious flow. When I'd read three, I met Dennis for the first time.

'He didn't know how the numbers should be done. My problem was to find a way that was consistent without being boringly consistent and that got into and out of the mimes organically in a way that sustained the meaningful theatricality of them. Halfway through I thought I knew how to do it. That was to go in black and white with the numbers in colour. I was in love with the idea but it was Dennis who thought it was wrong and he was right. It would have been a spectacular gimmick but it would have altered the dramatic balance. It's already enough that they burst into song.'

A vestige of Haggard's idea survives in reverse. When Eileen travels to London, some establishing footage of the Great Western express is inevitably in monochrome and then so is the number, 'Radio Times', that she mouths with her fellow passengers.

Author of the monograph *Lew Stone: A Career in Music*, Ken Trodd was ideally placed as producer. 'Ken made a gigantic contribution as a source for the numbers,' says Haggard. 'But I do remember – and I say this with considerable affection – that he was uncertain how it could work, he had to be brought round. Once I'd got the surreal thing about it, I was up for it all the way, more sure even than Dennis, not surprisingly because I was busy trying to make it work. He had a writer's understandable anxiety that the whole thing was a disaster.'

Six weeks were spent filming scenes and numbers on location, particularly in the Forest of Dean where a new generation of children followed in the footsteps of those who had appeared in *A Beast with Two Backs*. The rest was in the studio. 'Dennis hadn't done much filming then. He was a studio writer so we were now in a routine with which he was familiar. He came to the producer's run of episode one. We ran the first scene on the marked-out set in the rehearsal room and, as we walked to the next set, he gripped my arm with a fierce glint in his eye and said "It's going to work." I said "Well of course." I was in the middle of it when your conviction is about the process, not necessarily the result. You just know it feels good.'

Rewriting was minimal. 'We had a sandwich session early on and he did a little work on episode two at my prompting. I might say "Can't we have a better number there" and Ken would get excited and give me twenty-five more songs which was wonderful.'9

Much of the talk in the serial is about the songs. In the Gloucester pub where he picks up the local good-time girl, her men friends scoff at Arthur's foolish claim that he is himself a tunesmith. Their idea of a song is 'Roll Me Over in the Clover': 'that's what all the songs are about', they reckon, and of course this is true enough.

But for Arthur, who wants to be rolled over in the clover as much as anyone does, the songs come to embody all his yearning: 'It's looking for the blue, in'it?' he tries to tell his fellow salesmen. 'And the gold ... It's pennies from Heaven and we can't see 'em ... For Christ's sake, we're not here for very long ... It's inside yourself.' 'It's just a business, Arthur,' they protest. But from the very outset he hears the songs' eloquence, pitying Joan and alerting the viewer: 'Don't you ever listen to the words in these songs?' 'That's not real life,' she says defensively but songs speak for her, too, as they speak, Potter suggests, for all of us.

Joan is less free (or less ready to be free) than Arthur. He wants sex but she wants romance, except when *he* wants romance when she thinks it silly and retreats to realism. 'I can tell what's real from what's make-believe,' she protests later and he cries, 'All my life I've wanted someone with me who sees what I can see.' That is what Eileen gives him.

Potter was glad to expound the songs' potency: 'You can almost lick them they are so sweet and yet they have this tremendous evocative power, a power which is much more than nostalgia ... They seem to represent the same kinds of things that the psalms and fairy tales represented, that is the most generalised human dreams, that the world should be perfect, beautiful and loving ... A lot of the music is drivel in that it's commercial and never too difficult but it does possess an almost religious image of the world as a perfect place.'[10]

The songs are used throughout to express, in straightforward, ironic or subversive ways, the inexpressible. At least that is the theory. Despite Haggard's best efforts, however, there is a diminishing return on their value and, while there is only so much choreographic variety Tudor Davies can find for non-dancers and an inevitable limit to what can be achieved in context and in relatively naturalistic studio sets, this is largely due to the failure of conviction in the working out of the story.

The gradual decline in point and pith can be illustrated by the difference between, say, the cunning use of 'That Certain Thing' in episode two to show that seeing the bank manager (Peter Cellier) is a form of wooing and that Arthur aims high and misses just as he usually does in his romantic quests; and how gratuitously, in episode six, Arthur dances a buck-and-wing with a corn dolly to Kern and Fields's 'Pick Yourself Up' while waiting in the barn for Eileen to find food. The latter is all too clearly an exercise in marking time.

After two episodes of dexterity and economy (significantly, the first is much the shortest in the whole serial, the second the shortest but two), Potter is in love with his characters. This marks an advance. 'The thing that one loves about great writers,' says Piers Haggard (himself a descendant of a fine writer, Rider Haggard), 'is that, whatever their distress at the human condition, they love their people. You certainly feel that of Shakespeare and Chekhov and Dickens, that their hearts ache. In a lot of Dennis's work, his lip curls for the human condition and it's not a very pleasant experience. I directed one of those. But I think both *Pennies from Heaven* and *Blue Remembered Hills* contain a love of humanity.'

But love of your characters can lead you to indulge them and yourself. In episode three, powerful and beautiful writing is allowed to grow at the expense of pace and story. The opening scene contains key material including Arthur's reckless candour when he declares to Joan, 'I sometimes think if I had the chance and it was a dark night I'd fuck my own grandmother' (the 'fuck' was dropped out on transmission). But it's a two-handed sequence and it lasts more than twenty minutes.

The scene where Warner the headmaster shrinks from confronting Eileen with her sin is, though overdeveloped, beautifully turned and deeply felt in the way it suggests all that neither character can bear to say. Supremely, it needs no climactic number to remake the point yet, lackaday, the baleful inevitability tugs at the scene and here it comes, 'I Love You Truly' making explicit and banal all the scene's pining subtext.

Episodes five and six see a disastrous fall-off in narrative drive culminating in the calamity of the court sequence. The palpable fact that there is simply not a case against Arthur means that the court proceedings have no basis in reality and the dénouement is fatally undermined. Herbert Ross's disfavoured movie version of the tale at least has the good sense to jump directly from arrest to scaffold without parading the largest hole in a rapidly fraying plot.

How did it come about that *Pennies from Heaven* is, as a script, overwritten, overlong, repetitive and undisciplined? One answer is bracingly simple: Ken Trodd has almost never worked with a script editor. There are few writers who do not benefit from a candid and practical opinion offered by someone steeped in the script. Producers cannot afford the time to fulfil this function. But writers need it, none more than inspirational, driven writers whose work is personal, private and full of doubt and anxiety and rapture and longing.

'I think now one would want to trim it down a bit,' Piers Haggard admits. 'Later in his career, Dennis got so arrogant and powerful that he would have seen off any script editor. Only a powerful producer could handle him and he even saw off Ken for a while. And Ken wouldn't really fight him on those script things.'

That *Pennies* never fulfils its great promise is heart-breaking for it so deftly combines a beguilingly light surface with the ingredients of the kind of inexorable tragedy that worked so well in *Where the Buffalo Roam*. Aside from narrative failure, the difficulty with *Pennies* is with the women. The fate of irrelevance befalls even Joan once Arthur leaves her. The scenes with Dave King's broadly comedic inspector are of a much lower order than their equivalents in episode one when Nigel Havers, delivering some of Potter's much-relished salesman *shtik*, calls on Joan to ply her with a rubbishy 'beauty aid' and thereby enacts a 'visitation play' writ little.

But if Joan is from the unreconstructed male chauvinist's blacklist – a snobbish, frigid, pedantic scold – Eileen is no less a fantasy, stepping from a pedestal into the gutter. That Potter had a clear ideal is evidenced by Cheryl Campbell's report of his declared reaction to her. 'When he clapped eyes on me at the read-through, he found it very hard to swallow his disappointment,' she laughs, 'because I was the antithesis of what he'd imagined, which was some dark-haired, large-eyed, palpably erotic creature and I was sitting there with my long blonde hair that you could sit on looking like something that had fallen off the top of the Christmas tree.

'But he said that as soon as I started to speak the thing fell into shape so that was OK. When he saw the first episode, which was the first time he really spoke to me, his arthritic hands grasped mine and he gave me this big hug and said how thrilled he was and he was very moved.'[11] Campbell's self-description evokes none more vividly than Rapunzel whose tale Eileen reads to her class. Haggard got her to play on the connection when, in her semi-strip for Arthur, she thrashes him with her hair. Later an established tart in the pick-up pub sneeringly calls her Snow White. The unsettling underside of fairy tales makes for one of Potter's oft-used textures if not texts.* And fairy-tale women tend to be emblematic.

At the time, Campbell says, 'I did feel extremely right for the part. I was very shy and extrovert which is a peculiar mixture and I didn't understand it fully in myself. I also didn't realise straightaway what an idealised version of a woman it is and that's why it was so popular, set against the wife who's also an archetype. Dennis did tend to write like that and did so more and more and I found it more and more difficult

---

* Reviewing Bedtime Stories, a series of dramas based on fairy tales, in 1974, Potter wrote: 'Growing up dwindles down the witches' bogles and boggarts of the night into humdrum paranoia and the furiously thrilling foot-stomping of a gesticulating Rumpelstiltskin into the prosaic mouth-froth of a Bernard Levin.' The first two dramatisations, by Andrew Davies and Alan Plater (Potterites both), he accounted failures.[12]

to watch, to be honest. But it was a part that covered such a wide range that there would be something in it for anybody to play.' Happily, she is so bold and instinctive in the role that she bridges the hiatuses in its execution.

The only character fully realised is Arthur. And he is very finely achieved, with none of the bursts of writerliness that mar some of Potter's earlier characters with yearnings for a greater light. When Arthur gives voice to his spirit, he stays triumphantly in character and idiom.

'I feel empty,' he says at the beginning. 'Me, I'm a blank.' This might suggest an everyman waiting for the viewer to project on to him and it is true that you find yourself wanting him to prevail despite his sins both venial and venal; at the same time, though, he is an individual full of feeling and potential. He is an idiosyncratic man and a contrary onè, kind and mean, dauntless and craven, sweet and vicious, inspired and squalid. He is a booby who stumbles into every trap, especially those he makes himself; he is a tragic figure fated to fall, attended by his inescapable nemesis; he is a Christ figure, preceded by a John the Baptist, who brings a message out of the east, preaches a gospel to deaf ears and, though innocent, is sacrificed only to rise from the dead. Like every Potter hero, Arthur is redeemed.

The religious intent is manifest, not just in Haggard's centring of churches in his location-establishing shots and iconographic allusions like Joan in her winged dressing-table mirror suggesting a triptych of the Madonna; but in glancing references, like the Accordion Man's to busking 'wherever two or three – or preferably four busy streets intersect'.

In any break with the demands of reality Potter found the stirring of religion. The moment a Potter man pauses in buying or selling, clerking or soldiering, he is spiritual man; it might be in no more elevated an activity than trying to make sense of his marriage. Reviewing a BBC production of Ingmar Bergman's teleplay *Scenes from a Marriage*, Potter wrote that it 'is, I suspect, a drama of religious yearning that does not know that it is . . . What Bergman more than half wants to do is to treat marriage as a sacrament, not a contract. A brave affirmation, qualified away into near despair.'[13]

Ahead of transmission of *Pennies*, he declared: 'What I really want to do is to write a sort of religious drama without mentioning God or any of those hang-ups which make that sort of drama so difficult. To state the politics sounds ultra-reactionary: "No matter what happens, life is all right". But there is some sense in which you can actually assume the ultimate optimism, no matter the degradation, the miseries that the world inflicts on you. The final claim is not that it doesn't matter – it matters in your ligaments, your emotions, your betrayals – but that there is some sense of order, a rationality that is sheer optimism.'[14]

The author and his masterpiece

Femmes fatales:

Kika Markham
in *Double Dare*

Gina Bellman in
Blackeyes

Darkness into light on
Hammersmith Bridge:

Michael Gambon in
The Singing Detective

Cheryl Campbell and
Bob Hoskins in
Pennies From Heaven

Childhood in adulthood:

Janet Henfrey, Johnny Wade and Keith Barron in *Stand Up, Nigel Barton*

Janine Duvitski, Helen Mirren and Dinah's pram in *Blue Remembered Hills*

Betrayed by the words:

Hywel Bennett and Megs Jenkins in *Where the Buffalo Roam*

Patrick Malahide and Janet Suzman in *The Singing Detective*

Betrayed by lust:

Gina Bellman and
Michael Gough in
Blackeyes

Robert McNaughton
and Glynis Barber in
Visitors

Authority figures led a dance:

Four consultants in *The Singing Detective*

Five officers in the Ministry of Defence in *Lipstick On Your Collar*

Fantasy figures:

Arthur consults his bank manager (Peter Cellier, Bob Hoskins) in *Pennies From Heaven*

Louise Germaine in *Midnight Movie*

An observation of C. S. Lewis may serve here: 'There are two things inside me, competing with the human self which I must try to become. They are the Animal self, and the Diabolical self. The Diabolical self is the worse of the two. That is why a cold, self-righteous prig who goes regularly to church may be far nearer to hell than a prostitute. But, of course, it is better to be neither.'[15] Arthur, the 'filthy beast . . . low, low, disgustingly low', is saved; Joan, the 'stuck-up bitch' who wouldn't dream of going out to work herself, is damned. Where Arthur is moved to consider throttling Joan with his tie in a 'real' emotion, Joan fantasises dancing on Arthur's coffin, a poisonous, secret desire.

For all that America is a loudly god-fearing country, not much of the spiritual survives in the 1981 Hollywood rendering of *Pennies from Heaven*. It had been Piers Haggard's notion that there was a movie in the work: 'I'd have very happily done it again and I rang Ken about halfway through making the serial and told him so. He said "That's a good idea" but Dennis was against it. He felt we'd done it. Then when someone came up with the money he was all for it. It ended up in the lap of Herbert Ross who didn't understand it *at all.*'

What Ross loses in thoughtfulness and implication, he gains in production value and lickety-split. The songs perform a different function in the movie. The integrity of the original recordings is no longer preserved; instead they are built up with interpolations and new arrangements so that they furnish the basis for extended production numbers.

So the sense of the characters calling down a common culture to articulate universal feeling is replaced by routine movie-musical expressions of themselves (as opposed to all of us) through song in voices whose otherness is no more disconcerting than the routine dubbing of non-singers. We are not invited to make connections, just (in the good old showbiz tradition) to enjoy the show. The film actually works better as an affectless musical yarn than the serial does as a parable in an unprecedented mode but the ambitious failure is infinitely preferable to the steady compromise. In any case, MGM's deal on the movie took the BBC version completely out of the public domain for several years.* Thereby the movie forfeited any claim to be considered as a moral work.

---

* Potter also wrote a 'novelisation' of the film. It is calamitously bad, couched in an American idiom too inaccurate to be viewed as parody and reading as if written to order in a couple of days. The book has no solution to the loss of the numbers and there is a palpable bump where each used to be. 'Arthur usually had a song in his soft and squelchy heart,' Potter writes desperately. One chapter begins: 'The shine had gone off the apple, and the glow had left the cherry'.[16] Only a Puritan more severe than Potter himself would condemn the wish to make money out of a success but the step down to that much-contemplated state of prostitution is short. It could hardly be an accident that, in dedicating the book to the movie's producer 'for seeing and believing', he contrived to misspell her name.

Piers Haggard had every reason to be bitter but it didn't quench his enthusiasm for Potter at the height of his powers which, for Haggard as for many, is represented by the next work: 'I think his greatest masterpiece is *Blue Rememered Hills*. It's incredibly concentrated, it's truly imaginative, it's dramatically flawless and it catches right at his roots.'

The story has the absolute directness of legend, the power of universality and the iron logic of man's fall. It works a mechanism of classical simplicity. It is set in an Eden, beyond which is the unseen but ever-present corrupt world, riven, vile and full of real danger and imagined menace.

The Second World War is in its late stages. Seven children play in the Forest of Dean. John (Robin Ellis) and Peter (Michael Elphick) contest the pack leadership, the golden boy emerging triumphant over the more loutish Just William. Angela (Helen Mirren) is growing aware of her power to bestow favours while her less alluring friend Audrey (Janine Duvitski) can only keep up a sharp-tongued commentary. Willie (Colin Welland) is fat and weak, enthusiastically bending with the wind. Raymond (John Bird) is an assimilated oddity, the boy with a knack for gadgets. It's Donald (Colin Jeavons), easily belittled by the nickname Donald Duck, whose reclusiveness is too alienating for the pack to appreciate. Their senses inflamed by the thrill of a distant siren, perhaps indicating an escaped Italian prisoner, the gang shut Donald in the barn, perceiving too late that he has started a fire inside. He perishes. Fearful grief turns to closing ranks around an account to give the grown-ups.

The plot needs no labouring; nor does the resemblance to Golding's *Lord of the Flies*. The trick is that, as in *Nigel Barton*, the kids are adults. Willie is at first in long-shot being self-absorbed and unbridled. Only in mid-shot do we see that the boy is a man. He gallops through a field as a Spitfire, his 'great fat arse'[17] in grey flannel shorts, and the compact is sealed between us; we accept the convention without qualm. For its first audience, the realisation that it would *all* be like this, that there could be no intrusion from the outside world, no adult *deus ex machina*, was what made it gripping.

Uniquely in Potter's work, the film heeds the dramatic unities of time and place. Its ambit can barely be half a mile. Its action is continuous and in real time. Both camera and author are objective. The story certainly has a fateful tread – the unwitting killing of Donald is prefigured by the frenzied slaughter of a squirrel – but no other times or lives are projected. The frame of reference is naturalistic, the dialogue authentically 'heard', the observation documentary-keen. A gentle plonk of leavening music is most sparingly used.

Potter had looked hard at his own and other children and remembered in the most clear-eyed way he ever achieved. This is his own boyhood he sees 'shining plain'. The blue hills are the Malverns, backdrop to the Forest of Dean. Although Housman's untitled poem, which furnishes Potter's epilogue as well as his title, posits an image of childhood as 'The happy highways where I went / And cannot come again', Potter often revisited his own highways, both happy and anguished.

'When we dream of childhood,' he said ahead of transmission, 'we take our present selves with us. It is not the adult world writ small, childhood is the adult world writ large. We may mature with age, but we do not change.'[18] And of adults playing children: 'The adult body acts as a kind of magnifying instrument which, because it has to loosen up and let go, reminds us more of just how mobile and swift movement is in the childhood world and yet how long time is. Time is always an eternity when you're a child and the physical movement only emphasises that sort of sheer present tenseness.'[19]

If, in filming, you start to doubt the writing's cohesion, want to play with it or point it, the structure will collapse. You must also trust to the informal forest idiom. Director Brian Gibson says he could take the leap with the play 'because the thing about Dennis's writing, unlike so many writers, is that it always plays better than it reads. Here in Hollywood,* it always reads better than it plays because it's actually written for reading. While it felt a pretty bold risk at the time, I knew from experience that it was a risk worth taking.

'So we met with Dennis in a Greek restaurant in Bayswater. He was drinking Retsina and gargling it like a seven-year-old. Ken arrived late and Dennis spat Retsina at him and Ken got very irritated. There was this silly playfulness, he was still in the space he'd taken for writing the play.

'A few days later we sat down and discussed it. The only thing I didn't much care for was the ending. There was a greater sense that Donald Duck had killed himself – the others feeling culpable and then remorseful and then rationalising it – that wasn't there in the richness it is now. I think that was an important rewrite. He also had the adult actors suddenly replaced by children at the end and we decided to keep the adults, not to change the grammar. But otherwise, as so often with Dennis's writing, very little was changed compared with other writers.'

The documentaries made by Michael Apted for Granada, beginning with *Seven Up* in 1963 and revisiting the same children septennially,

---

* Gibson was speaking between shots on his mobile from a location shoot.

had reached *Twenty One* not long before Gibson began shooting. Gibson showed the latest and then the first film to his cast. 'I said "Don't worry about playing a kid, you'll get the childishness, just play the character." That gave them specificity. Otherwise we wouldn't have known how to get started. Concentrating on childishness, we would just have had a load of big kids running around and no character.'

Before going off to the forest location in Dorset (*not* Dean), the cast had ten days in a rehearsal room and, unusually, Potter appeared often. 'He was very supportive,' Gibson recalls. 'I was nervous and he took me for a drink and said "You've got to accept your own talent." It was very confidence-giving, coming from him. I'd been a Potter fan since the *Nigel Barton* plays. To try to translate his vision was a great honour. So it was a moment I treasure.'[20]

With *Pennies from Heaven*, Potter's historic association with drama on tape and in the studio had been buried. Everything henceforward would be film. Bright omen though *Blue Remembered Hills* might be, Potter on film would prove to be a very mixed blessing.

Half a Sixpence

'At least with London Weekend we know their value
system.'

Dennis Potter[1]

Late in 1979, BBC Radio caught up with Potter the playwright when an
adaptation of *Alice* went out as an Afternoon Theatre. *Traitor* followed
eighteen months later. Though he was brought up on wireless culture,
Potter never wrote directly for the medium. This is a great pity: the
architecture of his kind of drama would have worked unusually
well in sound only and stimulated much new experimenting with
technique.

Rather than looking for a new form, Potter was looking for a new
power infrastructure. For some time he had been pondering the
workings of the business in which he had made his career, as he told
Martin Jackson in January 1979: 'The big broadcasting institutions have
to be broken down and replaced by smaller creative units. Basically
the broadcasting authorities don't like plays on TV. They are awkward
and expensive.'[2]

Galvanised by his new status and his new medication, he was now
ready to take a much tighter control on his destiny. Kenith Trodd was
ready too. They had learned from the experience with Kestrel and the
connection then opened up with LWT was still exploitable. So Potter
and Trodd set up a company named for their greatest success, PfH, and
began negotiations with Michael Grade, then Director of Programmes
at LWT.

Potter was no businessman but he was full of fire and fight about
the possibilities. 'I am cocking a snook at the BBC,' he told Séan
Day-Lewis. 'There is a genuine crisis of management at the BBC and

one of the most damaging consequences of that is that the cutbacks in budget, initiative and enterprise in the drama department are serious enough to warrant moves like this ... But I still think, saving the presence of London Weekend people, that the BBC is the place to be and in a way my move is a move to get back to it as well as at it.'³ There goes Dennis Potter, biting the hand that has fed him for years *and* the hand now proffered for the future, confident that while both hands may be withdrawn in momentary hurt they will soon be thrust back at him, clutching wads of money.

Doing the rounds of media correspondents, he gave each a slightly different story, it ever being his custom to present a moving target. Another version went thus: 'I decided that I shouldn't be so reclusive and selfish and that I ought to be looking at the whole of my industry ... I've written more single TV plays than any other writer and I regard TV drama as *the* national theatre. I decided that I didn't want to see it all washed away. It's where my loyalty lies. So I vowed to myself that there would be a few bloody changes. And now that I've got the power – because people respect my work – and the opportunity, I can do something.'⁴

The latest disenchantment with the BBC had two specific focuses. One was the trimming of a commission offer from six 75-minute plays to five at 50-minutes. The other concerned PfH's first grand gesture which was to acquire the rights to the splendid twelve-novel sequence by Anthony Powell, *A Dance to the Music of Time*, written between 1951 and 1975.

'Potter has to create, not a serial like *The Forsyte Saga*,' explained Peter Fiddick, 'but twelve separate plays, each being a version of one complete novel: the aim is not just an "adaptation" for television, but in effect to find a play to stand for the book, as he did so successfully with Edmund Gosse's autobiographical study in *Father and Son*.'⁵

The PfH team took the proposal to the BBC. Potter claimed that Alasdair Milne joked with them – 'Trodd and Potter? I thought "No way!"'⁶ – but that joke backfired and in the end all the company was left with was a format fee. By a process too enervating to follow here, the BBC took over the project and, a few years later, failed to produce a dramatisation of the books by Ken Taylor. In his journals, Anthony Powell notes that at a dinner party 'the name [*sic*] of Dennis Potter and Ken Trodd came up in connexion with their running out on *Dance* TV project, the Potter episode, indeed, having buggered up the whole prospect of TV production of *Dance*'.⁷

So PfH sat down with Michael Grade. The result was an agreement for LWT to finance and service six location-filmed dramas by Potter plus a one-off film written and directed by Ken Campbell and a two-parter, *The Commune*, written by Jim Allen and to be directed by Roland Joffe (together they had made *The Spongers* at the BBC). It was a significant move, coming only a matter of months before the nascent Channel 4 began to tender commissions to an independent sector emerging in response. But the first three Potters were very modestly budgeted at £832,000 and Trodd said later that he thought Grade's notions of movie-financing were 'a bit euphoric'.[8]

Once in production, the three Potter plays soon racked up an overspend of £150,000. When *The Commune* was seen to be headed for an additional bill almost twice as big, Grade pulled the plug, formally rescinding the contract on 27 July 1980. He told the *Guardian* the following day: 'There is a lack of regard for the internal disciplines you have got to have in this business . . . I have worked very hard to make it clear that this is a partnership, not just cosmetic, not just an LWT takeover . . . But the lesson of it all really is the very great difficulty of a truly independent production company trying to work in partnership with an existing broadcaster.'[9] This was a dispiriting end to Potter's lordly plans for PfH to be 'raising its own finance from broadcasting and other organisations and making films for showing on television at home and in the cinema abroad'.[10] Always a dreamer.

The plays that did get made enjoyed mixed fortunes. *Blade on the Feather*, a slightly uncanny post-Anthony Blunt intrigue (though the writing was largely done pre-Blunt), is *Message for Posterity* revisited via *Traitor*. Retired Intelligence man Jason Cavendish (Donald Pleasence) lives in some style with his much younger wife Linda (Kika Markham) and his daughter by an earlier marriage, Christabel (Phoebe Nicholls). A stranger, Daniel Young (Tom Conti), calls at the house in time to administer mouth-to-mouth resuscitation to Cavendish, stricken by a seizure while the women are engrossed in a game of tennis.

Cavendish has an old comrade in his manservant Jack Hill (Denholm Elliott) and the pair warble together 'The Eton Boating Song' from which the film's title is taken. But the visitor, who casually beds Christabel, precipitates disturbing memories and behaviour: Cavendish dwells on a professional hit and Linda apparently kills herself in the shower. Young emerges as a vengeful agent for the Soviets and the slayer of Linda. Facing death at the hands of the man who so recently saved his life, Cavendish crumbles and is revealed as a double agent rationalising his treachery in terms of class politics. It seems that Jack in turn has betrayed Cavendish.

Much of the film is wilfully opaque but director Richard Loncraine's account of its origins goes some way towards explaining why: 'It was originally going to be directed by Joe Losey and for whatever reason Losey didn't do it. It was a piss-take of Losey's movies, *Accident** being the one it was most obviously derivative of. The idea, I suppose, was that Losey would direct a pastiche of one of his own movies. I didn't look at *Accident* again, I just did it as a very stylised film because that was the only way you could approach it.'[11]

According to press reports at the time, Losey walked off the picture because he despaired of ever getting it cast. Among those said to have turned down the roles of Cavendish and Hill were Laurence Olivier, Alec Guinness, James Mason, David Niven, Dirk Bogarde and Robert Morley. Ken Trodd was quoted as saying that 'all these performers flirted with the idea of playing the lead parts and in my opinion funked it at the last minute. Distinguished actors said they would not appear because they were concerned about the implications'[12] by which is meant the implications of playing, as it were, Anthony Blunt. Perhaps these players detected also the lack of conviction that remains lurking under the film's handsome surface.

The house which is the central setting is a fine greystone manse with a white first-floor balcony clamped onto it like a parasite on a big old host. Cavendish's recall of his seizure in the garden contains an allusion to Antonioni for he can hear the tennis game but the court is empty. There are many passing pleasures, not least Elliott's cod gentility as the bibulous butler. And all right-thinking people will support Cavendish on the issue of jam roll and custard, even if the custard in the film is distinctly lumpy.

But if Cavendish has a gratuitously surprising past as a children's writer, *The Emperor's New Clothes* ought to have been his text. Cross-references to other Potter works are perversely mystifying. Daniel Young ('a young Daniel come to judgment' again provides Potter with his name) tells the story of Bobby's objection to the waiter sweeping up while he is eating in *Joe's Ark*, then says it is his own experience. Alone, he has a childhood memory of dropping a book – Cavendish's book, as it turns out – into the polar bears' enclosure at the zoo, an image which recurred unexplained in *Paper Roses* and seemed to appeal especially to the figure of the television reviewer. What private doodles are these? Is it a game of scattering meaningless clues to supply exercises for earnest future students?

Like all Potter's directors since Gareth Davies, Richard Loncraine found the writer handed over the project and stayed away. 'I rewrote

---

* Joseph Losey's 1967 film was scripted by Harold Pinter from a novel by Nicholas Mosley. The destructive relationships between Oxford dons on languorous summer days in a comfortable mansion are presented in an elusive and ultimately circular manner.

the scenes I didn't like and I don't think he noticed or he didn't care. His attitude to dialogue and stuff was very odd. In my opinion he'd write a scene of genius and then one of absolute rubbish, almost as if he was trying to catch you out, to see if you'd spot it. He was always testing people to see if they would take the bullshit. I think he did with his audience as well. But he also got lazy and recycled the same ideas too many times. I think he looked down on his audience, he thought the world was full of arseholes and he patronised them. I saw the bitterness in the guy but he had a very quick brain. He was a genius, really, but some of his last stuff was diabolical.'[13]

The second LWT/PfH film was *Rain on the Roof*, a veritable pot-pourri of thematic revisitations, not least the visitation theme. The title is an Al Bowlly number, the imagery is full of the Bible, the marriage is vile and adulterated, the sex is sought but bitter, the disturbed boy cannot read, the memories are of an overbearing father, the medication is corrupted by cheese, there is a damaged hand, a stabbed throat and an air of brooding menace, willed violence and inexorable tragedy. You could hardly invent a more comprehensive parody of a Potter play.

John (Malcolm Stoddard) works in Bristol and lives well on it in the country. His marriage to Janet (Cheryl Campbell) is drowning in resentment about sex and barrenness and he cheats on her with Emma (Madeline Hinde), the wife of his colleague Malcolm (Michael Culver). A backward boy, Billy (Ewan Stewart), spies on the house, throws a stone at John and is let in by Janet who is prepared to teach him to read. Billy is assailed by images of his now dead father (William Bond) and by epileptic fits. His claimed solace is that he has seen Christ. The encounter eventually leads to Janet's seduction of him. John discovers them and beats her. Yet Billy becomes part of the household and, despite John's boorish remarks, dines with them and their friends. But the party breaks up, Billy runs away, then returns and stabs John. The terrorised Janet gives him another reading lesson.

The symbolism is not of a cryptic kind. A bird flutters trapped in the greenhouse. Billy's hand bears a stigma. Janet cradles Billy in a calculated *pietà*. John's milieu is Potter's favourite shorthand for untruth, the advertising business. And the names of Janet and John stand for the first reading book, itself a kind of fall.

The dialogue of this play seems unusually downright: 'You're quite a Puritan, aren't you?', 'I'm a very neurotic woman', 'We'll never be clean'. 'I'm afraid I refused to say one of the lines,' Cheryl Campbell confesses. 'Janet was supposed to get out of the bath, admire herself in this full-length mirror and, expecting him to knock at the door, utter the immortal line "Have I got a surprise for you, Billy boy!?" I said "I'm sorry – no way!" It's just got nothing to do with real women. So it was a tricky part to play. But that's not to say that being tricky means there wasn't a grain of something there, perhaps something rather pure or truthful or incisive or illuminating.

'I think people had begun to regard his work as too sacred to tackle and they weren't tough enough with him. That's why Ken was such a wonderful producer for Dennis because he wasn't afraid to say what he thought. They could thrash things out and I think that's absolutely necessary for a writer. An actor needs that with a director and a writer needs it with a producer. You need another pair of eyes and ears, sympathetic but sharp.'[15]

In *Cream in My Coffee*, Jean and Bernard Wilsher (Peggy Ashcroft, Lionel Jeffries) stay at a white palace of a hotel on the front at a once-fashionable seaside resort. Their marriage is soon seen to be drained of affection. Bernard is on a severe regime for his health, scoffing at another man's coughing, then racked himself. They bicker over rights and territories. Jean watches a girl in the pool making out she's in danger: 'naughty girl'[16] she muses. The hotel is staffed by 'foreigners' and has a dreary trio dutifully strangling Beatles melodies. Bernard is perplexed by Jean's observation that 'the band are playing *Yesterday*'. On the beach Bernard 'makes a scene' with a 'yobbo' over his radio.

Jean looks forward to 'Thirties Night' at the hotel but it proves to be only a modern group singing about 'the movies'. She tries to enter into the spirit of the evening but Bernard is transfixed by the mosaic ball, then attacks Jean with his rolled newspaper. He is wheeled out on a stretcher, followed by an abject Jean. What precipitated Bernard's behaviour was the past coming up to meet him. They have been here before.

The present is shadowed by the couple's stay at the same hotel forty years earlier. Young Bernard (Peter Chelsom) is a son of the manse who has defied his imperious mother (Faith Brook) to go away with what she calls 'a little flibbertigibbet from the post office': Jean (Shelagh McLeod). The youngsters spoon to the Palm Court orchestra playing 'On Cloud Nine'. Bernard jokingly calls Jean 'a loose woman' but the class differences are inevitably apparent and the magic begins to unravel, she calling him 'bully' and he her 'ninny', neither unjustly.

Into the breach steps Jack Butcher (Martin Shaw), the mid-Atlantic lounge lizard who croons with the hotel band. When Bernard is summoned home by the death of his father, Jean is easily conquered by Jack. Phoning her, Bernard proposes, then breaks with his mother. Jean is distraught, fearing that Jack will 'talk about me to your cronies', tearful to see Bernard arriving back at the hotel, only to stumble as he rushes towards her.

The implications of the film are profoundly depressing: that a cross-class union is doomed to bitter regret, that a woman taken advantage of has lost her advantage, that the mistakes of youth shadow a whole life, that people must needs behave according to type. The film's sympathies would seem to lie, however ugly his behaviour, with Bernard. He it is who makes a grand and romantic sacrifice and has a brave and noble sentiment to throw at his mother in the dark, heavily ornate house: 'I shall miss Father's money much less than I shall miss him'. Beside that, Jean is indeed a gauche and weak creature.

Jean grows into her fate, to be forever banal. Ashcroft signals her inner vacuum with the edgy radiance of her beam. This is a woman who fears she will not get it right, not out of a good-hearted consciousness of innocence (like the woman in the Joyce Grenfell sketch flying from her narrow life to her son's new family in the States) but because she is, in truth, just a flibbertigibbet from the post office. The crooner snares her only because, as her own generation would say, she has 'no character'.

As a story, it has a moral without much conviction. As a tragedy, it is without dimension. It is, in all conscience, a small film that follows a sorrow of a small order. Somewhere inside *Cream in My Coffee* is a very exact little film about endurance and settling for what you get. Instead PfH put up an edifice that is as handsome, curlicued and boomingly empty as the Eastbourne Grand in winter. Gavin Millar's lush and ingratiating direction is nothing if not leisurely, bathing the little story in atmosphere and texture. After the edit, Potter said it had 'come out as a two-hour film' (which is 40 minutes longer than the transmission cut) and considered that 'it needed that space to be done decently'.[17] Perhaps he thought he was writing *War and Peace*.

The three PfH/LWT films went out on successive Sundays in the autumn of 1980. Among the lukewarm reviews – 'a Rolls Royce production of a second–hand Vauxhall Viva script'[18] wrote Michael Church of *Blade* – was a magisterially devastating analysis in *New Society* by that sage of the North, Albert Hunt, a long-time specialist in teledrama.

Hunt argued that Potter presents a pessimist's view of the world, contrived through the way in which he heightens the dialogue and consciously loads quite simple words, actions and objects with significance:

> 'I didn't want to write for the theatre,' Dennis Potter has stated
> ... But to enter the world of Potter's plays immediately after
> watching *Shoestring* or *The Professionals** is to move into theatre
> – and theatre of a particularly limited kind. It's the kind in which
> elaborate sets offer us an illusion of real life, in which performers
> try to invest everyday actions with universal significance and
> in which we're asked to find meaning between the lines ...
> [Potter] puts television 'drama' into a special category, and clings
> to the idea of the writer as someone different, a person with an
> 'individual vision'. But to see the writer as someone different is
> also to see the writer as isolated, separate from his audience,
> which is perhaps why Dennis Potter writes so many plays about
> isolated – and therefore despairing – people.[19]

Hunt's shifting of the ground from 'individual' to 'different' to
'separate' to 'isolated' to 'despairing' has a certain specious force
but these states remain discrete, not organically connected to each
other. It does not follow that the individual must needs despair. The
argument is much less persuasive in contemplating some of Potter's
'individual visions' than others.

Nor is it generally true that Potter renders 'an illusion of real life'
which is what naturalism attempts to do. Potter's own view, elucidated
three years before Hunt's, is one to which this book has by its nature
subscribed:

> The television play is virtually the last place on the box where
> the individual voice and the personal vision is central to the
> experience. In the bombardment of electronic images, the
> perpetual blitz of meanings and messages, most of which
> authenticate the habits and attitudes of society, the play has
> the chance to show that the world is not independent of our
> making of it and, more, that the other programmes, too, are
> engaged in making the world even as they purport merely to
> reflect it. It follows, I think, that television writers should be
> prepared, if they can, to give more attention to the *activity* of
> drama itself rather than just jog along unconcerned about forms,
> naturalist forms, that are taken for granted.[20]

* Mainstream Sunday night drama of the time.

As it turned out, Potter would have nothing new on British television for five years after *Cream in My Coffee*. If disillusionment played a part, it was a small part. Offers of Hollywood money had a rather more decisive influence.

22

Alice Is At It Again

'I wanted to see if I could write American. Not just the
language but the ways of thought and life. And, touch
wood – sorry, knock on wood – I have managed so far
to do it.'

Dennis Potter[1]

Dennis Potter's first adventure in Hollywoodland was the movie of
Pennies from Heaven, which was made for MGM through director
Herbert Ross's own company and so failed to provide what might have
been an important stepping-stone to the big time for PfH. The road
to Hollywood is paved with the bodies of writers and their aborted,
adopted, kidnapped and abused babies. Compared with many, Potter
emerged relatively unscathed as well as financially secure and with
an unlikely Oscar nomination.

Potter and Ross also worked together on a script of a ballet-based
project called *Unexpected Valleys*, although Ross had already filmed
the essentials of the story in *The Turning Point* of 1977. There was a
Los Angeles-set version of *Double Dare* that looked likely to be made.
There was an American original set in New York and called *Midnight
Movies*. All came to nothing. If Potter was once starry-eyed ('I have
my first film-script all lined up,'[2] he eagerly told his *Sun* readers in
1968, a mere thirteen years before his first film got released) he had
to learn the hard way how the real world of fantasy functioned.

The first roadshow movie credited 'screenplay by Dennis Potter'
was Orion's attempt to cash in on the mega-dollar-earning detection
thriller with a Cold War background, *Gorky Park* by Martin Cruz Smith.
The conviction that what sells on the page will sell on the screen is one
of the myths that sustains Hollywood. But Smith's kind of complex

plotting, like that of the current golden goose of popular fiction John Grisham, allows no more than a bare skimming in a movie which results in a mixture of the thin and the elliptical. Though he made a decent professional job of filleting and pointing, Potter got no nearer transposing the paradoxically dense urgency of Smith's prose than have the dramatisers of Grisham.

Michael Apted, a diligent English director brought up in the Granada/BBC teledrama tradition but resident in Hollywood for fifteen years, is not the man for this sort of project and the movie got away from him in production problems as well as in artistic terms. The novel has an enticing fatefulness which Potter tries to preserve but, even shooting under the grey day and black night skies of Helsinki, the film's gloss fights the story's gloom. Ideally, it would be monochrome like the Wajda trilogy, an idea almost as uncommercial as the movie proved.

Potter's next public outing was launched a long way from the power breakfasts of Hollywood. *Sufficient Carbohydrate* is the only one of his original stage ideas to go the distance, opening at the little Hampstead Theatre on 7 December 1983 and transferring for a short West End run at the Albery. It is so strongly reminiscent of middle-period Osborne – of *Time Present* and *The Hotel in Amsterdam* and especially *West of Suez* – that it almost hurts.

The note Potter hits much more strongly than Osborne – aside from the sustainedly bilious, at which he challenges the grandmaster of caustic spleen himself – is the religious, even the religiose. Referring to the play, he wrote of 'the radiance of the religious sense of the world . . . once glimpsed as a child – a theme from which I, too, can never wholly escape.'[3] So Jack Barker, who throughout is drunk or getting drunk or sleeping off drunkenness, is yet looking out for a ship on the horizon and therefore, in Potter's theoretical view of human endurance, he is redeemable and indeed redeemed. 'It took me a long, long time to realise that I actually *was* on a journey,'[4] says Jack, framing the authentic voice of the playwright who now walks with (at least a simulacrum of) God.

The play is set, as is *West of Suez*, on a holiday island. Jack and his colleague Eddie work for a food processing company called Greenacre, making for much executive venom and allowing Potter to recycle a ludicrous discussion of the sexual instability of mushrooms last heard in *Schmoedipus*. Among the ingredients which make the play repellent in a gratuitous, destructive way is its crude anti-Americanism. In the televersion, reset from the Greek isle to the Umbrian retreat of Marvel Meal Inc, American Eddie cries, 'Look at this: you have to *cut* the bread. What a backward country'[5] and Michael Brandon's delivery suggests that he is in earnest, as all nasty jokes are. In both versions, Jack Barker and Eddie Vosper have the equivalent of a cock-size competition on the subject of Keats, the intended wrong-footing based on Potter's presumption that we do not expect Americans to have any literary culture. Their conspicuous exclusion from the game reminds us that in Potterland, women have even less culture than Americans.

The requisite partner-swapping is asymmetric because Jack is too drunk to participate. Eddie's wife Lucy, having had her eye blacked by Jack, ends up with her teenaged stepson Clayton ('I thought justice was a *woman*,' he cries when spurned later in the telefilm). But at least the sense of yearning and the possibility of 'radiance' informs the stage play. *Visitors*, the 1987 rewrite and Potter's first television one-off for seven years, drops the promise of a ship in favour of a gang of terrorists drawing closer, precipitating uncanny symbols – a severed hand running with ants evokes Buñuel's *Un Chien Andalou* – and eventually slaying the grown-ups in a cut-price version (no less risible for that) of the *Dynasty* bloodbath. Evidently, the furies arrive only in Clayton's wish-fulfilment.

Piers Haggard directed *Visitors*. 'I'd done a number of silly things since *Pennies* and I thought I really ought to get back to the challenge of this. There are pages and pages of it which really crackle. You think "Oh, I haven't read stuff like *this* for ages!" It was fun to do and of course doing it in Italy was attractive. But it is very, very dark. It's another self-projection, I suppose. That central character [Jack] is always pushing out the boat, always pressing the barrier of aggression and seeing how far you can push it. Which Dennis himself used to do, to see what would happen if you went on and on saying things you weren't meant to say.'[6]

After *Sufficient Carbohydrate*, the public heard nothing from Potter for almost two years, apart from the publication of the texts of *Blue Remembered Hills*, *Joe's Ark* and *Cream in My Coffee* under the Jack Barker-like title *Waiting for the Boat*. The sourness of the collection's reluctant preface, already remarked upon, suggests he was in a difficult place.

Late in 1985, Potter was back on television on both sides of the Atlantic with a big and expensive dramatisation, in what the Americans would call a mini-series, of the most important book he ever rendered: *Tender is the Night* by Scott Fitzgerald. Published in 1934, it was the last novel the American completed and it survives in two versions, the original and the 1951 revision based on Fitzgerald's incomplete attempt to place the events of the book in chronological order. Potter elected to follow the restructured reading.

The story breaks elegantly into six episodes based on location. The initial proximity to the First World War allows a favourite Potter image: soldiers on a train. Fitzgerald and Potter minutely trace the relationship, conducted across Europe, between the neurologist 'Lucky' Dick Diver (Peter Strauss) and the heiress patient, Nicole Warren (Mary Steenburgen), whom Diver treats – setting himself to transform her 'hysterical despair into [the] normal unhappiness . . . which is the usual lot of mankind'[7] – marries and at last leaves, Nicole noting (in a line of Potter's, not Fitzgerald's): 'He delivered me at the expense of himself'.

The dramatiser does a superb job, organising and making specific the pain that tends to wash in a rather general way through the book and self-effacingly articulating standpoints he would reject in his own work, especially Diver's plea to Nicole at the end of part one: 'Try to forget the past' (a line from the novel). Betty Willingale, initially the project's script editor, points out that 'what Dennis did so terribly well was to lift narrative and turn it into dialogue and I thought he found a rather beautiful poetic quality every now and then.

'It's a fine book but it's also a mess of a book and as a basis for a popular series it's a bugger actually because where do you begin? We got a lot of stick for not starting on the beach, which is what everyone remembers about the book, and then flashing back, but that was a deliberate decision and I was with Dennis totally on it. He gave himself much more work that way. And he did it very faithfully. Curiously enough it was the Americans who suggested radical and daft changes and I used to say to them "we're doing one of *your* great classics!" But I'm not for doing books word by word, that's why you need playwrights to do them, people like Dennis who can enter the ethos of the book with a playwright's eye.'

During pre-production, producer Jonathan Powell was elevated to BBC Head of Drama and Willingale took over the producer's job. 'I didn't know what I was walking into. It was the BBC's first really big co-production and we couldn't bring any of it into Britain because we had American actors and that would have contravened Equity regulations. So one didn't have the help of the BBC to hand or the back-up to retrieve anything that didn't work. All in all I have to say I wasn't as beady as I usually was about the scripts. The BBC had put in *more* money but the financial injection from Showtime was considerable so I got pressures from the Americans which I resisted tooth and nail. That I kept from Dennis.

'But occasionally there were scenes he'd skimped and twice I had to ring him from France or wherever we were with scenes that weren't working. He moaned a lot naturally but I very graciously gave him overnight and the next day he phoned it in and I must say he did wonders. But it was needs must. He stayed interested in it, came to all the previews and talked about it and was very supportive. Nobody liked it of course, including people in the BBC, and it got a terrible press. But funnily enough, Dennis *loved* it. He even liked Peter Strauss.

'He didn't like me, though, but I didn't take offence at that. But we clashed horribly on the music. He was always very hot on music and he'd written in what he wanted on the scripts and I changed it because it was all ten or twenty years too late. Dennis was furious. I said "Scott Fitgerald was said to have the best ear for music of his generation so we're going to trust him." Dennis said "Oh, well, if you're going to be as pedantic as that . . ."'[8]

The next Potter screenplay to go before feature film cameras was a throwback almost to the start of his creative writing career. *Dreamchild* recreated some of the scenes written for *Alice* twenty years earlier, even using some of the same lines, but adding an after-story, which becomes the movie's main traffic, about the child Alice visiting New York as a woman of almost eighty. This is an important piece in the canon.

The widow Alice Hargreaves (Coral Browne) travels to the New World with her young companion Lucy (Nicola Cowper) to receive an honorary degree from Columbia University as part of the Lewis Carroll centenary celebrations. She had not expected to be an object of interest and is alarmed by the town's expectation that she will in some unfathomable way be 'Alice': 'That's intolerable, quite intolerable. It would be difficult enough at my age to be what I once was but utterly impossible to be what I never was.'[9] But the huzza unlocks memories of her childhood (Amelia Shankley) and of the readings by Dodgson (Ian Holm) and the vague misgivings of her mother (Jane Asher).

Jack Dolan (Peter Gallagher) bests the newshound pack and breaches their suite. Though Mrs Hargreaves is severely practical – 'one should always address oneself to things as they actually are' – she is warmed by his charm. Jack appeals to her practicality by pointing out that she stands to make a lot of money out of her Carroll connection: 'Dollars or pounds?' she shoots back.

After a comic interlude at a radio station, Mrs Hargreaves believes she understands marketing. Jack has fixed for her to endorse the all-star Paramount talking picture of *Alice in Wonderland* (indeed released in 1933) but Lucy is distraught by these shenanigans.

Jack's professed affection and the grand but gracious regrets of Mrs Hargreaves put things right. Jack sits up working on the investiture speech.

At the ceremony, Mrs Hargreaves is astonished to hear a choir sing 'The Lobster Quadrille' and finds the past keeps breaking in on her thoughts. She departs from her text to say: 'At the time I was too young to see the gift whole, to see it for what it was, and to acknowledge the love that had given it birth. But I see it now at long long last.'

Dreamchild is Potter's commemoration of his own first journey to the New World, if not at eighty certainly at a mature age. And it is easily the most good-hearted of all his conjunctions of American verve and English reserve. Embodying blithe old-world hypocrisy, Mrs Hargreaves announces, 'I've never heard of anything so reprehensible in all my life' before embracing the reprehensible with a will.

The rest of the film rather falls away from this centre. The posited romance between Lucy and Jack is the least effective because the most hand-me-down (moreover this Lucy registers little and this Jack's looks are too daytime-soap for the role). There are extracts from the book with life-size models by the Jim Henson Creature Shop but these are too physically unyielding and too pedantically redolent of madness and dark imaginings. That young and old Alice visit them turn and turn about is a pleasing conceit, however.

Finally the flashbacks to childhood are as honeyed as required, Potter selecting and buffing up the most acute material from his old play. His swift sketch of Dodgson is so acute, for he was as sensitive to yearning as any writer. The earlier difficulty of Alice being too old is resolved here with the help of retakes and film cutting but by a perverse paradox Dodgson is now far too old in the person of Ian Holm, cast perhaps to reproduce his fine performance in the similar but much more substantial role of J. M. Barrie in Andrew Birkin's television three-parter *The Lost Boys* (BBC, 1978).

Gavin Millar brings more attack to it than to *Cream in My Coffee* and the interiors are beautifully underlit by Billy Williams. Potter acted as executive producer in tandem with the experienced Verity Lambert. The film was not a box-office success but it retains a particular following.

Co-producers of *Dreamchild* were Ken Trodd and Rick McCallum, the latter of whom had acted as executive producer on the *Pennies* feature. Potter's next movie was very much McCallum's baby, a big-screen rewrite of *Schmoedipus* under the title *Track 29*, a phrase from the old Harry Warren/Mack Gordon number 'Chattanooga Choo Choo'.

McCallum reckoned to have walked the script round 170 companies before striking a deal with HandMade Films. Not that he found its executives entirely supportive. 'None of us have even met George Harrison,'* he told the magazine *Producer*. 'Denis O'Brien who runs the company is the only person I know who suffers from jet-lag going from one holiday to another.'10

Track 29 was another Joseph Losey movie that never materialised. Losey left the project (then called *Tears Before Bedtime*) when Jewish investors objected to his casting of Vanessa Redgrave, known for her pro-Palestinian views. His successor was the nearest Potter ever came to working with an *auteur*, Nicolas Roeg. Roeg's own work (*Bad Timing, Don't Look Now, Insignificance, Walkabout, Eureka, The Man Who Fell to Earth, Performance*) suggests someone who would enjoy a meeting of minds with a purveyor of bad dreams, painful sex, alien beings, emblematic presences and ruined childhoods.

'I really enjoyed Potter,' Roeg says. 'He liked teasing people and he was proud of his learning. I remember seeing him in a restaurant with some people from Los Angeles. He waved me over and introduced me and I saw they were thrilled by and in awe of his intelligence which he was using as a shillelagh on them. He hid behind his intelligence but when things got to his heart, whether hurting or pleasing, he let the emotional side of his vocabulary come through.

'For a time during pre-production we got quite close. He'd come round for the evening whenever he could and talk about his life and what he was doing with his work. We'd range far and wide but all things are connected and I like that when one's working with a writer. It's not just born inside a boiled egg, it's connected to all kinds of things.

'In the first draft there was a sense of rape† I didn't want in *my* fantasy about the characters. I came to him saying I wanted to do this script but he understood that I wouldn't just ask what he wanted. We clashed and springing from that I was able to use his themes and he was able to adapt to my feelings about the human condition. We were addressing a continuing theme in Dennis's work which he felt he'd never got right. People tend to write the same play, make the same movie over and over again from different points of view. Like painters. John Bratby painted his wife for years – forwards, backwards, standing up, sitting in the bath. You never quite get it, never get every angle of it.

* The former Beatle set up HandMade in the early 1980s.
† By all accounts the first draft was as much a rewrite of *Brimstone and Treacle* as of *Schmoedipus*.

'He was at the point of wanting to direct himself so he was absorbed by translating from the page to the screen and how not everything is in the dialogue and stage directions, the way the feeling works behind it. His dialogue was so good, it was never just progressing the plot.

'He wasn't able to get to the set at all, first because we were in America and second because he was in one of his relapses.* We worked right up to when it was creeping back on to him. As soon as I'd finished a cut I arranged a screening for him and he was quite pensive about it. He said, "I've tried to get behind this theme many times, Nic, and this is the first time I really think it works." Whereupon we had a few large ones for the relief of it. It cleared his decks. We had a very good evening.'

Roeg's perception of HandMade Films differs from that of his producer. 'They were very good, George Harrison particularly. He said "go for it" because nobody really knows what's commercial anyway. George is one of the most commercially successful people we've had in this country over the last 30 years so who's going to tell him "yes, George, but you don't know what's commercial"?'[12] He roars with laughter.

Track 29 relocates the essentials of *Schmoedipus* in the American South and the prodigal, now bearing the *Brimstone* name of Martin (Gary Oldman), is a boy fostered in England. (He shares Potter's birthday.) Dr Henry Henry (Christopher Lloyd) is a geriatric clinician conducting a discipline-based relationship with Nurse Stein (Sandra Bernhard). Both model railroad freaks, they attend an enthusiasts' convention where Henry enthusiastically makes the keynote address.

Linda Henry, *née* Carter (Theresa Russell), is stifled in their strange house and Martin's arrival (much anticipated) releases memories of her teenage seduction by the fairground man (Oldman) and provokes a spiralling fantasy about bursting out of her cage. After Martin has apparently hacked Henry to death over the wreckage of the model railway, Linda metamorphoses from girly to womanly woman and walks out, leaving a pool of blood spreading on the ceiling but still hearing the voice of the perplexed Henry.

The most extensive developments from *Schmoedipus* to *Track 29* are to the husband's story, capped in the new version by Henry's inspirational speech to the convention, naturally parodying the evangelistic rhetoric of American religion both spiritual and secular (capitalism). Henry appeals to the 'long ago when we knew who we were, what we were and where we were going'.[13] Pastiche was never one of Potter's strong suits but here he hits it off, assisted by vivid

---

* 'The wind had got into my house again,' Potter said, 'and the tiles were falling off me.'[11]

staging. Overall, the script works the most convincing American idiom he ever caught. There is nice play with the meanings of 'mother'.

Oldman's games are rougher than the more ingratiating Tim Curry and the glimmer of adult eroticism is more pronounced. Roeg gives it huge panache and satirical bite and enjoys an orgy of movie references: *Cape Fear, Psycho, Strangers on a Train, King Kong* and more. Endearingly, the quintessentially British animation series *Dangermouse* plays on Linda's perpetually flickering television.

Relishable though it is, *Track 29* did little for Potter's status as a bankable name in Hollywood. But the year before it was made, he had returned to his best and favourite medium to create nothing less than his masterpiece and, most unexpectedly, to enhance his American reputation far more enduringly than through any of his supposedly America-friendly interventions in the world of the movies.

Someone in a Tree

'You in show business?' 'Just the opposite of show business. I'm in the hide-and-seek business. My name is Philip Marlowe.'

Raymond Chandler, *Playback*[1]

The Singing Detective is a summation of Potterana. It is his *Hamlet*, his *Ulysses*, his *A la recherche du temps perdu*, his *Seven Pillars of Wisdom*, his *Life and Opinions of Tristram Shandy*, his *White Album*. It is a *vade mecum* of his themes and concerns and characters and obsessions and techniques. As long as television survives and is archived and studied, it will be viewed, discussed and reinterpreted.

A number of different stories are interlaced. On the baseline is a pulp detective story, notionally a novel but realised here in an imagined dramatisation. This is '*The Singing Detective* by P. E. Marlow': it's 1945 in London. Mark Binney (Patrick Malahide) is directed to a pick-up joint called Skinskapes. Prowling in its bowels, he finds a murdered man. At the bar he meets a Russian hostess Sonia (Kate McKenzie), observed by two traditional hoods (Ron Cook, George Rossi). Sonia accompanies Binney to his flat and cavalierly chews up his money. With the hoods watching the building, Binney has his way with Sonia, then is brutal and accuses her of being a spy. She flees.

The Singing Detective himself (Michael Gambon) rehearses singing (not miming) between shows at the Laguna *palais de dance*. He has a catchphrase: 'Am I right? Or am I right?'[2] Binney seeks his help, fearing that Sonia has come to harm and that he will be the fall guy. 'I get the jobs the polite guys pass over,' the detective says. That night the hoods call on the sardonic Binney ('You look like strays from some bad film') to tell him that Sonia is drowned.

The detective, unapologetic for 'my unhelpful, paperback-soiled, little side-of-the-mouth, mid-Atlantic quips', believes Binney trades in Nazis. Binney angrily pays him off. The flat is now watched by a woman miming 'Lili Marlene'; she makes herself known to the detective but the hoods shoot her. Dying in his arms, she confirms that Skinskapes is a front for dealing in Nazi rocket scientists.

The hoods come to the Laguna to take out the detective but there is a shoot-out and they run. The detective finds Binney at his flat, stabbed through the throat. He hides when the hoods arrive. We learn that they are Intelligence leg-men. They deplore being dispensable, 'padding, like a couple of bleedin' sofas . . . our roles are unclear'. But in a final shoot-out, it is the author who gets the *coup de grâce*.

P. E. Marlow's novel is being laboriously read in an eighties hospital ward by Reginald Dimps (Gerard Horan), a recuperating petty crook. In the next bed, Mr Hall (David Ryall) regularly complains that Reginald is no company and fulminates against the nurses; when they attend him he is squirmily ingratiating. Reginald eventually discovers that the same Philip Marlow (Gambon) is a patient in the ward and he makes himself known to him: 'I bet you lie there all day long just thinking of murdering people, eh?'

This is exactly what Marlow does. He is being treated for psoriatic arthropathy, which is severe at the outset, making him vindictive, thinking of the other patients as 'rats' and railing against the brisk and prissy Nurse White (Imelda Staunton). But he likes pretty Nurse Mills (Joanne Whalley) – 'You're the girl in all those songs' – and when she greases his flaking skin he tries unavailingly to think boring thoughts (Bernard Levin, Clive James) to deter his erection. He tells her of imagining a cat in the bed. 'Sometimes, sometimes these hallucinations are better than the real thing, you know. People can sing in them – or dance, I don't mind, I don't mind. I like pictures.'

Sure enough, the high comedy of the consultant's round becomes a musical number ('Dry Bones') in response to Marlow's despair: 'Talk about the Book of Job. I'm a prisoner inside my own skin and bones.' The medicos only understand physical symptoms and look away from emotion. In the next bed, the chirpy Ali (Badi Uzzaman) suffers a fatal heart attack and Marlow weeps for his own impotence.

Dr Gibbon the psychotherapist (Bill Paterson) discomfits Marlow by seeking clues about him in his detective novel: 'Isn't it clear that you regard sexual intercourse with considerable distaste or, what is more to the point, with fear?' Cantankerous old George Adams (Charles Simon) is installed in the vacated bed. When he threatens to haunt his wife (Joan White), she smacks him and he blubs like a child. 'He's not strong enough to give me one back,' she explains. 'Not now, he isn't.'

Visited by his estranged wife Nicola (Janet Suzman), Marlow pretends to be asleep. Gibbon warns Marlow that 'chronic illness can be an extremely useful shelter . . . a cave in the rocks into which one can safely crawl'. Old George gets carried away recalling the easy sex in the war. Marlow is spellbound as he goes into a fatal spasm. He's reflective about death when Nurse Mills greases him, but still can't control his libido.

Nicola brings news of a man named Mark Finney who wants to make a movie of *The Singing Detective*. 'My advice is to take the money and run,' she says. Marlow wrote a screenplay before he met her which, according to Nicola, he destroyed. 'Ah well. Easy come, easy go,' he says. She thinks he should 'write about real things in a realistic way'. Dr Finlay (Simon Chandler) leads an invasion of evangelists into the ward. Marlow is disturbed by a word-association exercise with Gibbon. It emerges that his mother drowned herself in the Thames. Exorcising childhood ghosts, Marlow manages to walk again.

Mr Hall is unimpressed by Marlow's improvement: 'you don't have to make a song and dance about it, do you'. Nicola takes him home. The reconciliation with Nicola comes only after Marlow has elaborated a self-vexing fantasy that she is in cahoots with Finney (Malahide) to pass off his screenplay as theirs; that he eavesdrops while Finney betrays Nicola in a smarmy phone-call to Hollywood ('it's basically your money, control-wise'); that Nicola is livid ('you're a killer') and is discovered later to have stabbed Finney in the throat; and that Nicola throws herself off Hammersmith Bridge. Before departing, Marlow radiantly tells a perplexed Nurse Mills: 'Nicola isn't in the river.'

The last major strand is Marlow's memory of wartime childhood, surveyed by the boy Philip (Lyndon Davies) sitting in the treetops in the Forest of Dean and making vows for his own future: 'I'll find out things . . . I'll find out who done it.'

Philip lives with his parents in the cramped cottage of Gran (Maggie Holland) and silicotic ex-miner Grancher (Richard Butler). His Londoner mother (Alison Steadman) is maddened by Grancher spitting in the grate, by being dependent and by the spinelessness of her gentle husband (Jim Carter). The rows drive the boy in on himself, self-blaming. Mr Marlow comes alive with his much-appreciated singing (miming) in the working-men's club where Raymond Binney (Malahide) is chairman.

Up his tree, Philip sees his mother being led astray by Binney: 'Thou doosn't want no angel, doos't?' The boy is impelled to climb down and crawl through the ferns. He sees Binney's white bottom and his mother's legs in the air. He stays through the post-coital banter which makes his mother cry. In the working-men's club, Philip imagines everyone gossiping while his father sings on oblivious.

His schoolmates berate him with cries of 'Clever dick'. The teacher (Janet Henfrey) is exhilarated about troop advances and gets the whole class singing 'It's a Lovely Day Tomorrow'. She undertakes a terrifying investigation into the identity of the child who has left faeces on her desk, invoking God's wrath. Philip's snivelling catches her eye and she applies pressure until he cracks and names Raymond Binney's son Mark. The rest of the class embrace the lie and confirm it.

His mother takes him to live in London. The train is full of soldiers and Philip day-dreams of the war ending and of a scarecrow saluting from a passing field before being shot up by the soldiers. Thinking of her adultery, Mrs Marlow weeps but, when the soldiers try to comfort her, Philip is fiercely protective.

Mrs Marlow's own people in Hammersmith irritate her as much as her in-laws. The boy is unhappy, his accent mocked, his father seemingly a touchy subject. In an underground station, she notices a rash on his arm. He pleads to go home, accuses her of 'shagging' Binney and runs away.

After his mother's drowning, Philip goes home. His dad meets him off the train and they walk through the forest, speaking evasively of 'the accident'. The boy runs away when his father tries to tell him that he loves him. Up his tree, Philip vows: 'Doosn't trust anybody again. Doosn't give thy love. Hide in theeself.' He comes down and stalks his dad who, clenched in himself, is suddenly roaring his grief. The boy takes his hand. Up his tree he declares, 'When I grow up, I be going to be a detective.'

This précis teases out and renders linear lines of story which duck and weave in Potter's telling. Even so *The Singing Detective* is reassuringly accessible from moment to moment as well as viewed overall, due as much to Jon Amiel's immensely detailed and sure-footed direction as to Potter's less obviously anguished tone (for once he entirely keeps the shrill out of highly personal material).

That the action proceeds in Marlow's calculating mind – or, when he cannot control his body temperature, in his fevered mind – allows Potter considerable licence to be obscure but he rarely exercises it. The pair of hoods, designated First and Second Mysterious Man, do range freely, appearing as miners in the working-men's club (an unscripted Amiel touch, this), walking into the ward (where, mysteriously, Nicola sees them too), running into the forest and returning to the hospital to twist Marlow's crooked joints before being worsted there by the

Singing Detective. As pawns in a larger game, they are Rosencrantz and Guildenstern figures.*

Structurally, the serial is remarkably bold. Conjunctions inspired by memory allow time and perspective to flow freely. The ground shifts everywhere so that what at first appears as a neutral image reliably retrieved from memory emerges later as a projection. Details of the period tale, avowedly fictional, are revealed instead to be drawn from memory (Sonia is after all a whore whose services Marlow hired). Identities change: the drowned woman is successively Sonia in fiction (and fact?), Mrs Marlow 'disguised' as the fictional 'Lili Marlene' agent and Nicola in a wish-fulfilment. Levels of perception intersect so that Marlow sits claw-fisted in pajamas in the working-men's club and the scarecrow, haunting the ward, is a mouldering image of Philip's teacher.

The theme of transference of guilt is again central. The great betrayal in the classroom is given a quite distinct spin on this occasion, allowing Philip a mitigating circumstance. The casting of the same actress as the teacher should not obscure the fact that she (unlike Miss Tillings in *Stand Up, Nigel Barton*) puts unbearable pressure on the boy to name a guilty party: the vengeful malice of Nigel has dwindled into Philip's induced trespass.

For all the sparky writing invested in Marlow's defensive sarcasm throughout his scenes with Gibbon, there is unwonted benignity here in the depiction of psychotherapy. We see Marlow actually relieved by expressing his guilt. That he might achieve redemption is less clear. *The Singing Detective* seems to be the least deliberately religious of the post-*Son of Man* works, notwithstanding the image of Marlow, shot full-figure from above, irresistibly Christ-like in what can only be described as a loin-cloth as he lies 'crucified' by illness and the impenetrable incantations of Pharisaical consultants.

The role of musical numbers is different to that in *Pennies from Heaven*. They are not expressions of otherwise mute longings here, except accidentally. Rather they are evocative period pieces for the 'performers' (Marlow *père* and the Singing Detective) to deliver with, as it were, the proper flavour (Marlow miming a ditty by the *siffleur* Ronnie Ronalde is a particularly poignant example of how outmoded is the 'speciality act'); or else they are Marlow's hallucinations.

Jon Amiel tells the story of beginning work on the serial: 'I was directing *The Silent Twins* at the BBC and Ken Trodd came into my office in that sidelong way that he specialises in and put these six scripts on my desk. So I started reading and I realised halfway

---

* The proliferation of echoes of *Hamlet* through the serial deserves a study in itself.

through the first one that my hands were actually shaking. I felt absolutely convinced that I was in the presence of a masterpiece and I was terrified both that I might not be asked to do it and that I *would* be asked to do it. In fact I was only asked after five or six more eminent and obvious choices had turned it down for various reasons.

'I remember meeting Dennis with photographic clarity. It was lunch in his then favourite Italian restaurant. He was a tremendous creature of habit, he knew what he liked which was what he knew. I was really in awe of him but I was determined to prove that I wasn't just scared – which I was, completely – so I must have come over as insufferably cocky. I felt strongly that the script wasn't quite there and I'd decided that he would be someone who would appreciate the full-frontal approach rather than a tiptoe, so I jumped in. He grabbed his favourite tipple of the time, Gévrey-Chambertin, with his buckled hands, and he looked at me rather as Sebastian must have looked at the Roman soldiers as one arrow after another entered his body. The meeting ended fairly neutrally and we agreed to meet again a couple of days later. The situation was complicated by the fact that Ken and Dennis were in the midst of a full-scale marital split and Dennis was turning to Rick McCallum as his new producing partner. I had the temerity to say that I thought it was very important Ken stay on the project. It needed his in-fighting skills to protect it inside the BBC.

'When I got to the second meeting, Dennis was already drunk and Rick was there grinning with anxiety. Dennis greeted me with "Jon, you're looking a lot older than when I last saw you" and he proceeded to be vile for two hours in a way which only those who've had detailed dealings with him can quite appreciate. He was always at his most cutting when he had one person as his audience and another as the butt. He was very good at it and being pissed only made him better at it. After all, he was a man whose brain and tongue were his only weapons in an effectively useless body.

'I felt that the only way to deal with him was to get just as drunk but I only ended up with a savage headache, feeling I couldn't face the prospect of bearing this abuse right through the production. The language had been very ripe and I finally called him a patronising cunt. Another of his techniques was to look at you in a quizzical and innocent way – "Jon, have I hurt you? What did I say?" – which is even more infuriating. I'd like to say I walked out after that magnificent statement but the evening just petered out.

'Next morning I called Rick and said "I can't work with him. Nothing's worth it." Rick was very conciliatory and said that Dennis felt a bit guilty and would like to meet one more time. Shortly after that, Rick jumped ship in favour of Nic Roeg's *Castaway* which Dennis felt as an acute betrayal.

'Very gingerly, I went to the same restaurant a week later. Dennis was always obsessively on time and furious if you were late which I tend to be, so I deliberately arrived early. He came in and put a *Pepys' Diary* on the table and humphed a bit and said "I was buying a new copy of this so I thought I'd get you one as well."

'As it happened I'd bought him a book too. He said "Christ, Amiel, can't I ever get one up on you?" I couldn't know at the time but that was the last moment of conflict we ever had. What followed was extraordinary. I started in on what I wanted to do with the last episode and I was halfway through proposing the mysterious men come into the hospital and he said "yeah-yeah-yeah, shut up, hold on, okay, they'll come in – and what else?" And I found Dennis was letting me in on the process. I would get halfway into a thought and Dennis would shut me up. I had to learn to trust he would get it, which he always did. The thing he hated more than anything was being told what to do.

'When we'd finished eating, Dennis said "come back and we'll do some more". So we went to his flat in Paddington and talked for another hour or two about structure and plotting until he got tired. Then I called Ken who was getting anxious and I said we went back to Dennis's flat and he said "You did *what?* You went to his *flat?* I've never been to his flat!" I hadn't realised that this was an immense gesture of trust and inclusion, taking me into the *sanctum sanctorum*.

'The following meeting was the first time Dennis made me cry. He told me the history of his illness and the treatments he'd had and their side-effects, completely dispassionately and without any self-pity. It was so appalling that the tears rolled down my cheeks. When we left the restaurant, I offered him a lift and he said he'd rather walk. I watched him go, this very thin man, six foot one or two but stooped and with a very stiff walk. And I found myself intensely moved by him. I did really grow to love him in a way that quite astonished me. I'd always expected to admire him, I'd never expected to like him and I certainly never expected to love him deeply. Much later in a radio interview, he said we were like brothers on the script. Frankly I never had that good a relationship with my own brother but I was very touched.

'We agreed after the third meeting that I would direct it. There was a very short pre-production schedule, about two and a half months for seven hours of very complex material. About a week into it, Dennis rang and said "You'll be very pleased to hear I've decided to rewrite the whole lot!" I remember this wave of panic and nausea washing over me. What he did was the most amazing feat I've known any writer accomplish. He actually did what he threatened. He literally rewrote every episode from beginning to end. There was not a scene he didn't touch in some way and many he changed dramatically. He was beginning a very severe attack of his illness at the time. Yet he did one episode a week in ledger books in his beautiful longhand with hardly a crossing out. I've never known a writer edit himself like that. He got to the end and the last episode, though greatly improved, still wasn't quite right so he sat down and did it again. I had location managers tearing their hair out because they didn't know what to look for for episode six.

'There was a day he dropped in on rehearsals. He watched Patrick Malahide working on a scene. Patrick's an intensely analytical actor and he needed to map out the precise boundaries of each of the three characters he was playing. At the end of the scene he looked very nervously at Dennis who said "What you've got to understand about this character is that he simply doesn't exist, he's a figment of somebody's imagination." And I watched Patrick completely crumble – all the boundaries he'd carefully constructed just fell to pieces. In retrospect it was very funny and typical of Dennis's impatience with the process. At that point, I was feeling sufficiently in control not to be concerned and in the end it precipitated quite a few things that turned out to be useful for Patrick. So that was Dennis's contribution to rehearsals.'

Was he conscious of writing a masterpiece? 'I think so. He vigorously denied that it was autobiographical but it was at the very least intensely personal. After the read-through – which was an event in itself: Dennis read the role of the schoolteacher, quite brilliantly – he was absolutely white. I asked if he was OK and he said "I hadn't realised it was so close to the bloody bone." He had meant to fictionalise more but in practice that white glint shone through every page.

'He berated me for some small details as we went along but the truth is that I cut large chunks of text and made considerable changes without warning him* and he never commented once. One of the traps of his work is that he writes with such specificity and authority that the temptation is to treat the text as some golden treasure map that must be adhered to. If you want to change it, you damn well better replace it with something as specific and as intensely felt. That was what I discovered in working on it and it was an incredibly liberating discovery. That he never

* Episode five as produced departs wholesale from the structure of the published text.

intervened in that was another of the many surprises of working with him.'[3]

Alison Steadman, cast as Mrs Marlow, remembers Potter 'skulking in a corner of the rehearsal room. He didn't make himself known to the actors, no going round saying "hello". I was a bit nervous of him, to be honest, because he did have that reputation for not suffering fools gladly and I thought he might not like what I was doing.

'I found the story of my character very painful. But he'd written her with such understanding, brilliant for a man. There wasn't a moment I thought "Oh, I don't know why she's saying this" or "I don't quite believe that." When she's in the forest with Raymond, she says, "You've been here before, haven't you . . . You're no good." It's lightly said but there's this dawning behind it that she's being used but she can't get out of it. It's not until afterwards that she can't handle it and breaks down. I thought that was so moving and so true.'

The seduction scene in the forest was at the centre of the serial's passing notoriety. 'That scene was an ordeal mentally and physically. As well as the emotional stuff in it, we got scratched and bitten. And I hadn't seen it before it went out because the schedule was so tight.

'The morning that episode was shown, I went to my local newsagent and I saw the front of the *Sunday Today*, a paper which no longer exists, thank God. Colour pictures were still rare in newspapers but there was a colour photo of me – not in character, of *me* – under this headline: "BBC Braces Itself for Biggest Sex Shock Ever!" The newsagent went "Whoa-hey, nudge nudge" and I grabbed the paper, ran home, threw it down the hall and shouted for Mike.*

'I kept thinking "How explicit can it be?" So I phoned Jon Amiel in editing and he put a tape straight in a taxi. While I waited, I phoned my parents and said "don't invite the neighbours in and keep a low profile!". Then I sat and watched it and of course it was fine. Far from being embarrassed about it, I was proud of it. The very idea of it ever being cut was ludicrous because it was such a central obsession of Marlow's, the mother and the lover and the whore. It just shows how things get out of hand. Mind you, the viewing figures went right up!'[4]

Amiel's theory is that 'it was all to do with the Beeb-bashing period that Thatcher and Murdoch joined forces on so that he could advance his interest in Sky. It was whipped up by the Murdoch press. Dennis enjoyed all that stuff. He liked his bad boy reputation and being the excoriating critic.'

---

* Steadman, who is married to the director Mike Leigh, is the most game of players. She has also, as it were, undergone natural childbirth in *Our Flesh and Blood* and mastectomy in *Through the Night*.

Reactions to the serial in the business confounded Amiel's expectations. 'The first surprise was how little recognition the television establishment gave it. The BAFTA awards that year were a sick joke. That Dennis could be sitting there getting progressively drunker and not hear his name mentioned once was simply a crime. It got thirteen nominations from the membership but just two awards. I decided Dennis would get the Writer's Award but that went to the guy who wrote *Only Fools and Horses*. As usual, the British were suspicious of extraordinary achievement – not mine, although I'm proud of it, but Dennis's.

'But the Americans embraced it with a whole-hearted enthusiasm that astounded me. When an agent first said "I want to get it shown over here", I said "Oh, please don't bother. They're not going to get it. It's very English, it's very complicated, it's a scabby man railing and swearing. Unlike American shows, it *does* stop still for more than two minutes. It'll be just embarrassing." But it was shown widely on PBS and it re-established Dennis in Hollywood. The movie of *Pennies from Heaven* had been an expensive disaster.

'The great sadness for me is that we never found anything else to do together. He put a lot of emotional pressure on me to do *Christabel* but it felt like a step backwards for me and no amount of loyalty to Dennis would make me feel it was the right thing for me to do next.'

Whether it was the right thing for Potter is a speculation that must be largely futile. Coming between ambitious personal projects, *Christabel* would have felt like a good opportunity to exercise his craft without punishing his psyche. But as Graham Fuller points out in *Potter on Potter*,[5] he himself optioned the book on which the four-part serial is based after its republication in 1982 and he must have been drawn to its title, *The Past is Myself*. He told Fuller his title-change was in order to indicate his priorities but he would surely have taken much pleasure in being able to give the project the title of one of the most haunting of Coleridge's poems.

The Past is Myself is a memoir of the circumstances of the early years of an unusual mid-century marriage. The book is artlessly engrossing, written with candour and intelligence. Potter's version is more ruthlessly shaped and pitched. He begins, like an old showbiz pro, with the build-up to the wedding – a chance for Christabel (Elizabeth Hurley) to look lovely – and it is not until he speaks the vows that we enjoy the *frisson* that her lawyer groom Peter (Stephen Dillon*) is a German. The couple settle in Berlin.

* The actor now styles himself Stephen Dillane.

Thereafter it quickly takes the form of a personal story laid against momentous events: the rise and fall of the Nazi regime. Part of what makes it such a conventional narrative is that the technique of opening up an alien experience by filtering it through a stranger who more resembles the reader or viewer is very well-worked. Potter's Christabel indeed makes a virtue of her alienation: 'What have *we* got to do with politics?'6 What she begins to learn is the importance of small gestures of defiance – throwing cigarettes to POWs, taking on a Jewish maid who passes for Aryan.

Potter smuggles in his touches: Christabel reads *Alice* to her two sons. Despatched for safety to the Black Forest, she is sent by the villagers to talk to a captured American airman who, waking, takes her for an angel. Returning to Berlin to sue for the imprisoned Peter, she is engaged in conversation by an SS man who chillingly describes killing Jews.

'One of the first things Potter said to me after I was cast,' says Elizabeth Hurley, 'was "I have to say to you what I said to the real Christabel and that is that this is now *my* Christabel and *my* Peter and of course it's going to differ from the real Christabel and Peter. We've moved into fiction and you have to detach yourself from the initial reality and make the movie". That was important for me because I thought her book was superb – I loved her second book too, about living in Ireland – but for dramatic purposes I had to put it aside. He was involved in the audition process but after that he was very sick.

'The rehearsal wasn't sitting about in jeans and tee-shirt pretending to be in an air-raid shelter. It really was a great deal of discussion and Christabel and Peter came to those. It went from trivial things like costume etiquette and eyebrow plucking to things that, as an actress, you rarely have the luxury of asking. It's really very difficult to imagine the feeling of walking along a corridor into a Gestapo man's office where you're going to be interrogated in your attempt to save your husband's life and she was there to ask. Of course you can chose to do what she did or do your own thing but to *know* that is wonderful.

'Very often when you first work on a script you have the intention of changing as many words as you can, especially if they're ineptly written, but with someone like Dennis Potter you very rarely do. In fact I don't think I changed a word. I think his prose reads like poetry. It was a strange script, in some ways quite stylised and beautiful, and it played more simply than it read.

'I think he was absolutely the best person to do it. Some Americans who held the rights before had said "We gotta make this movie exciting, develop an affair between you and Adam or whatever" and Christabel was horrified. I sat with her when she saw it for the first time and it was so moving for her. It wasn't *her*, it was very different but very moving nevertheless. She thoroughly approved of it. But it was a great shame that it wasn't a huge success. Not a lot of people saw it but I think people who did were moved by it, people stuck with it and weren't disappointed that it wasn't singing and dancing and sexy, Dennis Pottery things.'[7]

The following year's project wasn't singing and dancing either but it was certainly sexy and intensely Pottery. And those who were moved by it were mostly moved to anger.

24

Deep Purple

'How many times, she wondered, would allegedly sympathetic accounts of the manifold ways in which . women were so regularly humiliated be nothing more than yet further exercises of the same impulse, the identical power?'

Blackeyes[1]

Much of Potter's work is haunted by the promise of a woman. She is precisely depicted as tall, dark ('raven-haired') and large-eyed. He battens most keenly on the eyes. In a virtuoso essay of 1972 about the strange conjunctions of television ('the mutation of poor old Maigret into bumbling Count Rostov'*), Potter makes what seems like a stray aside, an adumbration of work several years in the future. 'Somewhere, my love, somebody is rehearsing *Black Eyes*'.[2] And Potter eventually gives his vision the name of Blackeyes.

She is first brought into focus in his third novel, named for her, a fitfully brilliant exercise taking up the new free-flowing style that Potter had found in his previous novel, *Ticket to Ride*, to which this chapter will return. *Blackeyes* interlocks different accounts of the same story – formally two, with others working in a subterranean way.

'The lovely Jessica', as the novel's opening words describe her, is a green-eyed former model. She has told various stories about her career to her disreputable uncle, Maurice James Kingsley, who thereupon turned them into a novel, *Sugar Bush*, his first to be published in

---

* The actor Rupert Davies, cast in *War and Peace*, was most familiar on television as Simenon's sleuth – a character, oddly enough, recreated in the 1990s by Potter's Marlow, Michael Gambon.

many years. *Blackeyes* presents both Kingsley and Jessica in, as it were, an objective way. Reading *Sugar Bush*, which is extracted through her eyes (as well as through Kingsley's), Jessica 'had to start all over again, dismantling his narrative, reclaiming herself'. And so Jessica's version also takes over the narrative, though only when the 'objective' story is concerned with her dealings. Potter is handling conflicting realities simultaneously, one supposedly reclaiming 'truth' from the other though of course Jessica is not objective either – it is 'a vengeful game' for her. This theme of breaking free from someone else's account, someone else's fiction, will take centre-stage in Potter's very last work, *Cold Lazarus*.

In a quite haunting way, the story of Blackeyes, the Jessica fictionalised by Kingsley, takes on a life of its own, independent of both its 'creators'. In Kingsley's account, Blackeyes/Jessica blankly sleep-walks through a process in which she allows herself to be exploited. 'You let yourself be rogered by any Johnny who cared to ask,' Kingsley thinks in Jessica's company and it summarises his stance in his fiction. The history of his perception of her (it is not a great surprise) is that Uncle Maurice abused Jessica as a child.

But in the interstices between Kingsley's fictionalisation and the account of her life that Jessica owns – both in the sense that she 'possesses' it and in the sense that she 'admits' to it, at one level to her uncle, at another to herself – Blackeyes, a character on a page just as, in the end, both Kingsley and Jessica are, begins to take on an independent life; this transcends the yarn (clearly 'Kingsley's invention', simultaneously cerebral and cheesy) of her exploitation and death by drowning, a list of the men who have 'rogered' her tucked, with thunderous resonance, into her vagina. Modulating her own seeming passivity, she announces ('with precision' says the narrator, but *which* narrator?): 'I am not a prostitute.' This allows her to 'do the sex' on her own terms.

The 'erotic dream girl straight off the posters' is, Kingsley later perceives in pensive mood, 'possessed by the kind of beauty which provokes as much hatred as admiration'. And inevitably Kingsley invests Blackeyes with the pleasurable pain of his own longings. Jessica concludes 'that Kingsley had been writing about himself, mixing his own eccentricities into the girl's thoughts. A nasty image came walking towards her: the old man's grey-tufted head perched wrinkling and simpering on the young woman's slender body, a grotesque transplant.' The image of the writer's severed head will recur in *Cold Lazarus*.

A further perspective is revealed in the book, that of 'I', the seemingly uncharacterised narrator: 'I have used the old fellow's narrative as the basis of my own account'. Potter, who has such difficulty leaving things unsaid, sacrifices perspective in favour of this intrusive commentary, even if he is alive to every last irony in the 'authorial' aside: 'You will understand, of course, that this and what follows is as much an embarrassment to me as if I had been caught whacking myself off in a room with closed curtains'.

Potter must have intended, even while writing the novel, that this allusive, elusive, illusive material should be filmed, though not necessarily by himself. Rick McCallum, who developed the project as a domestic television serial and a movie for export and eventually produced it as a BBC four-parter, revealed that it was offered to Nicolas Roeg. 'I think it was a little bit mean-spirited for him'[3] is McCallum's assessment.

So Potter took the helm himself. This was widely though not universally thought to be ill-advised. Reviewing *Ticket to Ride* in 1986, I had written: 'You can feel Potter's movie experience, sense him "seeing the shots" and panning for you, tracking, pulling focus, dropping in filters and cutaways and, especially, editing with a highly developed rhythmic grasp. He *must* direct a movie.'[4] The writer who could say frankly 'I'm not a novelist'[5] wrote his second and third novels as if they were montages. Part of the result of (part of the reason for?) developing this fugitive fluidity was to keep more control, to make his vision so personal, so resistant to interpretation by other directors that he *had* to direct.

Blackeyes the serial garnered the most vitriolic reviews of Potter's career. Apart from the sheer vexation of being perplexed, critics were troubled by what they saw as an exploitative approach to women. The tabloids took up the cry of 'Dirty Den', derived from the *EastEnders* character: Potter ought to have rather enjoyed the implications of being twinned with a personage out of fiction but all the evidence suggests that he was too stunned to enjoy any of it.

Reassessment is in order. Certainly Potter misjudged the impact of his own images and should have anticipated that his detached stance, even as expressed in his own sardonic voice-over, would invite the judgement that to show is to endorse. From way back, Potter was opposed to offering easy moral stances in his work. So his strong feelings about the exploitation of women – and he clearly had such feelings even if they seemed to be at variance with his own voyeuristic sensibility – would never be more than *implied* in *Blackeyes*, even without the elliptical nature of the serial.

Twenty-one years earlier, Potter reviewed a teleplay set in the world that *Blackeyes* inhabits:

So here we go again. Round and round the mulberry bush or the pillow-case or the zoom lens, up to our glazed eyeballs in the joys of the Permissive Society. Last night's ITV play *The Photographer* began with the throaty click-click of the camera recording the frozen pose of a weary model. Sounds and sights of a new dream world, measured by the thousandth of a second and wrapped in glossy magazine covers to glimmer mockingly back from a hundred draughty little bookstalls on dirty station platforms.[6]

Potter is nothing if not a moralist. *Blackeyes* is no more to be condemned out of hand than Michael Powell's *Peeping Tom* or Alfred Hitchcock's *Vertigo* or even Brett Easton Ellis's *American Psycho*. All four works address degrees of objectification of women and – in exploring the phenomenon of that objectification – knowingly, calculatedly indulge it.

But the tone *is* problematical in *Blackeyes*. Potter tries to be light and playful. He has chuckly little jokes, some of them relatively private. Blackeyes (Gina Bellman) is sent to a modelling assignment requiring fair-skinned blondes with blue eyes by an agency called PfH. The copy of Kingsley's (Michael Gough) book that Jessica (Carol Royle) is reading can be seen to be Potter's *Blackeyes*. Al Bowlly and Bill and Ben the Flowerpot Men are dragged in kicking and screaming as cultural reference points.

And the writer-director's voice-over raises a question about Potter's confidence in his material. When the lascivious businessman Jamieson (Colin Jeavons) has Blackeyes astride him with Potter's camera (it has to be said) dwelling on her breasts, the voice-over asks pertly: 'Was that a real orgasm do you think?', then adds as if the answer is not to be trusted: 'No, no, all false of course.' The actors must have wondered whether this game would ever end.

'You have to imagine this if you must,' he says, drawing a veil over the abuse by Kingsley of the child Jessica and drawing a line between what art may demonstrate and what suggest. Maybe that is the work's true macrosubject. Life is a demonstration, art a suggestion, and the sovereignty (a word now appearing in Potter's essays) of the human being is not to be plundered for the delectation of others. Hence his demonising of Rupert Murdoch as orchestrator of tabloid values.

'I wasn't familiar with his work,' says Gina Bellman, remembering her call to read for the title role. 'But I responded very much to the title of the piece because I'd been told all through childhood that I had these very dark, melancholic eyes. So it struck a chord with me. I think Dennis was someone who was drawn to melancholy in people. We just talked about many things including feminist issues and he asked me really provocative questions like "What's it like to be an attractive woman in the 1980s?" He asked me to read from the book which was also a nice change from reading a script with a casting director's assistant. So it didn't really get scary until after I got the job.

'Dennis was always incredibly specific about shots and the costume and the look, very involved in every visual detail. But he didn't know how to get a performance out of an actor. So it became an intellectual process. We talked for hours about the content of the piece but creatively you were out on a limb, really. He was such an intense human being and so brilliant in so many areas but he had the concentration span of a child. When he was shooting it, he got bored with the writing and started to change it. When he was editing, he got bored with the direction. While I'm still very proud of *Blackeyes* and think it's ground-breaking material, the flaw in it is that it ended up being a different serial from the original script because he got bored and started changing his mind. That's why the narration suddenly appeared. I think it would have been much more lucid if he'd stuck to the script.

'His moods reflected his state of health. If he was feeling unwell he'd be in a bad temper and then he'd want to change things. He would come to the set very ill and then you'd never see anyone drink so much or smoke so much or eat such rich food. Other times he'd be in less pain and then he was really sweet and we'd have a thoroughly wonderful day's shoot. He was in his element and thrilled to be doing what he'd longed to do. It was a joyful time for everyone involved. It was total harmony through the most fabulous summer. He'd been a recluse for a long time and suddenly he was God.

'I was completely in awe of this brilliant man and I think he was in awe of my youth and energy. I would race around on my roller-skates. We struck up this weird and wonderful friendship. He became very possessive of me and I had to make myself available to have dinner with him every night on location to discuss the next day's shooting. He was being a Pygmalion character.

'He would talk literature and poetry and tell me about his old involvement in politics and his childhood and parents and family life and rave on about journalists. If he was being interviewed, he liked to have me there to watch him destroy the journalist's confidence. And he encouraged me a great deal with my acting and my performance.

'I found it an incredibly dark piece and felt enveloped in darkness by it. But he was always ready to talk about it. He was such a contradiction because there was a part of him that really was a dirty old man and another part that was so honourable and so gentlemanly and so wanted to address an issue that he thought important. He was always going on about being a puritan but a true puritan couldn't have come up with the stories he did.

'I think now there was quite a lot of nudity that was unnecessary but at the time I trusted him implicitly. And I'm still committed to the message of the piece. I believe we had to enter into exploitation to a degree in order to show it. It wasn't till people kept asking if I had felt exploited that I realised that I only felt exploited by the press. Then there he was saying publicly "I had to fall in love with the actress playing Blackeyes." Nothing happened between us but I had to live with all the speculation that that provoked.'[7]

That Bellman bewitched Potter was inevitable, given her resemblance to his long-nurtured fantasy, his new control as implementer as well as originator of his vision, his relish for emotional blackmail and psycho-danger games, her youth and undoubted talent. Perhaps losing his middle-aged heart and some of his reason to a young woman was preordained by William Hazlitt, with whom Potter so identified. 'To what state am I reduced, and for what?' Hazlitt wrote. 'For fancying a little artful vixen to be an angel and a saint, because she affected to look like one, to hide her rank thoughts and deadly purposes. Has she not murdered me under the mask of the tenderest friendship?'[8] It is a poignant connection that Potter's eldest child, Sarah, bears the name of both Hazlitt's wife and his beloved.

Although *Ticket to Ride* was written before the novel *Blackeyes*, the latter was dramatised sooner and so has taken precedence here. *Ticket* is the superior book. Faber did Potter no favour by blurbing it as 'a brilliant psychological thriller'[9] for the expectations thereby generated draw attention to conventional ingredients. After parody – which Potter could not do though he thought he could and persisted in so doing, witness the never accurately 'heard' hip journalist Mark Wilsher in *Blackeyes* – disclosure is the least satisfying literary gambit and it is not his forte either. The novel opens with a man in the grip of amnesia. In a simile that rings with defiance, he even has his protagonist peer 'like a detective' in the search for history and identity.

John is in obscure flight from home and past. Flight turns to quest. Dream and hallucination fuse memory and encounter. Images turn experience into symbol, symbol into experience. We are full-pitch into obsession and breakdown, paranoia and schizophrenia, priapism and death. And there is no let-up, 'there could be no escape into silence'. In the midst of the delirium, Potter places a burst of exquisitely timed and turned dinner-table comedy, followed by black family ritual. Here the central imagery comes into focus. John's sexual disgust is grounded in the obsessional, sublimating knowledge of wild flowers that so exercised his cleric father.

The flower/genital axis – Potter writes for instance of 'the recollection of a breathless descent into the tendrils of a plant, and the seep of mauve which came from its bloom' and he has John's father chide the boy with the highly resonant injunction: 'Please don't say um. Never say um. You are not a bumble bee' – this pollination/penetration parallel, directs us to the book's epigraph and its author, D. H. Lawrence.

The quotation is from Lawrence's poem 'Shadows' in which that equally perfervid novelist/playwright weaves a shiver of flower-dream-God-renewal magic. There is an irresistible reminder too of the vivid classroom scene in *Women in Love* where the predatory Hermione intrudes on Birkin's lesson about catkins and asks, 'When we have knowledge, don't we lose everything but knowledge? . . . If I know about the flower, don't I lose the flower and have only the knowledge?'[10]

In *Ticket to Ride*, Potter writes deeply about the urge to know and the loss that knowledge brings. His conclusion, which corresponds to the end of 'Shadows' – 'God is breaking me down to his own oblivion / To send me forth on a new morning, a new man'[11] – comes out of a too orderly wish to resolve the patterns of hurt. The arrival is less than the journey.

The most slippery aspect of the writing – it too suggests Lawrence – is the familiar preoccupation with woman as whore. Emboldened by his depiction of Mrs Hargreaves in *Dreamchild* (the film was released as he was beginning the novel), Potter makes one of his rare attempts to write from a woman's perspective – though formally filtered through the imaginings of a man (just as the greater part of Jessica's story in *Blackeyes* will be rewritten by Kingsley) – in the interwoven torments of John's seemingly abandoned wife Helen. That Helen used to be a prostitute may be a fixation of John's but it restricts the role of women in John's fracturing world-view, making all of them actual whores or women who, to a racked, heterosexual, puritan man, *behave* like whores.

The only woman not so characterised is John's fleetingly recalled mother, reduced by a cleft palate to a private sound-language like that of the paralysed Pattie in *Brimstone*. Nothing is desultory (a 'jobbing Scot' gardener is called Milne and that is neither private nor a joke) and even the mother's disability resonates with notions of secret silence, violence and perversion.[12]

281

The peculiarly musing, drifting style of *Ticket to Ride* suggests a ride described two years earlier in a stream-of-half-consciousness on the Intercity express: 'My wine-moistened lip deliberately lifted in a deliberately mannered imitation of a supposedly fractional disdain as I continued to stare out of the scudding, momentarily sightless window . . . Fortunately there was nobody in the opposite seat, unless it were the momentary phantom of my younger, more priggish and much more disdainful self . . . Perhaps it is impossible to compose neatly consecutive thoughts on the rattlingly straight, fast track between Swindon and Paddington.'[13]

The title *Ticket to Ride* is an effective hook. It implies a traveller who knows his destination even if the route is obscure. The title of the film version, *Secret Friends*, picks up the subject of discussion in the dinner-party scene of both book and film, that of the imaginary playmates of solitary children. John himself had a naughty *alter ego* into whom he channelled his hatred of his father. Again, this theme will inform *Cold Lazarus*.

The myriad questions which haunt the newly amnesiac John in the book are resolved into a central demand in the film – 'What have I done?'[14] – and this points the link to Christ in *Son of Man*: 'Is it me?' – emphasising the shape of the narrative as a journey out of the wilderness. Potter's own direction also finds an edgy, gallows comedy which the book never hints at, especially in the figures of the two (reduced from three) businessmen (Ian McNeice, Davyd Harries) on the train who eat in unison and attempt to make the appropriate noises over John's (Alan Bates) plight. As a comic pair who turn up 'mysteriously' in John's fantasy of his wife Helen (Gina Bellman) playing out a prostitute role in a hotel (c.f. *Double Dare*), both past and present, the businessmen now evoke the *film noir* hoods from *The Singing Detective*.

The end of the film, like that of the novel, is touched with bathos. John literally wakes from his nightmare ('I dream of the gutter') and is offered agony-auntish advice by Helen: 'It's not possible to live out a fantasy . . . It's too dangerous.' They look at his flower reproductions on the train.

Secret Friends was made as a feature film but received very limited theatrical release before joining the Film on Four repertoire for Channel 4 (which had financed the enterprise). The production company was Whistling Gypsy which Potter had set up with his agent Judy Daish and his daughter Sarah; its name was taken from the song associated with Alf Tracey, 'the Street Singer'.

'While we were doing *Blackeyes*,' says Gina Bellman, 'he gave me *Ticket to Ride* and said "I want to do the movie and you'd be perfect for the part.' I loved the book and was really keen to do the part. Then I didn't hear anything more. After *Blackeyes*, we'd meet for lunch every two or three months and he'd say he was still trying to set up *Secret Friends*.

'When *Blackeyes* got all that attention, he was such a fighter and such a strong spirit that at first he reacted in a sort of "fuck you" way. But he was devastated by the way it was received. I think if it had been released as a feature film, it would have had a completely different impact but he wanted to provoke people in their front rooms. With time his confidence was knocked and he got increasingly nervous about doing another film.

'I started to represent the failure of *Blackeyes* for him and he said "I'm not sure I want you to do it now" and I said "That's fine" and he said "But I made you a promise". A lot of game-playing went on but I ended up doing it. I was thrilled to work with Alan Bates.

'As soon as I was hired, Dennis started taking out all his frustrations on me. He had become quite controlling of me on *Blackeyes* but I'd gone off for a year and a half and worked with other directors and done some theatre and that was difficult for him to accept. I was meeting him on different terms. And I addressed the role in a much deeper way than I approached Blackeyes. He was bitter that I had grown and moved on and found other experiences when his heart was broken by how *Blackeyes* had been received.

'On the first day on the set, I came and met the crew and then Frances [Barber] and I had a scene to do. Frances is a fantastically brilliant classical actress and Alan was there too so I felt very intimidated. We did a camera rehearsal and then Dennis said in front of everybody "Gina, are you going to play the whole film in that New Zealand accent?" I haven't spoken in a New Zealand accent since I was ten. He always used to say "Here comes the Kiwi" and it was a fond reference on *Blackeyes* but this was a spiteful and undermining comment to make me feel like a silly outsider in front of a classical actress and a great film actor. And the bullying and the little comments were constant through the shoot. He'd go out of his way to intimidate and undermine me. We fought miserably and that rubbed on other people involved. He had his entourage, his agent and so on. And I was definitely in the enemy camp because I wouldn't pander to his tantrums and his bullying. He was a *real* bully.

'It was very difficult to bear and we hardly spoke after *Secret Friends*. I know what a complex man he was and I love him deeply and I don't think the two things contradict. We stopped being close when I couldn't cope with his mind-games any more.'[15]

25

You Keep Coming Back Like a Song

'Would someone with a hard face please protect me from those sickly and sugared old tunes?'

Dennis Potter[1]

The outcry over *Blackeyes* and the box-office failure of *Secret Friends* had a deplorable effect on Potter as a writer. He ran for cover and safety and tried to appeal to an old audience with familiar material and techniques. The result was a six-part serial that runs well nigh six hours and has nothing to say.

Lipstick on Your Collar was made by Whistling Gypsy for Channel 4 with Potter acting as executive producer and a new ally, Renny Rye, as director. With the exception of the American producer of the *Pennies from Heaven* movie (a double-edged compliment as noted earlier), all Potter's books and texts are dedicated to various combinations of his wife and children, save the text of *Lipstick* which is inscribed 'To Renny Rye who made the difference . . .'[2] Some would argue, of course, that this only shows just how much Rye was Potter's creature.

The basis and indeed the bulk of the raw plot of the new serial was the play *Lay Down Your Arms* made by Kestrel for LWT twenty-three years earlier. Other reworkings derive from *The Singing Detective*: life in a west London terrace and the situation of a man confined – earlier in bed, here to a desk – projecting production numbers around fellow 'inmates'.

The main setting is the War Office at the time of Suez. The embarrassing fact that the Suez crisis broke three years before the release of the serial's title song illustrates the lack of proper rigour in its making. Private Francis Francis (Giles Thomas) – perhaps a Welsh cousin of *Track 29*'s Dr Henry Henry – reports to the Russian section in the translation department of the War Office. He's staying with his long-suffering Aunt Vickie (Maggie Steed) and puritanical Uncle Fred (Bernard Hill) in their Fulham terrace house. By extraordinary coincidence, the voluptuous Sylvia (Louise Germaine), who lodges upstairs and for whom Francis soon nurses an unrequited passion, is married to his brutal corporal, Peter Berry (Douglas Henshall).

Sylvia is also lusted after – less romantically, more doggedly and with the advantage that he can run to folding money for favours – by the organist at the cinema where Sylvia works as an usherette, Harold Atterbow (Roy Hudd).

Meanwhile, Francis' fellow private, Mick Hopper (Ewan McGregor), who observes all and frequently fantasises about it, is immediately smitten at the arrival of Lisa (Kymberley Huffman), the niece of the American placeman in the War Office, Colonel Truck Trekker (Shane Rimmer). While the officers (Peter Jeffrey, Clive Francis, Nicholas Jones, Nicholas Farrell) idle the hours away or fret about the state of the world, the young men's pursuit of romance is of much greater interest to them (and, it is assumed, to us). Eventually, after Berry has been run down and killed by the hysterical Atterbow, the couples find they were mismatched.

Whatever a mismatched-couples plot might suggest, *Lipstick on Your Collar* is no 1950s version of *A Midsummer Night's Dream*. The difference between the Shakespeare and the Potter is that one is an invocation of magic that presents a complex story resolved with wit and legerdemain while the other is a rehash of tricks without a context, the needlessly elaborated story of which just trundles along and then stops dead.

Inexplicably, Potter and Rye fall into exactly the trap which Herbert Ross dug for himself in the *Pennies* movie, that of making the numbers entertainments for their own sake rather than organic ingredients. In this regard, *Lipstick* falls far short of both its fellow serials-with-numbers *Pennies from Heaven* and *The Singing Detective*, the first of which made the bold leap into lip-synch recordings of the day and then used them – with a few exceptions in later episodes – tellingly, the second deploying the device much more sparingly but with unrivalled flair. The *Lipstick* numbers are neither organic nor especially striking. Like numbers in the stage musicals of recent years, they are characteristically extended well beyond their worth. The song lyrics fail to follow the function established by the integrated musical of fifty years earlier, that of advancing the plot. Rather they impede it. And there are so many routines, *three* in the first War Office sequence alone. If this smacks of desperation, there is every reason for the makers to despair.

The one setting that Rye makes work with some style is the

Fulham Broadway Odeon, hearteningly full of patrons. Despite Potter's favoured emphasis on the modesty of his origins, visits to the pictures (unthinkable to Winifred Foley) occurred often enough. Seeing *My Gal Sal** on television, Potter recalled it as 'the first full-length film I was ever taken to see. A prim little boy who used to hoot at all the mushy kissing ... *My Gal Sal* of course was not quite the gal I thought I remembered. Past summers are always the most glorious ... I missed the slurping lollipops and the squeaking tip-up seats and the derisive howls whenever two giant lips smacked together on the big bright screen.'[3]

For his *Desert Island Discs* selection in 1977, Potter chose Reginald Dixon playing 'Somebody Stole My Gal' on the mighty organ at the Tower Ballroom, Blackpool: 'I was brought to London when I was ten, between VE Day and VJ Day, and went to ... what was then called the Gaumont Cinema in Hammersmith, now called the Odeon, I believe, and to my astonishment this great thing rose out of Hell [laughs] or wherever it had come from and all the lights dipped down and there was this marvellous thing making this sound.'[4] This image provides the only true magic in the serial as Hudd's Harold Atterbow, ludicrously majestic, rises astride his gleaming instrument and then, with a gleeful flourish, introduces the imperishable tune 'The Whistler and His Dog'.

The cinema also furnishes each episode's opening sequence. Once the ugly and garish titles, centred – unthinkably – on *la plus noire* of Potter *bêtes noires* the jukebox, are over, Rye begins rather aptly with a projector beam cranking into life and aiming at the viewer's brain. Newsreel footage plays to the packed house. (A report pointing the resemblance of Sylvia to Diana Dors is heavy-handed.) This device might even score a ten but for the fact that episode five breaks the convention, a *faux pas* that again suggests laxity.

After redundancy, prolixity is the serial's worst sin. The tedium of the War Office work is exemplified all too well. Some business with a coded message on the red scrambler (it turns out to be a racing tip 'from Mr Philby')[5] is so ponderous that it threatens to overlap the next episode. The protracted business of Uncle Fred leaving for work as if for the trenches is funnier as an idea than as a routine.

The young men are as earnest and fogeyish as Potter himself at their age. Francis complains of everything changing for the worse. Later the supposedly hip Hopper rails against change too. Francis, who believes in 'the redemptive power of love' but agrees with Sylvia that he just wants 'to be shagged', tells his aunt in all seriousness that

---

* A 1942 Fox 'naughty nineties' musical starring Rita Hayworth and Victor Mature.

he doesn't want to 'make the same mistake Pushkin ... made'. No indeed.

In this elaborated wasteland, such boldness and fun as exists is more than usually welcome and most of it resides in Roy Hudd's performance as Atterbow. Whether he is lighting up at the prospect of ten bobs' worth of 'snog' or finding simultaneously the pathetic and the menacing in a line like 'A man can only take so much, you know. Only so much', Hudd brings a true artistry to his performance. His presence is a reminder that all his life Potter wanted comedy specialists in his work, sometimes getting them (Stanley Baxter, John Le Mesurier, Bill Maynard, John Bird, Lionel Jeffries, Dave King) but frequently failing to do so (he wanted Tony Hancock to play Jack Hay the agent in *Vote, Vote, Vote*, Hudd, Penelope Keith and Spike Milligan to lead *Pennies from Heaven*, Max Wall and Jimmy Jewel for *Blade on the Feather*). Not surprisingly, he wrote a role in *Karaoke* which only Hudd could really bring off.

I talked to Roy Hudd at the end of his Christmas run in his own version of *Babes in the Wood*. He and his villain, old Potterite Keith Barron, slipped in a gag about Potter the night I was there, to my gratification. 'And it got such a laugh that I kept it in for the rest of the run!' laughs Hudd. 'And it was purely for you.'

For all the comedy of Atterbow, he is a driven man and there is much pain in the part. How does someone like Hudd reach that? 'Dennis said "What do you think when you read it?" I said "Well, he's a thoroughly bad egg, isn't he." He said "That'll do." When we'd done, he said "Do you know, you made me cry in that part. You brought pathos to it which I never saw in the first place."

'It was so beautifully written. It's *all* in the script, you didn't need to work anything out. His dialogue is so brilliant that every "um" and "er" is in the right place. You daren't busk it at all. The pauses give you just the time you need to think. I'm terrible at learning lines but the easiest I've ever had to learn – I'm not being pretentious here – are Shakespeare's and Dennis's. They both have a wonderful flow, a fabulous rhythm. You know that if you leave a word out you've done it wrong. That rhythm is very much a comic's thing. Dennis had that like there's no tomorrow.

'I'd done bits of straight comedy before and Dennis knew them all. He knew everything I'd done. And Atterbow made a tremendous difference to my career. The work I've been offered since has been good-class work, terrific stuff. I couldn't believe it when I got the part because I was a fan. But I was so delighted that it opened so many doors.

'Someone left me, as people do in their wills, a collection of scripts and there was a file of sketches for *The Dick Emery Show* and there were five pieces written by David Nathan and Dennis Potter, submitted and – I might tell you – rejected. So I sent one to Dennis with a note made of cut-out letters from the paper saying "Dear Dirty Den – Any more nonsense from you and I shall show this to the press. There's plenty more where this came from!" Dennis *screamed*.

'He was a great music-hall fan and remembered a lot of old jokes. So we spent a lot of time swapping stories. I used to have him laughing for twenty minutes but then I could see it was getting painful and he'd say "Go on, bugger off." But he was interested in *every*thing. Bloody brilliant. You're writing about an exciting man.'⁶

Potter showed his pleasure in Renny Rye's work by giving him the director's job on his last one-off drama, *Midnight Movie*, made by Whistling Gypsy for the BBC in 1993 but not transmitted until Christmas 1994, six months after Potter's death. It is a piece poised between genre parody and self-parody, both coarse and kitsch.* In some quarters it has been hailed as Potter's best work since *The Singing Detective*. Rather, it comes perilously near the bottom of the heap.

Amber Boyce is the daughter of the late British film actress Mandy Mason (both played by Louise Germaine). Temporarily based at Shepperton Studios, Amber's boorish American producer-husband James Boyce (Brian Dennehy) takes a large house in Surrey. The solicitor who arranges things, Henry Harris (Jim Carter), happens to be a Mandy Mason devotee, the house happens to have been the major location for her imperishable sixties chiller *Smoke Rings* (of which Henry knows the dialogue by heart) and the movie itself happens to be the BBC's Midnight Movie the night that Henry accepts an invitation to another of Potter's competitively destructive dinner parties.

Harris cannot stay away from Amber even though she is dangerous – at some level of either his consciousness or hers, she takes lovers only to kill them. Does he make love to her? If so, is he in danger? Meanwhile her relationship with her husband veers between brutality and infantilism.

Matters are resolved after a fashion by Harris seeming to receive a visitation from Mandy Mason and then deducing that Boyce was responsible for her death. This lays the ghost and Amber and Boyce are reconciled.

---

* A BBC press release description of the piece as 'a celebration of the art of cinema' would surely be thought tongue-in-cheek if Potter had not furnished the phrase himself.⁷

Renny Rye has the good sense to go at it like a train so that the extent to which the film is a mere farrago is masked. But he fails to achieve that tuppence-coloured delirium that would allow us to exclaim, as Boyce does of *Smoke Rings*: 'My God, it's so bad it's great!'[8] one of the most sought-after accolades in the business. From what little we see of *Smoke Rings* itself, it appears to be a touch over-produced for a true Hammer Films outing, missing that bargain basement look in colour and lighting. (The first direct spoof in the film is actually of the opening shot of *Secret Friends*.)

Another of Boyce's aphorisms may have struck a louder chord: 'Writers? They should be chained up in cellars like the old days.' Some at the BBC thought that the cellar was the place for *Midnight Movie*. 'The whisper from Television Centre,' reported the *Daily Express*, 'is that the picture is so dire it has plunged BBC executives into a gloom of despair. "It is absolutely unspeakable," says one.'[9] The same report claimed that Potter had sunk £500,000 of his own reserves into the project. If so, he can hardly have recouped it.

The missing ingredient in all Potter's work since *Christabel*, aside from critical/commercial success, was Ken Trodd. It had been their longest estrangement.

'I think it was always fractious,' says Trodd, 'and grew more so as time went on and his sense of who he was and who he needed to be got greater. I don't know whether it was just luck that I wasn't there for the dimmer work. But I couldn't have made *Blackeyes* or *Secret Friends*.

'Back in the early days, we were effective allies in the battles, particularly against the BBC and in the general conspiracy of getting his work on and keeping him working, a lot of time under the conditions of all that illness. He was, as we all know, a very ungregarious man and one of the reasons he made an ally of me was that I was a known quantity who happened to be in the right position at the right time. He could easily have had producers who didn't feel as much affinity with the work as I did, however abrasively.

'And one began to identify with the cause of making his work *work* and that sustained quite a long time. Obviously there were currents in the relationship, demands being made and implied that couldn't be met, both professionally and personally. There was a rhythm of disappointment there over a long period. When we formed PfH, he wanted me to make only his work. I had relationships with other people, a taste for other things. So that was a slight.

'The other aspect of it was that he became a control merchant. All writers do because they control what goes on the page and to a great extent he was in control in the sense that his work was usually done, it was done the way he wanted and done to acclaim. But apart from people who wouldn't give him money when he wanted it, I was the only intellectual, emotional, internal resistance to that process. I was inside and privileged and yet awkward and with a mind of my own, difficult I'm sure without any of those qualifications either. And I never acted grateful the way he thought I should. Over a period I did become a whipping boy to him. And I did instinctively have a specific wariness, before it became obvious, about his not wanting a shadow of being upstaged.

'One thing I never found a way to do – and I don't see how I could have done – was to strike the right balance between enthusiasm and criticism when I received the first draft of anything. He never wanted to wait for me to have time to assimilate. He always wanted feedback. The most memorable example was when he delivered a script which I took to Italy where I was going with my girlfriend on some quite other project. And Dennis rang the hotel that night and we had the most blazing row, on my side about my sense of being invaded too soon – I'd almost literally had the script just in time to take on the plane – and on his side whatever, fury at not being given the right response. So this battle raged in the room and at the end of the long and bloody call I tore up the script and deposited it in the bin.

'The next morning, Elizabeth and I went down to breakfast and Roy Battersby,* who had the next room, was already there and he rose and came towards us saying "Oh, I'm so glad. I couldn't decide whether to break the door down." He thought I'd been killing her. It did have a wonderful symbolism. It was the jilted lover on the phone, not the one in the room, who was being attacked. That sense of "you've left me, you've gone off to another country with a woman to do somebody else's work and I can't go" happened again and again when I went away. It was often quite titanic.'[10]

---

* Superb director of television and film dramas, such as *Leeds United!*, *Winter Flight* and *Olly's Prison*.

Please Don't Talk About Me When I'm Gone

'I called it *Karaoke* because – oh, you know, the song or
the story of our lives is sort of already made up for us.'
Daniel Feeld, *Karaoke*[1]

On 14 February 1994, Dennis Potter received confirmation that his
pancreas was cancerous, that the liver bore secondaries and that his
time was limited, perhaps to three months. He already knew that
his wife Margaret, 'the steadfast one' as he so often called her, was
terminally ill. She had undergone a mastectomy a year before and he
had been caring for her as far as he could. At the end of 1993 she had
been advised that she might look forward three years, but not more.

Potter had work to finish. The previous year, his series for the BBC,
Karaoke, had been, in Ken Trodd's phrase, 'knocked back to him'[2] and
he had effectively destroyed it and begun again. By now he planned a
sequel, *Cold Lazarus*.

News of Potter's condition spread through the business. Melvyn
Bragg, appraised by Michael Grade, suggested that Potter might be
up for an interview on the channel he now most trusted. And of
course he was. Fortified by champagne, black coffee, cigarettes and
a flask of liquid morphine, Potter sat down with Bragg, five weeks
into his death sentence, and held the television audience spellbound
for eighty minutes.

For Potterites, it was a last hurrah for familiar themes and allusions
and a lifting of the veil on the work in progress. For viewers to whom
Potter had become a more nebulous figure, it was a rediscovery that
he was not Dirty Den or the author merely of *Pennies from Heaven*.
For us all, it was a thrilling, dangerous teeter across the tightrope,
a farewell public mind-game, a vintage piece of hide-and-seek, a
splendid affirmation of the sovereignty of the human spirit, a last

ecstatic roll on the grass before the old dog was taken indoors for his blessed release. Nobody who saw it – and it seems as if somehow the entire nation saw it – missed the sense of a unique testimony. Yes, he was an exciting man.

The delight in the old Sankey hymn, 'Will There Be Any Stars, Any Stars in My Crown', was just a little more calculated than it might have looked, for the children's choir version plays its part in *Karaoke*. Potter still knew how to be a crowd pleaser and how to make a planned effect appear spontaneous. But the phrase that gleamed in the night was 'the blossomest blossom'[3] which he could see from the window where he was writing, an image of the vividness of the precious *now*, an image made even more resonant by the certainty that, however ill he was, Potter would himself see out, perhaps had already seen out, that blossom's span. Even if it were a bit of an old soft-shoe, this was still the expression of a true and felt emotion and everybody felt it fully with him. 'Not that I'm interested in reassuring people,' the old street-fighter could not resist adding, 'bugger that.'

At the time of the recording, Margaret was enjoying some remission and, in her sister-in-law's phrase, 'was making plans for her widow-hood'.[4] But a few weeks later she suddenly took a turn for the worse. It was discovered that the cancer had got into the bone and spread widely. After that it was quick. Margaret Potter died on 29 May, a Sunday, and was buried on the Friday. Her husband, determined to attend, was defeated by his own illness. But he knew the arrangements and asked for a similar service for himself. From that moment, he sank steadily and died on Tuesday 7 June.

A surprising amount of work can still be anticipated. The film *Mesmer*, a project much championed by its star Alan Rickman, is still mired in legal difficulties at the time of writing. There are other features that look likely: *The Flipsider* from Paramount; *Opium Blue* from Autumn Pictures; *James and the Giant Peach*, an animation script for Disney from a story by Roald Dahl that stops sounding improbable when it is remembered how fascinated Potter always was by children's stories; and, for the BBC, *White Clouds*, a dramatisation of Tim Parks' novel *Cara Massimina*. The latter is a strange choice for Potter – or Potter is a strange choice for it. His third project set in the Italy he never visited, the novel reads like a pre-emptive heterocynical corrective of Alan Hollinghurst's masterly *The Folding Star*. Parks' style, using much internalising that is apt to defeat even the finest dramatisers, falls somewhere between the knowing comedy of Michael Carson and the exquisite pinioning of Angus Wilson.

But the keenest interest will focus on *Karaoke* and *Cold Lazarus*, for first screening in 1996 by both the BBC and Channel 4 because that was what Potter wanted and he was always uniquely successful at getting his way. It would not be appropriate to forejudge these linked four-part serials. This book has taken as a given that drama, whether for television or theatrical release, lives its full life in production not on the page.

Broadly, both serials demand that a playwright, found to be dying in the first, cryogenically preserved for 374 years in the second, be *let be*. The serials propose deliberately to queer the pitch for such a book as this. *Karaoke* plays familiar but none the less well-conceived games with the notion of the author as puppet-master and the nightmare of the puppets dancing unaided. Playwright Daniel Feeld (the spelling perhaps announces that the character is deeply *felt*) is soon back in hospital. 'I remember when I could make the whole ward *sing*,' he says, a touching reference. There is a *galère* of characters as rich as anywhere in the earlier works and a relationship more tender than all predecessors. It is fine news that Roy Hudd takes the 'smashing part'[5] that seems most resistant to life on the page. And yes, there are songs.

Cold Lazarus is a new development though perhaps well cogitated. In a book review as long ago as 1968, Potter observed with a shudder: 'The biologist, it seems, has joined the nuclear physicist as a front-runner in the great race towards – well, what? Transplanted heads, perhaps . . . Brains kept alive in a bottle?'[6]

And this is the world of Potter's last work as he weaves a metaphor of his own unreliable memories still being plundered and misunderstood in centuries to come, an agony only to be relieved by the friendly hand of oblivion. It would be a chilling vision – it *is* a chilling vision – but it is presented with pawky comedy, larger-than-life characterisation and the kind of fitful futurology that a smart director can soon sort out.

So Potter did not go quietly into that good night. 'It really is Dennis getting the boot to everyone finally and completely,' says Roy Hudd of *Cold Lazarus* in which he is briefly spotted across the centuries. 'It is quite a piece, that one.' The writer as severed head in the deep future will undoubtedly take its place as one of television's abiding images. It emphasises a sense of Potter himself that has been uncovering itself in the course of this book, one somewhat distinct from his own abrupt and slightly curious annotation in the middle of his triumphant James MacTaggart Lecture: 'If anyone cares to look, really look, at my work over the years, they would not take too long to see how the great bulk of it is about the victim, someone who cannot explain, cannot put into the right words, or even cannot speak at all'.[7] After quite a lot of real looking, I would suggest that the subject is a slightly different figure, one more suggestive of Potter himself and not so ingratiatingly altruistic as that not quite convincing claim might propose. This figure is the prisoner.

Ken Trodd thinks so. 'Very much that. And *him* in prison, a resentment that occasionally I felt passingly guilty about, him in prison and producing the work and me being healthy and all over the place and the beneficiary in a way.'[8] What ultimately lifts *Cold Lazarus* is the sense of the imminence of freedom, of release. The transcendent aura also settled on that Channel 4 interview and made it almost unbearably compelling.

Roy Hudd remembers: 'My last brush with Dennis was him phoning to say "It's good news and bad news: it's all systems go on *Karaoke* and you're playing the part and I'm very pleased with it". So I said "What's the bad news?" and he said "I've got eight weeks to live." I've cried twice in my life about death. One was the comedian Billy Dainty who was my best pal and the other was Dennis. Later he needed to phone me about something and I got so choked up that he never spoke to me again. He hardly knew my wife but he would speak to her, and send all the instructions about *Karaoke* through her. But the interesting thing is that *Karaoke* changed after that. It became about a writer dying of cancer. And it's Dennis.'[9]

'I interviewed him for the *Sunday Telegraph* about *Lipstick*,' says David Nathan. 'We sat in his office at Twickenham and went through a bottle of wine and we got the interview out of the way. He was saying some nice things about me, we hadn't seen each other for a long time. And it was gradually getting darker, the sun was going down. We didn't turn the lights on, we just sat and talked and talked. Margaret was just getting over her operation and was supposed to be fully recovered. He said "As soon as she gets through convalescence, I'll be in touch." I didn't really believe it because he'd said things like that before and never did. And then as we got up, he did something so untypical of Dennis. He hugged me and kissed me on the cheek. That was the last time I saw him. When we watched his last interview, I dropped him a note. I didn't expect a reply.'[10]

'I believe quite definitely that he would not have done work of this quality if he had not been dying,' says Kenith Trodd. 'Something major became him in life in the leaving of it. All that I would add, which is sentimental, is that he came back to me in the end and I'm doing my best to stay with him for the end.'[11]

'Lastly,' writes Lewis Carroll, concluding *Alice's Adventures in Wonderland*, 'she pictured to herself how this same little sister of hers would, in the after-time, be herself a grown woman; and how she would keep, through all her riper years, the simple and loving heart of her childhood; and how she would gather about her other little children, and make *their* eyes bright and eager with many a strange tale, perhaps even with the dream of Wonderland of long ago; and how she would feel with all their simple sorrows, and find a pleasure in all their simple joys, remembering her own child-life, and the happy summer days.'[12]

Notes and Sources

DP = Dennis Potter; WSG = W. Stephen Gilbert; WAC = BBC Written Archive Centre

Title page

1 DP, 'Strachey & Co: At the End, the Barren Branches', review of *Lytton Strachey: The Years of Achievement 1910–32* by Michael Holroyd, *The Times*, 24 February 1968.

Preface

1 DP, *Alice*, The Wednesday Play, BBC1, 13 October 1965.
2 DP, 'Into His Own Trap', review of *Couples* by John Updike, *The Times*, 9 November 1968.

Introduction

1 Rowland Morgan, Digitations column, *The Guardian*, 10 December 1994; Morgan's source is Hansard, vol. 248, no. 154, col. 1185.
2 *Factfile 1995*, ITC, December 1994.
3 A radio licence was also available for £1. 5,423,207 sound licences and 9,255,422 'combined' licences were sold in 1959. The BBC reckoned to receive 87½ per cent of the licence revenue after Treasury and Post Office deductions. Source: *BBC Handbook 1960* (BBC, January 1960), pp. 195, 222.
4 This represents an increase of 2,012.5 per cent over three and a half decades, as compared to a percentage increase in the cost of living index over the same period of 1,070.7 Source: Central Statistical Office.
5 There is now no radio licence, either separate or combined. The only

concession on the cost of the licence is a reduction for a registered blind person of £1.25, which in the particular circumstances may strike many as an unusually paltry privilege. In February 1995, some 19,870,000 colour and 789,000 monochrome licences were held. Source: Television Licensing Centre, Bristol.

6 Rowland Morgan, Digitations column, *The Guardian*, 12 November 1994. Morgan's source is BARB/Continental Research, *Marketing Week*, July 1994.

7 Quotations are from *Radio Times* billings, 2 July 1959.

8 I am unable to locate a specific source for this observation but Anthony Smith, now president of Magdalen College Oxford, confirms in a letter to me of 21 March 1995 that this was indeed his view in the early seventies.

9 Quoted by WSG in 'In and Out of the Box', *Plays & Players*, March 1975.

10 Ibid.

11 Ibid.

12 This and subsequent short quotations are from my notes of Sydney Newman speaking at the first *Guardian* Lecture to be held at the Museum of the Moving Image, 22 September 1988.

13 Quoted by Marjorie Bilbow in 'The Compelling Challenges That Face Drama', *Television Today*, 30 May 1968.

14 Ibid.

15 This account is adapted from WSG, 'The Television Play: Outside the Consensus', *Screen Education*, Summer 1980.

16 Sydney Newman, *Guardian* Lecture.

17 This argument is adapted from WSG, 'Safety-Net Success', *New Statesman*, 5 August 1994.

18 *The Cherry Orchard* by Anton Chekhov, adapted by Trevor Griffiths, directed by Richard Eyre, BBC1, 13 October 1981.

19 This argument is adapted from the original draft of WSG, 'Are You Pottering, George?', *The Independent*, 20 October 1994.

20 DP, 'The Only Meat Was in the Cookery Class', In My View column, *The Sun*, 15 February 1968.

21 WSG, 'The Television Play'.

22 Ibid.

23 William Goldman, *Adventures in the Screen Trade* (Macdonald, 1984), Futura edn, p. 39.

24 WSG, 'Are You Pottering, George?'

25 Quoted by WSG in 'Safety-Net Success'.

26 The source of this quotation from John Hopkins cannot be traced but I suspect it originated on television, along with his observation that the best drama of the week was always Morecambe and Wise doing their routine in front of the curtains. Hopkins did tell Sonia Copeland in a newspaper interview: 'For me, writing for television means, ideally, that I'm writing for one or two persons at a time – drama at a level, ideally, from which they won't be able to escape from the logical conclusion of what I'm saying', *Sunday Times*, 25 May 1969.

27 WSG, 'Are You Pottering, George?'

28 Gus McDonald (Festival Chair), Introduction to Official Programme, published by *Broadcast* for the Edinburgh International Television Festival, August 1977.

29 Quoted by Steve Clarke in 'Screen Test for the Beeb', *Daily Telegraph*, 11 December 1993.

30 Stewart Lane, 'Who'll Win in the Series v. Play Battle?', *Daily Worker*, 8 August 1964.

31 T. C. Worsley, 'Minority Appeal', *Financial Times*, 17 March 1965.

32 George Melly, 'The Poor Relation in the Pecking Order', *The Observer*, 3 May 1970.

33 Quoted by Annalena McAfee in 'Play for Yesterday?', *Evening Standard*, 21 June 1990.

34 DP, introduction to the texts of *The Nigel Barton Plays* (Penguin Books, 1967), p. 11.

35 Quoted by Robert Cushman in 'Dennis Potter: The Values of a Television Playwright', *Radio Times*, 3 April 1976.

36 BBC Lunchtime Lecture, 26 January 1977.

37 Steve Clarke and Patrick Stoddart, 'Rechannelling TV's Big Screen Resources', *Sunday Times*, 28 January 1990.

38 Quoted by WSG in 'In and Out of the Box'.

39 Ibid.

40 Quoted by Philip Purser in 'Is the Writing on the Wall for the TV Play?', *Sunday Telegraph*, 24 March 1985.

41 Quoted in a survey by Cheryl Markosky, *TV World*, November 1986.

42 Quoted in 'In the Beginning Was the Script . . .', unsigned, *Television Today*, 29 January 1987.

43 Sue Summers, 'The New Golden Age of Film', *The Independent*, 9 March 1988.

44 Hugo Davenport, 'Screen Gems from West One', *Daily Telegraph*, 6 February 1993.

45 Quoted by Jay Rayner in 'Screen Saviour or Sinner?', *The Guardian*, 15 March 1990.

46 Quoted in Clarke and Stoddart, 'Rechannelling TV's Big Screen Resources'.

47 Quoted by Bob Woffinden in 'Dramatic Decline at the BBC', *The Guardian*, 15 May 1989.

48 George Faber, 'Are You Listening, Dennis?', *The Independent*, 13 October 1994.

49 WSG, 'Are You Pottering, George?'

50 Quoted by Gordon Burn in 'Television is the Only Medium That Counts', *Radio Times*, 8 October 1970.

Chapter 1

1 DP, 'Some Sort of Preface . . .', *Waiting for the Boat* (Faber and Faber, 1984), p. 23.

2 Ibid., p. 12.
3 Quoted by John Wyver in 'How to Turn a Difficulty into Child's Play', *The Guardian*, 26 January 1979.
4 Joseph Heller interviewed by Christopher Bigsby, *Kaleidoscope*, Radio 4, 24 September 1994.
5 DP, *Traitor*, Play for Today, BBC1, 14 October 1971.
6 DP, 'Back – to Weave Dreams Out of My Own Wallpaper', Dennis Potter column, *The Sun*, 21 October 1968.
7 DP, 'A Rainy Day in London Town – How I Love It!', Dennis Potter column, *The Sun*, 27 May 1968.
8 DP, 'A Touch of Reality', television review, *New Statesman*, 11 April 1975.
9 Brian Walden, 'Potter and Potterisms', *The Isis*, 13 May 1959.
10 DP, 'The True Kingdom,' *The Isis*, 21 May 1959.
11 DP, 'Seething Trouble', television review, *New Statesman*, 18 April 1975.
12 DP, 'Telling Stories', Stand column, *New Society*, 15 May 1975.
13 DP, *Hide and Seek* (André Deutsch, 1973), Quartet edn, p. 40.
14 William Shakespeare, *The Merchant of Venice*, Act IV, sc. i.
15 DP, '"Nightmare" Turned Out a Gem', television review, *Daily Herald*, 10 November 1962.
16 DP, 'Heigh-Ho, It's the Old Theme', television review, *Daily Herald*, 3 December 1962.
17 DP, 'Streets Behind Steptoe', television review, *Daily Herald*, 5 July 1963.
18 DP, 'Everybody's Confessing', television review, *Daily Herald*, 3 April 1964.
19 DP, 'Sinners! Don't Ring the BBC, They'll Wring You', Dennis Potter column, *The Sun*, 5 August 1968.
20 DP, 'A Subject of Scandal and Concern', television review, *Sunday Times*, 22 May 1977.
21 DP, 'Dennis Potter Exposed', Dennis Potter column, *The Sun*, 20 May 1968.

Chapter 2

1 DP, Foreword, *The Changing Forest: Life in the Forest of Dean Today* (Martin Secker & Warburg, 1962), p. 7.
2 Winifred Foley, *A Child in the Forest* (BBC Publications, 1974), p. 13; expanded from its serial form for *Woman's Hour*, Radio 4, March 1973.
3 DP, 'Changes at the Top', *The Isis*, 22 May 1957.
4 DP, *The Changing Forest*, p. 14.
5 DP, 'Why I'm Glad to be British', Dennis Potter column, *The Sun*, 8 April 1968.

6 DP, 'What It Means When a Village Loses Its Living', In My View column, *The Sun*, 21 February 1968.

7 This and subsequent quotations from Margaret Potter and June Thomas, interview with WSG, 6 October 1994.

8 For instance, in an unsigned obituary, *Daily Telegraph*, 8 June 1994.

9 Anthony de Lotbinière, interview with WSG, 10 March 1995.

10 Foley, *A Child in the Forest*, p. 23.

11 Joyce Latham, *Where I Belong: A Forest of Dean Childhood in the 1930s* (Alan Sutton, 1993), p. 103.

12 This and subsequent quotations from Iris Hughes, interview with WSG, 6 October 1994.

13 Quoted in letter from Iris Hughes to WSG, 16 February 1995.

14 Latham, *Where I Belong*, p. 113.

15 Letter from Iris Hughes.

16 DP, 'Why I'm Glad to be British'.

17 DP, 'Changes at the Top'.

18 DP, *The Changing Forest*, p. 49.

19 Ibid., pp. 44–5.

20 Ira W. Sankey, *Sacred Songs and Solos* (Morgan & Scott Ltd). The book bears no date but from the Preface it may be imagined that Sankey (1840–1908), a Pennsylvania American, was still well remembered: 'In this Revised and Enlarged Collection . . . will be found most of the old favourites sung by Mr Sankey in the great Revival Meetings conducted by Mr Moody during three notable campaigns in this country . . . It is almost superfluous to say that *Sacred Songs and Solos* has found favour in all parts of the world where the English language is spoken.'

21 Eliza E. Hewitt (1851–1920), 'I Am Thinking Today of That Beautiful Land', *Sacred Songs and Solos*.

22 Off-air transcript from *An Interview with Dennis Potter* with Melvyn Bragg, Without Walls Special, LWT for Channel 4, 5 April 1994. A version of the text is published in DP, *Seeing the Blossom* (Faber and Faber, 1994).

23 DP, 'Holy Creepers', television review, *New Statesman*, 25 October 1974.

24 DP, 'New Shoes Don't Come Only at Whitsun', Dennis Potter column, *The Sun*, 3 June 1968.

25 DP, *The Changing Forest*, p. 54.

26 Book title, *The New Priesthood* by Joan Bakewell and Nicholas Garnham (Allen Lane, 1970).

27 DP, *The Changing Forest*, p. 56.

28 Ibid., pp. 64, 66.

29 DP interviewed by Melvyn Bragg, *The South Bank Show*, LWT for ITV, 11 February 1978.

Chapter 3

1 DP, *Stand Up, Nigel Barton*, The Wednesday Play, BBC1, 8 December 1965; text published in *The Nigel Barton Plays* (Penguin Books, 1967).
2 DP, *The Glittering Coffin* (Victor Gollancz, 1960), p. 41.
3 DP, 'Some Sort of Preface . . .', *Waiting for the Boat*, pp. 33–4.
4 DP, *Moonlight on the Highway*, Saturday Night Theatre, Kestrel Productions-LWT for ITV, 12 April 1969.
5 Kenith Trodd, interview with WSG, 21 March 1995.
6 Trodd: this and subsequent quotation, interview with WSG, 20 April 1995.
7 Alan Bennett, interview with WSG, 31 January 1995.
8 DP, 'Death After Life', *The Isis*, 30 October 1957.
9 DP, 'Looking Back at Those Days in the Forces', television review, *Daily Herald*, 22 April 1963.
10 DP, 'But Where Was the Green Field Beyond?', In My View column, *The Sun*, 24 January 1968.
11 Angus Wilson, *The Old Men at the Zoo* (Martin Secker & Warburg, 1961), Penguin edn, p. 71.
12 Trodd, interview 21 March 1965.
13 Roger Smith, interview with WSG, 30 January 1965.
14 Sir Keith Thomas, letter to WSG, 13 February 1995.
15 Francis W. Steer, *Archives of New College Oxford* (Phillimore & Co., 1974).
16 Stephen Hugh-Jones, 'Union Report', *The Isis*, 7 November 1956.
17 Brian Walden, interview with WSG, 15 March 1995.
18 Quoted in Union Report, *The Isis*, 21 November 1956.
19 Michael Gregory, theatre review, *The Isis*, 20 February 1957.
20 Union Report, unsigned, *The Isis*, 8 May 1957.
21 DP, 'Changes at the Top'.
22 Alan Hancock, theatre review, *The Isis*, 29 May 1957.
23 Smith interview.
24 DP, 'The Wolfenden Report', *The Isis*, 6 October 1957.
25 DP, *The Changing Forest*, p. 72.
26 DP, Union Report, *The Isis*, 23 October 1957.
27 DP, 'Union Damns Union', *The Isis*, 6 November 1957.
28 DP, 'Death After Life'.
29 DP, *The Glittering Coffin*, p. 101.
30 Richard Hoggart, *The Uses of Literacy* (Chatto & Windus, 1957), Pelican edn, p. 14.
31 Ibid., pp. 247–8.
32 Ibid., p. 294.
33 Union minutes book, 21 November 1957.
34 Frederic Reynolds, 'Union Uproar', *The Isis*, 27 November 1957.
35 'Oxford Union Uproar: Libel Action Threat', unsigned, *Oxford Mail*, 22 November 1957.

36 'Undergrad Tribunal Set Up', unsigned, *News Chronicle*, 23 November 1957.

37 Arthur Chesworth, '"Political Plot" Row at Oxford', *Daily Express*, 26 November 1957.

38 Alan Smith, '"Filthy Smear" Shouts Walden in Union Riot', *Cherwell*, 23 November 1957.

39 Kenneth Trodd, 'Historic Vote Supports Vice Law Reform', *The Isis*, 27 November 1957.

40 Union minutes book 22 November 1957.

41 'Oxford President Criticised', unsigned, *The Sunday Times*, 15 December 1957.

42 'Verdict on Oxford Union Ex-President', unsigned, *The Observer*, 15 December 1957.

43 Walden interview.

44 Jonathan Cecil, interview with WSG, 8 February 1995.

45 Trodd interview.

46 Lewis Rudd, interview with WSG, 11 April 1995.

47 Ibid.

48 News, unsigned, *Isis*, 22 January 1958.

49 DP, 'The New Establishment', *Isis*, 22 January 1958.

50 DP, Union report, *Isis*, 26 February 1958.

51 DP, 'It's a Woman's World', *Isis*, 5 March 1958.

52 DP, 'The Referendum and After', editorial, *Isis*, 12 March 1958.

53 DP, 'Labour Club Blues', *Isis*, 12 March 1958.

54 DP, *The Glittering Coffin*, p. 5.

55 DP interviewed by Alan Yentob, *Arena*, off-air transcript, BBC2, 30 January 1987; a version is published in DP, *Seeing the Blossom*.

56 Smith interview.

57 Trodd interview.

58 Walden interview.

59 DP, 'Thank God for the Navy', editorial, *Isis*, 30 April 1958.

60 DP, 'Base Ingratitude?', *New Statesman*, 3 May 1958.

61 Smith interview.

62 Cecil interview.

63 DP, marginal comment, *Isis*, 21 May 1958.

64 Ibid.

65 Cecil interview.

66 Quoted in Lewis Smith, Comments, *Isis*, 4 June 1958.

67 'Manners Maketh Man', editorial, *Isis*, 18 June 1958.

68 Stephen Hugh-Jones, 'The Case for the Defence', *Isis*, 18 June 1958.

69 Covered in three *Daily Express* stories: 'Ex-Editor Potter of The Isis "Carpeted"', unsigned, 18 June 1958; 'Professor Waits at His Home But (So Far) No Apology', unsigned, 19 June 1958; 'Ex-Editor Apologises', unsigned, 20 June 1958.

70 'Manners Maketh Man'.

71 Smith interview.

72 DP, 'Small Victim', *New Statesman*, 21 June 1958.

73 John Bowen, interview with WSG, 22 March 1995.
74 Norman Willis, letter to WSG, 20 March 1995.
75 Cecil interview.

Chapter 4

1 DP, *Follow the Yellow Brick Road*, The Sextet, BBC2, 4 July 1972; text published in *The Television Dramatist*, selected and introduced by Robert Muller (Paul Elek, 1973).
2 BBC Written Archive file TEL1/C/1273/11372.
3 Lord Ashley, interview with WSG, 31 January 1995.
4 Lord Mayhew, interview with WSG, 27 January 1995.
5 Quoted in script of *Class in Private Life*, programme 2 of Does Class Matter? series, BBC TV, 25 August 1958 (WAC TEL1/C/1273/11372).
6 Mayhew, script of *Class in Private Life*.
7 Ashley interview.
8 Fred Cooke, 'Miner's Son at Oxford Felt Ashamed of Home: The Boy Who Kept His Father Secret' *Reynolds News*, 3 August 1958.
9 DP, *The Glittering Coffin*, p. 71.
10 WAC TEL1/C/1273/11372.
11 Mayhew, introduction to Does Class Matter?, *Radio Times*, 10 August 1958.
12 WAC TEL1/C/1273/11372.
13 DP, *The Glittering Coffin*, p. 71.
14 Ashley interview.
15 Mayhew interview.
16 This and subsequent quotations from correspondence by courtesy of Lord Mayhew.
17 Trodd interview.
18 DP, letter to Mayhew, 30 November 1958.
19 Mayhew, letter to WSG, 11 February 1995.
20 Rudd interview.
21 'Editorial Idol: Dennis Potter', unsigned, *The Isis*, 15 October 1958.
22 Nicholas Deakin, 'Off with the Motley', editorial, *The Isis*, 15 October 1958.
23 News, unsigned, *The Isis*, 15 October 1958.
24 'Hearts in the Dark', unsigned editorial, *The Clarion*, October 1958.
25 Peter Jay, Union Report, *The Isis*, 5 November 1958.
26 News, unsigned, *The Isis*, 19 November 1958.
27 DP quoted in 'Brecht Play for Labour', unsigned, *Cherwell*, 29 November 1958.
28 Smith interview.
29 DP, letter to the proctors, 31 December 1958.
30 Cecil interview.
31 'Proctorial Fine Controversy Grudgingly Paid' (*sic*), unsigned, *Cherwell*, 28 January 1959.

32 Ibid.
33 News, unsigned, *The Isis*, 4 February 1959.
34 William Shakespeare, *Julius Cæsar*, Act I, sc. ii.
35 Raymond Williams, *Culture and Society* (Chatto & Windus, 1958; reissued Hogarth Press, 1993).
36 DP, 'And Bow Twice . . .', Potter column, *The Isis*, 4 February 1959.
37 DP, 'The True Kingdom', *The Isis*, 21 May 1959.

Chapter 5

1 DP, 'Clocking Out', television review, *New Statesman*, 21 March 1975.
2 Leonard Miall, interview with WSG, 11 February 1995.
3 DP interviewed by Roy Plomley, *Desert Island Discs*, Radio 4, 17 December 1977, transcript WAC.
4 DP, 'Rally Round Patriots, Before Wireless Goes the Way of Empire', Dennis Potter column, *The Sun* 1 July 1968.
5 Alasdair Milne, interview with WSG, 30 January 1995.
6 Michael Peacock, interview with WSG, 2 March 1995.
7 *Panorama* general file, WAC T32/1, 200/2.
8 *Panorama* production file, WAC T32/1, 246/2.
9 Ibid.
10 Ibid.
11 Ibid.
12 Sir Robin Day, *Grand Inquisitor* (Weidenfeld & Nicolson, 1989), p. 125.
13 Day, letter to WSG, 23 January 1995.
14 *Panorama*: WAC T32/1, 246/2.
15 Peacock interview.
16 Ibid.
17 DP, 'Back on the Pioneer Trail', In My View column, *Daily Herald*, 6 July 1963.
18 DP, 'That Sweet Smell', television review, *New Statesman*, 17 May 1974.
19 DP, 'Panorama Without the Pomposity', television review, *Daily Herald*, 26 March 1963.
20 DP, 'Serious Bit of Strip-Tease', Dennis Potter on Television, *Daily Herald*, 28 March 1964.
21 DP, 'This Was a Great Night in the City', television review, *Daily Herald*, 27 July 1962.
22 Quoted by Philip Purser in 'A Playwright Comes of Age', *Daily Telegraph*, 2 April 1969.
23 DP, Forest of Dean paper, 21 January 1960, WAC T32/446/1.
24 Ibid., 25 January 1960.
25 De Lotbinière interview.
26 Ibid.
27 Memo, Grace Wyndham Goldie to de Lotbinière, 10 February 1960, WAC T32/446/1.

28 Quotations from DP, *Between Two Rivers*, BBC TV, 3 June 1960.
29 Memo, Kenneth Adam to Leonard Miall, 1 July 1960, WAC T32/446/1.
30 Miall interview.
31 De Lotbinière interview.
32 DP, *The Changing Forest*, p. 72.
33 DP, *The Glittering Coffin*, postscript, p. iii.
34 Ibid., postscript, p. ii.
35 Ibid., p. 22.
36 Ibid., p. 50.
37 Ibid., pp. 58–9.
38 Ibid., p. 60.
39 Ibid., p. 113.
40 Quoted on the dust jacket of *The Glittering Coffin* from a review by Douglas Brown, *News Chronicle*.
41 Alasdair MacIntyre, book review, *New Statesman*, 13 February 1960.

Chapter 6

1 DP, 'Dead Muster', television review, *New Statesman*, 10 January 1975.
2 Memo, Kenneth Adam to Leonard Miall, 26 November 1959, WAC T32/1,579/1.
3 Memo, Grace Wyndham Goldie to Kenneth Adam, 13 May 1960, WAC T32/1,579/1.
4 Memo, Goldie to Adam, 16 September 1960, WAC T32/1,579/1.
5 Memo, Adam to Goldie, undated, WAC T32/1,579/1.
6 Letter, Christopher Burstall to Richard Hoggart, 4 October 1960, and Hoggart's reply, undated, WAC T32/1,579/1.
7 Graham Fuller (ed.), *Potter on Potter* (Faber and Faber, 1993) p. 3.
8 Chris Dunkley, 'Small Screen Pioneer', *Financial Times*, 8 June 1994.
9 Miall interview.
10 Ashley interview.
11 Various documents, *Bookstand* contracts file, WAC R94/2,952/1.
12 Grace Wyndham Goldie, *Radio Times*, 13 October 1960.
13 Duty Clerk's log, 16 October 1960, WAC T32/1,579/1.
14 DP, *Bookstand* script, item on *Out West* by Jack Schaefer, BBC TV, 5 March 1961, WAC 32/449/1.
15 Memo, Adam to Miall, 17 February 1961, WAC T32/1,579/1.
16 Memo, Stephen Hearst to Goldie, 19 April 1961, WAC T32/1,579/1.
17 Memo, Adam to Stuart Hood, 30 May 1961, WAC T32/1,579/1.
18 Quoted in Alasdair Milne, *DG: The Memoirs of a British Broadcaster*, (Hodder & Stoughton, 1988), Coronet edn, p. 50.
19 Memo, Stuart Hood, 2 June 1961, WAC T32/1,579/1.
20 Memo, Hearst, 8 June 1961, WAC T32/1,579/1.
21 DP, 'Flogged All Round the Campus', *The Times*, 17 February 1968.
22 Letter, DP to Christopher Burstall, 2 October 1961, WAC T32/1,579/1.

23 Hearst, letter to WSG, 24 January 1995, and interview with WSG, 28 January 1995.
24 Dick Taverne, interview with WSG, 3 February 1995.
25 DP, *The Glittering Coffin*, pp. 122–3.

Chapter 7

1 Fuller (ed.), *Potter on Potter*, p. 10.
2 DP, *The Glittering Coffin*, p. 89.
3 David Nathan, interview with WSG, 1 February 1995.
4 DP, 'Oh, That Smug, Arrogant Ostrich!', As I See It column, *Daily Herald*, 4 November 1960.
5 Announcement, unsigned, *Daily Herald*, 5 November 1960.
6 Smith interview.
7 Nathan interview.
8 DP, 'Fly-Over in My Eyes', *Daily Herald*, 18 November 1961.
9 DP, 'Mr Flanders Finds Life Exciting', *Daily Herald*, 6 February 1962.
10 DP, 'Gloom Unconfined', television review, *The Sunday Times*, 31 October 1976.
11 DP, 'The Quiet Battle of Nob Hill', *Daily Herald*, 2 March 1962.
12 Quoted by Nicholas Wapshott in 'Knowing What Goes On Inside People's Heads', *The Times*, 21 April 1980.
13 Fuller (ed.), *Potter on Potter*, pp. 12–13.
14 Margaret Potter interview.
15 DP, 'Violence Out of a Box', television review, *New Statesman*, 29 November 1974.
16 DP, introduction to *Brimstone and Treacle* (stage play text, Eyre Methuen, 1978).
17 DP, 'Some Sort of Preface . . .', *Waiting for the Boat*, p. 20.
18 DP, 'Occupying Powers', the James MacTaggart Memorial Lecture, Edinburgh International Television Festival, 27 August 1993, televised Channel 4, 23 August 1994; text published in *Seeing the Blossom*, p. 51.
19 John Diamond MP, 'The Miner of the Forest', *Daily Herald*, 17 April 1962.
20 DP, 'Fake Beer But Real Good Fun', television review, *Daily Herald*, 19 March 1964.
21 DP, 'Occupying Powers', in *Seeing the Blossom*, p. 45.
22 Ibid., p. 55.
23 DP, 'Hurrah for the Gogglebox', In My Opinion column, *Daily Herald*, 31 August 1962.
24 DP, 'Praise Be for a Bold Experiment', In My View column, *Daily Herald*, 8 September 1962.
25 DP, 'The Most Exciting Ever', television review, *Daily Herald*, 27 March 1963.
26 Alan Blyth, Playbill, *TV Times*, 22 March 1963.

27 DP, 'This Was a Glorious Wallop', In My View column, *Daily Herald*, 30 March 1963.
28 DP, 'TV is an Electronic Yo-Yo', Dennis Potter column, *Daily Herald*, 28 December 1963.
29 Ned Sherrin, proposal document, 7 February 1962, WAC T32/1,649/1.
30 Memo, Stuart Hood, 3 August 1962, WAC T32/1,649/1.
31 Nathan interview.
32 DP, 'This TV Newcomer Smiles As She Bites: The Herald Reports How Auntie Found the Acid', news report-cum-review, *Daily Herald*, 26 November 1962.
33 David Nathan and DP, 'Mother's Day', *That Was the Week That Was*, BBC TV, 23 March 1963, published in *That Was the Week That Was* edited by David Frost and Ned Sherrin (W. H. Allen, 1963).
34 Memo, Cecil Madden to Ned Sherrin, 28 January 1963, *TW3* file, WAC T32/1,649/2.
35 Letter, DP, 18 June 1963, and reply, E. Caffery, 20 June 1963, WAC RCON T18.

Chapter 8

1 DP, *Vote, Vote, Vote for Nigel Barton*, The Wednesday Play, BBC1, 15 December 1965; text published in *The Nigel Barton Plays* (Penguin Books, 1967).
2 Ron Brewer, DP obituary, *The Independent*, 8 July 1994. Sadly the editor of *The Independent*'s gazette page failed to keep Mr Brewer's covering letter; I have made every effort to locate him but failed.
3 Taverne interview.
4 DP, *Arena* interview, *Seeing the Blossom*, p. 64.
5 Quoted by Barry Norman in 'What the Class Barrier Did for Dennis Potter', *Daily Mail*, 13 December 1965.
6 DP, 'Party Political Bores', Dennis Potter on Television, *Daily Herald*, 9 May 1964.
7 'Not a Stain! Shining Bright!', unsigned leader, *The Sun*, 17 September 1964.
8 DP interview, *The South Bank Show*.
9 DP, 'Facts Among the Fiction', Dennis Potter on Television, *Daily Herald*, 27 June 1964.
10 DP, 'Too Much Whisky', television review, *Daily Herald*, 3 May 1963.
11 DP, 'The Funny Side of Politics', television review, *Daily Herald*, 16 December 1963.
12 DP interview, *The South Bank Show*.
13 Stanley Baxter, interview with WSG, 6 March 1995.
14 Memo, James MacTaggart, 8 March 1965, WAC T5/1,026/1.
15 Fuller (ed.), *Potter on Potter*, p. 19.
16 *Brewer's Dictionary of Phrase and Fable* (1870); 14th edn revised by Ivor H. Evans (Cassell, 1989).

17 Nathan interview.
18 DP, 'Stories with an Ending', Dennis Potter on Television, *Daily Herald*, 22 February 1964.
19 Smith interview.
20 Quotations from DP, *The Confidence Course*, The Wednesday Play, BBC1, 24 February 1965, script in WAC.
21 William Hazlitt, 'On the Fear of Death', first published in *The London Magazine* and collected in *Table Talk* (1821).
22 Baxter interview.
23 Gilchrist Calder, interview with WSG, 4 February 1995.
24 Adrian Mitchell, television review, *The Sun*, 25 February 1965.
25 Richard Sear, television review, *Daily Mirror*, 25 February 1965.
26 Letter, Ayton Whitaker, 1 April 1965, WAC T5/1,026/1.
27 DP, 'The Face at the Window', Unread Classics series, *The Times*, 3 August 1968.
28 Ibid.
29 Virginia Woolf, 'William Hazlitt', *The Common Reader*, Hogarth Press 1932
30 Hazlitt, 'Mr Coleridge', *The Spirit of the Age* 1825.
31 DP, 'The Face at the Window'.
32 Fuller (ed.), *Potter on Potter*, p. 21.
33 Quotations from DP, *Vote, Vote, Vote for Nigel Barton*.
34 DP, introduction to *The Nigel Barton Plays*, p. 12.
35 Gareth Davies, interview with WSG, 24 February 1995.
36 DP, 'Cooked Geese', television review, *New Statesman*, 15 February 1974.
37 Memo, R. S. Meakin, 21 April 1965, WAC T5/691/1.
38 DP, introduction to *The Nigel Barton Plays*, p. 17.
39 Announcement, unsigned, Sydney Newman's office, 23 June 1965, WAC T5/691/1.
40 'Dose of BBC Jitters', unsigned, *The Observer*, 27 June 1965.
41 Memo, Paul Fox to Huw Wheldon, 23 June 1965, WAC T5/691/1.
42 DP, introduction to *The Nigel Barton Plays*, pp. 17–18.
43 DP, 'Occupying Powers', *Seeing the Blossom*, p. 35.
44 Announcement, WAC T5/691/1.
45 Smith interview.
46 Letter, Roger Hancock to Sydney Newman, 28 June 1965, WAC T5/691/1.
47 Letter, Sydney Newman to Roger Hancock, 5 July 1965, WAC T5/691/1.
48 Commissioning document, Tony Garnett, July 1965, WAC T48.
49 Davies interview.
50 Memo, Michael Peacock to Michael Bakewell, 11 August 1965, WAC T5/691/1.

Chapter 9

1 DP, *Blue Remembered Hills*, Play for Today, BBC1, 30 January 1979, published in *Waiting for the Boat* (Faber and Faber, 1984).

2 Smith interview.
3 Quotations from DP, *Alice.*
4 Rosalie Crutchley, interview with WSG, 1 February 1995.
5 George Baker, interview with WSG, 18 April 1995.
6 Memo, Michael Peacock to Michael Bakewell, 27 July 1965, WAC T5/834/1.
7 Davies interview.
8 Memo, Sydney Newman to Michael Bakewell, 14 October 1965, WAC T5/834/1.
9 Quotations from DP, *Stand Up, Nigel Barton.*
10 Davies interview
11 DP, introduction to *The Nigel Barton Plays*, pp. 19–20.
12 Fuller (ed.), *Potter on Potter*, p.30.
13 DP, *An Interview with Dennis Potter*, in *Seeing the Blossom*, p.13.
14 Quoted by Barry Norman in 'What the Class Barrier Did . . .'
15 DP interview, *The South Bank Show.*
16 DP, *Arena* interview, *Seeing the Blossom*, p.63.
17 Fuller (ed.) *Potter on Potter*, pp. 23–4.
18 DP, 'Telling Stories.'
19 Davies interview.
20 DP, *Arena* interview, *Seeing the Blossom*, p.66.
21 DP, Introduction to *The Nigel Barton Plays*, p. 22.
22 DP, *The Glittering Coffin*, p. 72.
23 DP, 'Prickly Pair', television review, *New Statesman*, 8 February 1974.
24 Tony Garnett, *Radio Times*, 2 December 1965.
25 Derek Malcolm, television review, *The Guardian*, 9 December 1965.
26 Julian Holland, television review, *Daily Mail*, 9 December 1965.
27 Philip Purser, television review, *Sunday Telegraph*, 12 December 1965.
28 Maurice Richardson, television review, *The Observer*, 12 December 1965.
29 Nancy Banks-Smith, television review, *The Sun*, 9 December 1965.
30 Adrian Mitchell, television review, *The Sunday Times*, 19 December 1965.
31 DP, introduction to *The Nigel Barton Plays*, p.17.
32 Nancy Banks-Smith, television review.
33 James Thomas, television review, *Daily Express*, 16 December 1965.
34 Kenneth Eastaugh, television review, *Daily Mirror*, 16 December 1965.
35 Mary Crozier, television review, *The Guardian*, 16 December 1965.
36 Quoted by Wapshott in 'Knowing What Goes On Inside People's Heads'.
37 Ron Brewer, obituary, *The Independent.*
38 DP, 'Occupying Powers,' *Seeing the Blossom*, p.36.

Chapter 10

1 DP, 'Ward 10 – from the Inside', television review, *Daily Herald*, 31 July 1963.

2 Letter, Roger Hancock, 19 May 1965, WAC T48.
3 Commissioning brief, 11 January 1966, WAC T48.
4 Quotations from DP, *Emergency – Ward 9*, Thirty Minute Theatre, BBC2, 11 April 1966, script from WAC.
5 Trodd interview with WSG, 1 May 1995.
6 DP, 'Prejudice, It Seems, is Multi-Coloured', In My View column, *The Sun*, 26 January 1968.
7 DP, 'The Night I Realised I, Too, Fear the Stranger', Dennis Potter column, *The Sun*, 29 April 1968.
8 Richard Brooks, 'Return of Politically Incorrect Den', *The Observer*, 14 February 1993.
9 DP, 'Alf Takes Over', television review, *New Statesman*, 20 October 1972.
10 Davies interview.
11 Nancy Banks-Smith, television review, *The Sun*, 12 April 1966.
12 Acceptance document, WAC RCONT 18.
13 Letter, Rosemary Hill to DP, 4 April 1966, WAC T48.
14 Quoted by Wapshott in 'Knowing What Goes On . . .'
15 Quotations from DP, *Where the Buffalo Roam*, The Wednesday Play, BBC1, 2 November 1966.
16 Davies interview.
17 Memo, Kenith Trodd, 29 July 1966, WAC T5/698/1.
18 Teleprint, CAPPS Wales (Programme Services Controlller), 8 August 1966, WAC T5/698/1.
19 DP, 'Serious Bit of Strip-Tease.'
20 Letters, production file, WAC T5/698/1.
21 Memo, Gareth Davies to Lionel Harris, 15 September 1966, WAC T5/698/1.
22 Memo, Gerald Savory, 20 October 1966, WAC T5/698/1.
23 Memo, Huw Wheldon, 21 October 1966, WAC T5/698/1.
24 Memo, Savory, to Michael Peacock, 24 October 1966, WAC T5/698/1.
25 DP, 'Why, in the Name of Auguish . . .?' In My View column, *The Sun*, 2 February 1968.
26 Memo, Savory to Harris, 26 October 1966, WAC T5/698/1.
27 Memo, Davies to Savory, 26 October 1966, WAC T5/698/1.
28 Maurice Wiggin, television review, *Sunday Times*, 3 November 1966.
29 Peter Black, television review, *Daily Mail*, 3 November 1966.
30 S. R. C., television review, *Daily Telegraph*, 3 November 1966.
31 Nancy Banks-Smith, television review, *The Sun*, 3 November 1966.
32 James Thomas, television review, *Daily Express*, 3 November 1966.
33 Kenneth Eastaugh, television review, *Daily Mirror*, 3 November 1966.
34 Stanley Reynolds, television review, *The Guardian*, 3 August 1967.
35 Minutes, Controllers' Meeting, 15 November 1966, WAC T5/698/1.

Chapter 11

1 DP, 'Telling Friday', television review, *New Statesman*, 10 November 1972.

2 Commissioning document, Kenith Trodd, 8 August 1966, WAC T48.
3 Letter, Trodd to DP, 21 December 1966, WAC T48.
4 Memo, Gerald Savory to Huw Wheldon, 9 November 1966, WAC T5/994/1.
5 Hunter Davies, 'Trials of a TV Man', Atticus column, *Sunday Times*, 30 October 1966.
6 Memo, Savory to Wheldon, 7 November 1966, WAC T48.
7 Telegram, Mary Whitehouse to Savory, 7 December 1966, WAC T48.
8 Letter, Manchester Humanist Society, WAC T5/994/1.
9 Stanley Reynolds, untitled, *The Guardian*, 16 February 1973.
10 Quoted in *Daily Mail*, 7 December 1966.
11 Quoted in *Daily Sketch*, 7 December 1966.
12 Correspondence, *Almost Cinderella* file, WAC T5/994/1.
13 Reported in *The Times*, 8 December 1966.
14 Letter, Savory to DP, 5 January 1967, WAC T5/994/1.
15 Quoted by Purser in 'A Playwright Comes of Age'.
16 Davies, 'Trials of a TV Man'.
17 Quotations from DP, *Message for Posterity*, The Wednesday Play, BBC1, 3 May 1967; remade, Performance, BBC2, 29 October 1994.
18 DP, proposal document, 19 May 1965, WAC T48.
19 James Green, 'Talking TV', *London Evening News*, 7 September 1966.
20 Joseph O'Conor, interview with WSG, 12 March 1995.
21 L. P. Hartley, *The Go-Between* (Hamish Hamilton, 1953), Penguin edn, p. 7. The original is of course: 'The past is a foreign country . . .'
22 Davies interview.
23 T. C. Worsley, television review, *Financial Times*, 10 May 1967.
24 Letter, Savory to DP, 1 May 1967, WAC T5/994/1.
25 Thomas interview.

Chapter 12

1 DP, *Brimstone and Treacle*, BBC1, 25 August 1987; produced for Play for Today 1976 (stage play text, Methuen, 1978).
2 Fuller (ed.), *Potter on Potter*, p. 33.
3 Quotations from DP, *The Bonegrinder*, Playhouse, Associated Rediffusion for ITV, 13 March 1968, script held in BFI.
4 Stanley Reynolds, untitled, *The Guardian*.
5 Baker interview.
6 DP, 'The English at Play', As I See It, *Daily Herald*, 12 August 1961.
7 DP, 'Banana Skins on the NHS', Dennis Potter column, *The Sun*, 22 July 1968.
8 DP, 'Why Import This Trash?', television review, *Daily Herald*, 6 August 1964.
9 DP, 'Mimic Man', television review, *New Statesman*, 13 September 1974.

10 DP, 'A Guy Called St George', In My View column, *Daily Herald*, 20 April 1963.

11 Fuller (ed.), *Potter on Potter*, p. 34.

12 DP 'I Really Must Tell You I'm So Very Happy', Dennis Potter column, *The Sun*, 13 May 1968.

13 Letter, Michael Bowen to DP, 8 November 1966, WAC WE13/977/1.

14 Letter, DP to Bowen, 11 November 1966, WAC WE13/977/1.

15 Quotations from *Any Questions* transcript, BBC Light Programme, 6 January 1967, held in WAC.

16 The Gospel According to St John, 5:8.

17 Séan Day-Lewis, television review, *Daily Telegraph*, 14 May 1968.

18 Peter Black, television review, *Daily Mail*, 14 May 1968.

19 Nancy Banks-Smith, 'Now We'll Put a Stop to That Happy Feeling', *The Sun*, 14 May 1968.

20 DP, 'Dennis Potter Exposed'.

21 DP, 'Back to the Play! Critics? What Do They Know?', In My View column, *The Sun*, 23 February 1968.

22 DP, 'Some Sort of Preface . . .', *Waiting for the Boat*, p. 15.

23 Quoted by Cordell Marks in 'The Way a Writer Beat Arthritis' *TV Times*, 21 May 1970.

24 DP, 'Greenery-Yallery', television review, *New Statesman*, 14 July 1967.

25 William Hazlitt, 'The Periodical Press', *The Edinburgh Review*, 1823.

26 DP, 'The Sparks Leap into Life', review of *John Keats* by Robert Gittings, *The Times*, 23 March 1968.

27 DP 'Young Ibsen: Towards the Southbound Steamer', review of *Henrik Ibsen: The Making of a Dramatist 1828–1864* by Michael Meyer, *The Times*, 9 December 1967.

28 DP, 'Orwell: Despair and an Acre of Calm', review of *The Collected Essays, Journalism and Letters of George Orwell*, *The Times*, 5 October 1968.

29 DP, 'Occupying Powers', in *Seeing the Blossom*, pp. 50–1.

30 Quoted by Purser in 'A Playwright Comes of Age'.

31 DP, 'I Really Must Tell You . . .'

32 DP, 'For the Fever of Fear a Cure Called Hope', Dennis Potter column, *The Sun*, 26 August 1968.

33 DP, 'The Seed Crushers Versus the Yellow Peril', Dennis Potter column, *The Sun*, 30 September 1968.

34 DP, 'Lightning Over a Dark Field', review of *Bomb Culture* by Jeff Nuttall, *The Times*, 7 December 1968.

35 DP, 'I Really Must Tell You . . .'

36 Quotations from DP, *Shaggy Dog*, The Company of Five, LWT for ITV, 10 November 1968, script held in BFI.

37 DP, 'High-Tension Drama at Top Speed', television review, *Daily Herald*, 3 March 1964.

38 Davies interview.

39 Michael Billington, television review, *The Times*, 11 November 1968.

40 Peter Black, television review, *Daily Mail*, 11 November 1968.

41 Trodd interview, 1 May 1995.

Chapter 13

1 DP, *Blackeyes*, BBC-ABC-TV New Zealand/BBC2, 29 November–20 December 1989.
2 Graeme McDonald, interview with WSG, 13 March 1995.
3 McDonald, commissioning brief, 16 June 1967, WAC T48.
4 Kenith Trodd, memo to Assistant Head of Copyright, 6 September 1967, WAC RCONT 18.
5 McDonald, commissioning brief, 10 November 1967, WAC T48.
6 Quotations from DP, *A Beast with Two Backs*, The Wednesday Play, BBC1, 20 November 1968.
7 Germaine Greer, *The Female Eunuch* (Paladin, 1971), pp. 264–5.
8 Hoggart, *The Uses of Literacy*, p. 91.
9 Ibid., p. 142.
10 Davies interview.
11 McDonald interview.
12 Production notes, WAC T5/882/1.
13 Letter, McDonald to Lionel Harris on location, 3 April 1968, WAC T5/882/1.
14 Memo, Savory, WAC T5/882/1.
15 DP, 'Embalmed,' television review, *New Statesman*, 27 February 1976.
16 Lesley White, 'Smoke Gets in Your Eyes', *The Sunday Times*, 12 June 1994.
17 Stanley Reynolds, television review, *The Guardian*, 21 November 1968.
18 Shaun MacLoughlin, *Radio Times*, 14 November 1968.
19 Maurice Wiggin, television review, *The Sunday Times*, 24 November 1968.
20 Commissioning brief, WAC T48.
21 Russell Twisk, *Radio Times*, 10 April 1969.
22 Trodd interview, 1 May 1995.
23 DP, *Hide and Seek*, p. 72.
24 DP, 'It May Be That Twiggy Has the Right Idea After All', Dennis Potter column, *The Sun*, 18 March 1968.
25 Quotations from DP, *Moonlight on the Highway*.
26 DP, *Hide and Seek*, p. 19.
27 'Quoted' in Ambrose Bierce, *The Devil's Dictionary* ('Golgo Brone' is undoubtedly one of Bierce's pseudonyms), *Collected Works*, vol. 7 (1911).
28 C. S. Lewis, *Mere Christianity* (Fontana, 1955), p. 56.
29 Stanley Reynolds, untitled article, *The Guardian*, 16 February 1973.
30 Unpublished transcript of DP interview with John Wyver, 14 February 1978, for article 'Paradise, Perhaps', *Time Out*, 3 March 1978.
31 Russell Twisk, *Radio Times*.

Chapter 14

1 DP, *Sufficient Carbohydrate*, Hampstead Theatre, 8 December 1983 (Faber and Faber, 1983).

2 Fuller (ed.), *Potter on Potter*, p. 38.

3 e.g. *Daily Sketch*, 4 December 1968.

4 DP, 'My Text for TV Parsons', In My View column, *Daily Herald*, 17 August 1963.

5 DP, 'A Jazz Ration Please!', In My View column, *Daily Herald*, 5 October 1963

6 DP, 'Our Future . . . with a Touch of the Dr Whos', In My View column, *The Sun*, 19 January 1968.

7 Mary Craig, 'Potter's Way of Faith', *Catholic Herald*, 5 May 1976.

8 Quoted by Purser in 'A Playwright Comes of Age'.

9 Quotations from DP, *Son of Man*, The Wednesday Play, BBC1, 16 April 1969.

10 William Blake, 'The Everlasting Gospel', 1818.

11 Quoted in *Programmes from Heaven*, obituary round-up, *The Guardian*, 8 June 1994.

12 Davies interview.

13 Memo, undated, WAC T5/1,966/1.

14 'Christ the Man', unsigned 'Diary' report, *The Times*, 7 April 1969.

15 Sylvia Clayton, television review, *Daily Telegraph*, 17 April 1969.

16 Julian Critchley, television review, *The Times*, 17 April 1969.

17 Quoted by Purser in 'A Playwright Comes of Age'.

18 DP, 'More of This Beautiful Martian, Please', In My View column, *The Sun*, 7 February 1968.

19 O'Conor interview.

20 Quotations from DP, *Lay Down Your Arms*, Saturday Night Theatre, Kestrel Productions-LWT for ITV, 23 May 1970.

21 Christopher Morahan, interview with WSG, 7 February 1995.

22 'Potter Runs into a *!*! Problem', unsigned, *Daily Sketch*, 23 May 1970.

23 Letter, *Sunday Telegraph*, 31 May 1970.

Chapter 15

1 Bernard Shaw, *Maxims for Revolutionists*, appended to *Man and Superman*, 1903.

2 Quotations from DP, *Angels Are So Few*, Play for Today, BBC1, 5 November 1970.

3 Quotations from DP, *Schmoedipus*, Play for Today, BBC1, 20 June 1974.

4 Quotations from DP, *Brimstone and Treacle*.

5 DP, 'The Unkindest Cut of All – I Almost Giggled', In My View column, *The Sun*, 25 January 1968.

6 DP interviewed by Bernard Levin, *The Levin Interview*, BBC2, 17 May 1980, transcript WAC.
7 DP, 'Paper Thin', television review, *New Statesman*, 17 October 1975.
8 DP, 'It May Be That Twiggy . . .'
9 DP, *Brimstone and Treacle*, stage play text.
10 Davies interview.
11 Quoted by Gordon Burn in 'Men With Something to Say: Television is the Only Medium That Counts', *Radio Times*, 8 October 1970.
12 'Council to Protest About "Filth" on Television', unsigned, *Glasgow Herald*, 10 November 1970.

Chapter 16

1 DP, *Hide and Seek*, p. 25.
2 Nathan interview.
3 Quotations from DP, *Paper Roses*, Granada for ITV, 13 June 1971.
4 Trodd interview, 1 May 1995.
5 Fuller (ed.), *Potter on Potter*, pp. 42–3.
6 Quotations from DP, *Traitor*.
7 DP, 'The Nasty Side of an Awfully Nice Town', *The Sun*, 6 May 1968.
8 Gordon Burn, 'Men With Something to Say'.
9 DP, 'Bunting on the Brain', television review, *Sunday Times*, 5 June 1977.
10 Quoted by Susan Raven in 'Relative Values: Critic and Cricketer', *Sunday Times*, 14 August 1983.
11 DP, *With Great Pleasure*, BBC Radio 4, 5 June 1976; DP's handwritten script is in WAC.
12 Ibid.
13 Quoted by D. A. N. Jones in 'Playing Potter's Traitor: "The Best Part I Ever Had on TV"', *Radio Times*, 7 October 1971.
14 Quotations from DP, *Casanova*, BBC2, 16 November–21 December 1971.
15 John Glenister, interview with WSG, 29 March 1995.
16 DP interviewed by Colin Morris, *The Anno Domini Interview*, BBC1, 13 February 1977, transcript in WAC.

Chapter 17

1 DP, *Hide and Seek*, p. 2.
2 Oliver Gillie, 'Drug Gives New Life to Dennis Potter', *Sunday Times*, 20 March 1977.
3 Quoted by Wapshott in 'Knowing What Goes On . . .'
4 DP, 'Some Sort of Preface . . .' *Waiting for the Boat*, p. 17.

5 Quotations from DP, *Follow the Yellow Brick Road*.
6 Epistle of St Paul to the Philippians, 4:8.
7 DP, introduction to *Brimstone and Treacle*.
8 DP, 'Tea-Bag Rebels: Dennis Potter's Verdict After a Night with Red Danny', *The Sun*, 17 June 1968.
9 Quoted by Purser in 'A Playwright Comes of Age'.
10 Roderick Graham, interview with WSG, 14 February 1995.
11 Stanley Reynolds, untitled, *The Guardian*, 16 February 1973.
12 Quotations from DP, *Only Make Believe*, Play for Today, BBC1, 12 February 1973.
13 Séan Day-Lewis, 'Will the Devil Get His Due?', *Daily Telegraph*, 5 April 1976.
14 McDonald interview.
15 DP, *Hide and Seek*, p. 60.
16 'Some Sort of Preface . . .', in *Waiting for the Boat*, p. 31.
17 Quotations from DP, *Double Dare*, Play for Today, BBC1, 6 April 1976.
18 John MacKenzie, interview with WSG, 17 February 1995.
19 Unpublished interview with John Wyver.
20 Quoted by James Murray in 'What the Devil Are They Playing At?' *Daily Express*, 29 March 1976.
21 Quoted in 'Potter Play: Mrs W Seeks Prosecution', unsigned, *Evening Standard*, 8 April 1976.

Chapter 18

1 DP, 'A Note from Mr Milne', *New Statesman*, 23 April 1976.
2 McDonald interview.
3 According to Peter Fiddick, untitled, *The Guardian*, 22 March 1976.
4 DP, introduction to text of *Joe's Ark*, *Waiting for the Boat*.
5 Quotations from DP, *Joe's Ark*, Play for Today, 14 February 1974.
6 Peter Fiddick, television review, *The Guardian*, 15 February 1974.
7 Freddie Jones, interview with WSG, 31 January 1995.
8 DP, introduction to *Joe's Ark*.
9 DP interview, *The South Bank Show*.
10 Quoted in 'Ban on Rape Play Lifted', unsigned, *The People*, 26 October 1975.
11 'Satan Play Banned by BBC', unsigned (but almost certainly Martin 'Scoop' Jackson), *Daily Mail*, 20 March 1976.
12 Quoted by James Murray in 'What the Devil Are They Playing At?'
13 Quoted by Peter Fiddick in 'Potter Play Banned', *The Guardian*, 20 March 1976.
14 Quoted in 'Potter Will Try to Stop Showing of His Plays,' unsigned, *Television Today*, 25 March 1976.
15 Quoted by WSG in 'Cowgill Beefs,' *Time Out*, 25 March 1976.
16 Martin Jackson, 'Banned by the BBC,' *Daily Mail*, 27 March 1976.

17 Julian Graff, 'BBC Drama Producers Stand Up To Be Counted ...', *Broadcast*, 29 March 1976.
18 Quoted by Peter Fiddick in untitled article, *The Guardian*, 12 April 1976.
19 Craig, 'Potter's Way of Faith'.
20 Milne, *D.G.: The Memoirs of a British Broadcaster*, p. 86.
21 Charles Curran, *A Seamless Robe: Broadcasting Philosophy and Practice* (Collins, 1979), p. 318.
22 Milne interview.
23 DP, interview with Mary Craig, *Sunday*, Radio 4, 25 April 1976.
24 DP interviewed by Melvyn Bragg, *South Bank Show*, LWT for ITV, 11 February 1979.
25 David Leland, interview with WSG, 10 February 1995.
26 Richard Loncraine, interview with WSG, 11 February 1995.

Chapter 19

1 Quoted in Edmund Gosse, *Father and Son* (William Heinemann, 1907), Penguin edn, p. 49.
2 DP, 'Tsar's Army', television review, *New Statesman*, 13 October 1972.
3 DP, 'Dead Muster'.
4 Gosse, *Father and Son*, p. 44.
5 Ibid., p. 56.
6 Ibid., p. 102.
7 Ibid., p. 177.
8 Ibid., p. 199.
9 Ibid., p. 233.
10 Ibid., p. 241.
11 Quotations from DP, *Where Adam Stood*, BBC2, 21 April 1976.
12 DP, *The Singing Detective*, BBC-ABC/BBC1, 16 November – 21 December 1986, (text Faber and Faber, 1986).
13 Brian Gibson, interview with WSG, 2 May 1995.
14 Quoted by Angela Carter in 'The Kind of Stories That Countrymen Tell', *Radio Times*, 1 November 1973.
15 Betty Willingale, interview with WSG, 25 May 1995.
16 Christopher Ricks, 'Translating Hardy for TV', *Sunday Times*, 5 February 1978.
17 Quotations from DP's dramatisation of *The Mayor of Casterbridge* by Thomas Hardy, BBC2, 22 January–5 March 1978.
18 DP, *With Great Pleasure*.
19 David Giles, interview with WSG, 14 February 1995.
20 Thomas Hardy, *The Mayor of Casterbridge*, (*The Graphic*, 1886); Oxford University Press edn p. 181.
21 Ibid., p. 67.
22 Ibid. p. 297.

23 Milne interview.

Chapter 20

1 DP, *Message for Posterity.*
2 Oliver Gillie, 'Drug Gives New Life to Dennis Potter'.
3 DP, *The Anno Domini* interview.
4 DP, *Desert Island Discs.*
5 Quoted by Wapshott in 'Knowing What Goes On . . .'
6 DP, *Desert Island Discs.*
7 Quotations from DP, *Pennies from Heaven*, BBC1, 7 March–11 April 1978.
8 Milne interview.
9 Piers Haggard, interview with WSG, 8 April 1995.
10 Quoted by Ray Connolly in 'When the Penny Dropped', *Evening Standard*, 21 March 1978.
11 Cheryl Campbell, interview with WSG, 8 April 1995.
12 DP, 'Receding Dreams', television review, *New Statesman*, 15 March 1974.
13 DP, 'Vicious Circle', television review, *New Statesman* 14 March 1975.
14 Quoted by WSG in 'The Ultimate Optimism', *The Observer*, 5 February 1978.
15 C. S. Lewis, *Mere Christianity*, p. 91.
16 DP, *Pennies from Heaven* (Quartet/PfH (Overseas) Ltd, 1981).
17 DP, *An Interview with Dennis Potter*, in *Seeing the Blossom*, p. 19.
18 Quoted by Martin Jackson in 'Kids' Play for Mr Potter!', *Daily Mail*, 27 January 1979.
19 Quoted by John Wyver in 'How to Turn a Difficulty . . .'
20 Gibson interview.

Chapter 21

1 Quoted by Wapshott in 'Knowing What Goes On . . .'
2 Quoted by Martin Jackson in 'Kids' Play for Mr Potter!'
3 Quoted by Séan Day-Lewis in 'Playwright Potter Quits BBC', *Daily Telegraph*, 18 May 1979.
4 Quoted by Richard Grant, in 'For 17 Years I've Been Fantasising About How to Improve TV,' *Evening News*, 21 May 1979.
5 Peter Fiddick, 'Channel Switch', *The Guardian*, 21 May 1979.
6 Quoted by Grant in 'For 17 Years . . .'
7 Anthony Powell, *Journals 1982–1986*, (Heinemann, 1995) p. 79.
8 Peter Fiddick, report, *The Guardian*, 28 July 1980.
9 Ibid.
10 Quoted by Séan Day–Lewis in 'Potter Switches Screen', *Daily Telegraph*, 20 October 1980.

11 Loncraine interview.
12 Quoted in 'A Play That Blunted the Stars' Enthusiasm . . .', unsigned, *Daily Mail*, 21 May 1980.
13 Loncraine interview.
14 Quotations from DP, *Rain on the Roof*, PfH/LWT for ITV, 26 October 1980.
15 Campbell interview.
16 Quotations from DP, *Cream in My Coffee*, PfH/LWT for ITV, 21 November 1980, text in *Waiting for the Boat*.
17 Quoted in Fiddick report, *The Guardian*.
18 Michael Church, television review, *The Times*, 27 October 1980.
19 Albert Hunt, 'Plays Portentous', *New Society*, 6 November 1980.
20 DP, 'Realism and Non-Naturalism', paper to the Edinburgh International Television Festival, 1977, *Broadcast*, 22 August 1977.

Chapter 22

1 Quoted in Fiddick report, *The Guardian*.
2 DP, 'I Really Must Tell You . . .'
3 'Some Sort of Preface . . .', *Waiting for the Boat*, p. 17.
7 Quotations from DP, *Sufficient Carbohydrate*.
5 Quotations from DP, *Visitors*, Screen Two, BBC2, 22 February 1987.
6 Haggard interview.
7 Quotations from DP's dramatisation of *Tender is the Night* by F. Scott Fitzgerald, BBC-Showtime-Seven Network/BBC2, 2 September–28 October 1985.
8 Willingale interview.
9 Quotations from DP, *Dreamchild*, Thorn EMI-PfH, 1985.
10 Quoted by Amanda Lipman in 'Track Record', *Producer*, date unknown.
11 Fuller (ed.), *Potter on Potter*, p. 124.
12 Nicolas Roeg, interview with WSG, 8 February 1995.
13 Quotations from DP, *Track 29*, HandMade Films, 1987.

Chapter 23

1 Raymond Chandler, *Playback* (Hamish Hamilton, 1958), Penguin edn, p. 28.
2 Quotations from DP, *The Singing Detective*.
3 Jon Amiel, interview with WSG, 18 February 1995.
4 Alison Steadman, interview with WSG, 15 March 1995.
5 Fuller (ed.), *Potter on Potter*, p. 66.
6 Quotations from *Christabel*, DP's dramatisation of *The Past is Myself* by Christabel Bielenberg, BBC-AEN/BBC2, 16 November–7 December 1988 (text Faber and Faber, 1988).
7 Elizabeth Hurley, interview with WSG, 26 April 1995.

Chapter 24

1 DP, *Blackeyes* (Faber and Faber, 1980), p. 36.
2 DP, 'Tsar's Army'.
3 Quoted by Amanda Lipman, 'Track Record'.
4 WSG, 'Potter's Field', review of *Ticket to Ride* by DP, *The Listener*, 2 October 1986.
5 Fuller (ed.), *Potter on Potter*, p. 127.
6 DP, 'Show a Thigh and Up Pops a Sermon', In My View column, *The Sun*, 30 January 1968.
7 Gina Bellman, interview with WSG, 30 May 1995.
8 William Hazlitt's letter to Peter George Patmore, 1820, included in the anonymously published *Liber Amoris* (1823).
9 DP, *Ticket to Ride*, dust jacket (Faber and Faber, 1986).
10 D. H. Lawrence, *Women in Love* (Martin Secker, 1921), Penguin edn, p. 45.
11 D. H. Lawrence, 'Shadows', published in *Last Poems 1928–9*, now in *Selected Poems* (Penguin Books, 1972).
12 This analysis appeared substantially as WSG, 'Potter's Field'.
13 DP, 'Some Sort of Preface . . .', *Waiting for the Boat*, pp. 12, 14–15.
14 DP, *Secret Friends*, Film Four International-Whistling Gypsy, 1991.
15 Bellman interview.

Chapter 25

1 DP, 'Occupying Powers', *Seeing the Blossom*.
2 DP, *Lipstick on Your Collar* (Faber and Faber-Channel 4, 1993).
3 DP, 'Welcome Back to the Piffle of the Past', In My View column, *The Sun*, 8 February 1968.
4 DP, *Desert Island Discs*.
5 Quotations from DP, *Lipstick on Your Collar*, Whistling Gypsy for Channel 4, 21 February–28 March 1993.
6 Roy Hudd, interview with WSG, 27 January 1995.
7 Paul Almond, BBC news release, 1 December 1994.
8 Quotations from DP, *Midnight Movie*, Screen Two, Whistling Gypsy for BBC2, 26 December 1994.
9 Ross Benson, 'Gloomy Beeb Goes Potty', *Daily Express*, 2 December 1994.
10 Trodd, interview with WSG, 30 May 1995.

Chapter 26

1 DP, *Karaoke*, BBC-Whistling Gypsy, for transmission 1996.
2 Trodd interview.
3 DP, *An Interview with Dennis Potter*, *Seeing the Blossom*.

4 June Thomas interview; I am indebted to her for the detail of this account.
5 Hudd interview.
6 DP, 'Biological Revolution: But What Else?', review of *The Biological Time-Bomb* by Gordon Rattray Taylor, *The Times*, 27 April 1968.
7 DP, 'Occupying Powers', *Seeing the Blossom.*
8 Trodd interview.
9 Hudd interview.
10 Nathan interview.
11 Trodd interview.
12 Lewis Carroll, *Alice's Adventures in Wonderland* (Macmillan, 1865).

Appendix I

The Works of Dennis Potter

This is a comprehensive list of Dennis Potter's writings published professionally as teleplays, stage plays, non-fiction books and novels, together with productions on television, cinema screen and stage of his scripts and his dramatisations of other writers' work. Personal appearances on television and radio are also listed but the extent of his copious journalism can only be broadly indicated.

Key: DP = Dennis Potter
DN = David Nathan
prog = programme/edition/episode
tx = transmission time using 24-hour clock (i.e. 2130 is 9.30 pm)
m = minutes (programme length)
uc = uncredited
rpt = repeat

'Base Ingratitude?' *New Statesman* 3 May 1958
The vivid article about 'Welfare State Oxford' that caught the BBC's attention.

Town and Country BBC Home Service 29 May 1958. tx 1824 c.16m
'A programme for listeners in the South-East of England' in which DP gave a talk 'A View of Oxford from *The Isis*'.

'Small Victim' *New Statesman* 21 June 1958
On his resignation from the editorship of *The Isis*.

Does Class Matter? prog 2: 'Class in Private Life'
BBC Television 25 August 1958 tx 2130 c.30m
'An Enquiry by Christopher Mayhew MP' who interviewed DP in the latter's rooms at New College Oxford. (Rest of the series: prog 1: 'What is Class?'; prog 3: 'Class and the Nation'; prog 4: 'Class in the USA'; prog 5: 'Class and the New Generation') film cameraman A. A. Englander/film editor Larry Toft/producer Jack Ashley.

Panorama BBC Television
Introduced by Richard Dimbleby/associate producer David Wheeler/editor and producer Michael Peacock.

DP took a General Trainee Attachment with BBC Television Talks from 6 July 1959 to 30 September 1960, during which he researched items for three editions:

23 November 1959. tx 2035 c.45m
'Corporal Punishment', a studio report by Robin Day, and 'Hawks', a studio response by the actor James Robertson Justice to an earlier item on pigeons.

30 November 1959. tx 2035 c.45m
'Closing of Pits in the Forest of Dean', a film report by James Mossman produced by David Wheeler.

21 December 1959. tx 2035 c.45m
'Paperbacks', a film report by Robert Kee produced by Jack Ashley.

The Glittering Coffin Victor Gollancz Ltd, February 1960.
DP's first book, a polemic on the state of the nation

Tonight BBC Television 8 February 1960. tx 1845 c.40m
DP interviewed on *The Glittering Coffin*. Introduced by Cliff Michelmore with Derek Hart, Alan Whicker, Fyfe Robertson 'and including' John Morgan, Polly Elwes, Cy Grant/associate producers Alasdair Milne, Antony Jay, Gordon Watkins/editor Donald Baverstock.

The World of Books BBC Home Service 13 February 1960. tx 1400 c.35m
DP on *The Glittering Coffin*. Introduced by Robin Holmes.

The Brains Trust BBC Home Service 17 April 1960. tx 1615 c.45m
DP took part in an Easter Day special discussion 'in which the viewpoint of the younger generation is put by: Alasdair Clayre (age 24) Fellow of All Souls College, Oxford; James Mirrlees (age 23) mathematical wrangler at Cambridge; Dennis Potter (age 24) author of *The Glittering Coffin*; Shirley Williams (Chairman age 29) General Secretary, the Fabian Society'.

Between Two Rivers BBC Television 3 June 1960. tx 2125 c.28m
DP's personal report, which he wrote, narrated and briefly fronted, on change in the Forest of Dean. Sound recordists Maurice Everitt, Frank Dale/film cameraman Peter Sargent/film editor Leonard Trumm/producer Anthony de Lotbinière.

Tonight BBC Television 30 September 1960. tx 1850 c.39m
DP took part in a discussion on English personality based on publication of the pamphlet "The Chipped White Cups of Dover". Introduced by Michelmore with Hart, Whicker, Robertson, Morgan, Trevor Philpott, Elwes and Robin Hall and Jimmie MacGregor. Associate producers Jay, Watkins, Tony Essex/assistant editor Milne/editor Baverstock.

Bookstand First series BBC Television
Sunday afternoon series billed in *Radio Times* as 'a kaleidoscope from the world of books' for which DP dramatised extracts from (mostly) novels. Presenter Dick Taverne/script associate Dennis Potter/film editors Agnes Evan, Joe Sterling/studio designer Natasha Kroll/programme assistant Ian

Martin/drama sequences director John McGrath/director Christopher Burstall/ producer Stephen Hearst.

prog 1: 16 October 1960. tx 1610 c.40m
with Prunella Scales, Robert Christopher, Roger Smith, Robert Hardy. Included DP's dramatisations of scenes from *Hurry On Down* by John Wain (acted by Gerald Case, Philip Grout, Vernon Dobtcheff, Guy Vivian), *Under the Net* by Iris Murdoch (Anthony Hall, Alfred Maron), *That Uncertain Feeling* by Kingsley Amis (Shirley Tongue, Denys Graham) and *A Kind of Loving* by Stan Barstow (Charles Lamb, Brian Murray).

prog 2: 30 October 1960. tx 1610 c.40m
with Dr Tom Paterson, John Hadfield, Bob Roberts, Bryan Pringle, Mr Smith, Mr Freeman (miners). Included DP's dramatisation of scenes from Christopher Hibbert's *King Mob* (Ian MacNaughton, Roger Snowden, Noël Coleman) and *Absolute Beginners* by Colin MacInnes (Terence Stamp, Christopher Sandford, Graham Bell, David Baxter, David Coe, Lucinda Curtis, Suzanne Vagley, Elizabeth MacLennan).

'Oh, That Smug, Arrogant Ostrich!' *Daily Herald* 4 November 1960
'Son of a miner and author of *The Glittering Coffin*', DP guest-wrote the 'As I See It' column. He called Oxford 'my "big chance", my emancipation from the alleged puritanism, ignorance and sterile dogmatism of a small coalmining community'.

'Shoddiness is Strangling Soccer' *Daily Herald* 9 November 1960
Despite a front-page fanfare (5 November) for an anticipated series of 'Group 60 Reports' put together by Kenneth Trodd, Robin Blackburn, Perry Anderson, Roger Smith, Nigelfred Young and DP, this routine piece on declining gates and lack of glamour at northern soccer venues was the only report to emerge from the touring Oxford graduates.

Bookstand continued

prog 3: 13 November 1960. tx 1610 c.40m
with L. H. Rees, F. G. Walker, Valentine Dyall, Paul Marsh, Cecil Trouncer, Gary Watson, Clive Graham. Included DP's dramatisation of a scene from *The Turn of the Screw* by Henry James (Prunella Scales, Peggyann Clifford).

Ten O'Clock BBC Home Service 17 November 1960. tx 2200 c.30m
'The News and Comment from at Home and Abroad'. DP spoke on Immorality among Young People. Introduced by John Thompson.

Bookstand continued

prog 4: 27 November 1960. tx 1620 c.30m
with Murray Sayle, Len Howard, James Morris, Iona & Peter Opie. Included DP's dramatisation of a scene from Sayle's *A Crooked Sixpence* (Toke Townley, John Ringham, Michael Caine) and DP interviewing Morris on his book *Venice*.

prog 5: 11 December 1960. tx 1620 c.30m
with Mervyn Jones, Raymond Williams, Ann Murray, Dr Anthony Storr,

Mrs Anthea Holme and DP's scene from Williams' novel *Border Country* (Rachel Thomas, David Lyn, Susan Field, Pryser Williams).

prog 6: 8 January 1961. tx 1615 c.35m
(Burstall & Martin swap roles) with Fr Thomas Corbishley, Anthony Flew and DP's scene from *The New Writer's Guide*: *Romantic Fiction* (Susan Bennett, Peter Bowles) and his interplay of G. K. Chesterton's *Orthodoxy* with James Joyce's *Portrait of the Artist* (John Hussey, Robert Lang).

prog 7: 22 January 1961. tx 1620 c.30m
with George Benson, Raymond Williams, Anthony Hall, Joanna Vogel, Kenneth Seeger, Ian Fairbairn and DP's scene from *The Glass Key* by Dashiell Hammett (Frank Finlay, Allan McClelland).

prog 8: 5 February 1961. tx 1620 c.30m
(Drama sequences David Willmott) with Kenneth Farrington, Claude Bourdet, Anthony Quinton, Mrs Elizabeth Salter and DP's scenes from Camus' *The Outsider* (Julian Glover, Malcolm Russell), *Sinner, Saint and Jester* by Rafael Sabatini (Carleton Hobbs, Gloria Dolski, Henley Thomas) and Sabatini's *Destiny of Fire* (Brendan Brady, Marion Diamond).

prog 9: 19 February 1961. tx 1620 c.30m
with John Harris, Cyril Hartley, Cecil Ellison, Harry Bartholomew, George Tirebuck, Anthony Storr, Charles Rycroft and DP's scenes from *Covenant with Death* by Harris (Brian Parker, Alan Stuart, Geoffrey Denys, Henry Soskin, Paul Mead, David Brierley, Walter Hall, Rodney Bewes).

prog 10: 5 March 1961. tx 1620 c.30m
with Andrew Shonfield, Paul Johnson, Nikolaus Pevsner, Marcus Cunliffe, Miss Delia Corrie and DP's scene from Huxley's *Brave New World* (Peter Carlisle, Ian Keill, Court Benson) and DP's own presentation about Westerns.

prog 11: 19 March 1961. tx 1615 c.35m
with Leonard Miall, George R. Mowry, Isobel English and DP's scene from English's *Four Voices* (Vanda Godsell, John Ruddock, Jane Jordan Rogers, Betty Hardy) and DP's interview with Francis Chichester filmed at the latter's home.

prog 12: 2 April 1961. tx 1615 c.30m
(Drama sequences Peter Hammond) with Ritchie Calder, Dr Dudley Stamp, Anthony Carson, J. Steven Watson and DP's presentation on and scene from Wilfrid Sheed's Oxford novel *A Middle Class Education* (acted by Ronald Wilson, Clinton Greyn, Gary Watson, Robert Mill, Harvey Ashby, Jill Brooke, Diana Sallis, Martin Lawton, David Philpott, William Swan, Geoffrey Thompson).

prog 13: 16 April 1961. tx 1620 c.30m
with Stan Hugill, Bob Roberts, Muriel Spark, Stella McCloy, Edward Hyams and DP's interview with Hyams and scene from his novel *All We Possess* (Frank Coda, Pat Roberts, Allan McClelland).

prog 18: 25 June 1961. tx 1615 c.35m
with Francis Newton, Richard Wollheim, Arthur Calder-Marshall, Francis
Hope, Robert Kee, Albert & Pascal Lamerisse and DP's presentation on
The Jazz Scene and his interview with its author, Newton.

General Articles *Daily Herald* 12 August 1961–16 March 1962.
DP wrote fitfully on a variety of subjects, mostly for the leader page. He also
took on some book reviews.

Rene Cutforth With Something To Say BBC Home Service 30 August 1961.
tx 2042 c.13m
DP guest speaker. Producer Francis Dillon.

Ten O'Clock BBC Home Service 6 October 1961. tx 2200 c.45m
DP spoke on 'the Establishment'. Introduced by George Scott.

The Changing Forest: Life in the Forest of Dean Today Martin Secker and
Warburg, 9 April 1962 ('Britain Alive' series no.3).
DP's second book, 'a social enquiry into the Forest of Dean'.

Guest Reviewing *Daily Herald* 7 May–26 May 1962.
DP covered television as holiday relief for Alan Dick.

Bookstand BBC Television 30 May 1962. tx 2041 c.29 m.
DP interviewed Edna O'Brien. Introduced by Brian Parker/producer Christopher
Burstall.

Television Reviews *Daily Herald* 23 July 1962–29 August 1964.
DP became the regular reviewer. From 31 August 1962, he added a Saturday
column, 'In My View' (renamed 'Dennis Potter About' on 7 December 1963,
'Dennis Potter on Television' on 25 January 1964), for more considered
pieces. He also wrote occasional general articles and media news reports.

That Was The Week That Was First series BBC Television.
David Nathan and DP joined the writing team of the late-night satire show
which had begun on 24 November 1962. The pair contributed items to most
editions from late February.
Regular cast: David Frost, Millicent Martin, Timothy Birdsall, Kenneth Cope,
David Kernan, Roy Kinnear, Bernard Levin, Lance Percival, Willie Rushton,
Al Mancini.
Regular writers: John Albery, Brad Ashton, Christopher Booker, Caryl Brahms,
Quentin Crewe and Julian Holland, Frost, Gerald Kaufman, Herbert Kretzmer,
Peter Lewis and Peter Dobereiner, Jack Rosenthal, Steven Vinaver, Keith
Waterhouse and Willis Hall, Michael Whale (uc: Clement Freud, Ned
Sherrin).
Music Dave Lee/design Malcolm Middleton/producer Sherrin.

prog 7: 5 January 1963. tx 2235 c.50m
'Attlee' dialogue by DN and DP.
Cast minus Mancini, plus Michael Redgrave, Peter Holmes, Arthur Blake,
Anthony Bateman, the Marquess of Bath
Writers plus John Antrobus, Brian Glanville, Lady Glen-Coats, Richard

Ingrams, David Mason, Marion McNaughton, David Nobbs, Geoffrey Paxton (uc: Roger Woddis).

prog 11: 2 February 1963. tx 2220 c.50m
'Statesman' sketch by DN and DP.
Cast plus Rose Hill, Bateman, Blake, Richard Clarke, William Holmes.
Writers plus Alma Birk, Anthony Booth, Charles de Gaulle (*sic*), Glanville, Antony Jay, Paul Jennings, David Kossoff, Ian Lang, Leslie Mallory, Kenneth Tynan.

prog 14: 23 February 1963. tx 2245 c.50m
'Faith' sketch by DN and DP.
Cast minus Kinnear plus Peter Dolphin, David Harding, Kenneth Loach, Angela Simmonds, David Walsh.
Writers plus James Crossman, William Franklyn, Glanville, Jay, Lang, Peter McEnery, Rosenthal, Tynan.

prog 15: 2 March 1963. tx 2245 c.50m
'Nationalisation Pamphlet' and 'Canon Collins' by DN and DP.
Cast minus Kinnear plus Tsai Chin, Jacqui Chan, Dolphin, Geoffrey Wright, Janet Hall, Wendy Barry.
Writers plus Kenneth Hewis, Mallory, George Mikes, Bill Oddie, Rushton, Peter Veale (uc: Birdsall, Allan Davis, Levin, Mancini, Michael Wharton).

prog 16: 9 March 1963. tx 2230 c.50m
'Free Gifts' sketch by DN and DP.
Cast plus Fenella Fielding, Leila Guirst, Sally Ann Shaw, Norman St John Stevas.
Writers plus Barry Fantoni, Robert Gillespie, Jay, Mikes, Leon Rosselson.

prog 17: 16 March 1963. tx 2225 c.50m
'Critics' item by DN and DP.
Cast plus Alison Leggatt, John Church, Dolphin, Walsh, Horace James, Elroy Josephs, Shaw, Beryl Nesbitt, Loach, Nicholas Ward.
Writers plus Werdow Anglin, Monica Furlong, Gillespie, Joe Haines and Andrew Roth, Jay, Kernan, Mallory, Christopher Martin, Mikes, Frank Muir and Denis Norden, Jack Trevor Storey, Tynan (uc: Alison Eyles, Ingrams, Stuart Morris, G. E. Pattie, Donald Webster).

prog 18: 23 March 1963. tx 2315 c.40m
'Mother's Day' monologue by DN, DP and Jack Rosenthal.
Cast plus Peter O'Toole, Church, Walsh, James, Josephs, Hall, Greta Hamby, Corinne Skinner, Randolph Churchill.
Writers plus Sydney Carter, Martin Folkard, Haines and Roth, George Hopkins, Enoch Kent, Tony Marriott, Mason, Mikes, Noel Picarda, Peter Shaffer (uc: Rushton, Veale).

prog 19: 30 March 1963. tx 2245 c.50m
'Milly's Monologue' by DN and DP.
Cast minus Kernan plus Coral Browne, Kevin Scott, Doris Hare, Janet Rowsell, Guirst.

Writers plus Paul Boyle, Carter, Ian Davidson, Elaine Dundy, Robin Grove-White, Haines and Roth, Jay, the Lord Chamberlain (*sic*) (uc: Ingrams, Eric Sykes).
Designer Melvyn Cornish.

prog 20: 6 April 1963. tx 2235 c.50m
'South Africa' sketch by DN and DP.
Cast minus Kernan plus Frankie Howerd, Joan Heal, Heather Harper, Josephs, Ann Bullen, Jean Cragg, Val Denister, Diane Langton, Maggie Lee.
Writers plus John Bowen, Carter, Haines and Roth, Tony Hendra, Jay, Douglas Livingston, David Nobbs, Rosselson, Webster (uc: Michael Flanders, Derek Lowe, Mallory, Tom McGuinness and Mark Newell, Muir and Norden, Shaffer, Johnny Speight).
Designer Stuart Durant.

prog 21: 13 April 1963. tx 2230 c.55m
'Referee's Report' by DN and DP and 'Nabarro: What's My Line?' by DN and DP, Haines and Roth.
Cast minus Kernan, Levin plus Edith Evans, Vivian Pickles, Hazel Hughes.
Writers plus Bowen, Carter, Hendra, Jay, Livingston, David Nobbs, Rosselson, Webster (uc: Malcolm Bradbury, Ingrams).

Woman's Hour BBC Light Programme 16 April 1963. tx 1400 c.60m
Fourth billed of seven items: 'Aspects of University Life 3' including 'a working class view of Oxford' by DP. Introduced by Teresa McGonagle.
Item rpt Home Service/*Home for the Day* 12.5.63 tx 0910

Woman's Hour BBC Light Programme 25 April 1963. tx 1400 c.60m
Fifth billed of six items: 'Talk of Books and Writers', DP interviewed Wyndham Thomas on *The Cutteslowe Walls*. Introduced by Teresa McGonagle.

That Was The Week That Was continued:

prog 23: 27 April 1963. tx 2235 c.50m
'Predictions' sketch by Booker & Frost after DN and DP.
Cast minus Kernan, Levin plus Cleo Laine, Chin, Michael Chow, Walsh, Ronnie Curran, Lindsay Dolan, Peter Gordeno, Roy Gunston, Andrew Morrison, Marcel Peake.
Writers plus Stuart Harris, Mallory (uc: John Braine).
Designer Melvyn Cornish.

Woman's Hour BBC Light Programme 15 May 1963. tx 1400 c.60m
Fifth billed of six items: 'Ideas in the Air' discussion by Marghanita Laski and DP. Introduced by Marjorie Anderson.

That Was The Week That Was Second series BBC Television.

prog 1: 28 September 1963. tx 2230 c.50m
'Shakespeare Strip' sketch by DN and DP.
Cast minus Timothy Birdsall (who died) plus Robert Lang, Irwin C. Watson, Sir Cyril Osborne.

Writers plus David Climie, Haines and Roth, Hendra, John Mortimer, Mikes, Oddie, Peter Pagnamenta, Ross Parker, Woddis (uc: Ashton, Keith Watson).
Designer Ridley Scott.

prog 4: 19 October 1963. tx 2230 c.50m
'Smoker' item by DN and DP.
Cast plus Fred Emney, Renee Houston, Madge Brindley, Watson.
Writers plus Basil Boothroyd, David Cumming and Bernard Mattimore, Mortimer, Oddie, Rushton, Peter Tinniswood and Nobbs.
Designer Durant.

prog 6: 2 November 1963. tx 2235 c.50m
'Comic Postcard Artist' sketch by DN and DP.
Cast minus Rushton plus Barbara Staveley, Jenny Till, Valerie Field, Jill Bush, Maxine Spyrou, the Rita Williams Singers.
Writers plus Oddie, Tynan, Les Williamson (uc: Edward Luckarift, Colin Welch).

prog 8: 16 November 1963. tx 2230 c.50m
'Courtaulds' and 'Invalid' sketches by DN and DP.
Cast plus Watson.
Writers plus John Bird, N. F. Simpson, Tinniswood and Nobbs (uc: Oddie, Welch).
Designer Archie Clark.

prog 10: 30 November 1963. tx 2220 c.50m
'Father Christmas' sketch by DN and DP.
Cast minus Roy Kinnear.
Writers plus Nobbs and Tinniswood, Oddie, Kenneth Pearson, Jonathan Routh, Rushton (uc: Cumming and Mattimore, Griffith Hansen, Welch).

prog 12: 14 December 1963. tx 2225 c.50m
'Nottingham Theatre' item by DN and DP.
Cast plus Laine, Malcolm Muggeridge.
Writers plus Bird, John Cleese, Cyril Connolly, Mason, Mikes, Nobbs & Tinniswood, Oddie (uc: Ronnie Carroll, Cumming, Penry Jones).
Designer Michael Young.

prog 13: 21 December 1963. tx 2230 c.50m
'Lord Mayor' sketch by DN and DP.
Cast plus Patricia Routledge, Lang, Eira Heath, Oddie, Cragg, Elaine Carr, Peta Pelham, Elizabeth Newell.
Writers plus Nobbs and Tinniswood, Oddie.

prog 14: 28 December 1963. tx 2220 c.55m
Unspecified contribution by DN and DP to last edition.
Cast plus Lang, Brindley, Graham Armitage, Curran, Richard Garner, Gunston, Morrison, Roy Stait, Colin Partington, the George Mitchell Singers.

Writers plus Braine, Davidson, Lang, Mason, Roth and Haines, Shaffer, Tinniswood and Nobbs (uc: Cleese).

Unsigned Editorials *The Sun* 16, 17 September, 31 October 1964.
Of the leaders run by the new title during its opening weeks, these three read like DP.

The Confidence Course BBC1 The Wednesday Play 24 February 1965. tx 2140 c.61m
Narrator, Geoffrey Matthews; *Director*, Dennis Price; *Black*, Neil McCarthy; *Jones*, Artro Morris; *Thomas*, John Moore; *Hazlitt*, Stanley Baxter; *Hammond*, William Moore; *Rosalind Arnold*, Yootha Joyce; *Bloom*, John Quentin; *Greenway*, John Blythe; *Angela Walker*, Joan Sanderson; *The 'Unconfident'*, Michael Brill, Betty Duncan, John Devaut, Gilly Flower, Olive Kirby, Jack Le White, Jimmy Mac, Ronald Mayer, Diane Woolley.
Designer Lionel Radford/story editor Roger Smith/producer James MacTaggart/director Gilchrist Calder/writer DP.

(No recording is known to exist.)

Woman's Hour BBC Light Programme 23 June 1965. tx 1400 c.60m
'Ideas in the Air' with DP. Introduced by Marjorie Anderson.

Item rpt Home Service/*Home for the Day* 27 June tx 1130.

Look East BBC1 East Region opt-out 13 October 1965. tx 1805 c.25m
DP interviewed in Norwich studio on *Alice*.

Alice BBC1 The Wednesday Play 13 October 1965. tx 2105 c.72m
Rev Charles Lutwidge Dodgson, George Baker; *Alice Liddell*, Deborah Watling; *Mrs Liddell*, Rosalie Crutchley; *Dean Liddell*, David Langton; *Lorina Liddell*, Tessa Wyatt; *Edith Liddell*, Maria Coyne; *Rev Robinson Duckworth*, Malcolm Webster; *Alexander Macmillan*, Maurice Hedley; *Stotman*, John Moffatt; *Dormouse*, Peter Bartlett; *Mad Hatter*, John Bailey; *March Hare*, John Saunders; *Caterpillar*, Keith Campbell; *Mock Turtle*, Norman Scace; *Gryphon*, Frank Shelley; *Gardener*, Billy Russell; *Gardener's Boy*, Michael Harfleet; *Workman*, Colin Rix; *Ellen*, Suzanne Vasey; *John*, George Pensotti; *Thornton*, John Steiner; *Hargreaves*, Tony Anholt; *Balcar*, Gareth Forwood.
Film cameraman Charles Parnall/film editor Peter Pierce/costumes Lisa Benjamin/make-up Christina Morris/telerecording editor Howard Billingham/music Peter Greenwell/lighting Robert Wright/designer Michael Wield/producer James MacTaggart/director Gareth Davies/writer DP.

rpt BBC1 6.7.66 tx 2102

Points of View BBC1 19 October 1965. tx 1855 c.5m
DP answered viewers' comments on *Alice*. Presenter Robert Robinson/producer Christopher Doll.

Late Night Line-Up BBC2 7 December 1965. tx 2309 c.32m
DP interviewed on *Nigel Barton* plays by Denis Tuohy; also featuring Joan Bakewell, Michael Dean, Nicholas Tresilian, Philip Jenkinson/producer Mike Fentiman.

Look East BBC1 East Region opt-out 8 December 1965. tx 1805 c.25m
DP interviewed in Norwich studio on *Nigel Barton* plays.

Stand Up, Nigel Barton BBC1 The Wednesday Play 8 December 1965. tx 2140 c.72m
Nigel Barton, Keith Barron; *Harry Barton*, Jack Woolgar; *Mrs Barton*, Katharine Parr; *Jill Blakeney*, Vickery Turner; *Adrian*, Robert Mill; *Miss Tillings*, Janet Henfrey; *Reporter*, P. J. Kavanagh; *Georgie*, Johnny Wade; *Bert*, Godfrey James; *Senior Proctor*, Llewellyn Rees; *Junior Proctor*, Brian Badcoe; *Conrad*, Brian Hankins; *Scout*, Terence Soall; *Mrs Taylor*, Barbara Keogh; *Jordan* Peter Madden; *Arthur*, Alan Lake; *Ernie*, Edward Palmer; *President of the Union*, Charles Lewsen; *Tim*, Charles Collingwood; *Children*, David Scheuer, Ian Fairbairn, Harriet Harper, Pamela Withers; *Undergraduates*, Michael Burrell, Jonathan Dennis, Michael Davis, Bridget Wood, Sheila Dunn. Story editor Tony Garnett/telerecording editor Paddy Wilson/lighting Robert Wright/designer Richard Henry/producer James MacTaggart/director Gareth Davies/writer DP.
    rpt BBC1 19 September 1966 tx 2105; BBC1 19 August 1987 tx 2130

Vote, Vote, Vote for Nigel Barton BBC1 The Wednesday Play 15 December 1965. tx 2145 c.78m
Nigel Barton, Keith Barron; *Anne Barton*, Valerie Gearon; *Jack Hay*, John Bailey; *Hugh Archibald-Lake*, Cyril Luckham; *Woman*, Dorothea Rundle; *Lady Chairman*, Betty Bowden; *Lady Secretary*, Margaret Diamond; *Mrs Morris*, Aimee Delamain; *Smith*, Walter Hall; *Male Nurse*, Keith Campbell; *Old Man*, Harold Bennett; *Mr Harrison*, George Desmond; *Pedestrian*, Charles Rea; *Mrs Thompson*, Madge Brindley; *1st Questioner*, Michael Segal; *2nd Questioner*, Raymond Witch; *Toastmaster*, Fred Berman; *Mayor*, Arthur Ridley; *Journalist*, John Evitts; *Fat Man*, Arthur Lawrence; *Mrs Phillips*, Sonia Graham; *Sir Harry Blakerswood*, Russell Forehead; *News-reader*, Huw Thomas; *Hunters*, Barbara Atkinson, Agatha Carroll, Donald Hewlett.
Film cameraman James Balfour/film editor Bill Brind/music Ronnie Hazlehurst/story editors Roger Smith, Tony Garnett/telerecording editor Julian Farr/lighting Robert Wright/designer Julia Trevelyan Oman/producer James MacTaggart/director Gareth Davies/writer DP.
    rpt BBC1 19 September 1966 tx 2104; BBC1 19 August 1987 tx 2130

Line-Up Review BBC2 17 December 1965. tx 2311 c.39m
DP in discussion on *Nigel Barton* Plays and *The Power Game* introduced by Denis Tuohy. Producer Jim Smith.

Emergency – Ward 9 BBC2 Thirty Minute Theatre 11 April 1966. tx 2150 c.30m
Flanders, Terence De Marney; *Padstow*, Tenniel Evans; *Adzola*, Dan Jackson; *Nurse Angela*, Gillian Lewis; *Doctors*, Paul Carson, Anwer Begg; *Night Nurse*, Rowena Gregson; *Sister*, Evangeline Banks; *Vyshinski*, Raymond Witch; *Old Man*, John H. Moore; *Youth*, Philip Needs; *Nurses*, Sheelagh McGrath, Dean Anthony.

Costume Joyce Macken/make-up Cherry Alston/story editor Kenith Trodd/ designer Paul Allen/producer Harry Moore/director Gareth Davies/writer DP.

rpt 19 July 1967 tx 2034
(DP also recorded a trailer about the play, produced by Michael Appleton, for tx use earlier in the evening).
(No recording is known to exist.)

Late Night Line-Up BBC2 8 May 1966. tx 2240 c.37m
DP in discussion on *The Survivor* by Henry Williams. Introduced by Tony Bilbow/producer John Philips.

Line-Up Review BBC2 8 July 1966. tx 2301 c.41m
DP interviewed by Tony Bilbow on 'the star system'. Introduced by Michael Dean/producer Pat Ingram.

Woman's Hour BBC Light Programme 24 October 1966. tx 1400 c.60
DP in 'Ideas in the Air' recorded at the Bristol studio.

Where The Buffalo Roam BBC1 The Wednesday Play 2 November 1966. tx 2135 c.73m
Willy Turner, Hywel Bennett; *Mrs Turner*, Megs Jenkins; *Mr Jenkins*, Glyn Houston; *Grandad*, Aubrey Richards; *Mr Black*, Richard Davies; *Susan*, Denise Buckley; *Carol*, Rhiann John; *Willy's Father*, David Morrell; *Schoolteacher*, Dilys Davies; *Police Superintendent*, Brinley Jenkins; *Inspector*, Ieuan Rhys Williams; *Cinema Patrons*, Kate Jones, Emrys Cleaver; *Cinema Manager*, Hubert Hughson; *Newsreader*, Ronnie Williams; *Policemen*, D. C. Mills Davies, Dillwyn Owen, Harry Oatten.
Costumes Juanita Waterson/make-up Heather Stewart/armourer Jack Wells/ graphics Kevin Eccleston/telerecording editor Howard Billingham/lighting John Brockbank, Tony Escott/story editor Kenith Trodd/designer Julian Williams/producer Lionel Harris/director Gareth Davies/writer DP.

rpt BBC1 19 August 1967 tx 2106; BBC2 19 August 1976 tx 2142;
BBC2 19 July 1993 tx 2100
(DP recorded a trailer, produced by Maurice Kanareck)

Woman's Hour BBC Light Programme 2 December 1966. tx 1400 c.60
Ideas in the Air discussion with Patricia De Trafford and DP. Recorded at the Bristol studio/introduced by Daphne Hibberd.

Third Degree BBC Home Service West Region opt-out 9 December 1966. tx 2130 c.30m.
DP was the 'guest personality' in a university student quiz pilot – here Bristol versus Exeter – with quizmaster John Cleese, producer Brian Skilton. A series was (virtually) networked from 30 March 1967, with the same teams in the first prog, Max Robertson instead of Cleese and no DP. It ended after a second series.

Twenty-Four Hours BBC1 28 December 1966. tx 2220 c.41m
DP in discussion with James Dance MP, William Hamling MP on Jonathan Miller's production of *Alice in Wonderland*.

Chaired by Kenneth Allsop, introduced by Cliff Michelmore, producer John Dekker, editor Derrick Amoore.

The Look of the Year BBC1 1 January 1967. tx 2250 c.37m
DP in discussion with Joseph Losey, Sir Michael Tippett, Philip Toynbee. Chaired by Robert Robinson, producer Peter Montagnon, director Michael MacIntyre.

Any Questions? BBC Light Programme 6 January 1967. tx 2015 c.50m
From Chepstow Community College, Monmouthshire; DP in discussion with Anne Allen, Russell Braddon, Enoch Powell MP, 'travelling questionmaster' Freddy Grisewood, producer Michael Bowen.

rpt Home Service 8 January 1967 tx 1310

(*Late Night Line-Up* 25 January 1967. DP booked to discuss *Man Alive*, arrived in London but was too ill to appear.)

The World at One BBC Home Service 3 May 1967. tx 1300 c. 30m
DP interviewed by Mark Puckle on *Message for Posterity*. Introduced by William Hardcastle, producer Nick Barrett.

Message for Posterity BBC1 The Wednesday Play 3 May 1967. tx 2141 c.79m
James Player, Patrick Magee; *Sir David Browning*, Joseph O'Conor; *Gillian Player*, Patricia Lawrence; *Clara Browning*, Anna Calder-Marshall; *Richard Browning*, Geoffrey Chater; *Hawkins*, Donald Hewlett; *Thompson*, Gordon Whiting; *Miles*, Tony Holland; *Manservant*, Keith Campbell; *Newsreader*, John Benson; *Committee Members*, Ballard Berkeley, Lionel Gamlin, Walter Hall, Raymond Witch, John Saunders; *Police Sergeant*, Peter Welch; *Maid*, Betty Turner; *Karl*, John Golightly.
Story editor Kenith Trodd/designer John Cooper/producer Lionel Harris/director Gareth Davies/writer DP.

(No recording is known to exist.)

Bravo and Ballyhoo BBC1 West Region opt-out 13 June 1967. tx 2305 c.25m
DP's commentary on media coverage of Francis Chichester's voyage. Producer James Dewar.

rpt BBC1 4 July 1967 tx 2304

The Nigel Barton Plays Penguin Books 1967.
Texts of *Stand Up, Nigel Barton* and *Vote, Vote, Vote for Nigel Barton* with Introduction by DP.

Television Reviews *New Statesman* 14 July-1 September 1967.
DP wrote a few columns, this time in the political weekly.

Book Reviews *The Times* 21 October 1967–27 December 1969.
DP began a stint of substantial Saturday supplement pieces, intended to be weekly but dictated by the state of his health. There were occasional full-page articles too.

Television Reviews *The Sun* 16 January–23 February 1968
Overlapping his *Times* commitment, DP took a guest stint in the now daily 'In My View' column on television.

Talkback BBC1 4 February 1968. tx 2241 c.34m
DP attacked an episode of the BBC police drama *Softly Softly* with David Coleman 'before a statistically selected audience'. Producer Brian Winston, editor Richard Francis.

Column *The Sun* 11 March–21 October 1968
DP began a new column, 'Dennis Potter,' on general topics.

The Bonegrinder Rediffusion for ITV Playhouse 13 May 1968. tx 2030 c.78m.
George King, George Baker; *Gladys King*, Margaret Tyzack; *Sam Adams*, Weston Gavin; *Mr Baker*, Arthur Cox; *Mr Lapwell*, Brian Oulton; *Girl*, Linda Marlowe; *Pedestrian*, Geoffrey Sumner; *Betty*, Dianne Greaves; *Publican*, Charles Rea; *Policeman*, Anthony Dawes; *Commissionaire*, Walter Horsbrugh; *City Gents*, Jeremy Child, Eric Dodson; *Old Man*, George Belton; *Emma*, Phyllis Montefiore; *Bank Clerk*, Martin Potter; *Sid*, Charles Lamb; *Sally*, Terry Day; *Carole*, Liz Gebhardt; *Nina*, Dona Martin; *Chris*, Anthony Villaroel; *Ted* Kenneth Scott; *Strap Hanger*, Bill Horsley; *Attentive Girl*, Penny Barham; *Announcer*, Peter Forbes–Robertson.
Designer Fred Pusey/producer-director Joan Kemp-Welch.

Shaggy Dog LWT for ITV, The Company of Five 10 November 1968. tx 2220 c.51m
Wilkie, John Neville; *Johnson*, Ray Smith; *Parker*, Derek Godfrey; *Receptionist*, Ann Bell; *James*, Cyril Luckham; *Pedestrian*, Betty Bowden; *Girl in Lift* Jane Murdoch.
Costume Ernest Hewitt/music Norman Kay/designer John Emery/producer Stella Richman/director Gareth Davies/writer DP.

(No recording is known to exist)

A Beast with Two Backs BBC1 The Wednesday Play 20 November 1968. tx 2108 c.71m
Joe, Patrick Barr; *Ebenezer*, Denis Carey; *Micky Teague*, Laurence Carter; *Joan Teague*, Madeleine Newbury; *Rufus*, Christian Rodska; *Rebecca*, Geraldine Newman; *Jack Hooper*, Roger Gartland; *Will*, Terence Sewards; *Harry*, Anthony Andrews; *Inspector*, Basil Henson; *Nellie*, Audine Leith; *Mary*, Esther Lawrence; *Arnold*, Llewellyn Rees; *Policeman*, Ron Eagleton; *Organist*, Rica Fox; *Barmaid*, Rosalie Horner; *Dancing Bear*, Gina; *Boys*, Stephen Pudge, Eddie Blow, Kevin Toogood; The Berry Hill Silver Band.
Make-up Eileen Mair/costume June Wilson/sound recordist Derek Meadus/film cameraman Ken Westbury/film editor Howard Kennett/studio sound Colin Dixon/studio lighting Dennis Channon/script editors Shaun McLoughlin, Kenith Trodd/designer William McCrow/producer Graeme McDonald/director Lionel Harris/writer DP.

rpt BBC1 4 August 1987. tx 2132

Vote, Vote, Vote for Nigel Barton Theatre Royal Bristol: Old Vic Company 27 November 1968 for four weeks
Nigel Barton, Frank Barrie; *Anne Barton*, Patricia Maynard; *Jack Hay/Conrad/*

Scout/Jordan/Senior Proctor, Martin Friend; *Harry Barton/Harrison/Mayor*, Norman Tyrrell; *Mrs Barton/Mrs Phillips*, Thelma Barlow; *Jill Blakeney*, Carole Hayman; *Miss Tillings*, Janet Henfrey; *Georgie Pringle/Toastmaster*, Andrew Dallmeyer; *Adrian/Interviewer/Junior Proctor*, Neil Cunningham; *Archibald-Lake*, Ronald Russell; *Reporter*, Brian Ralph; *Chairman*, Marcia Warren; *Mrs Morris/Mrs Thompson*, Audrey Noble; *Tim/Male Nurse/President of the Union*, Charles McKeown; *Bert*, Laurence Carter; *other parts*, John Flanagan, Sarah Lewis, Gillian Rhind, Nicholas Willatt.
Costumes Audrey Price/sets Michael Swindlehurst/lighting Kenneth Vowles/assistant director David Benedictus (Thames Television trainee)/director Antony Tuckey/writer DP.

Moonlight on the Highway Kestrel Productions/LWT for ITV Saturday Night Theatre 12 April 1969. tx 2130 c.52m
David Peters, Ian Holm; *Dr Chilton*, Anthony Bate; *Marie Holdsworth*, Deborah Grant; *President of Bowlly Appreciation Society*, Robin Wentworth; *Gerald*, Frederick Peisley; *Old Londoner*, Wally Patch; *Landlord*, Arthur Lovegrove; *Barman*, Michael Burrell; *Medical Students*, Derek Woodward, John Flanagan; *Patients*, Harry Hutchinson, Bart Allison, Kathleen St John, Beatrice Greeve, Walter Swash, Daphne Riggs, Johnny Watson, Ursula Granville.
Designer John Clements/producer Kenith Trodd/director James MacTaggart/writer DP.

Son of Man BBC1 The Wednesday Play 16 April 1969. tx 2117 c.90m
Jesus Christ, Colin Blakely; *Pontius Pilate*, Robert Hardy; *Caiaphas*, Bernard Hepton; *Peter*, Brian Blessed; *Judas Iscariot*, Edward Hardwicke; *Roman Commander*, Godfrey Quigley; *Procla*, Patricia Lawrence; *Andrew*, Gawn Grainger; *Ruth*, Wendy Allnutt; *Centurion*, Clive Graham; *Zealot*, Brian Spink; *Young Officer*, Robin Chadwick; *Soldiers*, Godfrey James, Eric Mason; *Hecklers*, Hugh Futcher, Raymond Witch, Edmund Bailey; *James*, Colin Rix; *Philip*, Walter Hall; *Priests*, Keith Campbell, Edward Bennett; *Money-Changer*, Alan Lawrence; *Man in Crowd*, Paul Prescott; *Leper*, George Desmond; *Woman Possessed*, Polly Murch; *Beaten Samaritan*, Peter Beton; *Beggar*, David Cannon; *Boxers*, Roy Stewart, Dinny Powell; The Carmel College Choir.
Costumes Dinah Collin/make-up Sandra Hurll/story editor Shaun MacLoughlin/sound Bryan Forgham/lighting Robert Wright/designer Spencer Chapman/producer Graeme McDonald/director Gareth Davies/writer DP.

rpt BBC1 4 June 1969 tx 2107; BBC2 28 July 1987 tx 2130

Son of Man Reviewed BBC1 20 April 1969. tx 1815 c.31m
Robert Robinson chaired a discussion with DP and others. Producer Peter Ferres.

rpt BBC1 20 April 1969 tx 2312.

Son of Man Phoenix Theatre Leicester 22 October 1969.
Jesus Christ, Frank Finlay; *Pontius Pilate*, Joseph O'Conor; *Caiaphas*, Ian Mullins; *Peter*, David Daker; *Judas Iscariot/Priest*, Stephen MacDonald; *Roman Commander*, David Henry; *Andrew*, Stanley Lebor; *Procla*, Linda

Polan; *Captain/Heckler*, Noel Collins; *Ruth*, Liane Aukin; *James*, Nicholas Chagrin; *John*, Graham Berown; *Boxer/Centurion/Money-Changer*, Roy Boyd; *Zealot/Heckler/Brigand*, Andrew Neil; *Priest/Money-Changer*, Douglas Storm; *Leper*, Miles Greenwood; *Dove Seller*, Andrew Jarvis; *Boxer*, Paul Jaybee; *Serving Girl*, Penelope Nice.
Designer Franco Colavecchia/lighting Geoffrey Mersereau/director Robin Midgley/writer DP.

12 November 1969 transferred to The Roundhouse London

Review: Television BBC2 1 November 1969. tx 2230 c.40m
DP interviewed by James Mossman on the medium's potential. Producer David Heycock/editor Mossman.

Any Questions? BBC Radio 2 20 February 1970. tx 2015 c.45m
from Newent School, Gloucestershire; DP In discussion with Adrian Cadbury, Lady Antonia Fraser and Vic Feather. Chairman David Jacobs/producer Michael Bowen.

rpt Radio 4 21 February 1970 tx 1315

Heroes and Hero Worship BBC South and West for BBC1 1 March 1970. tx 1825 c.30m
Magnus Magnusson interviewed DP on *Son of Man*. Producer Peter Firth.

rpt BBC1 3 March 1970 tx 1550

Lay Down Your Arms Kestrel Productions/LWT for ITV Saturday Night Theatre 23 May 1970. tx 2210 c.78m
Private Robert Hawk, Nikolas Simmonds; *Major Gerald Hisscock*, Peter Cellier; *Major Freddy Wilson*, John Warner; *Major William Timps*, Graham Armitage; *Lieutenant-Colonel Jack Bateman*, Leonard Trolley; *Colonel Ulysses S. Feather*, Ken Wayne; *Mr Hawk*, Joby Blanshard; *Mrs Hawk*, Julia Jones; *Pete*, Michael Cashman; *Pat*, Therese McMurray; *Prostitute*, Renny Lister; *Corporal Harry May*, George Layton; *Julian*, James Cairncross; *'Nina'*, Elizabeth Hughes; *'Trepliov'*, Tim Hardy; *Nick*, Tony Caunter; *Fred*, David Webb; *Ernie*, John Levene; *Londoner*, Will Stampe; *American Tourist*, John Bloomfield; *His Wife*, Tucker McGuire; *People in Theatre*, John Foley, Rosemary Turner.
Designer Michael Yates/producer Kenith Trodd/director Christopher Morahan/writer DP.

Angels Are So Few BBC1 *Play for Today* 5 November 1970. tx 2122 c.63m
Michael Biddle, Tom Bell; *Cynthia Nicholls*, Christine Hargreaves; *Mrs Cawser*, Susan Richards; *Mr Cawser*, Erik Chitty; *Richard Nicholls*, Barrie Cookson; *Postman*, Godfrey James; *Storyteller*, Beryl Cooke; *Clergyman*, John Glyn Jones; *Interviewer*, Kenneth Ives; *Danish Girl*, Denise Buckley; *Old Lady*, Dorothea Rundle; *Timothy*, Matthew Davies.
Costumes Elizabeth Agombar/make-up Dawn Alcock/film cameraman John Turner/film editor Ken Pearce/lighting Clive Thomas/sound Norman Bennett/script editor Ann Scott/designer Stanley Morris/producer Graeme McDonald/director Gareth Davies/writer DP.

Son of Man André Deutsch 1970
Text of stage play (reissued by Samuel French).

Myth and Truth BBC1 23 May 1971. tx 1815 c.35m
Discussion on 'death and resurrection stories' with DP, Hilda Ellis Davidson, Dr John Robinson, Dr W. D. Hudson, presenter Magnus Magnusson; stories read by Peter Copley, Gary Watson. Producer R. T. Brooks.

rpt BBC1 24 May 1971 tx 1254

Paper Roses Granada for ITV 13 June 1971. tx 2215 c.52m
Clarence Hubbard, Bill Maynard; *John Chart*, Donald Gee; *Joe*, John Carson; *Mrs Hubbard*, Aimee Delamain; *The Critic*, Dudley Jones; *Messenger*, Joe Gladwin; *Harold Bladdy*, Desmond Perry; *Chris Payer*, William Simons; *Neighbour*, Rosalie Williams; *PC*, Peter Childs; *Ted*, Harry Beety; *Anne*, Kim Corlette.
Graphics Lyndon Evans/sound Peter Walker/film cameraman Ray Goode/film editor Don Kelly/designer Alan Price/producer Kenith Trodd/director Barry Davis/writer DP.

Traitor BBC1 Play for Today 14 October 1971. tx 2121 c.61m
Adrian Harris, John Le Mesurier; *James*, Jack Hedley; *Simpson*, Vincent Ball; *Blake*, Neil McCallum; *Thomas*, Jon Laurimore; *Sir Arthur Harris*, Lyndon Brook; *Lady Emma*, Diana Fairfax; *Michaelov*, Richard Marner; *Duty Clerk*, Terence Bayler; *Craig*, John Quentin; *Schoolmaster*, John Saunders; *Little Adrian*, Sean Maddox.
Costumes Susan Wheal/make-up Margaret Webb/film cameraman Elmer Cossey/film editor Peter Coulson/studio sound Brian Hiles/studio lighting John Treays/script editor Ann Scott/designer Tony Abbott/producer Graeme McDonald/director Alan Bridges/writer DP.

rpt BBC1 27 February 1973 tx 2127; BBC1 21 July 1987 tx 2130

Late Night Line-Up BBC2 14 October 1971. tx 2324 c.36m
DP interviewed on *Traitor* by Michael Dean; other regulars Joan Bakewell, Tony Bilbow, Sheridan Morley.
Producer Peter Carr/editor Rowan Ayres.

Casanova BBC2 six-part serial
Casanova, Frank Finlay; *Lorenzo*, Norman Rossington; *Barberina*, Christine Noonan; *Christina*, Zenia Merton

prog 1 *Steed in the Stable* 16 November 1971. tx 2125 c.57m
Messer Grande, Victor Baring; *Uncle*, George Benson; *Senator Bragadin*, Geoffrey Wincott; *Circospetto*, Christopher Hancock; *Senior Inquisitor*, Ronald Adam; *Inquisitors*, Peter Sherwood, Aubrey Danvers-Walker; *Carlo*, Igor Silic; *Dr Bellotti*, Basil Clarke.

prog 2 *One at a Time* 23 November 1971. tx 2121 c.56m
Valenglart, David Swift; *Anne Roman-Coupier*, Ania Marson; *Schalon*, Patrick Newell; *Helena*, Elaine Donnelly; *Caretaker*, Arthur Pentelow; *Rose*, Julia Cornelius; *Manon*, Brigid Erin Bates; *Anna*, Caroline Dowdeswell; *Concert Master*, Oliver Butterworth.

Scan BBC Radio 4 25 November 1971. tx 2045 c.45m
DP interviewed by Michael Billington on *Casanova*.
Producer Rosemary Hart.

Any Questions? BBC Radio 4 26 November 1971. tx 2030 c.45m
from King Edward VI Camp Hill School, Birmingham. DP in discussion with
Lynda Chalker, Bamber Gascoigne, Lord Stokes. Chairman David Jacobs/
producer Michael Bowen.

rpt Radio 4 27 November 1971 tx 1315

Casanova continued

prog 3 *Magic Moments* 30 November 1971. tx 2122 c.55m
Genoveffa, Lyn Yeldham; *Capitani*, Frederick Peisley; *Pantalone*, Hugh
Portnow; *Colombina*, Rowan Wylie; *Arlecchino*, Tim Thomas; *Il Capitano*,
Emil Wolk; *Man with Knife*, Christopher Martin (plus Marson, Newell,
Cornelius, Bates, Dowdeswell).

prog 4 *Window, Window* 7 December 1971. tx 2123 c.48m
Mme Morin, Jean Holness; *Damiens*, Simon Barclay; *Tiretta*, Richard
Dennis; *Mme Lenoir*, Claire Davenport; *La Lambertini*, Jo Anderson; *Mlle
de la Mare*, Sarah Benfield; *Man in Coach*, Norman Tyrrell; *Violinist*,
Norman McGlen; *Whores* Sue Bond, Enid Burton, Julie Desmond (plus
Swift, Marson, Cornelius, Bates, Dowdeswell, Baring, Yeldham, Wylie,
Thomas).

prog 5 *Fevers of Love* 14 December 1971. tx 2121 c.52m
Pauline, Valerie Gearon; *Mr Hart*, Norman Rossington; *Nun*, Gillian
Brown; *Streetcrier*, Lyn Turner (plus Newell, Marson, Cornelius, Bates,
Dowdeswell, Yeldham).

prog 6 *Golden Apples* 21 December 1971. tx 2123 c.58m
Feldkirchner, Graham Crowden; *Caroline*, Gillian Hills; *Dr Rapp*, John
Ringham; *Father Balbi*, Roger Hammond (plus Marson, Cornelius, Bates,
Dowdeswell, Yeldham, Gearon).

Costume John Bloomfield/make-up Pam Meager, Eileen Mair, Penny
Bell/sound recordists John Murphy, Derek Medus, Colin March, Basil
Harris/film cameramen Ken Westbury, John Wyatt, Stewart Farnell/film
editor Graham Bunn/studio sound Chick Anthony/studio lighting Dave
Sydenham/video editor Ron Bowman/designer Peter Seddon/producer
Mark Shivas/directors John Glenister (progs 1, 2, 4), Mark Cullingham
(progs 3, 5, 6)/writer DP.

rpt as re-edit BBC2 prog 1 9 September 1974 tx 2100 c.97m
prog 2 10 September 1974 tx 2101 c.99m

Woman's Hour BBC Radio 2 14 January 1972. tx 1402 c.58m
Fourth item of five: Ideas in the Air. DP and Stuart Hall discussed 'labelling
people' in Birmingham studio. Introduced by Maureen Staffer.

Follow the Yellow Brick Road BBC2 The Sextet 4 July 1972. tx 2121 c.69m
Jack Black, Denholm Elliott; *Judy Black*, Billie Whitelaw; *Dr Whitman*,

Fight and Kick and Bite

Richard Vernon; *Dr Bilson*, Dennis Waterman; *Colin Sands*, Bernard Hepton; *Veronica Sands*, Michele Dotrice; *Old Lady*, Ruth Dunning; *Nurse*, Nicolette Pendrell; *Staff Nurse*, Maureen Nelson.

Costumes Ursula Reid/make-up Sandra Shepherd/graphics Nicholas Jenkins/sound recordist Malcolm Webberly/film cameraman Brian Tufano/film editor Roger Waugh/studio sound Brian Hiles/studio lighting John Treays/script editor Margaret Hare/designer Spencer Chapman/producer Roderick Graham/director Alan Bridges/writer DP.

rpt BBC2 24 July 1973 tx 2102; BBC1 14 July 1987 tx 2130

Television Reviews *New Statesman* 15 September–15 December 1972
DP resumed his column for three months.

Real Time BBC2 4 January 1973. tx 2344 c.53m
DP in discussion with Keith Kyle and Brian Walden on *All in a Day* and *The Candidate*, introduced by Michael Dean.
Producer Philip Speight/executive producer Mike Fentiman.

Only Make Believe BBC1 Play for Today 12 February 1973. tx 2126 c.74m
Christopher Hudson, Keith Barron; *Sandra George*, Georgina Hale; *Doctor*, Laurence Hardy; *Michael Biddle*, Alun Armstrong; *Cynthia Nicholls* Rowena Cooper; *Mrs Cawser*, Susan Richards; *Mr Cawser*, George Howe; *Richard Nicholls*, Geoffrey Palmer; *Interviewer*, John Malcolm; *Danish Girl*, Monica Ringwald.

Sound Chick Anthony/lighting Robert Wright/script editor Ann Scott/designer Graham Oakley/producer Graeme McDonald/director Robert Knights/writer DP.

rpt BBC1 2 May 1974 tx 2126

Real Time BBC2 15 February 1973/. tx 2353 c.51m
DP, David Mercer and John Hopkins talked about their work to Michael Dean. Producer Philip Speight/executive producer Mike Fentiman.

Real Time BBC2 28 June 1973. tx 2331 c.50m
DP in discussion with Michael Dean. Producer Philip Speight/executive producer Mike Fentiman.

The Hart Interview BBC1 West Region opt-out 14 August 1973. tx 2215 c.25m
DP was the first subject of a new series. Presenter Derek Hart/producer Dennis Adams.

A Tragedy of Two Ambitions BBC2 Wessex Tales 21 November 1973. tx 2100 c.49m
Joshua Harlborough John Hurt; *Cornelius Harlborough*, David Troughton; *Joshua Harlborough Sr*, Paul Rogers; *Rosa Harlborough*, Lynne Frederick; *Selimar*, Heather Canning; *Squire Fellmer*, Edward Petherbridge; *Mrs Fellmer*, Betty Cooper; *Countryman*, Dan Meaden; *Farm Labourer*, Andrew McCulloch; *Clergyman*, John Rainer; *Principal*, Peter Bennett.
Costume Barbara Lane/make-up Shirley Channing-Williams/music Joseph

Horovitz/sound recordist Colin March/dubbing mixer Stanley Morcom/film cameraman Peter Hall/film editor Ken Pearce/designer Richard Henry/ producer Irene Shubik/director Michael Tuchner/writer DP after the story by Thomas Hardy.

rpt BBC2 21 May 1975 tx 2125

Hide and Seek André Deutsch/Quartet Books 1973
DP's first novel (reissued by Faber & Faber).

Kaleidoscope BBC Radio 4 23 November 1973. tx 2245 c.30m
DP interviewed by Paul Bailey on *Hide and Seek*. Producer Rosemary Hart.

Follow the Yellow Brick Road Paul Elek Ltd *The Television Dramatist* 1973
Teleplay text published in a collection selected and introduced by Robert Muller, comprising *End of Story* by Leo Lehman, *Another Sunday* and *Sweet FA* by Jack Rosenthal, *The Gorge* by Peter Nichols and *Robin Redbreast* by John Bowen.
DP wrote a Preface to his own text.

Television Reviews *New Statesman* 11 January–31 May 1974
DP resumed his column.

Joe's Ark BBC1 Play for Today 14 February 1974. tx 2243 c.66m
Joe Jones, Freddie Jones; *Lucy Jones*, Angharad Rees; *Bobby Jones*, Dennis Waterman; *John*, Christopher Guard; *Sally*, Patricia Franklin; *Daniel Watkins*, Edward Evans; *Doctor*, Clive Graham; *Waiter*, Azad Ali; *Chef*, Colin Rix; *Customers*, Emrys Leyshon, Margaret John.
Costume Sonia Kerr/make-up Joan Barrett/sound Ray Angel/lighting Dennis Channon/script editor Ann Scott/designer Stuart Walker/producer Graeme McDonald/director Alan Bridges/writer DP.

rpt BBC1 19 December 1974 tx 2127; BBC1 7 July 1987 tx 2130.

Schmoedipus BBC1 Play for Today 20 June 1974. tx 2127 c.67m
Elizabeth Carter, Anna Cropper; *Glen*, Tim Curry; *Tom Carter*, John Carson; *Ronnie*, John Horsley; *Blake*, Bob Hoskins; *Dorothy*, Carol Macready; *Man in Corridor*, Reg Cranfield.
Sound Brian Hiles/lighting Dennis Channon/designer Peter Seddon/producer Kenith Trodd/director Barry Davis/writer DP.

rpt BBC1 10 April 1975 tx 2126

Television Reviews *New Statesman* 6 September 1974–27 June 1975
DP again reviewed.

Late Call BBC2 four-part serial
Sylvia Calvert, Dandy Nichols; *Arthur Calvert*, Leslie Dwyer; *Howard Calvert*, Michael Bryant; *Ray Calvert* Tim Morand; *Mark Calvert*, Nigel Crewe; *Judy Calvert* Rosalyn Elvin; *Young Sylvia*, Danielle Carson; *Myra Longmore* Sarah Sutton.

prog 1 1 March 1975. tx 2015 c.52m
Mrs Longmore, Elizabeth Chambers; *Sylvia's Mother*, Mary Chester; *Farmer*,

Edward Brooks; *Farmer's Boy*, Peter Vaughan-Clarke; *Mr Martineau*, John Dawson; *Mrs Amherst*, Anne Blake; *Pat*, Patricia Mort; *voices*, Jean Anderson, Derek Benfield, Richard Easton.

rpt BBC2 6 March 1975 tx 1955; BBC2 1 May 1976 tx 1930

prog 2 8 March 1975. tx 2015 c.54m
Chris Milton, Geoffrey Adams; *Lorna Milton*, Fanny Carby; *Sally Bulmer*, Diana King; *Muriel Bartley*, Rosemarie Dunham; *Nicholas McArdle*, Geoff Bartley; *Wilf Corney*, Hugh Sullivan; *Jack Cranston*, James Appleby; *Renee Cranston*, Shirley Cain; *Caroline Ogilvie*, Maxine Casson; *Furniture Men*, Frank Jarvis, Arthur Lovegrove (plus Chambers, Chester).

rpt BBC2 13 March 1975 tx 1955; BBC2 8 May 1976 tx 2019

prog 3 15 March 1975. tx 2017 c.55m
Jack Parsons, Raymond Mason; *'Helena'*, Gail Grainger; *'Cliff'*, Nigel Winder; *'Alison'*, Alison Griffin; *Mandy Egan*, Alison Dowling (plus Adams, Carby, King, Dunham, McArdle).

rpt BBC2 20 March 1975 tx 1950; BBC2 15 May 1976 tx 1941

prog 4 22 March 1975. tx 2008 c.53m
Shirley Egan, Kathryn Leigh Scott; *Timbo Egan*, Philip Bond; *Herbert Raven*, John Cater; *Dr Piggott*, Hilary Minster (plus Adams, Carby, King, Dunham, McArdle, Sullivan, Dowling, Mason, Grainger, Winder).

rpt BBC2 27 March 1975 tx 1952; BBC2 22 May 1976 tx 2022

Costume Judy Allen/make-up Magdalen Gaffney/film sound Graham Hare/ film cameraman A. A. Englander/film editor Sheila S. Tomlinson/studio sound Richard Chubb/studio lighting Geoff Shaw/music Dudley Simpson/script editor Lennox Phillips/designer Spencer Chapman/producer Ken Riddington/ director Philip Dudley/writer DP after the novel by Angus Wilson.

Television Reviews *New Statesman* 10 October–7 November 1975
A further stint.

Television Reviews *New Statesman* 6 February–28 May 1976
Apart from a couple of book reviews (one a laceration of Clive James' collected television columns), DP now ended his long association with the magazine.

Double Dare BBC1 Play for Today 6 April 1976. tx 2141 c.65m
Martin Ellis, Alan Dobie; *Helen/Carol*, Kika Markham; *Ben*, Joe Melia; *Client*, Malcolm Ferris; *His Wife*, Linda Beckett; *Peter*, John Hamill; *Maid*, Elaine Donnelly; *Barman*, John Joyce; *Waiter*, Stanley Lebor; *Receptionist*, Sarah Nash; *Porter*, Colin Prockter; *Security Guard*, Ian Munro.
Costume Barbara Kidd/make-up Shirley Channing-Williams/sound recordist Andrew Boulton/dubbing mixer Alan Dykes/lighting Phil Meheux/film cameraman Philip Bonham-Carter/film editor Roger Waugh/designer Paul Joel/producer Kenith Trodd/director John MacKenzie/writer DP.

rpt BBC1 28 July 1977 tx 2157

Where Adam Stood BBC2 21 April 1976. tx 2126 c.77m
Philip Gosse, Alan Badel; *Edmund Gosse*, Max Harris; *Charles Kingsley*,

Ronald Hines; *Miss Marks*, Heather Canning; *Brackley*, Gareth Forwood; *Mary Teague*, Jean Boht; *Wagonette Driver*, Hubert Rees.

* spelled 'Phillip' in opening titles

Costume Jean Ellacott/make-up Ann Rayment/music Carl Davis/sound recordist Peter Edwards/dubbing mixer Alan Dykes/film cameraman Peter Bartlett/film editor David Martin/designer Gerry Scott/producer Kenith Trodd/director Brian Gibson/writer DP after the memoir *Father and Son* by Edmund Gosse.

Sunday BBC Radio 4 25 April 1976. tx 2015 c.35m
DP interviewed on his work by Mary Craig. Introduced by Clive Jacobs/ producer David Winter.

Thought For the Day BBC Radio 4 30 April 1976. tx 0745 c.5m
More from the Mary Craig interview recorded for *Sunday*. Producer Angela Tilby.

Any Questions? BBC Radio 4 6 August 1976. tx 2030 c.45m
from Hereford; DP in discussion with the Dean of St Paul's, Lord Mancroft and Sue McGregor. Chairman David Jacobs/producer Michael Bowen.

rpt Radio 4 7 August 1976 tx 1315

With Great Pleasure BBC Radio 4 5 September 1976. tx 1815 c.45m
DP introduced his own selection of favourite prose and verse, read by himself and Jane Barrie and recorded at the Van Dyck Theatre, Bristol University Drama Department. The chosen sources were: Psalm 35; *Rapunzel* by the Brothers Grimm; *Vitae Lampada* ('There's a breathless hush in the Close tonight . . .') by Henry Newbolt; *Just William* by Richmal Crompton; *Letter to William Gifford* by Hazlitt; *Ivanov* by Chekhov; *The Wasteland* by T. S. Eliot; *The Mayor of Casterbridge* by Hardy; *The Diary of a Nobody* by Grossmith; *In Memoriam* by Tennyson; *The Big Sleep* by Chandler; *Exequy* by Bishop Henry King. Producer Brian Patten.

rpt Radio 4 9 December 1979 tx 2315

Television Reviews *The Sunday Times* 10 October 1976–9 January 1977
DP began another frequently interrupted newspaper job.

And With No Language But a Cry BBC Radio 3 27 December 1976. tx 2125 c.20m
DP gave a Christmas reflection.

The Anno Domini Interview BBC1 13 February 1977. tx 1816 c.33m
DP interviewed by Colin Morris on 'his work, his illness and his religious beliefs'. Producer Dennis Sullivan.

extract *Pick of the Week* Radio 4 18 February 1977 tx 1930

Television Reviews *The Sunday Times* 3 April–31 July 1977
DP resumed his column for four months.

Nationwide BBC1 21 July 1977. tx 1754 c.56m
Kieran Prendiville reported from the location shoot of *Pennies from Heaven*

343

and interviewed DP and actor Bob Hoskins. Introduced by Frank Bough/ deputy editor Stuart Wilkinson/editor John Gau.

Late Night Line-Up BBC2 1 August 1977. tx 2352 c.50m
Among items in a one-off revival for the *Festival 77* season, introduced by Michael Dean, DP and Christopher Morahan discussed the past and present of the television play. Studio director Tom Corcoran/producer Philip Speight.

Kaleidoscope BBC Radio 4 7 September 1977. tx 2130 c.30m
DP and Marcel Ophuls at the Edinburgh Television Festival discussed 'the current problems of British television'.

Television Reviews *The Sunday Times* 2 October 1977–25 June 1978
More trenchant observations.

Brimstone and Treacle Crucible Theatre, Sheffield 11 October 1977
Mr Bates, Christopher Hancock; *Mrs Bates*, Ann Windsor; *Martin*, Sean Scanlon; *Pattie*, Adrienne Byrne.
Designer Lynda Harris/director David Leland.

Any Questions? BBC Radio 4 21 October 1977. tx 2030 c.45m
from the Subscription Rooms, Stroud, Gloucestershire; DP in discussion with Sheila Hancock, Simon Jenkins and Dorian Williams. Chairman David Jacobs/ producer Michael Bowen.

rpt Radio 4 22 October 1977 tx 1315

Tonight BBC1 7 November 1977. tx 2302 c.43m
DP was the subject of 'the Ludovic Kennedy Interview' introduced by Denis Tuohy. Producer Barbara Maxwell/editor Mike Townson.

Desert Island Discs BBC Radio 4 17 December 1977. tx 1815 c.35m
DP interviewed by Roy Plomley. His eight 'gramophone records' were: *Immortal, Invisible, God Only Wise* sung by the Treorchy Male Voice Choir; *Sons of the Brave* played by the GUS Footwear Brass Band (his choice when asked to reduce the list to one); *You Couldn't Be Cuter* sung by Al Bowlly with the Lew Stone Band; *Twelfth Street Rag* by Duke Ellington and his Orchestra; *Somebody Stole My Gal* played by Reginald Dixon; *The Clouds Will Soon Roll By* sung by Elsie Carlisle with the Ambrose Band; *Edie Was a Lady* sung by Bowlly with the Stone Band; *Roses of Picardy* sung by Gracie Fields. His book choice was 'the best possible collection of Hazlitt's essays' and his luxury the painting *Gas* by Edward Hopper. Producer Derek Drescher.

rpt (shortened) Radio 4 20 December 1977 tx 1227

A Christmas Forest BBC Radio 4 26 December 1977. tx 1415 c.45m
DP gave a talk in the Bristol studio on the Forest of Dean. Producer Brian Patten.

rpt Radio 4 23 December 1978 tx 1850

Serendipity BBC Radio 4 2 January 1978. tx 1740 c.15m
DP 'goes to the Archive Auction'. Producer Anthony Wall.

The Mayor of Casterbridge BBC2 seven-part serial
Michael Henchard, Alan Bates; *Elizabeth-Jane*, Janet Maw; *Donald Farfrae*,
Jack Galloway.

prog 1: 22 January 1978. tx 2006 c.52m
Susan Henchard, Anne Stallybrass; *Mrs Goodenough*, Avis Bunnage;
Newson, Richard Owens; *Carter*, Jeffrey Holland; *Auctioneer*, Leonard
Trolley; *Men at Fair*, Rod Beacham, Bernard Taylor; *Hoer*, Anthony Douse;
Waiter, Terry Francis; *Guest*, Denis Costello.
rpt BBC2 27 January 1978 tx 2224; BBC2 26 June 1979 tx 2126

prog 2: 29 January 1978. tx 2009 c.52m
Abel Whittle, Peter Bourke; *Buzzford*, Joe Ritchie; *Concy*, Douglas Milvain;
Longways, Clifford Parrish; *Nancy*, Deddie Davies; *Henchard's Maid*,
Patricia Fincham; *Priest*, Mischa de la Motte; *Farmers*, Antony Spicer,
Arthur Bridgeman; *Boy*, Steven Warner; *Man*, Stuart Fell (plus Stallybrass,
Holland).
rpt BBC2 3 February 1978 tx 2231; BBC2 3 July 1979 tx 2126

prog 3: 5 February 1978. tx 2007 c.53m
Lucetta Templeman, Anna Massey; *Jopp*, Ronald Lacey; *Fall*, Freddie Jones;
Lucetta's Maid, Gilly Brown (plus Holland, Fincham).
rpt BBC2 10 February 1978 tx 2248; BBC2 10 July 1979 tx 2126

The South Bank Show Dennis Potter: Man of Television LWT for ITV 11
February 1978. tx 2215 c.53m
The last of three items, DP was interviewed by Melvyn Bragg. Designer
Andrew Drummond/researcher Nigel Wattis/executive producer Nick Elliott/
studio director Peter Walker/producer Tony Cash/editor Bragg.

The Mayor of Casterbridge continued

prog 4: 12 February 1978. tx 2007 c.51m
Mr Joyce, Alan Rowe; *Clerk of Court*, Kenneth Waller; *Policeman*, David
Auker (plus Massey, Bunnage, Lacey, Brown).
rpt BBC2 17 February 1978 tx 2315; BBC2 17 July 1979 tx 2127

prog 5: 19 February 1978. tx 2007 c.51m
Commissioner, William Whymper; *Farmer*, Michael Miller; *Old Woman*,
Phillada Sewell; *Landlord*, John Flint; *Fiddler*, Jack Le White (plus Massey,
Bourke, Lacey, Holland, Parrish, Milvain, Rowe, Brown).
rpt BBC2 24 February 1978 tx 2310; BBC2 24 July 1979 tx 2126

All in the Waiting BBC Radio 4 23 February 1978. tx 2030 c.15m
A series of six talks for Lent: DP gave the first, about light and darkness,
under the title 'The Other Side of the Dark'. Producer Michael Mayne.

The Mayor of Casterbridge continued

prog 6: 26 February 1978. tx 2006 c.50m
Charl, Desmond Adams; *Prince Albert*, Lloyd McGuire; *Doctor*, Charles

345

West; *Councillor*, David Willitts (plus Bunnage, Jones, Bourke, Owens, Lacey, Rowe, Parrish, Milvain, Davies, de la Motte, Brown).
      rpt BBC2 3 March 1978 tx 2305; BBC2 31 July 1979 tx 2132

prog 7: 5 March 1978. tx 2020 c.53m
Labourer, Alan Collins; *Companion*, Alec Bregonzi; *Cook*, Trudie Styler (plus Bourke, Owens, Rowe).
      rpt BBC2 10 March 1978 tx 2316; BBC2 7 August 1979 tx 2127

Costume Christine Rawlins/make-up Elizabeth Rowell/music Carl Davis/sound Robin Luxford/lighting Hubert Cartwright/videotape editor Neil Pittaway/script editor Betty Willingale/designer Peter Kindred/producer Martin Lisemore/director David Giles/writer DP after the novel by Thomas Hardy.

Pennies from Heaven BBC1 six-part serial
Arthur Parker, Bob Hoskins; *Joan Parker*, Gemma Craven; *Eileen Everson*, Cheryl Campbell.

prog 1: *Down Sunnyside Lane* 7 March 1978. tx 2127 c.72m
The Accordion Man, Kenneth Colley; *Conrad Baker*, Nigel Havers; *Marjorie*, Rosemary Martin; *Barrett*, Arnold Peters; *Irene*, Jenny Logan; *Jumbo*, Robert Putt; *Will*, Keith Marsh; *Betty*, Tessa Dunne; *Carter*, Wally Thomas; *Pianist*, Sam Avent.
      rpt BBC1 1 December 1978. 2135; BBC2 7 February 1990 tx 2101

Start the Week BBC Radio 4 13 March 1978. tx 0905 c.55m
DP in discussion with Joan Bakewell, Michael Herr, Kenneth Robinson. Introduced by Richard Baker/producer Ian R. Gardhouse.

Pennies from Heaven continued

prog 2: *The Sweetest Thing* 14 March 1978. tx 2128 c.77m
Mr Warner, Freddie Jones; *Bank Manager*, Peter Cellier; *Dave*, Philip Jackson; *Maurice*, Spencer Banks; *Dad*, Michael Bilten; *Ted*, Roger Sloman; *Bert*, Roy Holder; *Alf*, Bill Dean (plus Colley, Peters, Logan).
      rpt BBC1 1 December 1978. tx 2303; BBC2 14 February 1990 tx 2100

prog 3: *Easy Come, Easy Go* 21 March 1978. tx 2129 c.87m
Blind Girl, Yolande Palfrey; *Miner*, Frederick Bradley; *Mrs Corder*, Bella Emberg; *Woman Patient*, Maryann Turner; *Police Constable*, Roger Forbes; *Detective Inspector*, John Malcolm; *Railway Passengers*, Betty Hardy, Frank Lazarus, Norman Warwick, David Rowlands (plus Colley, Jones, Jackson, Banks, Bilten, Dean).
      rpt BBC1 8 December 1978 tx 2137; BBC2 21 February 1990 tx 2100

prog 4: *Better Think Twice* 28 March 1978. tx 2128 c.77m
Tom, Hywel Bennett; *Barman*, Will Stamp; *Cafe Proprietor*, Tony Caunter; *Customer*, Tudor Davies; *Doctor*, Vass Anderson; *Youth*, Tony London; *Street Whore*, Phyllis McMahon; *Pub Whores*, Olwen Griffiths, Maggy Maxwell; *Policeman*, Howard Lew Lewis (plus Colley, Logan, Emberg).
      rpt BBC1 8 December 1978 tx 2320; BBC2 28 February 1990 tx 2100

prog 5: *Painting the Clouds* 4 April 1978. tx 2127 c.80m
Major Archibald Paxville, Ronald Fraser; *Police Inspector*, Dave. King; *Estate Agent*, Roger Brierley; *Michael*, Nigel Rathbone; *Tramp*, Paddy Joyce; *Waiter*, Alan Foss; *Man on Bridge*, Chris Gannon; *Busker*, Ronnie Ross; *Man in Queue*, Reg Lever; *Inspector*, Laurence Harrington; *Shop Manager*, David Webb; *Customer*, Robin Meredith (plus Colley).
     rpt BBC1 15 December 1978 tx 2132; BBC2 7 March 1990 tx 2100

prog 6: *Says My Heart* 11 April 1978. tx 2137 c.85m
Farmer, Philip Locke; *Judge*, Carleton Hobbs; *Prosecuting Counsel*, Peter Bowles; *Sergeant*, John Ringham; *Constable*, Tim Swinton; *Clerk of the Court*, Stanley Fleet; *Foreman of the Jury*, Hal Jeayes; *Arnold*, Mike Savage; *Horace*, Roy Boyd; *Chaplain*, Noël Collins; *Executioner*, Roger Heathcott; *Pedestrian*, Steve Ubels (plus King).
     rpt BBC1 12 January 1979 tx 2223; BBC2 14 March 1990 tx 2100

Costume John Peacock/make-up Jenny Shircore/choreography Tudor Davies/graphics Sid Sutton, Bob Cosford, Tom Taylor/film sound Mervyn Broadway/dubbing mixer Alan Dykes/film photography Ken Westbury/ film editor David Martin/studio sound Brian Hiles/senior cameraman Dave Mutton/lighting Dave Sydenham/videotape editor Howard Dell/video mixer Shirley Coward/designers Tim Harvey, Bruce MacAdie/producer Kenith Trodd/director Piers Haggard/writer DP.

Television Reviews *The Sunday Times* 10 September–26 November 1978
Potter's last stint of regular reviewing.

Brimstone and Treacle Eyre Methuen New Theatrescripts 1978
Text of the stage version with a new introduction by DP (reissued by Samuel French).

Blue Remembered Hills BBC1 Play for Today 30 January 1979. tx 2128 c.72m
Peter, Michael Elphick; *John*, Robin Ellis; *Willie*, Colin Welland; *Angela*, Helen Mirren; *Audrey*, Janine Duvitski; *Donald Duck*, Colin Jeavons; *Raymond*, John Bird.
Costume Andrew MacKenzie/make-up Ann Briggs/special effects Peter Day/ music Marc Wilkinson/sound recordist Dick Manton/dubbing mixer Alan Dykes/photography Nat Crosby/film editor David Martin/designer Richard Henry/producer Kenith Trodd/director Brian Gibson/writer DP.
     rpt BBC1 30 May 1980 tx 2144; Channel 4 19 May 1991 tx 2030

Kaleidoscope BBC Radio 4 31 January 1979. tx 2130 c.30m
DP talked about *Blue Remembered Hills*.

Brimstone and Treacle Open Space Theatre, London 7 February 1979
Mr Bates, George Cole; *Mrs Bates*, Margery Mason; *Martin*, Richard O'Callaghan; *Pattie*, Lynsey Baxter.
Lighting Matthew Richardson/designer Sue Plummer/director Robert Chetwyn/ writer DP.

The South Bank Show LWT for ITV 11 February 1979. tx 2230 c.53m
First of two items is DP interviewed by Melvyn Bragg on the Open Space production of *Brimstone and Treacle* and the BBC's banning of the television production. Designer Mike Turney/researcher Jamie Muir/ executive producer Nick Elliott/film sound Eddie Tyse/film cameraman Ernest Vincze/film editor Robert Hargreaves/studio director Peter Walker/ producer Tony Cash/editor Bragg.

Alice BBC Radio 4 Afternoon Theatre. 28 November 1979. tx 1515 c.45m
Rev Charles Lutwidge Dodgson, George Baker; *Alice Liddell*, Heather Bell; *Mrs Liddell*, Jane Thomson; *Dean Liddell*, Richard Bebb; *Lorina Liddell*, Alison Draper; *Edith Liddell*, Emma Bakhle; *Macmillan*, Philip Voss; *Stotman*, Peter Baldwin; *Ellen*, Brenda Kaye; *John*, Lyndam Gregory; *Thornton*, Tim Bentinck; *Hargreaves*, Philip Sully; *Baker*, Andrew Branch.
Adapter-director Derek Hoddinott/writer DP.

First tx BBC World Service 17 June 1979

The Levin Interviews BBC2 17 May 1980. tx 2031 c.30m
DP interviewed by Bernard Levin at the Bristol studio. Director Roy Chapman/ producer Colin Rose/editor John Shearer.

rpt BBC2 18 November 1982 tx 1650

Dennis Potter – Television Playwright National Film Theatre/National Film Archive 13–30 October 1980
Comprehensive season of DP's work, comprising the *Nigel Barton* plays, *Alice, Where the Buffalo Roam, The Bonegrinder, A Beast with Two Backs, Moonlight on the Highway, Paper Roses, Son of Man, Lay Down Your Arms, Traitor, Joe's Ark, Casanova, Follow the Yellow Brick Road, Only Make Believe, Schmoedipus, Double Dare, Where Adam Stood, Brimstone and Treacle, Pennies from Heaven, Blue Remembered Hills* and *Cream in My Coffee* as well as a *Guardian Lecture*.

Blade on the Feather PfH/LWT for ITV 19 October 1980. tx 2200 c.82m
Jason Cavendish, Donald Pleasence; *Daniel Young*, Tom Conti; *Jack Hill*, Denholm Elliott; *Linda Cavendish*, Kika Markham; *Christabel Cavendish*, Phoebe Nicholls; *Doctor*, Gareth Forwood; *Andrew Cartwright*, Bill Weston; *Young Daniel*, Joel Samuel; *Newsreader*, Alvar Lidell.
Sound recordist Alan Mills/photography Peter Hannan/film editor Jon Costelloe/designer Andrew Drummond/executive producer Tony Wharmby/ producer Kenith Trodd/director Richard Loncraine/writer DP.

rpt Channel 4 3 March 1983 tx 2130

Kaleidoscope BBC Radio 4 22 October 1980. tx 2130 c.29m
DP interviewed by Chris Dunkley about the NFT season. Introduced by Edwin Mullins, producer Richard Dunn.

Rain on the Roof PfH/LWT for ITV 26 October 1980. tx 2200 c.76m
Janet, Cheryl Campbell; *John*, Malcolm Stoddard; *Billy*, Ewan Stewart; *Emma*, Madeline Hinde; *Malcolm*, Michael Culver; *Vicar*, Allan Cullen; *Billy's Father*, William Bond; *Castle*, David Webb; *Postman*, Dave Royal.

Music George Fenton/sound recordist Syd Squires/photography Michael Reed/film editor Ray Helm/designer Bryan Bagge/executive producer Tony Wharmby/producer Kenith Trodd/director Alan Bridges/writer DP.

rpt Channel 4 10 March 1983 tx 2130.

Cream in my Coffee PfH/LWT for ITV 2 November 1980. tx 2200 c.91m
Bernard Wilsher, Lionel Jeffries; *Jean Wilsher*, Peggy Ashcroft; *Jack Butcher*, Martin Shaw; *Young Bernard*, Peter Chelsom; *Young Jean*, Shelagh McLeod; *Mrs Wilsher*, Faith Brook; *Hotel Porters*, Leo Dolan, Will Stampe; *Hotel Maids*, Dawn Perllman, Pik-Sen Lim; *Boatman*, Walter Sparrow; *Waiter*, Howard Attfield; *Vicar*, Robert Fyfe; *Girl in Pool*, Tracy Eddon; *Rock Group*, Famous Names.
Musical director Max Harris/costume Sue Formston/make-up Pauline Green/ sound recordist Andrew Boulton/dubbing mixer Colin Martin/photography Ernest Vincze/film editor Derek Bain/designer John Emery/executive producer Tony Wharmby/producer Kenith Trodd/director Gavin Millar/ writer DP.

rpt Channel 4 24 February 1983 tx 2130

Traitor BBC Radio 4 *Afternoon Theatre* 20 May 1981. tx 1502 c.48m
Adrian Harris, Denholm Elliott; *James*, Ian Ogilvy; *Simpson*, Alan White; *Blake*, Don Fellows; *Thomas*, Gregory de Polnay; *Sir Arthur Harris*, William Fox; *Lady Emma*, Jane Thomson; *Schoolmaster*, Jack May; *Cole Mackinson*, Jean Rogers; *Duty Clerk*, Danny Schiller; *Craig*, David Griffin; *Policeman/ Agent*, Martin Friend; *Michaelov/Man*, John Church.
Adaptor-director Derek Hoddinott/writer DP.

First tx BBC World Service

Pennies from Heaven MGM/Hera Productions 1981. c.108m
Arthur Parker, Steve Martin; *Eileen Everson*, Bernadette Peters; *Tom*, Christopher Walken; *Joan Parker*, Jessica Harper; *Accordion Man*, Vernal Bagneris; *Warner*, John McMartin; *Detective*, John Karlen; *Banker*, Jay Garner; *Al*, Robert Fitch; *Ed*, Tommy Rall; *Blind Girl*, Eliska Krupka; *Bartender*, Frank McCarthy; *Barrett*, Raleigh Bond; *Prostitutes*, Gloria Leroy, Toni Kaye, Shirley Kirkes; *Old Whore*, Nancy Parsons; *Boy*, Hunter Watkins; *Elevator Operator*, Jack Fletcher; *Young Policeman*, M. C. Gainey; *Motorcycle Police*, Arell Blanton, George Wilbur; *Father Everson*, Will Hare; *Newsboy*, Mark Campbell; *Hangman*, Jim Boeke; *Jumbo*, Joshua Cadman; *Schoolboy*, Mark Martinez; *Warden*, James Mendenhall.
Costume Bob Mackie/make-up Ric Sagliani, Dan Striepeke/choreography Danny Daniels/music consultant Kenith Trodd/musical director Marvin Hamlisch/special effects Glen Robinson/sound recordist Al Overton/sound editors Richard L. Anderson, Stephen H. Flick, Mark Mangini, Stephen Purvis, Warren Hamilton/photography Gordon Willis/film editor Richard Marks/designer Ken Adam/executive producer Rick McCallum/producers Nora Kaye, Herbert Ross/director Ross/writer DP.

Pennies from Heaven Quartet Books 1981
DP's novelisation of the movie script.

Brimstone and Treacle Namara Films/Alan E. Salke/Herbert Solow/Pennies from Heaven 1982. c.87m
Martin Taylor, Sting; *Thomas Bates*, Denholm Elliott; *Norma Bates*, Joan Plowright; *Patricia Bates*, Suzanna Hamilton; *Businessman*, Benjamin Whitrow; *Stroller*, Dudley Sutton; *Miss Holdsworth*, Mary MacLeod; *Clergyman*, Tim Preece; *Passer-by*, Elizabeth Bradley; *Man*, Hugh Walters; *Drunk*, Christopher Fairbank.
Costume Shuna Harwood/make-up Elaine Carew/sound recordist Tony Jackson/sound editor Alan Bell/music Sting, the Police, Michael Nyman/ photography Peter Hannan/film editor Paul Green/designer Milly Burns/ executive producer Naim Attallah/producer Kenith Trodd/director Richard Loncraine/writer DP.

Omnibus BBC1 16 May 1982. tx 2159 c.39m
DP interviewed on the *Pennies from Heaven* movie. Introduced by Barry Norman/editor Christopher Martin.

Kaleidoscope BBC Radio 4 7 September 1982. tx 2130 c.29m
DP interviewed by Chris Dunkley on the *Brimstone and Treacle* movie. Introduced by Natalie Wheen/producer Robin White.

Shakespeare in Perspective: Cymbeline BBC2 9 July 1983. tx 2045 c.25m
In a series broadcast to shadow the productions in the *BBC Television Shakespeare* project, DP spoke to camera on one of the late plays.
Director Sally Kirkwood/producer Victor Poole.

Gorky Park Orion/Eagle Associates 1983. c.128m
Arkady Renko, William Hurt; *Jack Osborne*, Lee Marvin; *William Kirwill*, Brian Dennehy; *Iamskoy*, Ian Bannen; *Irina Asanova*, Joanna Pacula; *Pasha Pavlovich*, Michael Elphick; *Anton*, Richard Griffiths; *Major Pribluda*, Rikki Fulton; *General*, Alexander Knox; *Golodkin*, Alexei Sayle; *Professor Andreev*, Ian McDiarmid; *KGB Agent Rurik*, Niall O'Brien; *Levin*, Henry Woolf; *Natasha*, Tusse Silberg; *Fet*, Patrick Field; *James Kirwill*, Jukka Hirvik Angas; *Valerya Davidova*, Marjatta Nissinen; *Kostia Borodin*, Hekki Leppanen; *Director*, Lauri Torhonen; *Babuska*, Elsa Salamaa; *KGB Agent Nicky*, Anatoly Davydov; *Shadowers*, Lasse Lindberg, Jussi Parvianen; *Russian Tea Band*, Black Pearls; *Rock'n'Roll Band*, Bad Sign.
Costume Richard Bruno/make-up Alan Boyle, Ken Lintott/sound recordists Simon Kaye, Dan Wallin/sound editor Michael Hilkene/photography Ralf D. Bode/film editor Dennis Virkler/designer Paul Sylbert/executive producer Bob Larson/producers Gene Kirkwood, Howard W. Koch Jr/director Michael Apted/writer DP from the novel by Martin Cruz Smith.

Sufficient Carbohydrate Hampstead Theatre 7 December 1983
Jack Barker, Dinsdale Landen; *Eddie Vosper*, Nicky Henson; *Elizabeth Barker*, Jennifer Hilary; *Lucy Vosper*, Jill Baker; *Clayton Vosper*, Rupert Graves.
Costumes Sheelagh Killeen/lighting Leo Leibovici/designer Tanya McCallin/ director Nancy Meckler.

Transferred to Albery Theatre 31 January 1984

Kaleidoscope BBC Radio 4 8 December 1983. tx 2140 c.19m
DP interviewed on *Sufficient Carbohydrate*. Introduced by Paul Vaughan/
producer Carroll Moore.

Midweek BBC Radio 4 1 February 1984. tx 0905 c.55m
DP interviewed on *Sufficient Carbohydrate*. Introduced by Libby Purves/
producer Pippa Burston.

John Dunn BBC Radio 2 1 February 1984. tx 1804 c.55m
DP interviewed on *Sufficient Carbohydrate*. Introduced by John Dunn/
producer Bill Bebb.

Whicker! BBC Manchester for BBC2 9 March 1984. tx 2125 c.40m
DP in discussion with James Anderton, Daphne Rae and Alan Whicker about
violence on television.
Director John Rooney/producer Jenny Danks/editor Ken Stephinson.

Questions LWT for Channel 4 17 June 1984. tx 1430 c.27m
In the first of a series of a 'what makes them tick?' nature, DP was interviewed
by Marcel Berlins.
Executive producer Jane Hewland/director David Coulter/producer Julian
Norridge.

Waiting for the Boat Faber and Faber 1984
Texts of three teleplays, *Blue Remembered Hills, Joe's Ark* and *Cream in My
Coffee*, with DP's essay *Some Sort of Preface* . . .

Round Midnight BBC Radio 2 18 September 1985. tx 2302 c.118m
DP interviewed on *Tender is the Night*. Introduced by Brian Matthew/
producer Robin Sedgley.

Tender is the Night BBC/Showtime Entertainment/The Seven Network,
Australia/Twentieth Century Fox for BBC2 six-part serial
Dick Diver, Peter Strauss; *Nicole Warren*, Mary Steenburgen.

prog 1: 23 September 1985. tx 2130 c.55m
Devereux Warren, Edward Asner; *Dr Dohmler*, Erwin Kohlund; *Franz
Gregorovius*, Jürgen Brügger; *Baby Warren*, Kate Harper; *Conte di
Marmora*, François Guetary; *Wounded Soldier*, Richard Linford; *Singing
Soldier*, Jean Alonge; *Major*, Keith Edwards; *Patient*, Rosario Serrano.
rpt BBC2 26 September 1985 tx 2200; BBC1 12 June 1987 tx 2155

prog 2: 30 September 1985. tx 2130 c.55m
Abe North, John Heard; *Rosemary Hoyt*, Sean Young; *Mrs Speers*, Piper
Laurie; *Tommy Barban*, Joris Stuyck; *Mary North*, Nancy Paul; *Albert
McKisco*, Dennis Creaghan; *Violet McKisco*, Toria Fuller; *Luis Campion*,
Vernon Dobtcheff; *Mrs Abrams*, Mary Ellen Rae; *Royal Dumphry*, Terrance
Condor; *Second*, Pierre Castello; *Doctor*, André Chaumeau.
rpt BBC2 3 October 1985 tx 2200; BBC1 19 June 1987 tx 2130

prog 3: 7 October 1985. tx 2130 c.56m
Maria Wallis, Tracy Kneale; *Jules Peterson*, Ruddy L. Davis; *Girl at*

Cemetery, Linsey Beauchamp; *Sergeant de Ville*, Stephane Freiss (plus Heard, Young, Paul).

rpt BBC2 10 October 1985 tx 2200; BBC1 26 June 1987 tx 2130

prog 4: 14 October 1985. tx 2130 c.50m

Hannah, Joanna David; *Helen*, Erin Donovan; *Her Mother*, Pat Starr; *Kaethe Gregorovius*, Astrid Frank; *Patient*, Barbara Atkinson; *Preacher*, Norman Stokle (plus Brügger, Harper).

rpt BBC2 17 October 1985 tx 2200; BBC1 3 July 1987 tx 2130

prog 5: 21 October 1985. tx 2130 c.55m

Morris, Timothy West; *Collis Clay*, Hutton Cobb; *Nicotera*, Marc–Samuel Hadjadj; *Director*, Frank Karla; *Carabinieri Captain*, Guido Adorni; *Dr Dangen*, Jean Reno; *Americans*, Matt Frewer, Rolf Saxon, William Hope; *Taxi Driver*, Teco Celio; *Police Officer*, David Pontremoli; *Patient*, Nicholas Amer; *Young Man*, Louis Selwyn (plus Young, Asner, Stuyck, Harper, David, Brügger, Frank, Condor).

rpt BBC2 24 October 1985 tx 2200; BBC1 10 July 1987 tx 2130

prog 6: 28 October 1985. tx 2120 c.52m

T. E. Golding, Jerome Willis; *Lady Caroline Sibley-Biers*, Amanda Hillwood; *Scot*, John Sessions (plus Young, Stuyck, Harper, Creaghan, Fuller).

rpt BBC2 31 October 1985 tx 2200; BBC1 17 July 1987 tx 2130

Costume Barbara Kidd/make-up Jean Speak/music Richard Rodney Bennett/ sound Terry Elms/photography Ken Westbury/film editor Tariq Anwar/ designers Derek Dodd, Peter Higgins/executive producer Jonathan Powell/ producer Betty Willingale/director Robert Knights/writer DP from the novel by F. Scott Fitzgerald.

Dreamchild Thorn EMI/Pennies from Heaven 1985. c.94m

Mrs Alice Hargreaves, Coral Browne; *Rev Charles Dodgson*, Ian Holm; *Jack Dolan*, Peter Gallagher; *Lucy*, Nicola Cowper; *Mrs Liddell*, Jane Asher; *Little Alice*, Amelia Shankley; *Sally Mackeson*, Caris Corfman; *Lorina Liddell*, Imogen Boorman; *Edith Liddell*, Emma King; *Hargreaves*, Rupert Wainwright; *Rev Duckworth*, Roger Ashton-Griffiths; *Baker*, James Wilby; *Marl*, Shane Rimmer; *Radio Producer*, Peter Whitman; *Sound Effects Man*, Ken Campbell; *Actors*, William Hootkins, Jeffrey Chiswick, Pat Starr; *Crooners*, Johnny M, Tony Mansell; *Editors*, Peter Banks, Derek Hoxby, Ron Berglas, Ron Travis; *University President*, Olivier Pierre; *Reporters*, Alan Sherman, Danny Brainin, Sam Douglas; *Announcer*, Thomasine Heiner; Voices: *Gryphon*, Fulton Mackay; *Mock Turtle*, Alan Bennett; *Dormouse*, Julie Walters; *March Hare*, Ken Campbell; *Mad Hatter*, Tony Haygarth; *Caterpillar*, Frank Middlemass. Costume Jane Robinson/make-up Jenny Shircore, Eddie Knight/sound recordists Godfrey Kirby, Sid Margo/sound editor Brian Blamey/character creation Jim Henson's Creature Shop/music Stanley Myers/photography Billy Williams/film editor Angus Newton/executive producers DP, Verity Lambert/ producers Rick McCallum, Kenith Trodd/director Gavin Millar/writer DP.

Saturday Review BBC2 25 January 1986. tx 2210 c.50m

First of three items was a discussion of *Dreamchild*, following an interview with DP. Introduced by Russell Davies. Director Jonathan Fulford/producer Kevin Loader/editor John Archer.

Interview rpt BBC2 1 January 1987 tx 1445

Woman's Hour BBC Radio 4 5 March 1986. tx 1402 c.58m
DP interviewed on *Dreamchild*. Introduced by Sue McGregor/producer Sue Davies.

Kaleidoscope BBC Radio 4 5 May 1986. tx 2145 c.30m
'Making Television Sing': DP interviewed on his career and *The Singing Detective*. Introduced by Paul Allen/producer Thomas Sutcliffe.

rpt Radio 4 6 May 1986. tx 1630

Ticket to Ride Faber and Faber 1986
DP's second novel.

Round Midnight BBC Radio 2 9 September 1986. tx 2302 c.118m
DP interviewed on *Ticket to Ride*. Introduced by Brian Matthew/producer Stella Hanson.

Kaleidoscope BBC Radio 4 12 September 1986. tx 2145 c.30m
DP interviewed on *Ticket to Ride*. Introduced by Michael Billington/producer Anne Winder.

Late Night Line-Up BBC2 3 November 1986. tx 2345 c.35m
For *Festival 50*, the magazine was revived in a week of nostalgic editions. DP was among those interviewed by Alan Rusbridger. Director Tom Corcoran/ executive producer Ian Keill/producer Trevor Dann.

Breakfast Time BBC1 14 November 1986. tx 0700 c.125m
Tony Wilkinson reported from the location of *The Singing Detective* and interviewed DP, Jon Amiel and Janet Suzman. Introduced by Frank Bough, Sally Magnusson, Jeremy Paxman.

John Dunn BBC Radio 2 14 November 1986. tx 1702 c.118m
DP interviewed. Introduced by John Dunn/producer Phil Hughes.

The Singing Detective BBC/Australian Broadcasting Corporation for BBC1 six-part serial
Philip Marlow, Michael Gambon; *Mark Binney/Mark Finney/Raymond*, Patrick Malahide; *Nurse Mills*, Joanne Whalley; *Young Philip*, Lyndon Davies; *Hall*, David Ryall; *Reginald Dimps*, Gerard Horan; *Mysterious Men*, Ron Cook, George Rossi; *Noddy Tomkey*, Leslie French; *Porter*, Geoff Francis; *Night Nurse*, Sharon D. Clarke.

prog: 1 *Skin* 16 November 1986. tx 2105 c.68m
Staff Nurse White, Imelda Staunton; *Sonia*, Kate McKenzie; *Amanda*, Sharon Bourke; *Dr Finlay*, Simon Chandler; *Ali*, Badi Uzzaman; *Registrar*, Thomas Wheatley; *Consultant*, Richard Pescud; *Sister Malone*, Mary McLeod; *Houseman*, Paul Lacoux; *Visiting Doctor*, John Matshikiza; *Barman*, Trevor Cooper; *Busker*, Nigel Pegram.

rpt BBC2 1 June 1988 tx 2125; BBC1 11 July 1994 tx 2210

Start the Week BBC Radio 4 17 November 1986. tx 0905 c.55m
DP interviewed on *The Singing Detective*. Introduced by Richard Baker/
producer Victor Lewis-Smith.

The Singing Detective continued

prog 2: *Heat* 23 November 1986. tx 2105 c.69m
Nicola Marlow, Janet Suzman; *Mrs Marlow/Lili*, Alison Steadman; *Gibbon*,
Bill Paterson; *Mr Marlow*, Jim Carter; *Schoolteacher/Scarecrow*, Janet
Henfrey; *George Adams*, Charles Simon; *Grancher*, Richard Butler; *Gran*,
Maggie Holland; *Mrs Adams*, Joan White; *Young Mark*, William Speakman
(plus Staunton, McKenzie, Chandler, Wheatley, McLeod, Cooper).
rpt BBC2 8 June 1988 tx 2125; BBC1 18 July 1994 tx 2210

prog 3: *Lovely Days* 30 November 1986. tx 2105 c.63m
Grandad Baxter, Wally Thomas; *Uncle John*, Ken Stott; *Aunt Emily*, Jo
Cameron Brown; *Mary*, Angela Curran; *Soldiers*, Niven Boyd, David
Thewlis; *Rita*, Claire Phelps; *Brian*, Neil Pittaway; *Mortuary Attendants*,
Errol Shaker, Astley Harvey (plus Suzman, Steadman, Paterson, Carter,
Staunton, Simon, Henfrey, Cooper).
rpt BBC2 15 June 1988 tx 2125; BBC1 25 July 1994 tx 2210

prog 4: *Clues* 7 December 1986. tx 2105 c.67m
Evangelist, Heather Tobias; *Harold*, Martin Camm; *George*, Darren Williams;
Hostesses, Emma Myant, Susie Ann Watkins (plus Suzman, Steadman,
Carter, Henfrey, Thomas, Stott, Brown, Curran, Bourke, Chandler, Simon,
Speakman).
rpt BBC2 22 June 1988 tx 2125; BBC1 1 August 1994 tx 2210

prog 5: *Pitter Patter* 14 December 1986. tx 2105 c.58m
Drummer, John Sheraton (plus Suzman, Steadman, Paterson, Carter,
Staunton, Henfrey, McKenzie, Speakman).
rpt BBC2 29 June 1988 tx 2125; BBC1 8 August 1994 tx 2210

prog 6: *Who Done It* 21 December 1986. tx 2105 c.76m
Policeman, Malcolm Storry; *Physiotherapist*, Tricia George; *Barbara*,
Samantha Bryant (plus Suzman, Steadman, Paterson, Carter, Staunton,
Henfrey, Thomas, Boyd, Thewlis, Speakman).
rpt BBC2 6 July 1988 tx 2125; BBC1 15 August 1994 tx 2210

Costume Hazel Pethig, John Peacock/make-up Frances Hannon/choreog-
rapher Quinny Sachs/graphics Joanna Ball/sound recordist Clive Derby-
shire/dubbing mixer Rob James/photography Ken Westbury/film editors Sue Wyatt, Bill Wright/designer Jim Clay/executive producer Rick
McCallum/producers Kenith Trodd, John Harris/director Jon Amiel/writer
DP.

The Singing Detective Faber and Faber 1986
Text of the serial.

Question Time BBC1 22 January 1987. tx 2200 c.60m
DP in discussion with Lady Grimond, Roy Hattersley, William Waldegrave.

Chair Sue Lawley/director Antonia Charlton/producer Anna Carragher/editor Barbara Maxwell.

Arena BBC2 30 January 1987. tx 2130 c.60m
DP interviewed by Alan Yentob. Film cameraman Remi Adefarasin/film editor Stephen Evans/researcher Jane Bywaters/producer Anthony Wall.

Visitors BBC2 Screen Two 22 February 1987. tx 2230 c.89m
Jack Barker, John Standing; *Eddie Vosper*, Michael Brandon; *Elizabeth Barker*, Nicola Pagett; *Lucy Vosper*, Glynis Barber; *Clayton Vosper*, Robert MacNaughton; *Maid*, Mara Minniti; *Watchers*, Christiana Sartoretti, Enrico Maciolini, Giorgio Pangaro.
Costume Robin Stubbs/make-up Deanne Turner/sound recordist Peter Edwards/music Marc Wilkinson/photography John Else/film editor Ken Pearce/script editor Sarah Curtis/designer Derek Dodd/producer Kenith Trodd/director Piers Haggard/writer DP.

Track 29 HandMade Films 1987. c.90m
Linda Henry, Theresa Russell; *Martin*, Gary Oldman; *Dr Henry Henry*, Christopher Lloyd; *Nurse Stein*, Sandra Bernhard; *Arlanda*, Colleen Camp; *Dr Bernard Fairmont*, Seymour Cassel; *Trucker*, Leon Rippy; *Dr Ennis*, Vance Colvig; *Receptionist*, Kathryn Tomlinson; *Redneck*, Jerry Rushing; *Counterman*, Tommy Hull; *Waiter*, J. Michael Hunter; *Delegate*, Richard K. Olsen; *Old Man*, Ted Barrow.
Costume Shuna Harwood/make-up Jeff Goodwyn/sound recordist David Stephenson/sound editors Rodney Glenn, Colin Chapman/photography Alex Thomson/film editor Tony Lawson/designer David Brockhurst/executive producers George Harrison, Denis O'Brien/producer Rick McCallum/director Nicolas Roeg/writer DP.

Brimstone and Treacle BBC1 25 August 1987. tx 2210 c.72m
Made for tx on 6 April 1976 but withdrawn, this screening was the climax to a nine-week season of DP's BBC teleplays.
Mr Bates, Denholm Elliott; *Mrs Bates*, Patricia Lawrence; *Martin*, Michael Kitchen; *Pattie*, Michelle Newell; *Passers-by*, Patricia Quayle, Esmond Webb, James Greene; *Businessman*, Paul Williamson.
Costume John Bloomfield/make-up Marion Richards/sound recordist Doug Mawson/film cameraman Peter Bartlett/film editor Tony Woollard/studio sound Tony Miller/lighting Dave Sydenham/designer Colin Shaw/producer Kenith Trodd/director Barry Davis/writer DP.

Did You See? BBC1 25 August 1987. tx 2325 c.25m
DP among interested parties interviewed, followed by a studio discussion about *Brimstone and Treacle*. Chairman Ludovic Kennedy/director Dominic Brigstock/producer Nicholas Barker.

Wogan BBC1 25 September 1987. tx 1900 c.41m
DP, George Melly and Sir Edward Dunlop on the chat show with Terry Wogan. Director David Taylor/producer Jon Plowman/editor John Fisher.

Blackeyes Faber and Faber 1987
DP's third and last original novel.

Gloria Hunniford BBC Radio 2 28 September 1987. tx 1404 c.86m
DP interviewed. Introduced by Hunniford/producer Colin Martin.

Kaleidoscope BBC Radio 4 28 September 1987. tx 2145 c.30m
DP interviewed on *Blackeyes*. Introduced by Michael Oliver/producer John
Boundy/editor Anne Winder.

Brian Matthew Round Midnight BBC Radio 2 29 September 1987. tx 2302
c.118m
DP interviewed on *Blackeyes*. Introduced by Brian Matthew/producer Stella
Hanson.

Wogan BBC1 15 July 1988. tx 1900 c.42m
DP, Frank Dileo, Robin Leach and Jane Seymour on the chat show with
Terry Wogan. Director John Burrowes/producer Peter Estall/series producer
Peter Weil.

Christabel Faber and Faber 1988
Text of the serial.

Christabel BBC/Arts & Entertainment Network for BBC2 four-part serial
Christabel Bielenberg, Elizabeth Hurley; *Peter Bielenberg*, Stephen Dillon.

prog 1: 16 November 1988. tx 2125 c.57m
Adam, Nigel le Vaillant; *Mr Burton*, Geoffrey Palmer; *Mrs Burton*, Ann Bell;
Aunt Ulla, Renny Lister; *Neisse*, John Burgess; *Krueze*, David Lyon; *Clarita*,
Nicola Wright; *Prof Bauer*, Guy Deghy; *Priest*, Robert Howard; *Jewish
Tailor*, John Barrard; *Hotel Manager*, Michael Egan; *English Gardener*,
Arthur Whybrow; *Newsvendor*, Jonathan Izard; *Nazis*, John Phythian,
Tim Killick; *Brownshirts*, Stewart Harwood, David Baukham; *Nicky*, Sam
Preston, James Stewart; *John*, Ryan Le Neveu, Ben Preston.

prog 2: 23 November 1988. tx 2125 c.57m
Dr Carl Langbehn, Sam Kelly; *Lexi*, Suzan Crowley; *Ilse*, Jessica Turner;
Albrecht, Adrian Rawlins; *Botho*, Hugh Simon; *Freda*, Barbara Marten;
Jacob, Frank Baker; *Soldier in Park*, Greg Crutwell; *German Teacher*, Sue
Withers; *Ilse's Son*, Oliver Taylor-Medhurst; *Patrol*, Annie Hayes, Tricia
Kelly, Maureen Bennett; *Prisoner of War*, Wayne Norman; *SS Colonel*,
Richard Cubison; *Clerk*, Wilfred Grove; *England Committee*, Paul Kiernan,
Louis Mellis, Roy Heather; *Older Nicky*, Toby Lawson; *Older John*, Andrey
Justice; *Pianist*, Max Harris (plus le Vaillant, Palmer, Bell, Lister, Burgess,
Lyon, Wright, Sam Preston, Le Neveu).

prog 3: 30 November 1988. tx 2125 c.58m
Frau Muckle, Pat Heywood; *US Airman*, Dennis Christopher; *Bausch*,
Jim Carter; *Alois*, John Boswall; *Station Master*, David Blake Kelly; *SS
Man*, Andrew Wilde; *Frau Lange*, Joanne Allen; *Edeltrout*, Emma-Louise
Harrington; *Hilde*, Laura Goodwin; *Volk*, Richard Ireson; *SS Officers*, John

Gillett, Christopher Leaver; *Gestapo Driver*, Simon Tyrrell; *Irate Woman*, Joolia Cappleman; *Soldiers*, Kim Kindersley, Paul M. Meston, Duncan Piney; *Older Nicky*, Alastair Haley; *Older John*, James Exell (plus le Vaillant, Kelly, Crowley, Lawson, Justice).

prog 4: 7 December 1988. tx 2125 c.54m
Old Lady, Edna Doré; *Lange*, Ralph Brown; *Officer*, Wayne Foskett; *Sergeant*, Danny McCarthy; *Receptionist*, Eric Allen; *Blonde Woman*, Eileen Maciejewska; *Soldier*, Neale McGrath; *Policeman*, Philip Bretherton; *Prisoner*, Will Tacey; *Dutch Youths*, Nicholas Teare, Mark Draper, Tom Lambert, Simon Adams; *Boy Soldier*, Lawrence Cooper; *Guard*, Ian Lowe (plus Crowley, Heywood, Carter, Boswall, Haley, Exell).

Costume Anushia Nieradzik/make-up Deanne Turner/music Stanley Myers/ graphics Barbra Flinder/sound recordist Peter Edwards/lighting cameraman Remi Adefarasin/film editor Clare Douglas/designer Jim Clay/executive producer DP/producer Kenith Trodd/director Adrian Shergold/writer DP after the memoir *The Past Is Myself* by Christabel Bielenberg.

The Media Show Wall to Wall for Channel 4 9 April 1989. tx 2115 c.52m
DP among writers talking about directing their own work. Introduced by Muriel Gray/producers Jane Root, Paul Kerr, Andy Lipman/editor Alex Graham.

Heart of the Matter BBC1 5 November 1989. tx 2215 c.39m
DP among Joan Bakewell's interviewees on satellite television. Producer Olga Edridge.

The Late Show BBC2 9 November 1989. tx 2320 c.40m
You Must Remember This: reactions to the theories of screen-writing 'guru' Robert McKee included those of DP. Director Peter Lydon.

Saturday Matters with Sue Lawley 11 November 1989. tx 2250 c.45m
DP included in a discussion about sex. Introduced by Sue Lawley/director John Kaye Cooper/producer Jon Plowman.

Blackeyes BBC/Australian Broadcasting Corporation/Television New Zealand for BBC2 four-part serial
Maurice James Kingsley, Michael Gough; *Jessica*, Carol Royle; *Jeff*, Nigel Planer; *Blackeyes*, Gina Bellman; *Narrator*, DP (uc).

prog 1: 29 November 1989. tx 2125 c.49m
Detective Blake, John Shrapnel; *Jamieson*, Colin Jeavons; *Stilk*, Nicholas Woodeson; *Pathologist*, Cyril Shaps; *Casting Director*, Ann Bell; *Constable*, Lee Simpson.

Start the Week BBC Radio 4 4 December 1989. tx 0905 c.55m
DP in discussion with Martin Jacques, Tina Shaw, Richard Cork. Introduced by Robert Kee/producer Marina Salandy-Brown.

Behind the Screen BBC2 4 December 1989. tx 1450 c.10m
DP interviewed by Neil Mullarkey on *Blackeyes*.

Blackeyes continued

prog 2: 6 December 1989. tx 2125 c.46m
Mark Wilsher, David Westhead; *Photographer*, Peter Guinness; *Little Jessica*, Hannah Morris; *Singer*, Dennis Lotis; *Stilt Man*, Nicky Bee (plus Shrapnel, Jeavons).

prog 3: 13 December 1989. tx 2125 c.51m
Sebastian, Charles Gray; *Nigel Bennon*, Christopher Guard; *Rupert*, Ian Gelder; *Colin*, Gary Love; *Charles*, Peter Birch; *Receptionist*, Samantha Gates; *Model*, Nikki Mace; *Bennon's Assistant*, Lucinda Fisher (plus Shrapnel, Westhead, Morris, Bee).

prog 4: 20 December 1989. tx 2125 c.51m
Commercial Director, Laurence Rudic; *Bert*, Roger Walker (plus Jeavons, Westhead, Love, Morris, Bee).

Costume Robin Stubbs/make-up Frances Hannon/music Max Harris/sound Peter Edwards/photography Andrew Dunn/film editors Clare Douglas, Michael Parker/designer Geoff Powell/producer Rick McCallum/director-writer DP.

The Talk Show with Clive James BBC2 21 January 1990. tx 2130 c.44m
DP in discussion with Robert Hughes and Helen McNeil. Introduced by Clive James/director Dominic Brigstocke/producer Elaine Bedell.

Kaleidoscope Extra BBC Radio 4 30 May 1990. tx 1645 c.15m
DP in discussion with Melvyn Bragg, Fay Weldon and Rose Tremain at the Hay-on-Wye Festival. Introduced by Christopher Cook/producer Lesley McAlpine.

Secret Friends Film Four International/Whistling Gypsy 1991. c.97m
John, Alan Bates; *Helen*, Gina Bellman; *Angela*, Frances Barber; *Martin*, Tony Doyle; *Kate*, Joanna David; *Vicar*, Colin Jeavons; *Mother*, Rowena Cooper; *Businessmen*, Ian McNeice, Davyd Harries; *BR Steward/Patient*, Niven Boyd; *Young John*, Martin Whiting; *Singer*, Roy Hamilton.
Costume Sharon Lewis/make-up Ann McEwan/music Nick Russell-Pavier/sound recordists John Midgley, André Jacquemin/sound editor Andrew Glen/photography Sue Gibson/film editor Clare Douglas/designer Gary Williamson/executive producers Robert Michael Geisler, John Roberdeau/producer Rosemarie Whitman/director-writer DP 'suggested by' his novel *Ticket to Ride*.

The Television of Dennis Potter The Museum of Television & Radio, New York City, New York, USA 23 January–31 May 1992
A complete retrospective to *Secret Friends*, the material organised under six headings. The season's invaluable booklet included a new essay, *Downloading*, by DP. Later the season was remounted in Los Angeles.

PM BBC Radio 4 19 February 1993. tx 1700 c.50m
Mike Donkin reported on the making of *Lipstick on Your Collar* including

an interview with DP. Introduced by Frank Partridge, Hugh Sykes/producer Rahul Sarmik.

Lipstick on Your Collar Channel 4/Faber and Faber 1993
Text of the serial.

Lipstick on Your Collar Whistling Gypsy/Channel 4 six-part serial
Private Francis Francis, Giles Thomas; *Private Mick Hopper*, Ewan McGregor; *Sylvia Berry*, Louise Germaine; *Corporal Peter Berry*, Douglas Henshall; *Colonel Harry Bernwood*, Peter Jeffrey; *Major Wallace Hedges*, Clive Francis; *Major Archie Carter*, Nicholas Jones; *Major Johnny Church*, Nicholas Farrell; *Harold Atterbow*, Roy Hudd; *Aunt Vickie*, Maggie Steed; *Uncle Fred*, Bernard Hill.

prog 1: 21 February 1993. tx 2100 c.58m
Lieutenant Colonel 'Truck' Trekker, Shane Rimmer; *Dream Girl*, Carrie Leigh; *Man in Cinema*, Damian Dibben.

rpt 16 August 1994 tx 2200

prog 2: 28 February 1993. tx 2100 c.58m
Brigadier Cecil Saunders, Frederick Treves; *Fletcher*, John Cater (plus Rimmer, Leigh).

rpt 23 August 1994 tx 2200

English File BBC Schools for BBC2 5 March 1993. tx 1200 c.30m
For the *New Approaches: Drama* course, DP was interviewed on his rewriting of *Blue Remembered Hills* for the stage.

Lipstick on Your Collar continued

prog 3: 7 March 1993. tx 2100 c.59m
Lisa, Kymberley Huffman; *'Nina'*, Debra Beaumont; *'Trigorin'*, James Snell; *Voice of Eden*, Bernard Brown (plus Rimmer, Leigh).

rpt 30 August 1994 tx 2200

prog 4: 14 March 1993. tx 2100 c.58m
Manager of Palais, Sean Baker; *Palais Man*, Michael Nielsen; *Dance Instructor*, Jean Fergusson; *Captain*, Jay Villiers; *Soldiers*, Andy Laycock, Daniel Ryan (plus Huffman, Rimmer, Leigh).

rpt 6 September 1994 tx 2200

Opinions: Britain 1993 Open Media for C4 21 March 1993. tx 2000 c.27m
In the last of 'five individual contributions on the state of Britain today', DP savaged media magnate Rupert Murdoch.

Lipstick on Your Collar continued

prog 5: 21 March 1993. tx 2100 c.60m
General, Terence Bayler; *Brigadier*, Tim Seely; *Lieutenant Colonel*, Roger Hume; *Inspector*, Jim Carter; *Policeman*, Che Walker; *'Arkadina'*, Allison Hancock; *'Masha'*, Carol Starks; *'Medvedenko'*, Geoffrey Larder; *Singer*, Stephen Tremblay (plus Huffman, Laycock, Ryan, Beaumont, Snell).

rpt 13 September 1994 tx 2200

prog 6: 28 March 1993. tx 2100 c.64m
Club Man, Wensley Pithey; *Private Mason*, Darren Lawrence; *Parachute Officer*, Rupert Baker; *Policeman*, Benedict Martin; *Mrs Atterbow*, Ysanne Churchman; *Vicar*, Geoffrey Drew (plus Huffman, Rimmer, Treves, Bayler, Seely, Hume, Walker).

rpt 20 September 1994 tx 2200

Costume Sharon Lewis/make-up Sallie Jaye/choreography Quinny Sacks/ pre-production consultant Kenith Trodd/director of photography Sean Van Hales/film editor Clare Douglas/designer Gary Williamson/co-producer Alison Barnett/producer Rosemarie Whitman/director Renny Rye/writer-executive producer DP.

Clive Anderson Talks Back Hat Trick for Channel 4 25 June 1993. tx 2230 c.32m
DP, Zsa Zsa Gabor and Lee Marek were the chat show guests/introduced by Clive Anderson/director Pati Marr/producer Lissa Evans/series produces Dan Patterson.

The James MacTaggart Memorial Lecture Edinburgh International Television Festival 27 August 1993.
Using the title *Occupying Powers*, DP gave the 18th annual lecture which traditionally opens the industry gathering. His address, a *tour d'horizon* of the state of British television, was also a restatement of his central themes and concerns. The description of the BBC Director-General John Birt and its Chairman Marmaduke Hussey as 'a pair of croak-voiced Daleks' has gone into the language.

Nine O'Clock News BBC1 27 August 1993. tx 2100 c.27m
DP's MacTaggart Lecture reported. Newsreader Martyn Lewis.

Right to Reply Special Channel 4 30 August 1993. tx 1905 c.47m
Subtitled *Dennis Potter in Edinburgh*, this follow-up to his MacTaggart Lecture asked him to defend his text in discussion with Will Wyatt, Mick Eaton and an industry audience. Chair Sheena McDonald/producer Julie Hall/editor Nicholas Fraser.

Potter on Potter Faber and Faber 1993
Book-length interview with DP conducted, annotated and introduced by Graham Fuller.

Without Walls Special LWT for Channel 4 5 April 1994 tx 2100 c.68m
Melvyn Bragg conducted the now legendary *Interview with Dennis Potter* in which DP spoke of impending death and of his life's work. Director Tom Poole/producer Nigel Wattis.

rpt 9 June 1994 tx 2130

Last Pearls, *Daily Telegraph*, 4 June 1994.
DP's only short story.

Late Show Special BBC2 7 June 1994. tx 2100 c.56m
Dennis Potter: A Life in Television was the BBC's substantial obituary to its

most dogged contributor. Reporter Kevin Jackson/producer Roger Parsons/ editor Mike Poole.

Dennis Potter in Edinburgh Channel 4 23 August 1994. tx 2310 c.68m
A recording of DP's James MacTaggart Lecture in full, given the previous year. Director Martin Kemp/producer Julie Hall.

Blue Remembered Hills Everyman Theatre, Cheltenham 15 October 1994
The production played one performance, then took a six-date tour of Gloucestershire theatres and halls before returning to the Everyman for a two-week run.
Peter, David Kennedy; *John*, John Readman; *Willie*, Peter Rylands; *Angela*, Annie Sutton; *Audrey*, Angela Bain; *Donald Duck*, Steven Deproost; *Raymond*, Julian Protheroe.
Lighting Michael E. Hall/designer Nettie Edwards/director Martin Houghton/ writer DP.

Message for Posterity BBC2 *Performance* 29 October 1994. tx 2130 c.97m
A new production of the 1967 play with an introduction by Brian Walden (whose son Ben took a small role).
James Player, Eric Porter; *Sir David Browning*, John Neville; *Gillian Player*, Sophie Thompson; *Clara Browning*, Abigail Cruttenden; *Richard Browning*, Ronald Pickup; *Hawkins*, Stephen Moore; *Karl*, Manual Harlan; *Thompson*, Bruce Alexander; *Miles*, Ben Walden; *Barnes*, Bev Willis; *Newscaster*, Steven Crossley; *Voice of Art Critic*, Brian Sewell; *Committee Members*, Annette Crosbie, Patrick Godfrey, Edward Petherbridge, Tony Haygarth, Nicholas Selby; *Policeman* Joe Jones; *Emily*, Sarah Louise Mayne.
Costume Les Lansdown/make-up Jill Hagger/music Carl Davis/sound Gary Clarke, Jonathan Hall/lighting Clive Thomas/camera John Corby/videotape editor Anthony Combes/script editor Michael Hastings/designer John Asbridge/ producer Simon Curtis/director David Jones/writer DP.

Seeing the Blossom Faber and Faber 1994
A single volume brings together transcripts of *An Interview with Dennis Potter* of 5 April 1994 (retitled *An Interview with Melvyn Bragg*); the text of *Occupying Powers*, the James MacTaggart Memorial Lecture given as the keynote address at the Edinburgh International Television Festival on 27 August 1993; and the *Arena* interview conducted by Alan Yentob and first broadcast on BBC2 on 30 January 1987.

Midnight Movie Whistling Gypsy for BBC2 Screen Two 26 December 1994. tx 2210 c.96m
Henry Harris, Jim Carter; *Amber Boyce/Mandy Mason*, Louise Germaine; *James Boyce*, Brian Dennehy; *Bob MacLean*, Colin Salmon; *Bertie*, Steven Mackintosh; *Mrs Morrey*, Anna Cropper; *Vic*, David Curtiz; *Anne MacLean*, Lucinda Ann Galloway; *Policeman*, Gerard Horan; *Inspector*, Anthony Pedley; *Sergeant*, Michael Gardiner; *Doctor*, Michael Poole; *Cabbie*, Robert Putt; *Old Lady*, Georgine Anderson; *Old Man*, John Cater; *Bertie's Girlfriend*, Melanie Ramsay; *Johnny*, Stephen Greif; *Detective*, Geoffrey Larder; *Barney*,

Mark Frost; *Children*, Kelly Moorhouse, Joshua O'Brien, Pietra Pittman, Amelia Whiston-Dew.
Costume James Keast/make-up Lisa Westcott/music Christopher Gunning/photography Remi Adefarasin/film editor Clare Douglas/designer Gary Williamson/ executive producers Ruth Caleb, Mark Shivas/co-producer Rosemarie Whitman/ director Renny Rye/producer-writer DP.

Visions of Heaven and Hell Barraclough Carey Channel 4 three-part series
For this series about information technology, DP had filmed an interview which was extracted throughout.

prog 1 31 January 1995 tx 2100 c.50m
prog 2 7 February 1995 tx 2100 c.51m
prog 3 14 February 1995 tx 2100 c.51m
Directors Leanne Klein, Mark Harrison

Blue Remembered Hills Crucible Theatre, Sheffield 7 to 23 September 1995
Peter, Steve Nicolson; *John*, Ken Bradshaw; *Willie*, Charles Dale; *Angela*, Poppy Miller; *Audrey*, Morag Siller; *Donald Duck*, Tristan Sturrock; *Raymond*, Roger Morlidge.
Dialect Penny Dyer/movement Caroline Salem/fights Terry King/music James McConnel/lighting Tina MacHugh/designer Kit Surrey/director Deborah Paige/writer DP.

Son of Man The Pit/Royal Shakespeare Company in repertoire 11 October 1995 to 13 January 1996
Jesus Christ, Joseph Fiennes; *Pontius Pilate*, John Standing; *Caiaphas*, Philip Locke; *Peter*, James Ellis; *Judas Iscariot*, Guy Lankester; *Roman Commander*, Trevor Ray; *Andrew*, Sean O'Callaghan; *Procla*, Julia Crane; *Captain*, Robert Oates; *Ruth*, Sasha Behar; *James/Servant*, Vivian Munn; *John the Baptist*, Colin Jarrett; *Centurion/Priest*, David Beames; *Boxer/Money Changer*, David Keller; *Boxer/Soldier*, Nigel Clauzel; *Agitator*, Quill Roberts; *Priest*, Simon Cook; *Soldier/Musician*, Lester Simpson; *Disciple/Musician*, Michael Gregory.
Music director Richard Brown/music John Tams/sound Tony Brand, Barbara Gellhorn/fights Terry King/lighting Andy Phillips/designer Hayden Griffin/director Bill Bryden/writer DP.

Karaoke Whistling Gypsy for BBC/Channel 4 four-part serial
In production for tx April-May 1996.
Daniel Feeld, Albert Finney; *Nick Balmer*, Richard E. Grant; *Lady Ruth Balmer*, Julie Christie; *Mrs Haynes*, Alison Steadman; *Arthur (Pig) Mailion*, Hywel Bennett, *Anna Griffiths*, Anna Chancellor; *Ben Baglin*, Roy Hudd; *Sandra Sollars*, Saffron Burrows, *Oliver Morse*, Ian McDiarmid; *Linda Langer*, Keeley Hawes; *Mrs Baglin*, Liz Smith; *Peter Beasley*, Ralph Brown; *Ian*, Simon Donald; *Peter*, Neil Stuke; *Brasserie Waiter*, Steven Mackintosh; *Angie*, Natascha McElhone; *Impatient Patient*, Matthew Scurfield; *Consultant*, Stephen Boxer; *Staff Nurse*, Katherine O'Toole, *Sean*, Clive Mendus, *Dean*, Tom Fisher; *Doctor*, Matthew Cottle; *Tom*, Paul Raffield; *Businessmen*, Tony Buto, Niven Boyd; *Barmaid*, Fay Ripley, *Woman on Phone*, Beth Goddard;

Dr Barker, Grant Russell; *Young Man*, Ewan McGregor; *Secretary*, Siobhan Flynn; *Occupants*, Sam Halfpenny, Martin Malone, Chris Larkin; *Yuppie Drinkers*, Charley Boorman, Giles Taylor; *Waiter*, Christopher Glover; *Nurses*, Vivianna Verveen, Cathy Murphy, *Hostesses*, Jody Saron, Katy Carmichael; *Japanese*, Yashinori Yamamoto, Takahashi Sudo, Togo Igawa; *Porters*, David Norman, Stewart Howson; *Arab*, Eddy Lemare; *Clive*, Arthur Whybrow; *Luigi*, Arturo Venegas; *Waitress*, Miranda Pleasance; *Receptionist*, Lucy Cohu; *Mailion*, G.B. (Zoot) Money; *Cabbie*, Robert Putt.

Costume Janty Yates/make-up Dorka Nieradzik/music Christopher Gunning/ sound mixer John Midgley/photography Remi Adefarasin/film editor Clare Douglas/designer Gary Williamson/executive producers Michael Wearing, Peter Ansorge/producers Kenith Trodd, Rosemarie Whitman/director Renny Rye/writer DP.

Cold Lazarus Whistling Gypsy for BBC/Channel 4 four-part serial
In production for tx in 1996.

Emma Porlock, Frances de la Tour; *Tony Watson*, Grant Masters; *Daniel Feeld*, Albert Finney; *Fyodor Glazunov*, Ciaran Hinds; *Luanda Partington*, Ganiat Kasumu; *Blinda*, Carmen Ejogo; *Kaya*, Claudia Malkovich; *Martiana Masdon*, Diane Ladd; *David Siltz*, Henry Goodman; *Andrew Milton*, David Foxxe; *Nat*, Jonathan Cake; *Nigel*, Richard Karlsson; *Bill*, Ian Kelly; *Manolo*, Antonio Elliott; *Celestine*, Lisa Shingler; *Beth Carter*, Tara Woodward; *Young Chris/Young Daniel* Joe Roberts; *Tramp*, John Forgeham; *Daniel's Father*, Adam Bareham; *Student Daniel*, John Light; *Jim*, John Higgins; *Ted*, Edward Woodall; *John*, Miles Harvey; *Beth's Mother*, Susan Porrett; *Preacher* Malcolm Rogers; *Harry Schumpet*, Harry Ditson; *Dr Rawl*, Donald Sumpter; *Police Commander*, Paul McNeilly; *Inspector General Challender*, Michael Culkin; *Guards*, Silas Carson, Jason Salkey, Peter Warnock, Steve Spiers; *Harry the Doorman*, Leon Greene; *Policeman*, John Altman; *Prison Guard*, Darren Bancroft; *Youths*, Craster Pringle, Simon Meacock.

Producers Kenith Trodd, Rosemarie Whitman/director Renny Rye/writer DP.

Appendix II

Titles and Their Origins

In naming his works, Potter often took the title or a line of lyric from popular songs of the last 150 years. In this list of his titles and their song origins, *w.*=words, *m.*=music

Vote, Vote, Vote for Nigel Barton: from 'Tramp, Tramp, Tramp ('The Boys Are Marching)', a US Civil War song of 1864, *w.m.* George Frederic Root (via an unofficial adaptation as a campaigning song, 'Vote, Vote, Vote for Billy Martin')

Where the Buffalo Roam: from 'Home on the Range' ('Oh, Give Me a Home Where the Buffalo Roam'), *c.* 1873, *w.*Brewster Higley, *m.*Dan Kelly

The Bonegrinder: from 'Fee Fi Fo Fum,' a traditional nursery rhyme ('I'll grind your bones until you're dead')

Moonlight on the Highway: 1937, *w.m.*Edgar Leslie, Joe Burke, Al Sherman; recorded by Al Bowlly

Lay Down Your Arms: 1956, *w.*Paddy Roberts, *m.*Mike Gerhard, Leon Land; recorded by Anne Shelton

Angels Are So Few: from '(You May Not Be an Angel But) I'll String Along with You', 1934, *w.*Al Dubin, *m.*Harry Warren for movie *Twenty Million Sweethearts*; recorded by Al Bowlly

Paper Roses: 1953, *w.*Janice Torre, *m.*Fred Spielman; recorded by Anita Bryant and by the Kaye Sisters

Follow the Yellow Brick Road: from 'We're Off to See the Wizard', 1939, *w.*E. Y. Harburg, *m.*Harold Arlen for movie *The Wizard of Oz*

Only Make Believe: from 'Make Believe', 1927, *w.*Oscar Hammerstein II, *m.* Jerome Kern for stage musical *Show Boat*

Double Dare: from 'I Double Dare You', 1937, *w.*Terry Shand, *m.*Jimmy Eaton; recorded by Al Bowlly

Pennies from Heaven: 1936, *w.*Johnny Burke, *m.*Arthur Johnston for movie *Pennies from Heaven*; series version recorded by Edward Molloy

Blade on the Feather: from 'The Eton Boating Song', 1865, *w.m.*William Cory

Rain on the Roof: 1932, *w.m.*Ann Ronell; recorded by Al Bowlly

Cream in My Coffee: from 'You're the Cream in My Coffee', 1928, *w.*B.G. De

Sylva, Lew Brown, *m*.Ray Henderson for stage musical *Hold Everything!*; teleplay version by Sam Browne

Ticket to Ride: 1965, *w*.*m*.John Lennon, Paul McCartney for movie *Help!*; recorded by the Beatles

Track 29: from 'Chattanooga Choo Choo', 1941, *w*. Mack Gordon, *m*. Harry Warren for stage musical *The 1940s Radio Hour*

Blackeyes: from 'Black Eyes' or, more commonly, 'Dark Eyes', 1926, *w*.Harry Horlich after Russian folk-song 'Otchi Tchorniya'; recorded by Al Bowlly

Lipstick on Your Collar: 1959, *w*.Edna Lewis, *m*. George Goehring; recorded by Connie Francis

As a gesture of solidarity, almost all the chapters of this book have been given titles similarly derived. These are their origins:

Live and Kicking: a quibble on 'Alive and Kicking', 1941, *w*.Ralph Blane, *m*.Hugh Martin for stage musical *Best Foot Forward*

Take Your Finger Out of My Mouth: 1927, *w*.Yellman, *m*.Schuster; recorded by Al Bowlly in Berlin with Arthur Briggs's Savoy Syncopators

You're Sure of a Big Surprise: from 'The Teddy Bears' Picnic', 1913, *w*.*m*.John W. Bratton, James B. Kennedy ('If you go down to the woods today / You're sure of a big surprise')

The Varsity Drag: 1927, *w*.B. G. De Sylva, Lew Brown, *m*.Ray Henderson for stage musical *Good News*

I've Got the World on a String: 1932, *w*.Ted Koehler, *m*.Harold Arlen for revue *Cotton Club Parade*

Won't You Join the Dance? from 'The Lobster Quadrille', 1865, *w*.Lewis Carroll for the book *Alice's Adventures in Wonderland*

Close as Pages in a Book: 1945, *w*.Dorothy Fields, *m*.Sigmund Romberg for stage musical *Up in Central Park*

It's Only a Paper Moon: 1932, *w*.E. Y. Harburg, Billy Rose, *m*.Harold Arlen for stage play *The Great Magoo*

Painting the Clouds with Sunshine: 1929, *w*.Al Dubin, *m*.Joe Burke for movie *Gold Diggers of Broadway*

I'm Learning a Lot from You: 1930, *w*.Dorothy Fields, *m*.Jimmy McHugh for movie *Love in the Rough*

Ridin' High: 1936, *w*.*m*.Cole Porter for stage musical *Red, Hot and Blue*

The Honeymoon is Over: 1958, *w*.Sheldon Harnick, *m*.Jerry Bock for stage musical *The Body Beautiful*

I Get Along Without You Very Well: 1939, *w*.Jane Brown Thompson, *m*. Hoagy Carmichael

I'm Beginning to See the Light: 1944, *w*.*m*.Harry James, Duke Ellington, Johnny Hodges, Don George

Who's That Knockin' at My Door? from 'Barnacle Bill the Sailor', 1931, *w*.*m*. Frank Luther, Carson Robinson

We Open in Venice: 1948, *w*.*m*.Cole Porter for stage musical *Kiss Me Kate*

Says Who? Says You, Says I!: 1941, *w*.Johnny Mercer, *m*.Harold Arlen for movie *Blues in the Night*

Sit Down, You're Rockin' the Boat: 1950, *w.m.*Frank Loesser for stage musical *Guys and Dolls*

Other People's Babies: (*aka* 'The Nanny's Lament'), 1934, *w.*A. P. Herbert, *m.*Vivian Ellis for stage musical *Streamline*

You Can't Keep a Good Dreamer Down: 1946, *w.*Johnny Burke, *m.*Jimmy Van Heusen for movie *London Town*: theme song of the comedian Sid Field.

Half a Sixpence: 1963, *w.m.*David Heneker, title number of stage musical

Alice Is At It Again: 1946, *w.m.*Noël Coward for stage musical *Pacific 1860* but cut and used as a supper club number

Someone in a Tree: 1976, *w.m.*Stephen Sondheim for stage musical *Pacific Overtures*

Deep Purple: 1934, *w.m.*Mitchell Parish, Peter De Rose

You Keep Coming Back Like a Song: 1946, *w.m.*Irving Berlin for movie *Blue Skies*

Please Don't Talk About Me When I'm Gone: 1930, *w.*Sidney Clare, *m.*Sam H. Stept

Index